CRITICS ARE ~~~~~~~~~~
KENNEDY'S ~~~~~~~

DOUB~~~~~

"*Double Enchantment* ~~~~~~~~~~~~~~~~~~~th twists, turns, gnomes a~~~~~~~~~~~~~~~~~~~~~ adult lovers of Harry Potter the fix they've been missing since the last book. Mysterious, witty and sensual. Don't be the last to discover this wondrous world."

—Barbara Vey, *Publishers Weekly*'s Beyond Her Book Blog

"I was again swept away by Ms. Kennedy's writing. She easily transported me into her fantasy world that I'm looking forward to visiting again. Kennedy knows how to bring magical fantasy to life!" —Night Owl Romance

"Kennedy's world is intriguing and filled with pageantry and adventure." —*Romantic Times BOOKreviews*

"*Double Enchantment*, like its predecessor *Enchanting the Lady*, is well...enchanting. A feel-good fairy tale set in a spellbinding world where magic is the order of the day...a place where good men come in many forms and good women are more than a match for anything the universe has to throw at them. I loved both these books and am looking forward to the next in the series." —Fresh Fiction, Fresh Pick!

"I am impressed that the intricacies of the descriptions given don't slow the story down. I thought Ms. Kennedy really outdid herself." —Once Upon a Romance

"The world feels real, as if I'm not reading a fantasy, but in fact a historical accounting of that time."

—Romance Reader at Heart

"A rousing good tale which illustrates what could happen when your inner wild child (suppressed for far too long) is given the chance to live free and have a bit of fun...Magical, bewitching, enthralling..." —Romance Reviews Today

ENCHANTING THE LADY

"*Enchanting the Lady* is a delightful gem of a historical fantasy. A highly imaginative depiction of Victorian London!"
—*USA Today* Bestselling Author Jennifer Ashley

"The imagination of J. K. Rowling and the romance of Julie Garwood all rolled up into one fabulous novel."
—Award-winning Author Erin Grady

"The latest from Kennedy is simply delightful, set in a fantasy-touched Victorian England that's imaginative, historically vigorous and ripe for further adventures. Felicity is a pleasantly unassuming heroine and is well matched in Terrence, while the identity of the villain will keep readers guessing until the very end."
—*Publishers Weekly*

"*Enchanting the Lady*, the first book in Kathryne Kennedy's planned historical paranormal series, will cast its own spell over readers with its fabulously imaginative setting and charmingly original characters."
—*Chicago Tribune*

"This captivating tale combines the excitement and edgy danger of a thriller with the treat of a romantic romp. Kennedy is going places."
—*Romantic Times BOOKreviews*

"The first in Kennedy's Relics of Merlin series, the novel takes a number of fairy tales, most notably Beauty and the Beast, and delightfully turns them on their collective ear. Playful prose carries the reader through this well-crafted, sexy romp of a story sporting an engaging cast."
—*Booklist*

ON THE PROWL

Philomena caught a flash of movement. She began to run toward the tower stairs, yanking up the hem of her nightgown when it threatened to tangle about her ankles. She'd forgotten to tie her robe and it floated behind her along with her loose hair. She'd almost reached the door of the tower when—

"Oof!"

She hit a solid wall of muscled fur. A confusing few moments of tangled limbs and growls of surprise followed, and then Sir Nico shifted to human and she found herself lying spread-eagled atop him.

"What on earth are you doing out here?" she demanded.

"I could ask you the same thing."

He smelled liked sweet grass and starlight. She could barely make out his features in the gloom, for she'd dropped her fairylight in the fall and it winked sadly at her from a few feet away. "I was hunting a ghost."

"Why am I not surprised?"

Phil suddenly realized that she could feel the rise and fall of his chest with his words. That the heat of his skin warmed the full length of her and his mouth lay only a heartbeat from her own. The deliciously wicked throb that ignited between her legs made her scramble to her feet. "Just what were *you* doing?"

He sat up, his arms propped carelessly atop his raised knees. "I was hunting too, my lady."

KATHRYNE KENNEDY

Enchanting the Beast

LOVE SPELL NEW YORK CITY

For my two best friends, David and Carla Lambert

A LOVE SPELL BOOK®

May 2009

Published by

Dorchester Publishing Co., Inc.
200 Madison Avenue
New York, NY 10016

ISBN 10: 0-505-52764-2
ISBN 13: 978-0-505-52764-6
E-ISBN: 978-1-4285-0677-0

The name "Love Spell" and its logo are trademarks of Dorchester Publishing Co., Inc.

Printed in the United States of America.

10 9 8 7 6 5 4 3 2 1

Visit us on the web at www.dorchesterpub.com.

ACKNOWLEDGMENTS

A special thank you to my wonderful editor, Leah Hultenschmidt, who had to work extra hard on this one. To all the Dorchester staff, who are frankly just amazing. And to Samantha Cable, Sabrina Ellis, Ali Thompson, Barbara Mueller and Tina LaVon, whose support means the world to me.

Enchanting the Beast

Long ago a great wizard was born with magic in his very blood. He lived for thousands of years and went by many names, but the one we know best is Merlin.

Merlin passed his magic down through his offspring, and the power made his children rulers. Some inherited more magic than others, and eventually titles reflected their gifts. In Britain, kings and queens held the strongest power. After the royals, dukes had the greatest magical abilities in that they could change matter. Marquesses could cast spells and illusions and transfer objects but not change them. Earls mastered illusions, while viscounts dabbled in charms and potions. Barons had a magical gift, which could be as simple as making flowers grow or as complicated as seeing into the future.

And then there were the baronets. Part man, part animal, the shape-shifters were Merlin's greatest enchantment . . . and eventually his greatest bane. For out of all mankind, they were immune to his magic.

Merlin created thirteen magical relics from the gems of the earth, a focus for some of his greatest spells. After Merlin's disappearance, his children tried to find the relics, since these items held the only magic stronger than their own. The relics proved to be elusive until his children discovered that the shape-shifters they so despised could sniff out the power of a relic.

Over the centuries the relics faded to legend. But the most powerful of Merlin's descendants did not forget, and shape-shifters became the secret spies of many rulers.

Chapter One

Lady Philomena Radcliff closed her eyes and called to the spirit of the late Lord Stanhope. She tried to ignore the excited breaths of the ladies within the séance circle, which she could clearly hear over the muted strains of ballroom music coming from behind the closed drawing room door.

"Lord Stanhope," Phil said, with as much theatrical brilliance as a stage performer. She spread her hands flat on the mahogany table. "Your wife wishes to speak with you one last time. Is your spirit still in this house?"

The withdrawing room smelled of candle wax and the clashing perfumes of the assembled ladies: Lady Stanhope, Lady Montreve, and their two daughters. And unfortunately, their daughters' silly young friends, who started to giggle as the silence lengthened.

It appeared that the late Lord Stanhope had chosen not to linger in the physical world.

Which didn't make one whit of difference to Phil. Lady Stanhope had paid her for some peace of mind and she would give it to her regardless. When Phil had been orphaned at a young age, she'd used her magical gift to support herself, quickly discovering that half of her job consisted of her theatrical ability to convince her audience. If the spirit she called made an appearance, she just considered it a bonus.

Her primary concern was to relieve the suffering of those that tragedy had left behind.

She opened her eyes. "We must combine our efforts. Lady

Montreve, will you douse the candles? Thank you. Now, clasp your neighbor's hand and concentrate on the late Lord Stanhope. Use your will to call him to us."

Lady Montreve's skirts swished and her hoops crackled as she took her seat again next to Phil. Her gloved hands trembled beneath Philomena's fingers, matching the rhythm of Lady Stanhope's grip on Phil's other hand. She gave both of the ladies a reassuring squeeze.

The ballroom orchestra finished its tune, and despite the multitude of guests in the other room, a quiet descended on the mansion. The fire crackled in the hearth, and the wind made a soft keening noise outside the glass windows. Phil lowered her voice to a husky whisper. "Keep concentrating, ladies. I can feel your will rising, calling out to Lord—"

The drawing room door burst open and the shadow of a large man loomed on the threshold. The circle of hands broke. Lady Stanhope gasped, Lady Montreve stifled a scream, and the other girls collapsed into a fit of giggles.

Philomena suppressed her urge to admonish them like a doddering governess and forced a smile instead. "If you don't mind, sir, we were in the middle of—"

"I'm quite aware of what's going on in this room, madam. If you will excuse the interruption, I would like to join you." He closed the door behind him, shutting out the light from the outer room, allowing the soft glow of the fireplace to highlight his features. The giggles abruptly died, and soft sighs of admiration issued from the mouths of several young girls.

Philomena could hardly blame them. She had never seen such a striking young man. Dark hair liberally streaked with blond fell in waves past broad shoulders that strained his old-fashioned evening coat. The firelight reflected glints of gold in his large dark eyes and played across the angular planes of his face, outlining high cheekbones. Even white teeth flashed as he performed a courtly bow.

Phil's stomach flipped and her hands broke out in a sweat inside her gloves. She struggled to hide her reaction before anyone noticed. Heavens, she was old enough to be his . . . well, older sister perhaps. But still, too old to be making a fool of herself by gawking at the beautiful young man.

Lady Stanhope recovered first. "I don't remember the pleasure of an introduction, sir."

Again, a flash of those even white teeth. Good heavens, were those dimples?

"I'm Sir Nicodemus Wulfson, Baronet of Grimspell castle."

Soft gasps accompanied his words and several of the younger ladies actually looked frightened. All baronets were shifters and immune to all magic. The aristocracy hated that "the animals" could see through the spells crafted to maintain their superior social status.

"I don't think . . ." Lady Stanhope began, ready to deny the gentleman's request.

Phil quickly stood. "It would be a pleasure for you to join us, Sir Nicodemus."

He turned those large, glittering eyes on her in surprise, his predatory gaze sweeping over her from head to foot. Phil felt heat rise in her cheeks. As usual, she'd dressed in the artistic style, eschewing the corsets and crinolines of her peers. Most of her friends were followers of the Pre-Raphaelite Brotherhood, but few of them had the daring to wear their medieval-style dresses out in public.

He surprised her with a sudden smile of approval. "Thank you, Lady . . . ?"

"Philomena Radcliff."

"The ghost-hunter," he acknowledged. "I've heard a great deal about you. It's a pleasure."

The Adonis stepped forward and took her hand, sweeping his lips across the top of her glove. Thank heavens for that layer of material, for he surely would have burnt her skin with the heat of his mouth. Phil quickly snatched back her hand and resumed her seat at the table, trying to ignore the flutter in her stomach. Lady Stanhope's older daughter eyed her with shrewd speculation, her lovely little mouth twisted with disdain.

Phil leveled a gaze on the girl that quickly made her look away. She wished she knew what it was about the young man that made her feel so unusual.

The screech of wooden legs over marble made them all turn to watch Sir Nicodemus drag a chair over to the table and squeeze between Philomena and Lady Stanhope. He sat with stealthy grace.

He looked up and flashed that brilliant smile again, taking in the entire circle of women. "I've always wanted to experience one of these table-turnings. It's gracious of you to allow me to join you." Despite his apparent lack of social standing a few of the youngest girls leaned forward and licked their lips.

Philomena pressed her lips together to prevent the same reaction. It was all well and good for young debutantes to react to him, but she had to be at least ten years his senior and it would only make her look like a complete fool. The man had too much charisma for his own good, but perhaps he needed it, given his nature. Because of her spiritual sensitivity she could sense his animal-self like a dark shadow surrounding him. She really should have allowed Lady Stanhope to reject him, for if she continued in her obvious fascination in him, she was sure to make a complete cake of herself.

But Phil's sense of justice could not allow her to shun him. So when Lady Stanhope hesitated to link her hand with the baronet's, Philomena hid her fear of the way she might react to his touch and slapped her gloved palm over his with forced bravado.

Tiny shivers traveled from his hand through her body.

She'd been correct. His touch flustered her more than the caress of his gaze. For a moment Sir Nicodemus stared at their clasped hands, his dark brows raised in surprise. Then he turned and glanced at her, that wolfish grin back on his face.

Phil abruptly blew out the candle and closed her eyes. Heaven help her if he set his mind on exploring that instant chemistry between them. "Now concentrate, ladies . . . and gentlemen. Lord Stanhope, we summon your spirit, please come to us." A soft tapping sounded at the window, most likely a tree branch in the wind, but Phil grasped at it. "Lord Stanhope! Is that you?"

Sir Nicodemus made a small sound of derision, but she could feel the rest of the circle tense with excitement.

Phil opened her eyes, fully prepared to cast an unfocused gaze at the corner of the room where she would pretend Lord Stanhope stood. His wife only wanted to tell him that she loved him. She hadn't had a chance to do so before he died. Who was she to deny the lady that satisfaction?

But Philomena caught a movement from the fireplace and her gaze met that of Tup. The young boy sat atop the mantel, his bare feet hanging over the edge, the glow of the fire shining through them. His brown hair was a mess as usual, his face so dirty that his hazel eyes stood out in startling contrast. Really, such a ragtag street urchin! Phil's heart squeezed a bit and warmth flowed through her.

"Tup," she whispered, trying to rise but anchored to her chair by the grip of Lady Stanhope and Sir Nicodemus.

"What's a tup?" murmured one of the girls.

"The ghost-hunter's spirit guide," Lady Montreve snapped.

Phil was vaguely aware of the shock that rippled around the table, including that of Sir Nicodemus. She could feel him watching her, like a predator studies his prey, waiting for the perfect moment to leap. But she ignored them all, intent on seeing Tup's ghost again. He wasn't strong enough to stay long in the material world.

The only thing she'd ever regretted about not marrying was that she would never have her own child. And then Tup had followed her home one day.

"I come to tell ye to stop that," he said, his large eyes blinking with sadness.

"What do you mean?" Phil asked.

"Cor, don't ye fathom that the man passed over into hell? And he *likes* it there."

Oh, dear. That meant that the man was as close to a demon as they came. No wonder using magic to summon a spirit was frowned upon. But since magical power was based on rank, only a royal could do that, or possibly a duke. Granted, ghosts would sometimes answer the call of a loved one . . . "But then why would he answer Lady Stanhope's call, Tup?"

Lady Stanhope gasped. Was Sir Nicodemus actually growling?

They couldn't hear Tup, of course, just Philomena's part of the conversation. She told herself to be more careful with her words.

"Not *her* call," the boy answered impatiently. "Hers." And he nodded at Lady Montreve.

Phil turned and stared at the lady, who refused to meet her gaze. But even in the weak glow of the firelight she could see the dark stain of color flooding the pretty woman's cheeks. Is that why Lady Montreve had come this evening? To see her lover one last time? Philomena glanced at Lady Stanhope. Did she know her husband had been having an affair with her friend? Was that the real reason she'd called the séance, to find out the truth of it?

Tup's eyes widened. "Crikey, I'm too late." And he disappeared.

Phil slowly turned her head. Lord Stanhope's specter

materialized beside Phil's assistant, Sarah, and floated toward their table.

"Reginald, is that you?" his wife cried.

But Lord Stanhope only had eyes for Lady Montreve. He circled the table until he stood behind the pretty woman. "Did you call me back for one more round, you doxy? Missing me already, eh?" He leaned forward, his face so close to the back of the lady's neck that Phil could see the tiny hairs on her skin move. "Don't think I don't know it's my money you're missing. But I learned some things in hell, my dear. And when I heard your call I decided I shouldn't have to wait to try them on you."

Lady Montreve shuddered. "I shouldn't have come. I didn't think it was possible . . ." The young girl sitting next to her recoiled.

"Don't break the circle," Philomena warned. "It's her only protection." She felt Sir Nicodemus's grip tighten but the young girl—Phil wished she could remember her name—on the other side of Lady Montreve was trying to twist her hand from the woman's grasp.

Phil saw Lord Stanhope's arm disappear into his lover's skirts. Lady Montreve screamed.

"What's happening?" Lady Stanhope cried.

"Stop it!" Philomena shouted.

Lord Stanhope ignored them all, his black grin twisted into a leer of sadistic pleasure. The young girl pulled her hand free from Lady Montreve's grasp. The circle was broken. Philomena didn't have a choice. "Let go of my hand," she told Sir Nicodemus. Bless him, he didn't ask questions or argue; he just released his grip.

Phil really didn't want to do this—oh, how she didn't want to do this. She took a deep breath and stepped into Lord Stanhope's black shadow and opened her soul to his. For one horrendous moment the man's spirit melded with hers. Shafts of burning cold swept through her veins. His twisted sense of pleasure shook her body with an evil joy that made her squirm with shame.

She tried to send his soul back then, demanding that he return to the other side. He laughed at her. Phil strengthened her will, fighting with everything she had. Convulsions shook her body and then the world went black.

When Philomena opened her eyes she squinted at the glare of light. Every candle in Lady Stanhope's drawing room must have been lit, including the gas and fairylights. Sarah leaned over her, that blunt face and those glossy black eyes reflecting her concern. "You're well, then?"

At a nod, her assistant retreated and Phil sat up, her head swimming for a moment. She clutched her temples, realizing with dismay that her hair had come undone and lay about her shoulders. She must have looked as bad as she felt. How long would it take before the taint of that man's evil left her soul?

"That was quite a performance," Sir Nicodemus drawled.

Philomena winced. "Can you lower your voice, please? My head aches." She glanced around the ostentatious room, with its silk-papered walls and gilt edging. She avoided his gaze. "Where is everyone?"

"Lady Stanhope left your payment on the table," he answered. Phil's eyes went to the thick stack of bank notes. More than enough to keep up her household for the next few months, with some left over for luxuries.

"Lady Montreve has probably retired to the country," he continued. "The gaggle of young girls are likely swooning over the experience to their beaux in the ballroom . . . and Lady Stanhope asked you to leave as quickly as you are able."

Phil nodded, and winced again. Well, she couldn't exactly blame either lady. They had certainly gotten more than they'd bargained for with this séance.

Sir Nicodemus held out his hand to help her rise. Philomena ignored the appendage and managed to wobble to her feet unaided. "Sarah, will you fetch the coach?"

Her assistant slid from the room, and the baronet raised a brow. "I see you have no prejudice against my kind. You should suit admirably."

"What do you mean?"

"Your maid. She's a were, is she not?"

Bright lights danced in Phil's vision. "How did you know?"

He shrugged those broad shoulders and Phil desperately tried not to admire them. Oh botheration, why hadn't the young man just left with all the others? She felt enough out of sorts without having to hide her attraction to him.

"There's a stillness about my kind," he replied. "Although I can't quite pin what type of were-animal she might—"

Philomena's knees buckled and she would have sprawled to the floor if not for his quick reflexes. Instead she found herself within his arms. She stammered excuses, yet did nothing to escape his embrace. "I'm afraid that the encounter with Lord Stanhope quite did me in. I do try to avoid contact with the spirits. I'm far too sensitive to their presence."

He smelled marvelous. Like country meadows and sweet grass, with a musky undertone that she couldn't quite define. He stood at least a head taller than her and his arms were layered with the thick muscles of a man, not the wiry strength of a young boy. And the heat of him . . .

"Are you all right, Lady Radcliff?" he murmured.

She looked up to find his face mere inches from her own. He'd bowed his head and his nostrils were flared. Heavens, was he *scenting* her?

"Quite. I think you can let me go now."

But neither of them moved. Philomena couldn't tear her eyes away from his. Golden flecks in those deep brown irises sparkled and appeared to move, as if to hypnotize her. His mouth moved closer to her own and she had the shocking thought that he might kiss her. Ridiculous. Phil stepped out of his arms, gathered up her shawl, and tried to flee the room.

"Lady Radcliff. Your payment?"

He held out her bank notes, a mocking smile twisting an otherwise extremely attractive mouth. She tried to snatch them from his hand, but he pulled the bills away from her.

"Why don't I carry these for you while I see you home?"

"That's quite unnecessary."

"Oh, but I'm afraid you're wrong. What if you were to swoon again?"

Phil narrowed her eyes. "I assure you, I'm not ordinarily given to fainting. If you hand me my money, sir, we will likely never see each other again."

The cheeky man pocketed her notes and gently clasped her arm. "Ah, but that's where you're wrong, Lady Radcliff." He opened the door to the drawing room, allowing the lights and music to surround them. And exposing them to the witness of a hundred gazes. "I have a business proposition for you. One that will be a hundred times more profitable than what Lady Stanhope has provided you."

Phil's ears pricked up; she couldn't help it. When one had experienced the feeling of an empty belly, the value of money held enormous attraction. When he guided her down the hall she didn't protest, even when he purposely led them past the open double doors of the ballroom. Magic had created a winter wonderland of sparkling snow that swirled beneath the dancers' feet. Huge icicles glittering with rainbow colors hung from the ceiling and crystal statues graced the ballroom floor. Phil sighed with regret at the beauty of it all. She had so looked forward to attending the ball after the séance.

Outside the doors of the mansion the true summer

weather enveloped them, the fog of the night making it almost difficult to breathe. Lady Stanhope's coach waited to take her home, the stomping unicorns standing before a pumpkin-shaped carriage.

Sarah hissed and scooted into the corner when Sir Nicodemus entered the coach. Phil leveled a glare at her assistant, then turned her attention on the young man.

"It must be difficult not to experience the illusions of magic, Sir Nicodemus. It's quite a delight for one to ride in a pumpkin." She ended her words with a brilliant smile.

His eyes widened and he stared in silence at her for a moment. Then he blinked. "I can see magic, Lady Radcliff. It's just a bit transparent to me. Like so many other things."

"Ah, like people, I presume?"

The carriage hit a pothole and a streak of white hair fell over his forehead, making him appear even younger. Phil wondered how old he was anyway, then dismissed the thought. It was none of her business and it didn't matter.

"Sir Nicodemus. If you believe I'm a charlatan, why mention a business proposition to me?"

He sighed and lounged back against the velvet padding, his glittering eyes studying her face. "Nico."

"I beg your pardon?"

"I wish you would just call me Nico."

Before Phil had a chance to respond, the coach lurched to a stop in front of her townhouse. For a moment she wished she lived a bit farther away from Lady Stanhope. "I'm sorry we didn't get an opportunity to discuss your business proposal. Perhaps if you call on me in the morning?" Phil gathered up the drapes of her gown and prepared to exit the carriage, but the heat of his touch on her arm made her freeze.

"I'm afraid my business can't wait until the morning," he said. "I detest the city, and now that I've found what I was looking for, I'd rather make the arrangements and leave."

The man always managed to say the most intriguing things. Despite her reluctance to invite him inside, she found herself doing so. She prayed as they made their way to her front door that it would be a quiet night. The only way she'd managed to afford a home within Mayfairy was to purchase a house no one else wanted—a former brothel haunted by its previous occupants. Of course, the noises and moving objects didn't scare her, but the images of the ghosts had proved to be entirely too enlightening.

"Sarah, will you light some lanterns, please?" Phil asked when they entered the drawing room. Sarah lit every candle and touched on every fairylight in her attempts to banish the shadows in the room, but too many still remained. Sarah took an inconspicuous seat in the corner of the room, silent but always watchful over her mistress. Sir Nicodemus took a seat near the fireplace, the banked coals turning the white in his hair a shade of red. Phil's eyes searched the room, noting how plain it appeared compared to Lady Stanhope's. But it did seem that the ghosts might be quiet tonight. She sat on the settee opposite the young man's chair and smiled with relief.

Sir Nicodemus drew her bank notes from his pocket and set them on the tea tray. He smiled a bit sheepishly. Quite becoming. "Sorry. I just wanted to make sure that you'd talk to me."

"I am most intrigued," Phil replied. "What could be of such importance that you felt the need for such coercion?"

He leaned forward, that dark shadow falling over his features again. "How did you know?"

"Whatever do you mean?"

"Oh, come now, you don't really expect me to believe in ghosts, do you? I'm not as gullible as my bro—well,

I believe in what I can see and hear, and I saw nothing. So how did you know Lord Stanhope was having an affair with Lady Montreve? Is that how you mediums manage to convince your clients, by digging up the dirt on them?"

Phil might have been offended if she hadn't sensed the desperation in his manner, as if he wanted to believe in her. A shadow of movement appeared behind his left shoulder, but she ignored it while trying to form her reply. "You do not believe in spirits?"

Her calm response took him aback. Phil smiled, but it quickly faded as she saw what appeared behind him. The ghosts that haunted this house were what she called a memory haunting, meaning that she couldn't interact with them and they never did with her. They just reenacted scenes from their lives over and over. It was Fanny who appeared tonight—and Fanny had a bit more awareness than the others.

"No, I don't believe in ghosts," Sir Nicodemus said. "But my brother does. And therein lies my problem."

Fanny crooked her finger at someone behind Phil, but she refused to turn her head and look. "Yet you believe in magic."

"Of course. Even though it doesn't affect me, I can still see and feel it."

"So why wouldn't you believe that I have the magical gift to see ghosts?"

A young man took Fanny's hand, and she led him over to a mattress that appeared to hover in midair. Usually Fanny's clients were older gentlemen. Phil narrowed her eyes suspiciously.

"Ah, but what I believe doesn't matter. I only need to know that you will be convincing enough to fool, ah, help my brother."

Fanny laughed, low and sultry, pulling her young client into her arms. He kissed her hesitantly, and she ran her fingers through his hair, pulling his mouth closer, practically devouring him.

"Royden thinks Grimspell castle has ghosts, you see. And that they've suddenly become angry and are haunting his dreams."

Phil tore her gaze away from the couple behind Sir Nicodemus and tried to focus her attention on him. Oh botheration, that proved worse. She imagined running her own fingers through his white-brown hair, pulling his mouth toward hers with the same intense hunger that Fanny displayed. What would it be like to feel those youthful lips on hers? To feel such a passion?

Sir Nicodemus's eyes glittered and he leaned forward. "Is something wrong?"

"No, ah, nothing."

Fanny slid the young man's shirt off his shoulders, running ghostly fingers down rippled flesh. She undid his belt, unbuttoned his trousers, and let his clothing fall away. His eagerness for Fanny was plain to see.

Sir Nicodemus pulled something from his coat pocket and handed it to Philomena. She took it but couldn't tear her eyes away from the vision.

"Those are first-class tickets to Norwitch, Norfolk. You'll have to hire a carriage to take you to Trollersby, and from there the locals will direct you to Grimspell castle."

Fanny was doing things with her mouth that had the young man's face twisted with sheer pleasure. Phil watched where and how Fanny moved her tongue to make her client moan the loudest. Whenever the haunting began, Philomena would swear to herself that she wouldn't watch. But she had yet to find the willpower to resist.

"As you can see," Sir Nicodemus said, raising his voice, "if you would be so kind as to *look,* there are several gems from our vaults—a down payment for your services."

That managed to get Phil's attention. Large emeralds

sparkled in her palm. She could only guess at the value, but she imagined it would keep her household for several years. "A down payment?" she whispered.

"Yes. You will get the remainder once you've convinced my brother that you've banished his ghosts. Do we have an agreement?"

Fanny squealed and Phil's traitorous gaze went back to the couple. Good heavens, she sat atop the young man. Phil tilted her head in studied amazement. Fanny rode him hard, up and down, until he cried out with a roar, his groin pushing her high off the bed with his climax.

"Lady Radcliff." Sir Nicodemus reached out and touched her hand. Philomena sprang to her feet, tickets and gems scattering across the polished wooden floor. They bumped heads as they both reached down to pick them up and for a moment faced each other in a crouch. Phil's cheeks felt hot and her body ached with a need that was entirely Fanny's fault.

Sir Nicodemus leaned toward her, as if he sensed her arousal and couldn't help but respond to it. The shadow of his were-self fell away, and tenderness glittered in his eyes. He reached out a hand and stroked her cheek.

Phil snapped her head back and stood. "I think you'd better go."

He rose as well, confusion clouding his features. "But . . . we have an agreement, then? You'll come to Grimspell castle?"

Philomena was so flustered she would have agreed to anything. "Yes, yes, of course. Just please go." Fanny laughed, and Phil turned to find the ghost's eyes staring straight at her. Her heart flipped in her chest with surprise and she opened her mouth to speak, but the vision faded.

Phil spun. "Sir Nicodemus."

He turned stiffly around to look at her from where he stood in the drawing room doorway.

"What are you?"

He didn't ask what she meant. "Surely you've guessed? My were-form is a wolf, Lady Philomena Radcliff. I eat young girls for dinner." And he turned on his heel and left.

Phil shuddered to think of what he did to older women.

Chapter Two

Nico took the first available train out of London. He couldn't stand the stench of the city, the press of so many people. He felt grateful that he'd found a convincing medium quickly, so he could return to the forests of Grimspell.

When he detrained at the station, he hired the first available coach, a ramshackle bit of wheels that lacked any illusion to hide the fading paint and cracked upholstery. Nico hardly cared. He put his face near the broken window and turned his nose toward Grimspell forest.

He sighed and closed his eyes, breathing in the scent of heather from the surrounding fields. Lady Radcliff's face formed in his mind. Whether a charlatan or not, the woman had the theatrical ability to fool his brother and give him some ease. Or so he hoped.

The road grew rougher the farther they went from the city, and he grabbed the leather strap to keep him in his seat.

How odd. When he thought about Lady Radcliff, a calm that he hadn't felt in years settled over him. He decided he would very much like to see the ghost-hunter again.

Would he feel that same tug of desire he'd felt in her drawing room? Damn, the temperature had risen faster than he could account for and she'd fairly vibrated with a lust that his body instantly responded to. He'd barely had enough control to hold his were-self in check. The beast had actually smelled her passion and the urge to howl had tightened his throat.

Did he flatter himself to think that he'd brought on that passion? No, it had to be something else. Perhaps she was mad. Well then, she should fit right in at Grimspell castle.

Nico's nostrils flared as he caught the sudden scent of his forest. Too impatient to wait a moment longer, he banged on the carriage top, and as soon as the coach shuddered to a stop he leaped out the door.

"Take my baggage on to the village," he told the coachman. "I'll walk from here." The pock-faced man scratched beneath his battered top hat and then lightly slapped the reins for the horses to move on, not saying a word.

Nico made his way through the trees, which grew smaller here at the outskirts of the forest. Pine needles crunched beneath his feet and gave off a sharp scent that he eagerly breathed in, finally clearing his senses of the stench of the city. The trees grew thickly together despite their smaller size, and soon the canopy above blocked the sunlight, creating a sheltered haven of gloom and shadows.

Nico smiled and shifted, his clothes disappearing into his coat of fur, his eyesight sharpening so that he could see the tiny nymphs high up in their tree boughs. His sense of smell and hearing became heightened as well. Through the swish of wind in the trees he could hear the chatter of the jeweled dragobirds. Beneath the loamy smell of leaf-covered earth he could scent the stickmen with their mossy hair and mold-covered clothing.

A human could not truly appreciate the beauty of Grimspell forest.

Nico snapped his jaw shut as he heard the sharp crack of a gun. He should have known that his contentment wouldn't last. The villagers weren't supposed to hunt in these woods, but they still persisted. And since Beatrice's death, the fools would shoot at anything that moved.

He took off toward the sound, scenting the two villagers before he saw them. Nico shifted to human before he approached. "What do you think you're doing? There's no poaching here, and you're liable to shoot a baronet."

One of the men bowed his head in a quick apology but the other narrowed his eyes at Nicodemus. "We weren't poachin', m'lord. We seen us a black wolf and we got us a right to protect ourselves."

Nico's stomach dropped and rage poured through him. Besides himself, there were two other weres in Trollersby. Sir Edgar Hexword and his daughter, Jane. Jane's wolf had a black coat.

"Get out of my woods," he growled. Nico towered over the two men. "If I catch you here again, I'll haul your sorry selves to the magistrate."

The smaller man quickly turned and fled, but the larger of the two took his time leaving. "Don't think just 'cause yer gentry that ye can get away with murder. 'Twas a wolf that killed yer young lady and jus' 'cause the magistrate found ye innocent don't mean that we all believe it."

Nico's hold on his were-self became tenuous. The desire to leap on the man, to feel him quake in terror beneath his snapping jaws, overwhelmed him. He stood with fists clenched, hardly daring to breathe, until the men disappeared from his sight. He finally let out a shuddering breath.

Jane.

He shifted and raised his nose, looking for any trace of her scent. He found none, but headed in the direction the men had been shooting, keeping alert for any sign of tracks. After circling a stand of oaks several times, he found the barest trace of paw prints. They were too large to be Jane's. But the elusive beast had left no scent and nothing but a ghost of a track. Nico howled in frustration.

After two years of searching, he'd found nothing significant that would lead him to Beatrice's killer. Nico turned and headed for Hallows Hall. The guilt that had left him in London shadowed him again as he thought of his former fiancée.

If only they hadn't fought the night Beatrice had been killed. If only his were-beast didn't enjoy the thrill of the hunt and lust for the kill. When she'd died, the wolf had been free to roam. Nico had welcomed the chance to put aside all his human concerns. The wolf had grown so strong that Nico kept to his beast-form for months. When Royden had finally come to fetch him, Nico had almost turned on his brother. He couldn't let that happen again.

He shook his head. He hadn't killed Beatrice. Her body had looked as if it had been mauled by a wolf, but it could have been some other animal. He just had to find it.

Hallows Hall sat on a low rise, with a view of the valley behind it. Sunlight crowned the old manor with a golden glow, highlighting the thread of gold that streaked through the local stone. Rose vines covered the front face of the building, most of them still in bloom and heavily scenting the air.

Nico shifted to human and strode up the drive. His brother would be annoyed if he found out Nico had visited his pack before returning home, so he'd best make this visit quick.

Before he reached the door, it swung open and Jane flew out, her black hair tumbling out of its bun and her soft brown eyes shining with joy. "Nico!"

He scooped her up into his arms and swung her around, her hoops rocking like a giant bell. Jane laughed, her freckled cheeks flushed with color. "You're finally back."

Nico set her down and tugged one of her curls. "I've only been gone a few weeks."

"Well, it felt like forever! Did you find a medium? What's she like? Do tambourines fly in the air at a séance?"

Nicodemus smiled at her questions. Although only a few years separated them, Jane always seemed so much younger to him. "Yes. You'll meet her yourself soon. And no."

He watched her match her questions to his answers and open her mouth to ask more. He laid a gentle finger across her lips. "I can't stay. I just got home and haven't even seen Royden yet. But tell me, have you been in Grimspell forest lately?"

"A couple of times, just to find out if you'd returned yet. Why?"

A deep male voice interrupted them. "Wulfson." Sir Edgar Hexword stood at the door, then shifted to wolf. He was slightly smaller than Nico's wolf but had the same coloring of brown streaked with white—although the white in Hexword's case looked more gray.

"Hexword," Nico replied, and then he too shifted to wolf, Jane quickly following suit. Sir Edgar drew back his lips and ears, tucking his tail between his legs and arching his back. Jane copied her father's movements. Nico responded by standing tall, with his ears up and forward, staring at Hexword and then his daughter, establishing his dominance over the pack again. With that out of the way, Nico shifted back to human and held out his hand to Sir Edgar Hexword.

The older man shifted to human and grasped Nico's hand in a firm grip. "How was London?" he asked.

Nico grimaced.

"Ah, well. I enjoy the city myself. The theatre and museums . . . I just wish I had more opportunity to visit."

Jane's mouth started moving while she shifted. ". . . and he found a woman who can talk to ghosts, Father. Could we invite her for dinner soon?"

Hexword raised a bushy gray brow.

Nico shrugged. "I don't know whether she actually communicates with the spirits. I don't even know if I believe in ghosts. But I think she'll convince Royden."

Sir Edgar nodded. "Why don't you come inside for a glass of brandy?"

Nico shook his head, his hair brushing his cheeks. "I have to get home. I just wanted to tell you that I caught some villagers shooting at anything that moves in my woods. Be careful if you hunt there, and use the roads when you can."

Hexword nodded. "It's gotten worse lately. But now that they know you've returned, I'm sure the villagers will stay out of the woods."

Nico frowned. "We'll see." He glanced at Jane, who looked more than a little frightened. He forced a smile. "I'm looking forward to introducing you to Lady Radcliff, the ghost-hunter. I think you'll find her interesting, to say the least."

Jane studied his face. "It appears that you do."

Nico felt his smile become genuine. "She's . . . not what I expected."

Hexword laughed and slapped him on the shoulder. Before Jane could ask what he meant, Nico shifted and loped back down the drive, following a well-worn trail back to Grimspell castle.

The old keep didn't glow in the sunshine; rather it seemed to suck the light into its old stones and swallow it. Nico passed through the gate where the outer walls had once stood, the forest taking over the fallen stone until it seemed that a layer of bush and bracken ringed the castle. When he walked past the stables, the dogs set up a racket, quickly recognized who had invaded their territory, and their growls became teasing instead of vicious.

Out of habit, Nico glanced up at the narrow windows of the keep before rolling in the soft dirt with the dogs. His parents hadn't approved of his playing with the animals, and Royden's wife, Edwina, appeared to feel the same way. Although he didn't much care what Edwina might think of him, he wouldn't want to offend her for Royden's sake. But it appeared that no one knew he was back yet, and so he rolled into the middle of the pack. Most of them were wolfhounds, but still, he was careful with teeth and jaws against their weaker strength. But he played with abandon, until his coat was covered in a fine layer of dirt. When he finally shifted back to human, the stable master greeted him and kindly brushed his clothes with a broom.

As Nico passed the inner walls, his steps grew slower. Something about the old place bothered him. His father had told him that his uneasiness was natural because he was a were, but had never fully explained what he'd meant. Perhaps he would have if he hadn't died a few years ago on that ocean voyage with Mother.

Nicodemus trudged up the stone steps and opened the massive wooden door, his sense of unease increasing. The interior of the keep had been remodeled so many times, only the outer walls repaired in their original form. He stepped into an entrance hall, which now held portraits of his ancestors and weapons and armor from the old storage rooms. The flagstone had been softened with wool rugs here and there, but his footsteps still echoed down the hall. He imagined Lady Radcliff walking these halls in her medieval-type dresses and decided she'd fit in quite well here. He passed the library, dining room, and withdrawing room, hearing the sweet sound of Edwina's singing coming from the music room.

Edwina had decorated the room when she'd married Royden, and Nicodemus couldn't say he cared for her taste. The powder-blue furniture and pink pillows clashed with the yellow-plastered walls. The piano held so many gewgaws that he couldn't see the polished surface of the instrument. But since the castle windows were all narrow, he did have to admit that the colors brightened the room.

And the acoustics were perfect for Edwina's angelic voice. Nico stood in the doorway and just listened, his eyes half closed with pleasure. Edwina was the daughter of Lord Magift, the local magistrate and Baron of Bargest House. She'd inherited the baron's level of power and had been given a magical gift of song. There wasn't a singer in London who could match the beauty of her full-throated voice.

In the corner of the room stood a table with three tiny marionettes playing an accompaniment. Strings that disappeared into thin air magically pulled their wooden arms to play their instruments, and tiny sparkles of light swirled around their curtained stage. Royden had bought it as a wedding gift for Edwina, and it was her most prized possession.

Royden looked up from the piano bench where he'd also been accompanying Edwina, and broke off the tune. "Nico! Welcome home."

Nico stepped into the room, ignoring the scowl on Edwina's face at the interruption of her recital, and kissed her on the cheek. Her face cleared and her natural prettiness returned. She patted her blonde hair and blinked her blue eyes at him. "Did you bring me my present?"

He'd almost forgotten. "It's in my baggage, which I'll have fetched from the village. But I found the bolt of fabric you asked for . . . and a few other things besides."

Edwina clapped her hands and flew out the door, calling for Dickens to send a boy to the village.

Royden smiled indulgently after his wife, but his expression didn't quite meet his eyes, which were ringed by dark circles. Although he'd always been a trifle pale, his face now looked like bleached parchment. Royden had taken after their mother and hadn't inherited their father's power of shape-shifting. Which meant that the lands and title went to Nico. But instead of being resentful, Royden had made himself indispensable to his brother. His management of the house and lands for these last few years had allowed Nico the freedom to search for Beatrice's killer.

But his illness, this belief that he was sensitive to the supposed ghosts of Grimspell castle, had put the burden of running the estate back on Nico. And Nico couldn't find the truth if he was tied up with all the details of the estate. Besides his genuine concern for his brother's health, Nico needed his help. "You're still not sleeping?"

Royden shook his head.

"Or eating?"

Royden sighed. "I just don't seem to have any appetite. Did you happen to bring back any sweets from London with you?"

Nico grinned. Royden's sweet tooth had caused him more trouble growing up than Nico's shifting, and it stood as a private joke between them. "It happens that I did. I'm sure Edwina will have my trunk here within the hour and I can tempt you with what I brought."

"Perhaps." Royden unsuccessfully tried to match his brother's grin. "Did you find a medium? A real one, that is?"

Nico turned and sat in the blue wingback chair next to the piano. He sat forward, pulled a pink lace pillow from behind his back, and leaned back again, tossing the bit of fluff onto the settee. "Well, let's see. I couldn't find a royal to speak to—the Hall of Mages was so backed up with requests that I would have had to wait for over a month for an audience—and there's only one duke I heard of who made a hobby of crafting ghost spells. He wasn't interested in our supposed spirits, however."

"Nico, just because you can't see them—"

He waved a hand. "I know, I know. But why haven't the castle ghosts haunted my dreams? And why would they suddenly become angry within the last few months? Even the duke couldn't show me a real ghost, and until I see one—"

"You're just not sensitive enough to be aware of them. You're incredibly stubborn and too skeptical for your own good."

"I went to London for you, didn't I?"

Royden ran his fingers over the piano keys. He knew how much Nico hated cities, London being the largest in England and therefore the worst. "Yes, you did. So you couldn't find anyone to come?"

"I didn't say that." Nico fidgeted with the fringe on the edge of the chair, watching Royden get frustrated with his silence.

As usual, Royden broke first. "But who's left? Earls can create illusions of ghosts, but that wouldn't help. I suppose a very powerful viscount could craft a potion or charm that might help us?"

Nico sighed. He couldn't even tease Royden anymore. His brother's health had rapidly deteriorated in his absence. "Not that I know of. But I did find a baroness who had an unusual magical gift. She can not only see spirits, but she can also hear and talk to them." Nico kept his doubts about Lady Radcliff's abilities to himself. Perhaps Royden's belief would help him. "She has agreed to help us."

His brother's eyes lit up. "When will she be here?"

"Within the week, I imagine. She supports herself with her gift and I paid her a hefty sum from the family treasure."

"Doesn't she have anyone to take care of her?"

"I don't believe so. I don't think it would matter to her anyway. She's of an independent nature."

Royden suddenly leaned forward and studied Nico's face. "Is she? How unusual. Tell me more about her."

Nicodemus felt his mood lighten and sat up straighter, visualizing the unique Lady Radcliff. "Her name is Lady

Philomena Radcliff. She refuses the conventions of current fashion and dresses in the most outlandish clothes . . . and they suit her entirely. She employs a shape-shifter as her assistant, and I swear the woman's were-form is some kind of snake."

Royden made a face.

"Exactly. Not many would employ shape-shifters in their households, Roy. It's not like here at Grimspell, where all of our castle servants are weres. And even I would hesitate to hire one that could shift into a snake."

"She sounds like a remarkable woman."

"And beautiful too. Did I mention her beauty?" His brother choked on a laugh, and only then did Nico realize that Royden had been teasing him. "Well, she is. And that's the last thing I'm going to tell you about her. Your curiosity will have to wait until she arrives, you ungrateful chap."

Two spots of color had appeared on Royden's cheeks. He stood up from the piano bench as if he had the legs of an old man. "I'm entirely grateful to you, Nicodemus. And I hope she can help. And . . . well, this is the first time I've seen you interested in a woman since Beatrice died."

Nico's gut twisted at the mention of her name, and he withdrew into the shadow of his were-self again. He had the urge to leave the castle, hunt through the forest again. Perhaps outside his own woods those tracks would pick up. He should search again beyond his lands—

"Nico, Joseph asked me to talk with you as soon as you returned." Royden swayed on his feet. "He's hiring the yearly lads for the harvest and would like our help in choosing them. I don't mind going, but . . ."

Nicodemus stood and grabbed his brother's arm to steady him. "The only place you're going is to bed to get some rest. I'll go see Joseph now."

Royden nodded and shuffled out the door.

Nico ran his fingers through his hair in frustration, a fine dusting of dirt from his romp with the dogs falling on Edwina's clean floor. He hoped Philomena Radcliff, charlatan or not, had taken the first train out of London and would be here soon.

For all of their sakes.

Chapter Three

Phil thoroughly enjoyed the journey to Norwitch. The locomotive traveled so very fast it just took her breath away with excitement. Occasionally she was sent to the country to perform a séance, but she'd never traveled so far from London. The inns in which they overnighted were quaint, and even more so the farther they went. Sir Nicodemus had provided first-class tickets, and even Sarah, who despised traveling, appeared to be quite comfortable.

When they entered the station at Norwitch, the smell of sheep's wool and boiled leather overwhelmed her. The city looked as if it had grown up in and around the trees, and a great cathedral and an old Norman castle dominated the skyline.

Phil would have liked to explore, but Sir Nicodemus had mentioned angry ghosts in his home. And although the baronet appeared to be as sensitive to otherworldly contacts as a block of wood, it sounded as if his brother was not. Despite their corporeal nature, angry ghosts could be harmful.

Sarah finally secured them a coach, and they left the city behind. The roads became rough enough that Phil wished she could have found a carriage with better springs, but the view from the window made up for the bumpy ride. Phil opened the window and breathed in the fresh, sparkling air. She couldn't put a name to half the plants she saw, but the riot of green and the color of the flowers made her feel peaceful, and she dozed for a while.

"I don't like the lookss of that," Sarah said.

The carriage gave a stupendous bounce, and Phil opened her eyes and glanced out the window. The rolling hills and meadows of heather had been replaced by the shadow of enormous trees. Their huge roots had spread to the road, which caused the coach to jostle so vigorously that Phil heard Sarah's teeth snap.

"I think it looks mysterious and—"

"Sspooky."

Phil held her hand to the roof of the coach as a bounce nearly smashed her coiffure against it. "I was going to say intriguing. Imagine what splendid pockets of nature lie within its sheltering boughs."

Sarah gave her a skeptical look, her narrow lips compressing into a fine line. A particularly rough patch made it impossible to speak for a time.

"All right then," Philomena continued. "Just imagine all the small rodents hiding in the undergrowth. And I would think bats would cloud the sky in the evening."

Sarah's glossy black eyes narrowed with interest, and she looked out the window with an altered perspective. Phil doubted if London provided her assistant with many a bat-snack, and although the subject was too delicate for discussion, she had read up on the habits of Sarah's were-form.

Boa constrictors particularly loved bat hunting. And Phil wanted Sarah to be happy, for she'd had so little happiness in her lifetime. Although most of the gentry treated their servants as nonentities, Phil had decided long ago that a happy servant made a loyal one. She paid more attention to them as a consequence and she'd never been disappointed in their service—unlike many of her friends.

The coach finally, mercifully, shuddered to a halt. Both Phil and Sarah climbed out with shaky legs. A charming chapel stood before them, with an ivy-covered parsonage nestled beside it.

"The village of Trollersby, m'lady." The coachman swept his battered hat in the direction of the thatch-roofed group of buildings.

"If you would wait but a moment," Phil told the coachman, "I will inquire as to the directions of Grimspell castle."

His eyes widened, and his mouth worked as if he would like to spit. "This here is as far as I can take ye."

Sarah hissed in her scariest way, but the man didn't even blink. He just turned and untied their trunks, lowered them quickly to the road, and his equipage disappeared in a cloud of dirt.

"Well, I never!" said Phil.

"He'ss more sscared of something else than he iss of me," Sarah muttered, looking decidedly put out.

Phil suppressed a smile, picked up her traveling bag, and decided the trunks would just have to stay where the coachman had dropped them, for they were too heavy to carry. She walked down the graveled path to the parsonage door, scattering a few chickens along the way, and boldly rapped the knocker.

A portly man with enormous mutton chops and a balding pate answered the door. "May I help you?"

"Are you the rector?"

He had very blue, very jolly eyes. "Reverend Cyril Jenkins, at your service."

"Lady Philomena Radcliff, from London. I apologize for disturbing you, but our coachman dropped us off at your doorstep . . ."

He smiled, revealing a large gap in his front teeth. "Ah. Yes, well, this is usually as far as a city coach will take you. Come in, come in." He held open the door, revealing a cozy front room with several crucifixes adorning the walls.

"It's most kind of you, I'm sure. But if you could just direct us to the nearest stable where we can hire another carriage to take us to Grimspell castle, we would be most obliged."

The twinkle in his eyes disappeared. "And what business would a lady have there?"

Sarah hissed at his tone. The reverend's eyes widened, and he took a step back.

"I'm sure that's none of your affair," Phil said in her most no-nonsense voice. "If you would just direct us to the stable."

Reverend Jenkins had started to sweat. "I meant no offense, ma'am. It's just that with all the goings-on up at the castle, I feel it's my duty to warn you."

Fully prepared for the man to whisper to her of ghosts and hauntings, Phil smoothed the front of her dress and tried for patience.

The reverend plowed on. "You do know that the owner of the castle is a were-wolf?"

Phil didn't blink. "Of course."

"And that he . . . well, just be careful, Lady Radcliff. He's a dangerous man."

"I'm sure Sir Nicodemus will be grateful to hear what you have to say about him."

The man took a step back in surprise. "As the Good Lord's servant, it's my duty to protect those in need of His guidance, m'lady. You can tell the baronet I said so."

Phil sighed. "The stable, Reverend Jenkins?"

"We don't have one. But if you would like to wait, James will be returning with my carriage shortly, and if you're still determined to pay a visit, I can manage to take you there."

Meaning he would lecture her for hours in an attempt to change her mind. Should she shock him by telling him why she was visiting Grimspell? She glanced at Sarah, whose eyes were shining with anticipation.

Philomena felt a yank on her skirt. One of the reverend's chickens was pecking the hem of her best traveling outfit. Sarah let out a hiss, and a cacophony of squawking followed, feathers flying in all directions.

"Can you direct me toward the castle?" she shouted over the noise.

The reverend swallowed hard and pointed a shaky finger. "It's down that road through the enchanted forest."

Sarah's tongue flicked out of her mouth, and she licked her lips in the direction the chickens had gone.

Phil had run out of patience. "Capital. It's a lovely day, and I think we shall walk it."

He glanced at her fine clothes and shook his head. "If you won't listen to the sound advice of a man of the cloth, at least heed my warning and stay out of the forest."

Phil dug through her reticule and gave the man a few shillings. "Would you be so kind as to rescue our trunks and have them delivered to Grimspell?"

He gave an exaggerated sigh. "Of course I will, if you're sure you wish to—"

"I assure you, I do. Come along, Sarah."

Her assistant gave one last lingering look at the scattered feathers and followed Philomena down the dusty road.

"I do believe that's one of the most shocking encounters I've ever had," Phil said, glad that her traveling suit was a few inches above the ground. Her garments lacked the hoops that would carry the cloth above the dirt. "I couldn't bear to stay in that man's presence another moment."

"Ssuperstitious, they are. Just because Ssir Nicodemusss is a were don't make him any more dangerouss than any other man."

The trees quickly swallowed the road, casting Phil in a welcome shade of coolness. "I imagine we'll encounter that sort of nonsense among many of the villagers, Sarah. Peculiar though, since the baronet has lived here all his life. You would think that familiarity would ease their fears."

The woods grew closer until Phil could hear rustlings in

the undergrowth. Her back had already started to ache a bit. Although her dresses were lightly boned, they didn't give her back the support a corset would have. She turned and glanced behind her at Sarah, who mimicked her mistress's style of dress in much plainer cloth, but Sarah didn't appear to be aching at all. Of course, she must keep in mind the suppleness and strength of Sarah's were-form.

Birdsong filtered through the depths of the forest, and the buzzing of a few bees among a patch of blooming nettles provided an accompaniment to their song. The leaves beside her rustled with the movement of some small animal.

Sarah cleared her throat. "Do you ssuppose it's really an enchanted foresst, mistress? I'm hungry."

Philomena shrugged. "Most probably. And until we find out the nature of the enchantment, I suggest we heed that bit of advice from the poor reverend and stay out of it."

"Lady Radcliff."

"Yes?"

"It appearss that you have ssomething stuck to the back of your sskirt."

Phil grasped the material in annoyance and spun it around to her front to study it. A small stick had attached itself to the cloth. She reached down to tug it free when it suddenly moved. She stifled a scream and suppressed the urge to run away. A sorry lot of good that would do her when it was attached to her skirt.

"What iss it?" Sarah breathed.

"It looks . . . why, it looks like a praying mantis, that's all." Phil grasped the stick again and gave it a much fiercer pull. The stick screamed. Sarah hissed, and this time Phil allowed the screech in the back of her throat to come out.

"Easy there," the stick said. "Do ye wanna break me?"

Philomena brought the cloth closer to her face. Two arms, covered in moss. Two legs with some darker substance covering them . . . mold? And yes, atop the spindly figure sat a tiny head with small black eyes and a hooked nose. He wore nothing but a loincloth made of tiny leaves.

Phil finally gathered enough moisture in her mouth to reply. "Of course not. But why, exactly, did you latch on to my dress?"

"Thought I'd catch a ride, is all." The stickman pulled his clawlike fingers out of the weave of the cloth and tumbled to the ground. "Thank ye, kindly. It was interesting." He gave her a creaky bow and walked back into the forest.

Phil headed up the road again, this time a bit faster. The little man had meant her no harm, but still, the encounter discomfited her. What if he'd decided to attach himself to her pantalets?

By the time she saw the crenellated turrets of the castle, she had a raging thirst and heaven knew how many blisters on her feet. Sarah lagged behind, and when she turned to give the woman a smile of encouragement Sarah smiled back, revealing her pointed teeth. Which is why Sarah rarely smiled, and it testified to her fatigue that she so forgot herself.

Philomena went through a gate that appeared to be attached to a solid wall of greenery, then froze when she saw Grimspell castle. It looked like something right out of a fairy tale, with its wall of towers protecting the stone keep beyond. Although the walls of the keep had been weathered to gray by time, the arched windows and corbelled cornices made it appear fanciful rather than dismal.

"Isn't it grand?" she whispered. Sarah gave her an odd look, but Philomena was too excited to notice. She couldn't wait to explore the inside. "Can you imagine the history within those walls?"

She hobbled forward as if in a trance, despite the pain in her feet, which had gone beyond aching and into sheer agony. She passed a building that smelled like the stable when suddenly she found herself in the midst of a growling, tumbling pack of dogs. Then Sarah stood at her right hand and shifted. Sarah's clothing melted into her skin, although it didn't matter what color material she wore—her scales always had dark black blobs on a brown background. She had teeth sharp as needles and no fangs . . . since boas strangled their prey to death. Phil had never actually seen Sarah feed and she really would prefer not to.

Sarah hissed and snapped at the dogs, quickly clearing a circle around them.

The largest of the beasts—almost twice as big as the rest of the pack—rolled out of a tumble and stood before her on all fours. Time stood still for a moment and Phil dared not breathe. What a magnificent animal! His head nearly reached her shoulders, his coat a glistening sheen of striped white and browns, and his brown eyes had golden flecks within them.

She recognized those eyes.

Perhaps a more ordinary woman—one who didn't talk to ghosts and live in a haunted house—might have chosen that moment to turn right around and run back screaming to the reverend's ivy-covered house. But all Phil could think about was her aching feet and nearly intolerable thirst.

"Sir Nicodemus, would you mind calling off your dogs? They are scaring Sarah." Phil felt relieved that her voice barely shook.

He turned and growled at the dogs until they lowered their heads and whined, slinking away. Then the baronet shifted to human and Philomena felt that peculiar flutter in her stomach again. She understood the unusual streaks of white in his brown hair now; they matched the fur of his were-self. He seemed taller than she remembered, his muscular shoulders even broader in just a thin linen shirt. He had a bit of a beard shadow and his hair, lacking the cord that had held it back in London, fell wildly across his cheeks and forehead.

Dirt streaked his trousers and the front of his white shirt. Why did men appear more rugged and handsome when they were scruffy, and women just appeared . . . well, scruffy?

Sir Nicodemus smiled, and his dimples made her heart race. "I think your assistant is scaring my dogs more than they are frightening her. Do you mind?"

Phil tore her gaze away from the handsome man. "Sarah. I'm perfectly safe."

Sarah swung her head around in that weaving, dancing way of hers and slowly shifted back to human. A few of the dogs barked in surprise, and Sarah hissed, her human throat just as capable of emitting the same menace. The beasts turned tail and disappeared into the stables.

"Well, that was quite a welcome," Phil said into the sudden silence.

Sir Nicodemus's narrow cheeks flushed with color. "I do apologize . . . had I known you were coming—"

Phil found his blush most endearing. "It's my fault, I'm afraid. I just couldn't bear to sit with that reverend and wait for a carriage."

He took a step forward, those full lips quirking. "Couldn't you? I'm rather glad to hear that."

He must know what the reverend had to say about him, and the fact that she had refused the rector's company appeared to cheer him immensely. He took another step nearer, until she could feel the heat of his body. "I don't play with the dogs that often, you see. It's just that I had been away for a while and they missed me."

"I would think that you would play with them quite often," Phil breathed, trying not to drown in his lovely eyes. "That's your nature, after all."

His smile widened, revealing those perfectly straight teeth. Although at this close proximity, Phil could make out the hint of fangs at the corners of his mouth. What would it be like to kiss him?

"You have a most accepting nature, Lady Radcliff."

"Do I?" Botheration, Phil had completely forgotten what they had been discussing.

"You must be tired," he said, curling his hand under her arm in the most casual way. "Let me show you to your rooms. I'll have Beth fetch you some refreshment. I've already warned her about your assistant—"

"That wasn't necessary," interrupted Phil, leaning on his arm rather heavily. She told herself that she should resist the desire to be closer to him, but her feet really were sore. "Sarah is perfectly civilized unless she thinks I'm in danger."

Sarah made a noise in the back of her throat.

"I meant no offense," he replied. "It's just that, well, Beth is a weasel and they don't much get along with snakes."

Phil slowly went up the castle stairs, noting how shiny and worn they appeared. She wondered how many knights and maidens had trampled up and down these very stones. "Perhaps you should provide us with a different maid."

"It wouldn't matter a great deal. I should warn you, Lady Radcliff, every servant here at Grimspell is some type of were."

"Really? How extraordinary."

Sir Nicodemus opened one side of the double wooden doors. It creaked quite satisfactorily. "Not really. The title of baronet is rather empty to most shape-shifters, as it doesn't necessarily come with an endowment, as Sarah can surely testify to. And most of the gentry aren't willing to hire a were, even if their natures are of a peaceful sort."

Phil nodded rather distractedly, trying to force her eyes to adjust to the gloom behind the doors. "I found Sarah starving on the streets of London—I know precisely what you mean. But I've never had a more loyal companion and her nature has protected me from dishonest clients more often than I can count."

Sarah made a soft, rather satisfied hiss from behind them.

Philomena's eyes had adjusted and her heart sank. The interior of the castle had been entirely redone. Besides the armor and weapons adorning the entry hall, it appeared to be designed to look like the interior of any ordinary mansion in London. She couldn't help a sigh of disappointment.

Nicodemus came to an abrupt stop. "Is something wrong?"

"Oh, no. It's just that . . . I so hoped to see a real castle."

He smiled indulgently and led her on. "This is a real castle. This floor was once the armory and guardrooms, and although it's been renovated into smaller, public rooms, a remnant of the original design can still be seen on the flagstones, see there?"

Phil looked down and nodded, noting the streaks of lighter stone where a larger wall must have once stood.

"And the only way to get up to the first floor," he continued, passing through a well-stocked library and opening a door, "is by the tower stairs."

The winding stairway looked sufficiently medieval. The ache in Phil's feet faded a bit as excitement propelled her up the stairs. Small windows emitted enough light for her to see her feet, and she could imagine again those who might have gone before her. A slight musty smell with a rather sharp undertone made her ask, "Do you still use the garderobes?"

She couldn't detect a trace of embarrassment in his reply. "Fortunately, we had some plumbing installed for necessaries. Although I should warn you, the water is never warm."

Phil stopped at the landing and pushed open the door. A long hall stretched out before her.

"This floor was once the great hall," Sir Nicodemus

said. "It has been divided into suites of bedrooms. The floor above us once housed the original castle lord's bedroom, but has been renovated into servants' rooms and a schoolroom. I can show it to you tomorrow, if you'd like."

Phil nodded with an eagerness that matched the tone of his voice.

He walked ahead, pointing out various bedrooms, including his, which was only a few doors down from the guest room into which he showed Phil and Sarah. To Phil's delight, her room held a large tester bed, complete with boxed canopy and hanging curtains. She had but to close the draperies to be in a room within the room.

"Through that door is a small chamber for Sarah. I thought you would be more comfortable with her nearby."

Philomena gave him a smile of such appreciation that he appeared dumbfounded for a moment.

"Yes, well. If you need anything, there are two pulls, one for the maid and another for the kitchen. We dine early here in the country, at six. I hope you'll be joining us?"

"Of course. I'm looking forward to meeting the rest of your family."

He backed slowly out of the room, as if hesitant to leave, and Phil found herself regretting that she wouldn't see him for several hours. They'd barely spent a moment in each other's company.

Then she chided herself for a fool. Why would such a beautiful young man have any interest in her society? "Until then, Sir Nicodemus?"

Sarah stepped forward and closed the door behind him, then set Phil's bag next to the wardrobe and went to investigate her own quarters.

Phil sat on an odd, v-shaped chair, and unlaced her boots with a groan. She wiggled her toes, and by the time she'd counted her blisters, a knock sounded on the outer door. "Enter."

A small brown-haired woman with beady black eyes and a rather pink nose hurried into the room. She took one look at Phil's feet and clucked, quickly setting her tray down. "How do you do, Lady Radcliff? I'm Beth. Shall I fetch some unguent for those poor feet?"

Before Phil had a chance to reply, Sarah emerged from her connecting room. The two servants stared at each other for a moment, both of them swaying back and forth in time with each other's movements. When one leaned left, the other followed. When one leaned right . . .

Phil felt quite mesmerized. "Sarah, this is Beth."

Sarah hissed. Beth hissed back, but with an entirely different inflection. For a moment the tension in the room felt palpable. Then both women suddenly smiled at each other.

"I thought I might fetch a salve for your mistress's feet," said Beth. "Would you like me to show you the kitchens?"

Sarah's eyes lit, and when Phil nodded, she followed Beth out of the room.

Phil stared at the tray Beth had left behind, her mouth so dry her tongue felt stiff. A pitcher speckled with condensation sat in the middle of the carved tray. She stood with a wince and hobbled over to it, picked up a glass, and shakily poured some of the colored liquid. Phil took a taste and closed her eyes in sheer rapture at the tartly sweet flavor. She shivered as the lemonade went down her throat.

She really should bathe her face and feet. But the bed looked so inviting. Phil gave in to exhaustion and collapsed across the heavenly soft surface, quite oblivious to the world for some time . . . until she felt a ghost.

The room's temperature lowered abruptly, and Phil's eyes flew open. Despite the daylight still streaming in through the narrow windows, she clearly saw the apparition when it floated through the shadows of her chamber.

The man looked like a medieval peasant, with coarse

clothing, a straw hat and split hose. He waved a scythe in front of him, not as if he mowed a field, but more like he warned off some attacker. Before she could blink, he went through the wall.

Phil sat up, pulling the counterpane around her shoulders, and waited for her chattering teeth to calm. Botheration, the ghost appeared to be a memory, with no awareness of her whatsoever. She sincerely hoped the castle held more interactive spirits, or she would have a difficult time finding out what was troubling them.

She wished that Tup could have come with her, but most ghosts couldn't travel far from the place they haunted. Oh, how she would miss him! And he might have been able to help.

Someone had fetched her trunk; she nearly tripped over it as she opened the small door into the washroom. When she saw the bath full of water, all other considerations flew from her mind. Sarah and Beth must have returned and prepared it while she'd been sleeping, and although the water was tepid, it felt perfect for the warm summer temperature.

Phil quickly shed her clothes, rubbing the small dents in her skin caused by the boning in her dress, and lowered herself into the water. Her feet stung like the blazes, but by the time she finished her bath and rubbed her blisters with some of Beth's salve, which she'd found next to the tub, she managed to slide into her silk slippers with barely a wince.

The clock on the mantel showed half past five, but she decided to go down to dinner early in the hopes of exploring a few rooms. She glanced in the cheval glass and decided that wearing her favorite blue-gray watered silk gown had been a good choice. The sleeves puffed at the shoulders and tightened down to her wrists and the double-layered skirt had sufficient fullness to approximate current fashion. Besides, the back had a train, and she could imagine herself a princess of the castle.

She almost laughed at her own foolishness, then decided that at her age, she could afford to be a bit foolish.

Phil hadn't heard a slither from Sarah's room but checked her assistant's chamber anyway. The woman hadn't even unpacked yet. She must have returned to the kitchens with Beth, and Philomena felt relieved that Sarah would be able to fit in with the rest of the staff while they stayed here.

With the approaching dusk, fairylights had been lit in the stairway, which gave the walls a rosy glow. In spite of her blisters, she fairly floated down the stairs, imagining that she ran to welcome home her errant knight, back from some daring quest.

The library smelled of old paper and rich leather. Phil wondered if any of the books contained an account of the castle's history and decided she would have to ask. Nary a ghost hovered about the room, so she went into the hallway and heard the echo of voices coming from an open doorway at the end of it. She studied the portraits of Sir Nicodemus's ancestors that lined the walls, deciding that all of them were extraordinarily handsome. He came from a long line of shape-shifters.

The deep sound of his voice almost made her jump.

". . . I know, but Joseph said some of the workers wouldn't hire on with me there. I'm sure he'll choose fine, Royden—he's been running the home farm for years."

Sir Nicodemus spoke from his position near the mantel, one booted foot atop the raised hearth, a glass of burgundy liquid in his hand. He seemed to sense her presence with an uncanny awareness, for as soon as she appeared in the open doorway he looked up.

His eyes met hers, and Phil felt a spark of something like lightning rip through her body. For a moment she could neither breathe nor move, trapped within the depths of his dark brown gaze. He seemed to look into her soul, to go beyond her superficial thoughts into the very recesses of her being. Phil lifted her chin. She wasn't frightened by what he might find there.

Then the moment passed, and she took a breath. The gold in his eyes glittered in the candlelight. He swept an approving gaze over her, from the top of her loose coiffure to the bottom of her flowing dress. And then he smiled. Rather wolfishly. "Lady Radcliff, how kind of you to join us."

Phil stepped into the withdrawing room. Decorated in soft peaches and greens, it exuded a peaceful aura. She didn't detect a sign of an otherworldly presence. Despite the modern furniture, the walls had been decorated with tapestries of knights and maidens, and wooden carvings of saints. Silver chalices adorned several tables, and she longed to study the intricate enamel work on the vases scattered about the room.

A couple sat on a lovely curved settee adjacent to the cold fireplace, and she turned to study them instead. The man stood at her entrance, his face similar in looks to Sir Nicodemus, but not nearly as handsome. His brown hair lacked the streaks of white and his brown eyes those glittering sparkles of gold. His mouth might have been just as full-lipped, but it was compressed into a thin line that reflected a man haunted by demons. Shadows darkened the skin beneath his eyes and made his complexion look even paler. He quickly rose and sketched a bow, a tentative smile relaxing his face.

The woman next to him stayed seated, her hands anchoring the hoops of her dress across her lap. Blonde-haired and blue-eyed, she had a flawless complexion with the dewy glow of youth. The practiced smile frozen on her face gave her the ethereal beauty that was so popular among the aristocracy of London.

Sir Nicodemus strode forward and gently grasped Phil's

gloved hand, leading her over to the couple. "Lady Philomena Radcliff, may I introduce my brother, Master Royden Wulfson of Grimspell castle, and his wife, the Honorable Edwina Wulfson, baroness-of-honor for Bargest House?"

Philomena frowned. There was something about that house name that sounded familiar, but she couldn't recall it. Then she realized that Royden had not inherited the shape-shifting abilities of his brother and had been given the honorary title of "master" for his stewardship of the castle. Although he would surpass Nicodemus's ranking when he assumed his wife's title upon her parents' death— assuming Edwina passed her magical testing.

Figuring out the status of lords and ladies always gave Phil a headache.

Master Wulfson reached out and clasped her hand with the intensity of a drowning man. "I do hope you will call us just Royden and Edwina . . . we're not much for titles here, are we, Nico?"

Sir Nicodemus shot his sister-in-law a look and then chuckled.

Phil felt his laugh vibrate all the way to her toes. "I would be honored. And you may call me Philomena."

"Oh," said Edwina. "Surely you're too old for us to call you by anything but your title." The woman possessed one of those irritating, high-pitched little-girl voices. The room wallowed in silence for a heartbeat. "I mean, it would be disrespectful, wouldn't it?"

Phil formed her lips into an indulgent smile. "Of course not. I insist that you call me Philomena."

Sir Nicodemus leveled a glare at his sister-in-law before giving Royden a rather pointed look at his hand, which still clutched Phil's rather tightly.

Royden let her go, and Sir Nicodemus guided her to another settee, this one cross-stitched with numerous flowering roses. He settled next to her as if he belonged at her side, leaned over and whispered, "Now you'll have to call me Nico too."

Yes, she remembered that he'd asked her to call him that in London. His breath had tickled her ear and managed to set off those tiny sparks in her body again. She really must find some way to control her attraction to the young man. "I will strive for Nicodemus," she replied, scooting away from him.

"It appears that I must be content with that . . . for now." He lounged back against the cushions and took a sip of his port, watching her with hooded eyes, an amused smile on his face.

"Shall I sing for you before dinner?" asked Edwina, her voice piercing the room like a knife. Phil noted the way the other woman kept glancing at Sir Nicodemus and herself.

"Ah, yes," said Nicodemus. "Edwina has the voice of an angel." Edwina preened under the praise.

"Can it wait until after dinner, dear?" Royden asked.

Edwina's eyes widened with shock. Phil thought this might be the first time anyone had ever turned down an offer to hear her sing.

"I've been most anxious to ask Lady Radcliff . . . er, Philomena, a few questions," Royden continued.

"I'll be happy to answer as many as I am able," Phil replied.

Royden sat down next to his wife, as slowly as an old man. "How do you propose to deal with Grimspell's ghosts?"

Phil felt Nicodemus tense. "I'm not quite sure," she answered honestly. The baronet relaxed. His brother did not.

"Surely you have some sort of . . . plan?"

She shrugged. "Until I find out what type of ghosts I'm dealing with, I'm afraid not."

"There are different types of ghosts?" Sir Nicodemus drawled. Edwina hid a smile beneath a dainty hand.

"Of course," Philomena replied. She had been prepared for Nicodemus's continued skepticism, so he didn't ruffle her in the slightest. "Some are so old, they are just shadows. Some are just memories, doomed to repeat the same actions over and over. And then there are those whose connection to the material world is so strong that I can manage to speak with them."

"You can really talk to them?" Royden asked with feverish intensity.

Phil held up a hand. "Sometimes, and that's only if they're in the mood to do so. Ghosts can be just as unpredictable as human beings."

"That's conveniently logical," Nicodemus muttered.

She ignored him, as did Royden. "But you can perform a séance and make them talk to you?"

She shook her head. "I can't make them, sir. Neither can I call them, not with any regularity, I mean. It helps if there's someone else in the room who has a special connection to the spirit. They'll come at a loved one's call, and sometimes I can act as intermediary." She didn't add that Tup usually helped her. He wasn't here, so she would have to do her best without him.

Sir Nicodemus looked as if he wanted to say something, but he glanced at his brother's face and swallowed his words.

"Well, this is all very fascinating, I'm sure," Edwina said. "But how are you going to help my poor Royden sleep at night?"

"If I can find out why the castle's ghosts are angry, perhaps I can figure out a way to appease them. Royden, do you mind if I ask you a few questions?"

He shook his head, but Phil felt Nicodemus lean forward, as if prepared to pounce on her if he felt his brother needed protection. Phil swallowed, all sorts of visions dancing through her head as she imagined him . . . pouncing. Blast Fanny and her haunting for teaching her things no spinsterish woman should know.

Royden's hand had started to shake. Nicodemus stood and poured another glass of port, handed it to his brother, then stood by his side. Philomena felt a little calmer with a bit of distance between herself and the shape-shifter. She just needed to avoid looking at him.

Royden drained his glass and nodded. "Ask me anything you wish."

"I'm assuming the ghosts have lain quiet for centuries. Do you remember when they started haunting your dreams?"

"Not exactly. It's been months since I first dreamt of them. It wasn't so bad at first, but then . . ." He shuddered.

Edwina put her arm around her husband. "At first I thought he was just having bad dreams," she said. "But then odd things started to happen . . ."

Phil leaned forward. "Like what?"

"Oh, little things. Like something not being where I had left it. Peculiar gusts of wind that come from nowhere. And then Royden's thrashing and crying became so violent that I had to move out of the room." Edwina blushed.

"This is the first I've heard of it," Nicodemus said.

Edwina's perfect skin turned an even brighter shade of pink. "It's not something I would ordinarily mention. But anything to help my poor Royden . . ."

Her husband scowled. Phil didn't think he liked to be called "my poor" anything. She quickly directed her next question to him. "Can you connect the beginning of your troubled dreams to any occurrences in the household? A new renovation, perhaps?"

Royden shook his head. "No, not that I can think of. We haven't dug up any old graves, if that's what you mean."

"I see," Phil replied. "But something must have changed,

and if we can't determine what that might be, perhaps we can ask the spirits themselves. Since they seem to be attuned to you, perhaps they will answer your call."

"Another séance, Philomena?" Nicodemus asked. "If I recall, the last one didn't go very well."

Phil's heart did a little skip at the sound of her name on his lips. He had such an extraordinarily deep voice that her name sounded like a passionate endearment. Botheration, this infatuation for the man was only getting worse. Her annoyance at herself made her reply sound more sharp than she intended. "Yes, Sir Nicodemus. A séance. Tonight."

Chapter Four

Nico wondered at Philomena's contrariness. The wolf in him could sense her desire, could almost smell it every time he got near her. And yet she acted as if his presence annoyed the hell out of her. He fought the urge of his were-self to grumble in confusion and instead downed the last of his port.

Cheevers announced dinner, his protruding lips trying unsuccessfully to form the words without sounding like a quack. Nico gave him a nod of approval anyway, knowing that the young man desperately wanted to impress their London visitor, and he held out his arm to Philomena to escort her in to dinner. He never would have made the attempt if it hadn't been for the instincts of his were-self. He would have thought she'd reject him.

After a brief hesitation, she took his arm and he suppressed a smile of satisfaction. How did ordinary men deal with ladies when they managed to completely hide their true feelings?

He sat next to her at the table, which appeared to discomfit her. Royden and Edwina sat facing them, Edwina chatting away about nothing as usual. Nico worried that his brother might collapse face-forward onto the table, so he watched him throughout the meal. Nico hoped Royden, who had scarcely slept and barely eaten, had the stamina to play the séance game tonight.

"I hope our fare isn't too simple for you, lady?" Nico asked.

Philomena contemplated her plate. "On the contrary. Without the heavy sauces that cover every dish in London, one can truly appreciate the flavor of the course. This is quite an exemplary sugar beet."

He watched with ridiculous fascination as she popped the vegetable into her mouth. She had an extremely kissable mouth. The wolf in him made him lean toward her and brush his arm against hers. The shock of that brief contact made him wonder again at his reaction to her. A mere touch had never managed to affect him so.

"You are a remarkable, woman, Lady Radcliff," Nico murmured.

She froze at the compliment. If he was having difficulty figuring out his own reactions to her, he feared he would never understand hers. Why did she seem so rigid with him?

"I'm afraid I don't know what you mean."

Nico shrugged. "You are so accepting. You embrace people without judgment—and most surprisingly, shapeshifters as well."

She spoke to her plate. She hadn't looked at him once since they sat down. "I talk to dead people, Sir Nicodemus. That has a tendency to alter my perception of the living. I'm acutely aware of the short time we have on this earth."

His attraction to the woman must be clouding his good sense. He was really starting to believe that she told the truth. That she did see ghosts. Nico brushed his leg against her skirts beneath the table. She pretended she didn't feel a thing. "Our castle is so old it's probably full of spirits," he said. "Surely you should have seen a few by now."

"Just one."

He froze in the act of reaching for his wineglass. "Have you, now? Why didn't you mention it?"

She finally turned and looked at him. Her pale eyes had darkened to a smoky gray in the candlelight, and the red in her hair made her dark brown curls fairly glow. She had a tiny nose that tipped up slightly at the end. With her round cheeks, it gave her a rather impish look. Nico licked his lips.

"I didn't mention the spirit because I didn't want to dishearten your brother. I cannot speak to a memory ghost and that's all he appeared to be."

Damn. He was starting to *want* to believe her.

"Did I hear you say ghost, Philomena?" Royden asked. Evidently Edwina had paused long enough in her prattle for him to overhear. As a matter of fact, his sister-in-law now stared at them with heated concentration.

Nico felt Philomena's sigh of dismay. "I saw one of your castle ghosts earlier this evening," she said. "But it was only for a brief moment."

Royden's eyes lit with excitement. He completely abandoned any pretense of eating his dinner. "What did it look like? If it should match one of the ghosts in my dreams . . ."

It would just be a coincidence, finished Nico silently.

But Philomena started nodding her head. "It would confirm that the ghosts were actually visiting you." She set down her fork and tilted her head in consideration. "He looked like a medieval peasant—"

"Straw hat?" Royden interrupted. "Thick coarse hose, rolled up above the knee?"

She nodded enthusiastically. "Yes, that's right. And he held a scythe—"

Roy clutched the edges of the table so hard Nico could feel it shake. "And he tried to chop your head off!"

Lady Radcliff froze, Edwina's mouth fell open, and Cheevers let out a stifled *quack*. Nico threw the footman a warning look. Proper servants pretended to be deaf even to the most outlandish statements from their employers.

"He did wave his scythe rather wildly," Philomena said.

Royden turned his gaze on Nico. "Does this prove it to you, brother? I am not mad. There's something wrong in this castle, and the spirits are trying to warn me."

Nicodemus covered his surprise at his brother's words. He hadn't realized Roy had been afraid that Nico might think he was insane. "It's why I went and fetched Lady Radcliff from London, now, isn't it?"

"But you didn't believe."

"It doesn't matter what I believe, Roy. What matters to me is that you get well again."

His brother hung his head, and Nico felt his were-self rising to the surface, smothering his human fear over what was happening with Royden. His vision darkened, and he suppressed a howl. He had the sudden, consuming desire to hunt. How had he forgotten his quest to find Beatrice's killer? He had to find him, to track him down and tear out his—

"Will you sing for me, Edwina?" Royden asked. "I have an overwhelming need to hear the sweet sound of your voice."

Edwina threw Lady Radcliff a rather triumphant smile and quickly rose from her chair, escorting her husband from the room. Her grin wavered a bit when Royden paused and said, "We will meet you in the music room for the séance, Philomena?"

She nodded and they left. Nico struggled with the wildness gathering inside him while Philomena calmly picked up her fork and began to eat again. For a moment they heard nothing but silence, and then Edwina's faint song curled into the room. Was it Edwina's song or Philomena's quiet nature that began to soothe him? Nico couldn't be sure, but the desire to flee into the forest began to fade.

"Edwina has a lovely voice," his dinner companion said. "I'm looking forward to hearing the full glory of it."

Nico leaned back in his chair, concentrating on his glass of wine.

"Tell me about your forest," Lady Radcliff said.

"What do you wish to know?"

She daintily wiped her mouth with a napkin and looked at him again. He felt the wildness of his were-self fade even more. "I'm told it's enchanted. Is it dangerous?"

Nico smiled. "No. Not the forest or its creatures. They are . . . mischievous but not dangerous." He twirled his glass, watching the red liquid slosh up the sides. "Unless I accompany you, though, I'd suggest you stay clear of it. We've had some poachers lately . . ."

Before his thoughts could track that gloomy thought, she spoke again. "What are the stickmen?"

The woman's curiosity knew no bounds. "How do you know about them?"

"When we were walking from the village, one of them . . . stuck himself to my skirt."

"Did he, now? What a smart stick."

She actually blushed. Nico leaned forward and swept his arm around the back of her chair. She froze, all her sweetness and charm hidden again, and pretended that his arm wasn't there.

"He told me he just wanted to catch a ride."

Nico set down his glass of wine. "They do that, the stickmen. They always want to see what's on the other side of the road." She held her hands loosely clasped in her lap. He rubbed his thigh, catching the silk of her dress with his movements.

"They . . . the stickmen . . . they won't harm anyone, though?"

Nico caught a fold of her dress with his fingers and began to rub it idly. "No. Although they've been known to lay traps for the hunters or anyone who has treated them unkindly. You weren't unkind to the stickman, were you?"

Philomena blinked. Now she had to ignore the back of his arm and his other hand rubbing the fabric of her dress. She did a jolly good job at both. "Certainly not."

"Well, then you'll have nothing to fear from them."

They both sat there, staring at each other for the longest time. Nico wondered why she didn't pull away from him again. It was almost as if . . . as if she were afraid to move.

So, he didn't annoy her. His were-instincts had been right; she desired him. And it terrified her. Her breath came in short little bursts of panic.

She suddenly flew to her feet. "We'd best join the others. After all, I'm here to help your brother and shouldn't get distracted by . . . well, just distracted."

Nico sighed and rose, taking Phil's arm and leading her to the music room. He would find a way to ease her fear of him, but in the meantime, his only desire was to banish the smell of panic about her. But when they stood at the threshold of the music room, her fear suddenly increased. "What is it?" he demanded.

"This room," Philomena gasped. "Can't you feel the hostile energy?"

Nico grasped her gently by the shoulders and spun her around. "It's all these clashing colors—" The marionettes suddenly began to play their miniature instruments, sparkles of light bursting from their little stage. He'd meant to make light of the situation, but Philomena's face twisted with what almost looked like pain. "Would you turn that thing off, Edwina?"

"I didn't turn it on," she huffed, rising from the settee where she'd been fanning a collapsed Royden. She slapped the button that turned off the machine. The music dragged a bit, then resumed at a screeching fast pace. "What's wrong with it?"

"It's made with magic," snapped Nico, as if that explained anything. "Royden, see if you can stop it."

"My stomach hurts," he groaned.

"Y-you must get him out of here," Philomena said. Her teeth had started to chatter. "I d-don't know how he's m-managed to stay in this room for this l-long."

Nico wanted to shake her. Surely she didn't need to employ this much dramatics to convince Roy of her abilities. Royden often had stomachaches; it didn't mean a thing. Instead Nico put his arm around Lady Radcliff and led her from the room. Her shoulders did feel a bit cold and when he sat her back down in the dining room her hands felt like ice, even through her gloves.

"Cheevers, get one of the maids to light a fire." The young footman, who'd suddenly appeared in the hallway, nodded. This late in summer they'd probably roast in here, but Nico couldn't be sure if Lady Radcliff's tremors were real or imaginary. "No, wait," Nico continued. "Go help my brother. He's had one of his spells. Bring him and his wife in here first."

"And Sarah," Philomena said. "Please have him fetch my assistant."

In all the excitement Cheevers forgot himself, and his stride waddled as he hurried down the hall.

Nicodemus warmed her hands with his. "You should be on the stage, madam."

She narrowed her eyes. "You are as spiritually sensitive as a block of wood." Her anger brought a bit of color to her cheeks and she quit shaking.

"No doubt. Are you feeling better?"

"Yes. You can let go of my hands now."

But she didn't pull away. Nico tightened his hold. "I assure you that I'm not insensitive to *you*. I understand that you earn your living convincing others that ghosts are real. But you needn't do so with me. As long as you convince Royden—"

Her eyes sparkled. "I assure you that what I felt in the

music room is quite real. How do you explain the magical music turning on by itself?"

Nico wanted this woman to be honest with him, and the fact that she continued this ridiculous act in his presence annoyed him. "It's magic, and magic can't be trusted. Remember, Philomena, I can see through any spell devised of man."

"But ghosts aren't magic. They are as real as you or I."

A hissing noise came from the doorway. Philomena blinked. "Sarah."

"Yess, my lady. I came as fasst as I could. What hass happened?"

Philomena pulled away from Nico with obvious relief. He sighed and took a seat, crossing his arms over his chest. Royden entered the room, the color back in his face, with Edwina not far behind.

"You felt it too?" asked Royden, taking a chair across from Philomena.

She nodded. "Have you ever felt anything like that in the music room before?"

Roy glanced at his wife. "Sometimes. But I didn't want to hurt Edwina's feelings. Her singing usually makes me feel better."

Philomena frowned. "Has anything dreadful happened in that part of the castle?"

"No more than anywhere else," Nico answered.

"Well then. Perhaps it's because you spend so much time in there, Royden. Since the spirits are drawn to you, their energy may be concentrated in that room."

"That makes sense," Royden said. Nico snorted.

She ignored him. "I think it's best if we perform the séance in here, then. I'm not sure if I can withstand that much hostile energy. Sarah, can you douse the lights?"

Nico waved Cheevers and the maid away from the door. He supposed they didn't need that fire now. Philomena looked fully recovered from the chill that had taken her earlier. Nico reached across the table for Edwina's hand and eagerly clasped Philomena's when she reached for him. Damn if he didn't find himself looking forward to her theatrics.

The acrid scent of snuffed candles tickled his nose, and the only remaining light came from a lantern that sat next to Sarah in the corner of the room. The were-snake turned down the wick until only a soft glow penetrated the shadows of the room.

"Take my hand," Philomena said to Nico's brother. "Are you holding Edwina's?"

"Yes." Royden's voice trembled with excitement. "What happens next?"

"I want you to close your eyes and *will* one of the spirits to come to you. But only one! Concentrate on the one that I saw earlier."

"The one with the scythe?"

"Err, I suppose so. Are there any others that seemed, well, less angry to you?"

"I'm afraid not."

"Him then."

The silence of the room engulfed them. Nico had to admit, the darkness added to the atmosphere, seemingly smothering them in a black cloak. His eyes adjusted until the light by Sarah seemed brilliant. The servant never took her eyes off her mistress. No wonder Philomena had called for her. He'd never seen a more formidable protector.

Nico shifted in his seat. Damn it, the woman didn't need any protection. He'd started falling for the entire drama. He mentally shrugged. So perhaps Royden would as well.

"I'm frightened," Edwina squeaked.

"We'll be fine as long as we don't break the circle," Philomena assured. She took a deep breath and intoned her next words. "Spirit of Grimspell castle, Royden Wulfson wishes to speak with you."

"No, I don't," Roy whispered.

Nico smiled. When they were children, his brother had once faced down a charging boar . . . and that same night, had crawled into Nico's bed because he feared the imaginary monsters under his own.

"*I* wish to speak with the spirit," Philomena amended. "I only want to help you. To find out what has made you so angry."

Nico really couldn't help admiring the ghost-hunter's abilities. She was so good at this. He couldn't wait to see what she'd do next. Both Royden and Philomena still had their eyes closed, but Edwina's were wide open and as round as saucers. Nico smiled at his sister-in-law, but he couldn't be certain she could see it in the gloom, so gave her hand a reassuring squeeze.

"Come to my call," Philomena said. "Wherever you may be, I command you to come."

Odd, how the castle seemed to almost groan. Nico had never noticed the many creaks and tiny sounds of the old fortress. He leaned forward and studied the darkened features of Philomena's face. The faint lamplight highlighted her full lips and the tip of her tiny nose. He'd never met a more beautiful woman in his life. Too bad she was a charlatan. He really could come to admire her.

He felt her tense. If he had been timing this, he would say that right about now would be the perfect time for her to pretend to see the medieval servant—

"Tup," she whispered. "What on earth are you doing here?" Her eyes opened and she looked at a spot right above the mantel of the fireplace.

Nico smiled with satisfaction.

"Is that the name of the castle ghost?" Royden asked.

"It's her spirit guide," Nico answered, remembering the name from the séance in London.

Philomena ignored both of them. "But how could you?

I've never known a ghost who could travel far from the place they haunted." Her head tilted to the side, and if Nico hadn't known better, he'd swear she was actually listening to someone. "No, no. Of course I'm glad you're here. But what do you mean, you're haunting *me*?"

"Can a person be haunted?" Royden asked.

"Apparently so," Nico answered.

"Will you both hush?" Edwina snapped.

"Well, I suppose it *will* remain a puzzle," the ghost-hunter said. "And I *am* very glad you're here, Tup. I've missed you dreadfully."

Nico blinked. It looked as if a spot of shadow, a bit darker than the smoky blackness of the rest of the room, detached itself from the fireplace and floated toward the table. He felt an unearthly cold between himself and Philomena.

Damn, now his imagination was acting overtime.

"Turn up the light, Sarah," Nico demanded. To his surprise, the servant did as he asked.

Nico turned his head and watched in disbelief as Philomena's hair smoothed back from her cheek and her skin indented as if she'd been poked. Or kissed. By someone or something named Tup.

It couldn't be a magic spell. He could *see* magic.

Philomena smiled, then stilled, as if listening again, and nodded her head. "I know. That's why I've come. Do you know what they are so angry about?"

A shiver started up Nico's spine. If he hadn't seen it for himself he would never have believed it. But no errant wind had swept aside the ghost-hunter's hair. No trick of shadow had made that indentation appear briefly in her cheek. His mind reeled at the implications.

And then Lady Radcliff sprang out of her chair, breaking hands with Royden. But Nico only tightened his grip. He remembered what had happened the last time she'd launched herself at something. He had thought she'd pretended to faint, that her convulsions were just the work of an extraordinary actress. Now he knew otherwise.

Philomena tried to fling herself across the table toward the fireplace. "Leave him alone!" she screamed, twisting her hand away from Nicodemus's. "Let me go, Nico! He might hurt Tup."

Sarah had turned the wick of the lamp all the way up. She lit a match and hurriedly tried to relight all of the candles in the room. Royden's eyes rolled up and he slumped to the floor, pulling Edwina down with him. Nico could see nothing but the hoops of her skirt over the edge of the tabletop.

"Philomena." Nico pulled her around to face him. Tears tracked a crooked path down her cheeks. "Tup will be all right. Do you hear me? If he's a spirit just like them, he should know how to fight them."

"But he's just a boy."

Nico felt something loosen in his chest. Damn, had he been jealous of a ghost? Because he felt relieved to learn that it had been a lad that had kissed her cheek. "Which means he'll be clever enough to outwit another spirit."

She let out a breath. "They're gone anyway. But yes— yes, of course. He grew up on the streets of London. He knows how to take care of himself."

Nico had only been guessing, trying to do anything to stop her from fighting the castle ghost herself. "Something happened to Royden." Assured that she'd be fine, he released her hand and went to his brother's side. Edwina looked even paler than her husband. She had climbed off of him and arranged her skirts, and now patted his face.

Nico squatted. "Royden. Can you hear me, man?"

Roy's eyes fluttered open. "Did you see them, Nico? Did you see the spirits that haunt me?"

Nico sighed with relief and didn't hesitate to reassure his brother with a half-truth. "Yes, of course I did. Now help me get you up, that's a good chap. Sarah, call Cheevers."

The woman slid toward the door. Cheevers must have been standing right behind it because he ducked inside before she even opened her mouth.

"Get my brother to bed." Nico glanced at Edwina's terror-filled face. "And send Mistress Wulfson her maid. And some brandy."

When they left the room, he turned toward Philomena. "I will see you to your room myself. No arguments."

She shrugged and followed him to the staircase, Sarah bringing up the rear. Nico struggled with what he'd seen this evening. He didn't particularly like being proven wrong. But somehow he felt relieved. Lady Radcliff had not been lying to him. She really could see ghosts. They really did exist.

He stopped outside her door but when he turned to go back to his own rooms she stayed him with a touch. "You . . . you believe me now." Her large gray eyes looked enormous with the memory of her tears in them.

Nico nodded. "I may be stubborn, but I'm not a blind fool. I saw the lad kiss you."

She smiled then, barely a lift of her full lips.

Nicodemus turned to Sarah. "I assume you have experience looking after your mistress?"

She nodded, her neck undulating with the movement.

"Will she be safe tonight?"

"I can answer for myself, Sir Nicodemus. I'm not even sure the ghost was intentionally attacking Tup. I don't think it would be even strong enough."

"Because it's a memory spirit."

"Yes."

"So they can't harm you or Royden either?"

Phil frowned. "No. I think I overreacted, you see. But I'm quite fond of Tup."

Nico narrowed his eyes in thought. "And yet they have harmed Roy by disturbing his dreams until he can neither eat nor sleep. I'm not sure how much longer his body can hold up." He fought down his frustration. How could he protect those in his care against ghosts? "So you'll both be safe tonight?"

"Quite safe, I assure you. Remember, that's why you hired me. To solve this haunting. This will not be my last encounter with your ghosts."

He didn't like it, but she was right. "Good night, Lady Radcliff."

He spun on his heel and went to his own rooms. But he left his bedroom door wide open behind him and slept lightly, listening for any sounds in the hall. He had always thought his brother sickly and prone to flights of imagination, but now he knew better. He didn't dare shift to wolf and hunt for Beatrice's killer like he did most evenings. Thanks to the estimable Lady Radcliff, he spent most of the night waking from the slightest sound, worried about her and his brother.

And planning a way to get closer to Philomena.

Chapter Five

Phil woke the next morning with a smile on her face. It took her a moment to realize the cause of it. Tup had followed her to Grimspell castle. She parted the curtains of the tester bed and glanced around the room, only slightly disappointed when she didn't see him. He didn't often appear during the harsh light of day.

Shafts of bright sunshine striped the room through the narrow windows and she cut through them as she went to the washroom. Phil splashed cool water on her face. Perhaps she shouldn't be so happy that Tup had come, because it meant that the lad was haunting her and not her London townhouse, as she'd always supposed.

It bothered her to think that she might somehow be responsible for keeping his spirit anchored to the material world. The lad's mother had abandoned him when he was no more than three years old . . . perhaps she had become a mother figure to him and that was why he felt drawn to her? Now she had another mystery, although she didn't regret his presence. Tup could help her communicate with the castle ghosts. And seeing his dear face last night had made her so happy, even though she'd been frightened when the castle ghost had appeared to threaten him.

Phil patted the water from her face with a cloth and blinked at her reflection in the mirror. Tup's presence also had the added benefit of convincing Sir Nicodemus that ghosts were real. Not that she cared one whit what he might think, of course, but it could make her task easier.

Sarah slid into the room, her uncanny sense of timing precise as usual, and helped Phil into her gown. She chose a dark brown poplin dress that looked sturdy enough for exploring. She hoped that Sir Nico would remember to give her a tour of the castle today, but if not, she would manage by herself. She intended to explore the place from top to bottom and the dark material would hide any dirt.

Besides, it made her hair look like dark mahogany and her eyes a smoky gray. Not that she cared whether she looked attractive or not . . . "Sarah, twist my hair into a bun today, will you?"

Phil sat in front of the vanity and the thin woman's deft fingers quickly did as she had asked. There, no curls to soften her features or make her look any younger than her forty years.

"I can't imagine stuffing my blisters into my walking shoes. Can you find something more suitable?"

Sarah smiled, as if she'd anticipated the request, and handed Phil a rather scuffed pair of sturdy leather slippers. When she stood, Phil barely felt her injuries. Her assistant handed her a loosely woven shawl and then quietly retreated back into her own room while Phil went downstairs.

When Phil entered the breakfast room and saw Nico standing by the window, her stomach did a curious flip. A beam of sunshine streaked through his hair, highlighting the unusual mix of white amongst the brown strands. He looked outside, toward his enchanted forest, and his eyes glinted with gold and a wildness that made her pulse race. She had the oddest thought. What would it be like to follow the wolf along his hunting trails?

He turned toward her as if he felt her presence and devoured her with his gaze for several long moments.

Withstanding this young man's charisma would be more difficult than solving the riddle of his ghosts.

"Where is everyone?" she asked, heading for the sideboard. The heavenly smell of fried ham glazed with honey, eggs scrambled with chives, and crumpets drizzled with butter made her stomach grumble. Phil unabashedly began to load a plate.

"Royden and Edwina are both still in bed," Sir Nicodemus replied. She ignored the way the sound of his deep rich voice made her heart skip. "After last night, I thought you wouldn't rise until noon, as well."

Philomena sat at the linen-covered table and scooped up a mouthful of eggs. Divine. The footman, Cheevers, set a glass of cold milk next to her plate and she washed down her food. "Ordinarily I wouldn't be up this early," she admitted. "But I was too excited to explore the castle."

She heard him take a seat opposite her, studiously avoiding his gaze.

"I'm looking forward to showing you my home," he murmured. Had he purposely lowered his voice to implicate something more in his offer?

Phil sliced a piece of ham and frowned. Was she seeing implications that weren't there? Her appetite suddenly fled, and she pushed her plate away. Sir Nicodemus sprang to his feet as if he'd been anxiously awaiting that signal and held out his hand to her. Phil ignored it and turned to Cheevers. "Would you mind fetching Sarah for me?"

The footman's eyes went warily from her face to Nico's but turned to do her bidding. Phil sighed and ignored the scowl on the baronet's face. "What an interesting jacket."

He shrugged. "It's common here. Apparently it's catching on with the young prince and his set."

Phil nodded. She doubted that Prince Albert would fill out the checkered and belted jacket quite the same way the baronet did. Did he get such broad shoulders from his were-animal?

"While we're waiting for Sarah, why don't I show you the chapel?" His face shone with eagerness and his eyes showed a hint of mockery. As if he knew she felt afraid to be alone with him. However, Phil would never have risen to the bait if he hadn't added, "It's been kept in its original state. You should see the archways carved into the solid stone, and the stained-glass windows . . ."

Phil took a step toward him. "Stained glass?"

He nodded and spun, and she found herself following him out to the hall and into a small morning room. Scattered papers covered two large desks, and household and estate account books were stacked in cases behind them. "We meet with most of our tenants in here," he said. "The room is narrow because of the chapel hidden behind the walls, here."

Phil clasped her hands. Hidden rooms. How delightful.

Sir Nicodemus pushed aside two oak panels to reveal an opening. He waved her through, and Phil didn't hesitate.

Sunshine streamed through several stained-glass windows high in the walls above them. The chapel ceiling had to be above the first floor; she could see a tiny alcove where the lord and lady must have viewed the mass. The walls had indeed been engraved with archways and stone columns besides. Phil quickly removed her gloves and stuffed them in the pocket seam of her dress before running her fingers across the carved surface.

When she reached the stone altar she felt a breath of cold air caress her cheek and stepped out of the way as a priest materialized behind the altar, holding a golden cup up to the heavens. She saw his mouth move but heard no words, and then she blinked and he disappeared.

"What is it?" Sir Nico demanded, suddenly standing next to her, his warm hands on her shoulders. She hadn't even seen him move. Phil recalled that Sarah had the ability to twist her body into amazing contortions; the baronet might have supernatural abilities in his human form as well.

"Just another ghost," she replied. The man might be insensitive to spirits, but apparently he sensed *her* reaction to them quite well.

"Just another ghost, she says," he muttered.

Phil sighed. "Can't you feel the peace in this place? Oh botheration, what am I thinking, of course you can't. Most ghosts are completely harmless, Sir Nico. You must resist the urge to clutch at me in alarm every time I see one."

"If you had only seen yourself last night . . ."

"I do apologize," Phil said. "I overreacted. It's just that Tup is so very dear to me."

"So you said." He took a step, closing the distance between them again. "Tell me about him."

Phil tried not to react to his nearness. His clutching had actually felt rather marvelous. "He's a street urchin who followed me home one day. I didn't even realize he was a ghost until the glass of milk he tried to drink just poured onto the floor. It's like that sometimes with a new spirit. I can't tell them from the living."

He played with the sleeve of her dress, rubbing his palms across the fabric. Sir Nico appeared to have the habit of absentmindedly fiddling with something. She stepped away, trying to discourage him from releasing his pent-up energy on her clothing, and studied the carved wooden cross hanging above the chapel altar.

"That must have made your life difficult," he said.

Phil shrugged. "Most people think I'm a bit mad."

"Is that why you've never married?"

Phil gave him a quelling look over her shoulder. "I beg your pardon?"

He leaned against the altar, his arms crossed over his

chest, his head tilted to the side, a thatch of white-brown hair falling over one eye. He didn't look the slightest bit intimidated. "Admit it, a beautiful woman like you doesn't stay unattached. Or have you been married?"

"Certainly not." Phil reined in her annoyance. She'd had several beaux over the years but not a one of them could tolerate her gift. "It is absolutely none of your business, young man. I'm here to do my job and nothing more. You must desist in this . . . unusual interest you have in my person."

"Why?"

Botheration, she hadn't been prepared for that response. He genuinely didn't understand her resistance. "How old are you?"

He scowled. So, perhaps he understood more than he appeared to. "Seven and twenty."

"And I am forty years old. It is highly inappropriate for you to be flirting with such an older woman."

"Are you worried about what others may think?"

Phil blanched. "Certainly not." That wasn't exactly why their age difference bothered her. She switched tactics. "Do you always flirt so outrageously with your guests?"

He closed the distance between them in a heartbeat. Really, she'd never seen anyone move quite that fast. "I assure you that I don't make a habit of flirting with women I barely know. Only you." He lowered his head and breathed in the scent of her. "I wish I knew why I have this overwhelming attraction to you, but I don't. Weres have a tendency to follow their natural instincts."

Phil swallowed. "Well, I do not. And I cannot do my job properly if you insist on making me uncomfortable."

He stepped back and looked deeply into her eyes and Phil's stomach flipped. To be fair, the way he made her feel wasn't entirely his fault. But she had to put a stop to this.

He slowly nodded. "Yes, I think I see the problem. And

I want Royden well again. I will endeavor to behave until you solve the problem of our ghosts, but after that . . ."

For a brief moment Phil felt the thrill of anticipation. Then she realized that after she finished her job she would leave Grimspell castle and never see him again. Her heart sank. There would be no after. Botheration, that's what she wanted, right?

She followed him out the door through multicolored shafts of light from the stained glass. He kept his word, behaving like a gentleman while he showed her around the keep, never once broaching another intimate subject to her. Phil didn't see another spirit, not even when they reached the gloomy basement of the kitchens.

"Cook has baked my favorite apple tarts," Nico said, and they settled at a scarred wooden table at which Phil imagined he'd spent many a lunch as a boy. While they ate cheese and tarts Phil amused herself by studying the servants. Cook was a bear of a woman, with thick arms and a gravelly voice. Her two helpers hopped around the kitchen at her beck and call, occasionally stopping to wiggle their noses in Phil's direction.

"Bear, and two rabbits?"

Nicodemus smiled and nodded.

Phil would have like to have stayed and talked, but she could tell that their presence in the servants' environs made the weres uncomfortable. Besides, the heat of the stove became intolerable. So when Nico suggested they leave, she followed him with a brief word of thanks to the cook. He showed her the scullery and pantry and then turned to go back upstairs.

"Wait a moment," Phil said. "Do you mean to tell me that's it?" Besides the chapel, every other room in the castle had been renovated. She'd so hoped to experience some element of the medieval era.

"What do you mean?"

"Isn't there a dungeon or anything?"

His smile did dangerous things to her insides. She must remind herself to quit making him do that. "Of course there's a dungeon, but I didn't think a lady would want to see it."

"Of course I want to see it. It hasn't been renovated like everything else, has it?"

He shook his head. "It even has some original torture devices—are you *sure* you want to go down there?"

Phil nodded decisively. "Quite."

"Somehow I knew you'd say that." He handed her a fairylight globe but took a lantern for himself. "If you suffer just one convulsion, I'm dragging you back upstairs, understand?"

She felt pleased that he worried about her and thought that was the source of his discomfort. But when they passed through a couple of moldy cellars into a stone chamber with roughly hewn walls, he stopped dead in his tracks.

"Sir Nicodemus?" Every muscle in his body had tightened. She touched his arm and he felt as unmovable as a rock. His nostrils flared and his jaw hardened and suddenly she could see the outline of his were-self surrounding him like an aura. "Nico?"

"I hate it down here," he growled. "I don't know why. I've always hated this castle and the feeling gets worse when I come down here."

Phil didn't know quite what to say. How awful, to hate one's home. She would never have guessed it. Perhaps he wasn't as insensitive as she'd thought. "You could be responding to the suffering that went on down here. It's a perfectly natural reaction."

He shook his head, his hair appearing to float around his face. The image of his were-form over his human one looked quite disconcerting. "It smells like evil. Yet faint, so faint . . ."

"I can go on by myself," she suggested, and suddenly realized that she'd forgotten all about Sarah. She guessed her assistant hadn't been able to find them in this rambling keep.

The baronet blinked and shook himself, his wolf shadow disappearing. "Don't be foolish. I said I don't like it down here, not that I'm afraid of it." He turned and met her eyes over the glow of his lantern. "I have yet to encounter anything I've ever been afraid of."

Phil caught the feral glimmer in his eyes and shuddered. She believed him. He didn't look the least bit afraid. Just angry. And dangerous. He strode forward, grasped the rusty iron ring of a heavy oak door, and pulled. The screeching of the hinges almost made her cover her ears. She followed him into a large open chamber, quickly scanning the stone room. No ghostly images remained inside the rusting cages, the wall shackles, or on the stained tables, thank goodness.

Spiderwebs shrouded the room, and Phil swiped at them as she made her way around the space. "It's even worse than I could have imagined," she said. "Quite satisfactory for historical purposes and completely ghastly otherwise. I can understand why you don't like to come in here."

Sir Nicodemus ignored her. He'd made his way straight across the room and had stopped in front of another large oak door, his hands fisted at his sides.

"What's in there?" Philomena asked, hurrying to his side. When he didn't respond, she touched his arm and felt the vibration of fury inside his body. "Nico?"

He stared at the door, his voice low. "Inside is a tunnel, leading to other tunnels. There's a complex maze of them beneath Grimspell castle. My father never told me who dug them or why, just that I had to stay out of them."

Phil considered his nature. "And did you?"

His mouth quirked. "It was on a dare, and I did it because this place made me feel . . . odd. I only disobeyed him that once, and I was never tempted to do it again. I got lost in that labyrinth and was almost buried alive when one of the tunnels collapsed." He took a deep breath. "Stay away from here, Lady Radcliff. I can already feel your mind calculating, wondering if this is where the castle ghosts are buried."

"Perhaps you should chain the door shut, if it's that dangerous."

He looked down at a rusty pile of metal. "It was chained, and bolted besides. Time has done its work, I see. I'll make sure the butler commissions a new lock."

Phil shivered. The dungeon had suddenly become cold. Not just cold, but so icy she could feel the hairs on the back of her neck prickle.

"Philomena?"

She couldn't respond. She had to see what lay behind her. Phil slowly turned, her eyes widening on the scene inside the shadowy chamber. A warrior stood on the left, chain mail covering his chest, a feather-topped helmet hiding his face. He raised a glowing blue sword and charged across the room to her right, where a weaponless man in a black robe waited for him, seemingly defenseless.

"What do you see?" Sir Nicodemus demanded.

"Look out," Phil shouted, but too late. The blue sword arced, and the robed man held out his hands . . . and a shaft of red light knocked the warrior back across the room. He scrambled to his feet, holding the sword in front of him like a shield, and it kept the red magic at bay.

"Damn it, Philomena," Nico snarled.

"Two men," she gasped. "One is a wizard and the other is a warrior with a magical sword—no, he's—good heavens, he's a were-wolf." His armor had disappeared into his fur, the blue magic of the sword suddenly shining in his fangs. The robed man changed as well, but he used a magic spell to make his body grow larger, almost filling the room.

"Dragon," Philomena whispered. She'd never seen anything quite so magnificent. Eyes of silver and scales of shimmering red, with a forked tail that lashed with fury and wings that spanned the width of the room. The two creatures lunged at each other, claws flashing, fangs gleaming. The sounds of their battle cries made her cover her ears.

"Sir Nico. Just this once you have my permission to clutch me." His warm arms slid around her, feeling like bands of steel. She sagged against him, watching with disbelieving eyes at a long-ago battle against a legendary creature and . . . "Your ancestor?"

"What?"

"I think . . ." The dragon gave a roar, quickly cut off by the wolf's fangs at his throat. The were had the same uncanny speed as Sir Nico. Every time the dragon threw him off, the beast pounced back at his throat. Despite the dragon's size, the were-wolf harried him until the larger beast tired. The wolf sprang for the dragon's throat and sunk his blue teeth deep. The dragon roared jets of crimson and yellow fire and tried to shake off his attacker. But the wolf held on until those luminescent wings twitched and stilled. "I think he might be one of your ancestors."

"Fighting in our dungeons. With a dragon?"

"Yes." Phil pulled away from him. She didn't care for his tone. The vision faded to black, and she sighed. "I would like to get out of here before that repeats again."

"Are you all right?" Sir Nicodemus asked.

"Of course," Phil replied, skirting her way around the room. Even though the dragon and the were-wolf were gone now, she hesitated to occupy the same space where they'd fought. She'd never seen anything quite like that before and didn't want to risk stepping into any residual feelings the fighters might have left behind.

When they reached the cellars and closed the door

behind them, Phil's legs gave way, and she collapsed atop a crate. Dragons had been outlawed ages ago and taking the shape of one was considered the darkest form of magic. She'd never thought to see one, even as a ghost. "I wonder what they were fighting over," she murmured to herself.

Nico lit his lantern and held it close to her face, studying her with a frown for a moment. "No convulsions?"

Phil smiled. "They were just old memory spirits."

"Ah. Good, then." He set the lantern on the floor. "They could have been fighting over our treasure."

"You keep it in the dungeon?"

"No, but maybe we did once, long ago. How old do you think the vision might be?"

"I'm not sure." Phil noticed the strands of cobwebs on the hem of her skirt and began to vigorously slap them off. "But the were-wolf—when he was in human form anyway— wore chain mail and a helm. Perhaps he lived here when the castle was new."

Nico crouched and helped her clean her skirts. But he didn't slap. He carefully swept his palm across the fabric. "Or maybe he built Grimspell himself. We have no way of knowing. Who won, anyway?"

Phil smiled. "The were-wolf."

"Against a dragon. Not bad." His hands swept up to her waist. Phil suspected that he now swiped at imaginary cobwebs. Before she could protest a hiss came from the entrance to the kitchens, and Sarah's head swayed around the doorframe.

"Ah, Sarah, you finally found us." Phil rose out of Nico's hands. "You missed the tour, but I shall tell you all about it." Her assistant's glossy black eyes narrowed on the baronet.

Sir Nico flashed a smile of even, white teeth. "I'll see you at dinner, Lady Radcliff?"

"Of course," she replied as she followed Sarah out of

the stuffy room. "I will need to perform another séance tonight."

His groan made her echo his smile.

Much to Phil's dismay, the séance that evening proved uneventful. Even Tup didn't make an appearance. When Edwina suggested that she entertain them with a song, Phil and Royden exchanged looks of alarm. But when they entered the music room, that hostile energy that had permeated it the night before had disappeared.

Edwina activated her magical marionettes and the little wooden men accompanied her in a piece from the operetta *Orpheus in the Underworld*. The song from Eurydice's death scene made Phil smile, Sir Nicodemus scowl, and Royden shudder. On the last note, Edwina's angelic voice faded to a silent room.

Phil sighed. She would never have thought that the girl's squeaky voice could emit such beautiful throaty notes. "You sing beautifully, Edwina."

The blonde shrugged her delicate shoulders and floated over to the magical stage, frowning at the wooden musicians. "I think there's something wrong with them. Didn't you hear that off note?"

"It sounded perfect to me," said Royden.

Edwina spun, her hoops swaying with her movements like an oversize bell. "There's no help for it, I suppose."

"What do you mean?" asked Phil.

"She means that magic has a tendency to be unreliable around shape-shifters." Nico's voice shook Phil for a moment. He'd been quiet most of the evening. She snuck a glance at him, admiring the cut of his dinner jacket and the way his white cravat made the skin of his face look a golden brown.

"Not really," Royden mused, his long legs stretched out in front of him on the low couch. "Magic just seems to have to work harder around so many weres. The weaker it is, the quicker it fades."

Royden didn't look so tired this evening. Phil smiled. "I wondered why you used so many candles instead of fairylights."

"This isn't London," he agreed, "where there are so many of the aristocracy that magic is in the very air you breathe. Here in the castle, where almost everyone is a shape-shifter . . . well, we don't have much need for magic anyway."

Nico stepped away from the piano and sat down next to Phil on the settee. Royden grinned and Edwina raised her delicately arched brows. "You seem disappointed, Philomena," Nico murmured.

"Why, not at all," she replied, unconsciously leaning toward him. He smelled incredibly good, as if he'd bathed in the fresh waters of a stream. "I find it quite peaceful."

"I suppose," he said, his fingers straying to the edge of her skirts, "that you don't need spells and potions to make your life more exciting. Not when you see otherworldly beings on a daily basis."

"That's true." Phil glanced down at his fingers. He'd caught up the edge of her white silk gown and had started to play with it. "But I think I would miss the magic of London if I stayed away too long."

"Ah, but we have magic here." He grinned, the shallow dimples appearing in his freshly shaven cheeks. "Remember, we have an enchanted forest."

"I would very much like to see it sometime."

"You shall. There's a particular glade I plan to take you to. Willows surround it and at sunset the water sprites dance on the surface of a small pond."

Phil felt herself falling under the spell of his charm. Again. She imagined the private setting, the two of them alone. What would his bare skin feel like beneath her hands?

What would his face look like if she used some of Fanny's skills on his body? In the past few years she'd learned what it could be like to be with a man in an intimate way. The haunting of her London townhouse had opened new ideas to her.

Phil embraced new ideas.

Edwina cleared her throat. "Do you have many *young* friends in London, Lady Radcliff?"

Nico's fingers stilled and he scowled.

"Why, no," she replied. "Why do you ask?"

Edwina shot a look at Nico but plunged ahead. "I just thought you might find our company boring. I'm sure your *older* friends are much more entertaining."

Phil smoothed her satin skirts, removing Nico's fingers from their folds in the process. "On the contrary. I find your company most invigorating."

"You are too kind," Edwina answered with a winsome smile. "But perhaps I will invite my mother for a visit. You are about an age. She has developed quite a fondness for knitting. Perhaps she can show you some of her stitches?"

Phil tilted her head at the girl. What an interesting creature. "I'm afraid I don't knit. I'd rather talk to dead people." She rose, her gown falling about her figure in a quite satisfactory manner. "And if you'll excuse me, I've had a rather tiring day. Come along, Sarah."

The were-snake emerged from a darkened corner of the room and followed Phil to the door. Both gentlemen had risen to their feet and she noticed with a frown that Royden swayed a bit. Nico, on the other hand, practically glowed with robust energy. He stepped forward and took her hand, bending to pass his lips over the top of her glove. Phil hid the shiver that went through her.

"Shall I show you the forest tomorrow, Philomena?"

"That's not possible," Edwina interrupted. "Is it, Royden?"

Nicodemus glanced at his brother, who shrugged. "I'm afraid she's right. It's time to bring in the grass at the home farm and I don't think I can oversee it this year. I was hoping you might manage it, Nico."

"Naturally," he replied. "Forgive me, but I had forgotten." Then his brown eyes lit. "Perhaps you would care to join me? If you're longing for magic, you'll find plenty of it at the farm—although probably not what you're used to. The area has few of the gentry but enough hedge witches to make up for it."

"Hedge witches?" Phil asked, her curiosity piqued.

"The illegitimate offspring of the local gentry. They don't have enough magic to qualify for a title, even if they were acknowledged, but their simple charms are helpful to the country folk."

Phil shot a glance at Edwina and sighed. As much as the outing interested her, the less time she spent in the baronet's presence, the better. He utterly destroyed her good sense. And she had a job to do. "Thank you for the offer, but I must decline." His face shadowed, and before Philomena could change her mind, she turned and practically ran from the room.

By the time Sarah had helped prepare her for bed, Phil was chiding herself for a fool. Why should she let that silly little girl make her decline an invitation that appeared to be a fascinating experience? Most spirits didn't appear in the daytime so she wouldn't be neglecting her job. She crawled beneath the blankets with a sigh. How often would she be able to participate in an actual harvest? She wondered about the hedge witches and of what type of charms they might be capable.

Phil turned and fluffed the feathers in her pillow. She might never again get the opportunity to find out. As she drifted to sleep, she also wondered whether her annoyance was really about a harvest, or whether she regretted not being able to spend another day in the baronet's company.

She yawned and her eyes drifted closed. It seemed as if only a few moments had passed when an icy coldness in the room woke her. But when she opened her eyes, she realized hours had gone by, because the moonbeams through her narrow window barely penetrated the deep dark of the night.

And revealed a warrior, clad in a feathered helm, who brandished a blue sword at the foot of her bed.

Chapter Six

Philomena sat up, her hair falling heavily about her shoulders. "Hello."

The warrior stood like a statue, neither blinking nor breathing. He looked more insubstantial than he had in the dungeons, with barely a glow from his magical sword. He'd opened the faceplate of his helm, and this close she could make out his features. She sucked in a breath at how much he resembled Sir Nicodemus.

"He don't know why he's here," said a familiar voice. Phil smiled and glanced at the mantel, always Tup's favorite perch.

"It's good to see you, Tup. Where have you been?"

He kicked his bare feet, the glow from the banked coals in the hearth shining through his toes. "Tryin' to figger out why the ghosts are angry. Ain't that what ye wanted?"

Phil frowned. "I don't want you getting hurt. I can solve this mystery by myself."

Tup gave her a rather cheeky grin. "Cor, now, there ain't much the old buggers can do to me. 'Cept maybe try and scare me. Most of 'em are as dead to the earth as that one."

The warrior suddenly turned his head and looked straight at Tup.

Phil started. "Are you sure of that?"

The boy disappeared halfway into the portrait above the mantel. "Sort of. None of 'em will talk to me. That's if I can find 'em, and likely as not they're never where I look."

The warrior raised his sword, then glanced over his shoulder. He strode toward her closed door and disappeared through it. Phil scrambled out of bed, threw on her robe and picked up a fairylight, the dust inside glowing at her touch. "If he won't tell us what's wrong, perhaps he can show us." Tup looked uncertain, but when she left her room she felt him right behind her. The warrior appeared in the hallway for a brief moment, then disappeared again, following a course long erased by the castle's renovations.

Phil stopped in frustration, waiting for him to appear again. "Where'd he go, Tup?"

"I told ye, they're hard to find."

His voice sounded so faint. Phil squinted in the gloom. "Are you all right?"

His features had faded to a mere shadow. "Tired now," he sighed. "I wish I could stay with ye longer."

"Me too. But you mustn't blame yourself . . ."

He disappeared.

And then, from the corner of her eye, Philomena caught a flash of movement. She began to run toward the tower stairs, yanking up the hem of her nightgown when it threatened to tangle about her ankles. She'd forgotten to tie her robe and it floated behind her along with her loose hair. She'd almost reached the door of the tower when—

"Oof!"

She hit a solid wall of muscled fur. A confusing few moments of tangled limbs and growls of surprise followed, and then Sir Nico shifted to human and she found herself lying spread-eagled atop him.

"What on earth are you doing out here?" she demanded.

"I could ask you the same thing."

He smelled like sweet grass and starlight. She could barely make out his features in the gloom, for she'd dropped her fairylight in the fall and it winked sadly at her from a few feet away. "I was hunting a ghost."

"Why am I not surprised?"

Phil suddenly realized that she could feel the rise and fall of his chest with his words. That the heat of his skin warmed the full length of her and his mouth lay only a heartbeat from her own. The deliciously wicked throb that ignited between her legs made her scramble to her feet. "Just what were *you* doing?"

He sat up, his arms propped carelessly atop his raised knees. "I was hunting too, my lady."

Phil swallowed. She imagined him running in his were-form through the forest, tracking his prey, the silent stealth of a deadly predator. "Oh." The word came out barely audible.

He looked up at her from beneath the fall of his hair. "Does the thought frighten you?"

Phil considered. "Not really. One must eat, you know. Whether it comes from the kitchen or forest, it's one and the same."

He laughed. "I find your practical nature quite appealing."

"Jolly good. I'd best get back to my room now."

Phil turned and he stood in front of her. *He stood in front of her.* Would she ever get used to how quickly this man could move?

"Before you go, I'd like to apologize."

Her mind reeled. She could think of several things he should apologize for. "For what, exactly?"

"For my sister-in-law." He moved a step closer and caught a curl of her hair between his fingers. "She's a silly chit, and you shouldn't allow her to make your decisions for you."

"I beg your pardon?"

He gently tugged the curl, and her scalp tingled. "You're not going with me to the home farm tomorrow because of what she said. You think people will talk if we're seen together."

"That's ridiculous." He kept fiddling with her hair, the strands tickling her neck.

"I agree. So why don't you come with me?"

"Sir Nicodemus, may I remind you that I have a job to do?"

"We'll be back before nightfall."

If he didn't stop . . . "You have a nervous habit of fiddling with my person, sir. That tickles."

He let go of the lock with a sigh. "If I promise not to fiddle with you and be a complete gentleman, will you go?" She couldn't understand why it was so important to him. He astonished her by echoing a similar thought.

"I don't understand why you're hesitant to go. You are my guest and we're nothing but friends, correct?"

She found herself nodding. The man had the uncanny ability to put her into a trancelike state. He had the strongest magnetism she'd ever encountered.

"Excellent. I'll see you first thing in the morning."

First thing in the morning turned out to be hours before the crack of dawn. Phil rolled over and snuggled back beneath the covers while Sarah answered the knock at the door. But the sound of Nico's voice telling them to hurry made her heart skip and energy pour through her body.

"Something practical," Phil said as she bounded out of bed. Sarah chose a dark red gingham dress with heavy boning and helped Philomena into it. Then her assistant went into her own room to change, and Phil struggled with a choice of mantelets. She kept being tempted by the lovely white one with red roses embroidered all over it, but finally chose the serviceable burgundy and a wide-brimmed bonnet with a matching ribbon.

She was glad for the warmth of the heavier coat when she saw the open cart that waited for them. Although Phil knew that when the sun came up the heat would be intolerable, the cold of early morning had her shivering. Fog wreathed the castle drive and obscured the surrounding forest, the chilly air making her breath frost white as well.

Nico had been strapping in the horses, murmuring to them and laughing. When he approached her, Philomena shivered even harder—and not from the chill. His hair spilled over his intense eyes, a half smile still curving his full lips, making those small dimples in his cheeks. He wore some type of heavy leather jacket, with wide sleeves and collar, which made his shoulders look even broader. He looked so incredibly masculine. And rugged.

"Good morn," he said, looking deeply into her eyes.

Sarah hissed and Nico sighed, helping her sluggish assistant into the rear-facing seat of the cart. Sarah blinked at him, even her eyelids moving slowly in the cold. He then assisted Philomena into the forward seat and sat next to her. She had to resist the urge to snuggle up to his warmth.

The horses started forward at a brisk trot, the cold air making her eyes tear. "Sir Nicodemus?"

"Yes?" He had such a deep voice for such a young man.

"The reins?"

"Yes?"

"They appear to be missing."

He leaned his head down, his breath warm against her ear. "Samuel and Charles are were-stallions. They know the way to the farm."

"Oh. Well, I daresay they will be most helpful with the harvesting as well."

"And they don't mind the presence of a were-wolf."

Phil tugged down the brim of her hat to shield her eyes from the wind. Of course he had a difficult time with ordinary horses. Even the two were-beasts occasionally rolled an eye at the predator sitting behind them.

Although the cart lacked the magical enhancements that she would expect in London, it made up for the lack with well-oiled wheels that carried them almost smoothly over the dirt roads. They eventually left the heavily wooded forest behind. Phil stopped shivering when the sun rose. She admired the open countryside, with its scattered ponds heavy with ducks and geese amid meadows full of daisies and red poppies and gorchids.

She was acutely aware of Nico's nearness but didn't speak to him again until they reached the farm. A large home with high peaked gables and a wraparound porch sat on a small rise amid fields of golden hay rippling in the breeze. Phil breathed in the sharp, clean scent of the air and wondered how she'd manage London's smoky fog when she returned.

Nico unharnessed the horses and they shifted to men, nodded to Phil and went in the direction of the outbuildings. She smiled at their matched stride, the way their long hair floated behind them just like their were-manes. Nico stood next to the cart, holding up his hand to help her down, watching her with a frown. "Samuel and Charles are both married."

Phil realized she might have been staring after the men with a bit too much appreciation. But really, human women had no defense against such masculine beauty. And had that been a note of jealousy she'd heard in his voice? She allowed him to help her down, and when he held her hand longer than quite necessary, she gave him a dazzling smile.

Sarah flowed down from her seat and joined them, giving a slight hiss of satisfaction when Nico dropped Phil's hand. As they walked toward the house Phil saw a cloud of insects buzzing over the hay. Only they didn't look like any bugs she'd ever seen before.

"Hayfairies," Nico said, his eyes still watching her. "They help us plant the crop and spend the entire summer playing in it, then help us harvest it. We'll make extra ricks for them to live in during the winter."

Phil started toward the cloud, excited to see a hayfairy at close range. Nico held her back. "They can be mischievous toward strangers. Why don't you wait to meet them later?"

She sighed and nodded, trying to curb her enthusiasm. Then she caught sight of a group of men and women dressed in the most outlandish-colored clothes, bits of leaves and twigs woven in their hair. They formed a circle around a shiny pile of scythes, tossing sparkling dust all over the tools.

"Please don't tell me I'll have to wait to meet them too."

Nico smiled and shook his head, leading her to the group. They chanted a few more words and then, one by one, turned to stare at Phil and Sarah. The baronet introduced the hedge witches, who nodded politely enough at her and Sarah, but kept giving Sir Nico the oddest glances. Before Phil could decipher those looks, a group of laborers filed out of one of the buildings, a stocky redheaded man in the lead. "Nico," he called. "I'm glad you could make it."

"Joseph," Sir Nicodemus replied, striding over to grasp his hand. "Good to see you again."

Although Joseph did appear glad to see Nico, many of the laborers' faces twisted into scowls. Surely they couldn't be prejudiced against shape-shifters, because they seemed quite at ease with their leader.

"Lady Radcliff," Nico said, bringing Joseph to her side. "May I introduce our bailiff, Joseph Eyre?"

"How do you do," Phil greeted him. "A were-fox, sir?"

Joseph's black eyes twinkled, and he didn't appear the slightest bit offended by her bluntness. "Well done, lady. My wife is as well, and wait 'til you meet our little 'uns." Then his eyes swung to Sarah and his grin faltered. He glanced at Nico, then shook his red head of hair as if chiding himself for his foolishness. "I'd like to visit more, but I'm afraid that the men need overseeing. Perhaps you should head up to the house and introduce yourself to my wife, Martha."

Apparently the hedge witches had completed charming the tools, because the workers started to pick them up and make their way to the fields. Samuel and Charles shifted to their were-forms and allowed the bailiff and Nico to mount them. "I'll oversee the north field," said the baronet, and Joseph nodded and went south. Nico glanced once at Philomena. "Will you be all right?"

"Why, of course," Phil replied. She had no shyness with strangers and wasn't some young girl afraid to be left unchaperoned. He gave her a relieved nod and a grin of admiration before he galloped off.

Phil and Sarah stood alone in the yard. To Philomena's dismay even the hedge witches had disappeared. She would have liked to have asked them about their charms . . . and see if she could discover why they had given such odd looks to the baronet.

"They accept me here," Sarah murmured.

Phil nodded, heading for the house. "They are used to all different sorts of weres, except maybe the workers. One or two seemed uncomfortable."

"It feelss good to be accepted."

"I know," Phil replied. Although many people hired her for her magical abilities, few could accept her ghost-talking as a part of their lives. A couple of beaux had tried, but it had been too disconcerting for them to live with for long.

She opened the front door when no one answered the bell. Her nose led her to the kitchen, where the smell of fresh-baked bread made her mouth water. A freckle-faced woman chopped vegetables on a cutting board, her hair a darker shade of red than Joseph's. Several other women bustled about the homey kitchen and a group sat around an oak table, shelling peas and gossiping. Their tongues stilled when Phil and Sarah entered the room.

"You must be Martha," Phil said, smiling at the redheaded woman.

"And you must be Lady Radcliff," she replied, hastily dropping her knife and bobbing her head with respect. "The master sent a message sprite ahead of you, letting us know that you would honor us with a visit. Please, let me show you into the parlor and I will bring you some tea."

"If you don't mind, I would much rather help here." Blank faces stared back at her. "I'm rather good at shelling peas."

Martha gave her a smile full of relief, obviously grateful that Philomena wouldn't put on airs. "Oh, any help would be appreciated, Lady Radcliff. There will be a lot of hungry men at the end of the day. Please, you may wash up over here—Mary, would you move out of the way, then? And Constance, give Lady Radcliff the blue bowl, yes, that's the one."

Martha introduced the ladies and girls, and Phil promptly forgot most of their names. There were simply too many to remember. She joined the women at the table while Sarah slid over to the bailiff's wife and silently made herself indispensable. Her assistant had a knack for that.

Silence reigned for a time until one of the younger girls gathered up enough courage to ask Phil about ghosts. She entertained them for a time with her stories, until they relaxed a bit with her, and started talking among themselves again. Since it was mostly gossip about people she didn't know, Phil only paid half her attention to them, as she wondered what Nico might be doing. Would he oversee the workers all day? Or did she have a chance of seeing him before evening?

". . . Sir Nicodemus."

"Shush, Gertrude," one of the women snapped. "Or Martha might hear you."

Phil's ears pricked at the sound of his name echoed from her thoughts. Martha had left the room with several buckets and a few ladies in tow. Philomena leaned forward, pretending to listen to a buck-toothed woman answer her question about the sharpening charm the hedge witches had put on the tools. But she focused her entire concentration on the conversation of the two women sitting next to her.

Apparently Gertrude wouldn't be shushed. "He should have had a proper trial like anyone else. But no, the gentry all have friends in the highest places and they're cleared with nary an inquiry. I tell you, it's just not right."

"It's not our place to question the law."

"Nonsense. If there had been a proper investigation we would have dismissed the charges. But now we can't be sure, can we? Admit it, Rowena; even you are uncomfortable having him here today. I can only imagine how the men must feel, with a killer right in their midst."

"Shush, Gertrude. I mean it. That kind of talk will only get you in trouble. Do you want *her* to overhear you?"

Since Martha had not returned from outside, Phil had the most uncomfortable feeling that they were referring to her. She couldn't ignore such a blatant invitation. The buck-toothed woman across from her finished her explanation and got up to take her full bowl to the worktable. Phil turned and gave both of the women a conspiratorial smile.

"Did you mention my employer? I thought I overheard his name." Rowena looked scandalized, but Gertrude had the most malicious smile of satisfaction on her face.

"I thought it only proper to warn you, Lady Radcliff. You seem like a kind woman, despite your tendency to see ghosts. And since you're staying in his home and all . . ."

"I am all anticipation," Phil assured her, trying not to throttle the younger woman.

"There's some that think . . . Well, did you know that Sir Nicodemus was engaged several years ago?"

Phil tilted her head.

"To a girl much younger than he is. Some said they didn't get along, that they had a fight the night she was murdered."

"That's only a rumor," the other woman interrupted. "And don't say *murder,* Gertrude. It could have been an animal."

"Nonsense. The girl was found in the forest with marks on her too large for any natural animal of the woods. Tooth and claw marks, Lady Radcliff. The size of a were-wolf's."

Phil's mind reeled. "Are you insinuating that Sir Nicodemus murdered his intended?"

"And got off because his brother is married to the magistrate's daughter—"

"Gertrude," snapped Martha, who had just entered the kitchen. She had the eyes and ears of her were-self, because their voices had been pitched much lower than those of the other chattering women around them. "You will leave this house at once. I will not have you spreading these vicious lies about the master. Not in my home."

Gertrude snorted and rose to her feet, her hoops swaying around her. "I'm only saying what everyone thinks."

The other women had fallen silent and now listened avidly. Martha's face turned beet red. "Hasn't Sir Nicodemus always been good to us? How many other tenants have as much meat on their tables as we do? How often has he come to the aid of one of our children?"

"That doesn't excuse his crime. Even if he did it in a fit of passion, he should be punished for it like anyone else."

Several women nodded. Martha picked up a wooden spoon and brandished it like a weapon. "Your *betters* have named him innocent and anyone who thinks otherwise will leave my home this instant."

Gertrude stomped out the door, throwing a look of entreaty at the women behind her. But although some appeared to share her suspicions, none rose to follow her. Philomena sat frozen in her chair, unable to believe what she'd heard. Nico accused of murder? Found innocent, but the villagers didn't believe the verdict? It explained the rector's unusual warning when she'd arrived in Trollersby. And the reactions of the hedge witches and laborers on the farm. She had thought their attitudes stemmed from prejudice against shape-shifters, to fear of Nico's predatory nature. It never occurred to her that there could be something more.

Ridiculous. Nico had been found innocent. The silly conjectures of a narrow-minded woman should not bother her. Martha appeared quite certain of his innocence. Still, an empty feeling in the pit of her stomach bothered her throughout the rest of the morning. Martha must have noticed her distress, because she suggested that Phil join the group of ladies carrying water to the workers.

"Would you mind bringing Sir Nicodemus his water? I wouldn't ordinarily ask but it appears that you have an interest in the farm and might want to see how the fields are cleared."

Martha handed Philomena a bucket and directed her to one of the paths between the rows of hay. The sun beat down on the golden heads of the crop, seeming to increase the heat tenfold. She felt grateful for the wide-brimmed bonnet she'd chosen, pulling it even farther down her forehead to shade her eyes. The bucket of water grew heavier with each step, and the tall hay blocked the occasional breeze.

Despite her discomfort, Phil felt such an exquisite sense of freedom that she loved every minute of it. She looked up at the blue sky, rose to her toes so she could catch a glimpse of the sea of golden hay, and searched for hayfairies. When she heard the faint swish of scythe through grass she slowed her steps, unwilling to break the feeling of peace that had fallen over her.

And then she felt something tickle her behind. Beneath her skirts. Phil slapped at her bottom and something slithered down her leg. She spun, the water sloshing over the bucket, stamping her feet, trying to see what manner of insect had gotten into her clothes. She hoped it wasn't poisonous.

But she didn't see a thing. So she hurried forward, entered a clearing of mown hay, and then skidded to a halt at the sight of Sir Nicodemus Wulfson, baronet of Grimspell castle. He bent slightly over, his scythe flashing so quickly through the dense growth that it blurred. He worked alone, and perhaps that was why he'd removed his shirt. The sun had already turned his skin a golden brown and his muscles rippled with every motion he made. Phil swallowed. She'd never seen anything more beautiful than his naked torso.

He froze and turned toward her, as if he'd felt her watching him. He'd tied a cloth around his forehead to hold back his hair, and it emphasized the gold in the dark brown depths of his eyes. Or perhaps the sun made those sparkles glitter so brilliantly?

"Is something wrong?"

Phil floundered. She couldn't very well say that the sweat that slicked his chest made it gleam like burnished copper. "Something got beneath my skirts." Oh, botheration, that sounded worse.

He dropped his scythe and put his hands on his hips, bending backward with a groan. She heard his back pop. "If only I hadn't promised to be a gentleman . . . Are you my water carrier?"

She offered up the bucket and then frowned. "I've spilled some, I'm afraid."

He shrugged, setting off a marvelous reaction through his shoulder muscles. Phil wished he'd quit moving. But he took the bucket, tilted back his head, and drank, the sinews in his throat working with an alternating rhythm. She could only stand and stare, completely transfixed.

Then he closed his eyes and poured the rest of the water over his head. It sluiced down his strong nose and chin, creating gleaming rivulets down his chest until the waist-band of his trousers absorbed the rest of it. "Ah. The witches always charm the water to keep it cool. I'm afraid that the jug I brought with me is already warm and you saved me from having to go back and fetch it."

Phil glanced across the space that Sir Nico had cleared, grateful to focus her eyes anywhere else but on him. She stared down the mown rows. "You did all of that?"

He grinned. "Joseph and I oversee the men; then when we have them spaced, we start working. I guess many landowners wouldn't do it, but with my were-strength I can clear as much as five men working together." He tossed down his bucket and unself-consciously flexed his arms. "Besides, it's good exercise." He took a step toward her.

Phil avoided his eyes, remembering what that woman had said about the murdered girl. That the marks on the dead woman's body hadn't been made by an ordinary animal. She stared at his chest, wondering exactly how strong he might be. To her chagrin she noticed that his nipples had puckered from the cool water. Drops of moisture sparkled like diamonds on the fine dark hairs that surrounded the peaks. Had she ever seen a man's nipples before? Maybe one of Fanny's ghostly customers—

"So, are you impressed?" he murmured.

It took her a moment to realize he referred to the amount of field he had cleared. "Certainly."

He raised his hand, stopping just short of touching her arm. "Can I stop being a gentleman?"

"Certainly not. You promised." Phil leaned down and retrieved the bucket. Botheration, her fingers shook. "I'd best get back to the house. The other women are preparing quite a feast, you know."

"They always do. What's wrong?"

"I—I'm not sure what you mean." Phil wanted to flee, but her traitorous feet stayed rooted on the cut hay.

"Why won't you look at me?"

Because she didn't want him to see the naked desire in her eyes. Because she didn't want him to see the fear that might be there as well. Phil tried, but she couldn't meet his gaze. He closed the remaining distance between them and although he didn't touch her, she felt surrounded by the sheer predatory strength of him.

Chapter Seven

Nico stared down at the top of her bonnet. She knew. He should have told her about Beatrice sooner. He should have realized that she'd find out from the gossipy villagers. But he'd told himself that it didn't matter. He was only her employer. Did that entitle her to his problems?

His nostrils flared as he breathed in the sweet scent of her, his were-self shadowing him now. Nico had to struggle against the beast to keep from touching her. He wanted her. Wanted her badly.

He silently groaned. He needed to make her trust him. At least enough to allow him in her bed so he could ease this desire for her. "They told you about Beatrice, didn't they?"

Philomena looked up at him in surprise, and he caught her gaze, searching those gray eyes for some answers. The beast inside could have howled at the ardor he saw within their depths. Nico had expected it. But behind that sultry look lay a hint of fear. Damn, he didn't need her answer, but she responded anyway.

"Was that her name? The name of your fiancée?" The bucket slipped from her fingers and hit the ground, but she didn't appear to notice.

The sun had dried the water with which he'd doused himself and made his skin itch. Nico rubbed his chest, watching with satisfaction as her eyes followed his movements. "Yes. And I suppose I'll have to tell you the entire story."

Her head tilted and she studied him, in that quiet, accepting way that she had. Her eyes were so pale in the sunlight that they almost appeared to glow. "As my employer, you don't have to tell me anything at all."

"But as your friend, I would like you to know. We are still friends, aren't we?"

"So you keep insisting."

"Well, we could be more . . ."

She huffed and Nico smiled. Some of her fear had disappeared, and he smelled her curiosity. He would take any advantage he could get. He turned and burrowed in the uncut hay, wrapping tops together to form a shallow sort of cave. "Will you sit and talk with me, lady?"

She frowned. Before she could form a refusal, he added, "Your nose escapes the rim of your bonnet. It's liable to get painfully red."

Her eyes widened in dismay, and with that confident grace of hers she settled into his shelter. Nico felt her tense as he sat beside her and made sure not to sit too close.

"Where on earth is your shirt?" she asked, an almost painful note in her voice.

Nico pointed down the mown pathway. "I think I left it back there."

She sighed with vexation, and he forced himself to smother a grin. Lady Radcliff wanted him just as much as he wanted her. But she couldn't quite settle her mind to the fact. He hoped he could change that.

So he spoke the truth. "I fell in love with Beatrice's gaiety, the way she viewed life as nothing but a lark. She was such a contrast to the darkness of my were-self." He felt his smile fade. "It took me a while to realize that along with that gaiety came a frivolous nature that knew nothing of loyalty or honor."

Nico tore the cloth off his forehead and let his hair shadow his eyes. He glanced at her from beneath that shelter and realized that he'd said it all wrong. "I found out that Beatrice had been unfaithful. When I confronted her, she said it meant nothing and I shouldn't take it so seriously."

Philomena's face creased in sympathy and encouraged Nico to continue. He twisted the cloth in his hand while he spoke. "I broke the engagement that night."

"The night she was murdered?"

Ah, she was quick. Nico nodded. "But I swear, I didn't harm her. She said that she wanted my title and she wouldn't allow me to leave her so easily. I don't know what she meant and I never had a chance to find out. Because they found her the next morning in the forest, her beautiful face and body . . ." He couldn't suppress the shudder from that memory. The wounds had been so deep.

Philomena laid her fingers over the cloth he clutched, stilling his hands. "Is that why you were accused? Because you'd fought that night?"

Nico looked up at her. The sun had brought out tiny freckles across the bridge of her cheeks and nose. Tiny lines radiated from the corners of her eyes. He adored every detail about her. "No one else knows about that."

Her eyes widened.

"At least, I didn't think anyone knew. But perhaps someone overheard us. Because too many people still suspect me of murdering her."

"What happened with the investigation?" she asked, her voice even and strong.

Nico dropped the cloth and turned his hand, lacing his fingers in hers. After all, she had touched him first. "They investigated all the weres in the parish. Any of those with teeth and claws. But we all had alibis and there wasn't enough evidence to convict anyone. Not even a scent of the killer could be detected on her body. Not a track could be found in the area where they'd discovered her."

Philomena gently twisted her hand from his grasp. "And so it remains a mystery and fodder for people's imaginations. Until the true killer is found."

Nico brushed at his arm, feeling the tickle of an insect. "And there you have my obsession. I have spent the last two years combing the woods for any sign of another beast. What animal leaves barely a track and no scent?"

Philomena frowned. "If Beatrice's spirit still remains attached to the earth, perhaps I can help you—ooh!" She wiggled her torso. "I think that insect is still inside my dress."

Nico narrowed his eyes, searching the tall golden stalks around them. "Be careful, it might not be—"

The soft drone of thousands of wings met his ears, and Nico groaned. He'd hoped they could talk a while longer. He wasn't sure that she believed him yet. Whenever he felt his were-self shadow him, her eyes still widened with fear. She seemed to have more experience with human nature than he did. Could she detect the doubt in his voice?

"Sir Nicodemus. There's a winged creature perched atop your head. And it is most definitely not a bug."

"They have come to bedevil me back to work," he said. "No doubt they are anxious for their winter ricks."

The ghost-hunter leaned forward, squinting at the tiny creature. Nico had an ample view of Philomena's breasts and couldn't speak for several moments. She had large, extremely lovely breasts.

"A hayfairy," she breathed. "Aren't you the sweetest thing I've ever seen? You're like a tiny person, except your skin and hair are the color of hay—ooh!" She sat back, her face turning beet red, and squirmed again. She covered her breasts with her arms and stifled a laugh.

"That's a hayfairy inside your dress, not an insect," Nico said. "They like to tickle." Fortunately, they knew *he* wasn't ticklish. Philomena twisted. Apparently she was.

She gasped. "That's a most inappropriate place . . ." She looked up to the top of his head. "Tell your friend to cease this instant."

Nico heard tiny laughter. "That's enough," he growled. "If you don't come out of her dress right now, I will be forced to go in and get you."

Lady Radcliff's eyes widened at his threat. Nico was looking forward to carrying out his promise, but the hayfairy emerged from the hollow between her breasts. He felt an unreasonable surge of jealousy.

Nico saw a blur of movement pass his face and join the flock that flew around them, their tiny wings picking up the sunlight in luminescent colors. The little fellow in Philomena's dress made a face at him before flying off as well.

"You'd best get back to work," she said, rising to her feet and stepping out into the sunlight. She looked up at the hovering flock. "They are dreadfully mischievous, aren't they?"

Nico stared at her. She'd smiled when she'd said it. She retrieved the bucket and glanced up at him. The smile had disappeared.

"Do you believe that I'm innocent?" Suddenly it seemed very important to him, beyond the need to gain her trust.

She pulled down the rim of her bonnet again, shading her eyes. Rather than give a direct answer, she said, "Along with seeing ghosts, I can often see people's auras."

"What's an aura?"

"It's the essence of a person, and it can change with his mood." She stared at him with those big gray eyes, and Nico fought the urge to hide from that penetrating gaze. "When I look at you, Sir Nicodemus, I often see the shadow of your wolf. I have to wonder how much of the beast controls you sometimes."

She turned and disappeared into the rows of grass. Nico stared after her for a moment, then, with a growl, picked up his scythe and attacked the hay with a vengeance. Why did he have to lust after a woman who saw too much? He knew he hadn't harmed Beatrice, but he was all too aware that he was capable of it. His were-self loved the hunt; the scent of blood and the copper taste of it in his mouth.

He didn't want to know that about himself. And Philomena was right. The wolf shadowed him far too often. He couldn't allow himself to get lost in his beast-form again.

By the end of the day Nico had cleared almost twice as much as he'd done in the morning. And he was no closer to finding a solution to any of his problems. He strode across the fields, heading for the stream with the rest of the men. Many looked at him askance and he could feel the condemnation in their eyes.

He plunged into his bathwater to cool his body and thoughts. He wanted to scream his innocence, but he knew it wouldn't do any good. Damn, but he was tired of being treated like a criminal. Whether Lady Radcliff believed him or not, she had at least offered to help. He decided he would accept her assistance to see if Beatrice's spirit still clung to the earth.

The servants had brought soap and left his change of clothing next to Joseph's.

"I'm starved," the bailiff said while changing into his clean clothes.

Nico shrugged. It took a while for his appetite to return after he worked. But he followed the rest of the men to the house, where tables had been set up in the yard. The sun had faded and the sky had darkened to a sapphire blue. One of the old gaffers had pulled out his violin, and the strains of his music filled the night air. When they finished the harvest, the feast would be larger and the tunes lively enough to dance to. But tonight, the lament of the strings matched the exhaustion of the workers.

Nico sat on a bench and watched the women carry out the platters of food, frowning when he didn't see Lady Radcliff among them. She didn't seem one to take on airs because of her title. After all, she'd consented to bring him his water. So he wondered where she'd gotten off to.

He felt a tug on his trouser leg. "Unca Neeko. Will you come play with me?"

Nicodemus bent down and looked into the freckled, earnest face. Joseph and Martha's children had always called him uncle, although the title was purely honorary. "Wouldn't you like to eat?"

Josette shook her pale red curls. "Mamma made us eat already so we wouldn't bother you men." She cast a cautious glance at her mother. "The boys won't let me play in the stack with 'em. Say I'm too little."

Nico grinned. "Well, we'll see about that, won't we?"

He took her tiny hand and allowed her to lead him into the barn. Fairylights illuminated the tall stack of hay that stood just beneath the loft. Josette's brothers, Jack and John, waited patiently at the loft's edge, their eyes fixed on the woman who stood next to the haystack beneath them.

Philomena.

"Now then, Tup. The other boys showed you how to do it. It's your turn." She held her bonnet in her hand and waved it like a flag.

Her head tilted upward at an empty space between the two brothers. Nico felt the hair rise on the back of his neck.

"He's scairt too," whispered Josette.

Nico crouched. "Who?"

"Why, that boy dressed in rags."

The two brothers stood back from the edge and suddenly whooped. Nico could swear he saw the hay shift, as if a body had slid down it.

"Well done, Tup," Philomena cried, clapping her hands.

She listened a moment. "Yes, of course you can do it again. But you must wait your turn."

Jack and John jumped from their perch onto the haystack and slid down with a volume of noise that only those two brothers could manage.

"I wanna go too," Josette said.

Nico took a breath and stepped all the way into the room. Philomena gave him a startled smile, then returned her attention to the loft, where her eyes followed an invisible figure down the haystack again.

"Josette wants to try it too," he announced.

The brothers frowned. "But, Uncle Nico," Jack said, "she's too little."

"Phil says she might get hurt," John added triumphantly.

Nico raised a brow at the nickname they'd used for the ghost-hunter. "Phil? I like that." Before she could respond, he caught Josette up into his arms and carried her to the ladder that led up to the loft. "Women are always too protective of children. That's why they need a man around."

Phil snorted but didn't protest when he led the little girl to the edge of the loft.

"Oh," Josette breathed. "It looks so far down." She turned and stared over her shoulder. "Tup says not to be scairt." And with that, she leaped over the edge.

Nico tried to ignore the cold sensation that crept over his skin, but he wasn't quite used to Phil's ghosts yet. When the little girl reached the bottom of the stack he jumped down himself, sliding down the stack much faster than the children had. He passed their landing spot and knocked Philomena off her feet and they tumbled together in the loose straw. She landed spread-eagle atop him.

"We really must stop doing this," she said. But she wore a smile.

Her hair had come undone, tumbling about her shoulders, the auburn strands shining red in the fairylight. He plucked a piece of straw from the curls. "It feels most natural to me."

Philomena playfully slapped his shoulder and stood. They watched the children for a time in companionable silence.

"So have you tried it yet?" Nico asked, nodding at the haystack.

"Certainly not."

"I'm surprised. You're always so eager to see and do new things. Or have you slid down a haystack before?"

"I can't say that I have."

"She's scairt," announced Josette, who had just slid to a stop in front of them. "Don't be scairt, Lady Phil. See, I'm not hurt."

Phil glanced at Nico and scowled at the expression on his face. "It's not ladylike."

"Coward," he murmured. "I'll go with you, if you want."

She gave him a withering glare and stomped over to the ladder, climbing it faster than he would have credited. Without the slightest hesitation she jumped onto the stack, a blur of flying skirts and petticoats. She came to a stop at the bottom and didn't move for several moments.

Nico's heart dropped. "Are you all right?"

She looked up and blinked, a smile spreading across her beautiful face. "That's the most fun I've had in ages."

He grasped her hand and helped her to her feet, following her up the ladder. He joined her at the edge of the loft. "Together?" he said, taking her hand again. Her eyes sparkled and they leaped into space, landing with a sliding thud onto the stack and swooshing too quickly to the bottom.

They grinned at each other and ran back to the ladder, jumping the haystack again and again until finally they were both breathless with laughter . . . and there was more hay spread out on the floor than left in the stack.

Nico glanced around. "Where did the children go?"

"To bed, I imagine," she replied, plucking straw from her

dress. "We should be ashamed of ourselves, stealing their haystack that way." But she didn't look the least bit sorry.

"And Tup?"

"He faded quite a while ago. He can't materialize for any great length of time."

Nico raised a brow. "The other children saw him."

"Of course. The young don't wear the veils of skepticism that most adults do."

"Neither do you, it seems." He stood and raked his fingers through his hair, bits of hay floating to the ground. "Come, I'd like to show you something."

She hesitated. "Isn't it rather late?"

Nico shrugged. "There's a full moon tonight, so we'll have no trouble finding our way home. Come on, Phil. I thought you were wanting a bit of magic?"

Her eyes lit and she followed him up the ladder without another word. Nico made his way to the dark side of the loft, opening the door onto the night. Phil looked down on the field of hay that butted up to the property, the moonlight bathing the tall grass with a heavenly glow, the gentle breeze making the stalks undulate in a pattern similar to waves on a lake.

Moonlight did breathtaking things to her features. He snapped his mouth shut and gathered armfuls of grass, making a soft nest for her to sit on. She sat with cultivated grace. "It's really a charming sight. I could quite fall in love with the country."

"There's more."

"What do you mean?"

"Shh. Just watch." Nico stood behind her, his wolf steeling him to patience, knowing just when it would be the right time to pounce on his prey. He saw the first wink of light before she did and watched it quickly grow into a whirlwind of glowing color. Lady Radcliff gasped and leaned forward.

The wings of the hayfairies glowed with their own internal light, multicolored hues of lavender, pink, and gold. They danced above the fields in a centuries-old tradition, whirlwinds of color that appeared to glitter from the flutter of each wing. Nico felt mesmerized for a moment himself, even though he'd witnessed it a thousand times before.

Then he sat next to Philomena and caught sight of her face and realized that even frolicking hayfairies could not hold him as spellbound as her beauty could. He fisted his hands against the urge to reach out and stroke her cheek, to run his fingers through the silken strands of her loose hair. His were-self growled at him to wait.

She sat frozen for the longest time, her eyes so wide they reflected tiny sparks of color from the dance.

"Sir Nicodemus." Her voice was low, so husky with promise that he didn't dare breathe. "I would like to forget, for just a moment, that I am forty and you are seven and twenty. I would like to be kissed in the moonlight, with straw in my hair and hayfairies dancing over fields of waving grass. Do you think you could retract your promise to be a gentleman?"

Nico let out a breath.

"Just for this moment, of course," she added.

Of course. Nico put his hand under her chin and stroked the firm line of her jaw with his thumb. He gently turned her face toward him, the wolf retreating so that he felt an unusual warmth flow through him as he lowered his mouth to hers. Her lips tasted sweet; she smelled of crushed hay and roses. Nico stroked his lips over hers, her mouth trembling beneath his. Something twisted inside his chest and he kept his touch light, his mouth relaxed and undemanding. He couldn't remember ever bestowing such a tender kiss upon someone. He had never wanted to.

He could have kissed her all night, but she pulled back,

staring into his eyes as if trying to see into his very soul. "The shadow of your wolf is gone."

Nico brushed the hair away from her face, then stroked the soft curls. "It's only a myth that the full moon makes us shift. But he's still there, always a part of me, I'm afraid."

She had opened her mouth to say something when they heard a hiss from behind them. Phil pulled away from him with a guilty start, and Nico didn't suppress the growl of frustration that rose from his chest.

Sarah appeared unaffected by the menacing sound. Her glossy black eyes blinked at him with studied indifference. "I thought you might be hungry, Lady Radcliff. They are packing away the food."

At the mention of food, Nico realized that his appetite had returned and his stomach growled louder than his voice had. Phil smiled and patted his shoulder. "Run along now; don't wait for me. I'll need Sarah to rearrange my hair before I go down. Really, Sarah, it's amazing how quickly a bun comes unraveled when sliding down a haystack."

She had dismissed him. Like a child. Nico felt himself shift to his were-form and he didn't stop it from happening, even when he saw the ghost-hunter's eyes flicker in fear. She'd said she would forget their age difference for only a moment, but he was bloody well tired of her using it as some sort of shield.

He purposely brushed his coat against Sarah as he passed her, his canine lips pulled back in a sneer. She didn't betray a shiver of intimidation. He suppressed a kernel of admiration for the were-snake. Almost two times the size of an ordinary wolf, he'd made many a man tremble in fear.

Nico shifted back to human to get down the ladder. He no longer felt the urge to jump down a haystack.

Nicodemus barely exchanged a word with Philomena on the way back to Grimspell castle. Samuel and Charles had worked the fields as well and their hooves dragged, their heads hanging in weariness. Nico hated to delay the men's return home to their families, but they would be passing by the place where Beatrice's body had been found, and for the first time in years he felt a small glimmer of hope that he'd be able to discover her killer. If, that is, Lady Radcliff still wanted to help him. He'd sulked since he'd left her in the loft.

"Samuel, Charles, would you stop here?"

They each rolled an eye at him but plodded to a halt.

"Why are we stopping?" Philomena asked.

He didn't look at her, just pointed through the dark stand of trees. "They discovered Beatrice's body near here. I'd like you to see if her spirit still remains, Phil. That is, if you're willing." He liked using the children's nickname for her. It suited her much better.

He heard her suck in a breath. "Are you sure you want to do this?"

Nico fisted his hands. So, she still didn't believe in his innocence. Then he turned and stared at her in surprise as another realization struck him. If he were guilty, Beatrice's spirit would expose him. Her question had been designed to protect him. "I have been looking for Beatrice's killer for two years. Her *real* killer. So yes, I'm absolutely certain I want to do this." He sprang down from the cart and held out his hand to her. She clasped it in a strong grasp and joined him on the dirt road.

Samuel and Charles suddenly looked alert when Nico turned to them. "We'll be as quick as we can." Samuel tossed his mane and Charles snorted.

"I can track the spot better in were-form," he told Philomena, and then glanced at Sarah, who'd slid down from her seat and stood at her mistress's side. "I'll carry Lady Radcliff on my back. In the dark, it's treacherous territory for a human on foot. If you want to accompany your mistress, you'll need to keep up."

Sarah nodded and shifted to snake. She was big enough to move fast, as long as she could get past any obstacles.

"On your back?" Philomena squeaked, her face a mixture of anticipation and horror. "I can barely sit a horse, Sir Nicodemus, much less a wolf!"

He smiled. She looked as anxious as a child. Ah, excellent. He lowered his voice and spoke in the manner he used when talking to Josette. "Don't worry, sweetie, you'll be fine. You'll have to ride astride—they don't make sidesaddles for wolves. Just remember to keep your legs tucked up and your head down in case of overhanging branches. Hold on to my fur, it won't hurt me."

She still hesitated.

"Come on, Phil. Don't be *scairt*." Nico emphasized the last word. Her eyes rounded in sudden realization and he hid his smug grin by shifting to wolf. Now maybe she would know how it felt to be treated like a child.

She muttered something under her breath but swung her leg over his back and wiggled to find her seat. Nico closed his eyes at such sweet torture. Then she leaned forward and wrapped her arms around his neck, burying her fists in his fur and keeping her head down as he had instructed. As soon as she tucked up her legs, Nico loped into the trees, Sarah slithering right behind them.

He kept his pace slow, although he wanted to run through the forest, his wolf-self longing for such reckless joy. Nico tried to keep to an open path, but several times he was forced to scramble over fallen logs and leap small gullies. Despite what she'd said, the ghost-hunter made an excellent wolf rider, molding herself to his back as if she were a part of him.

Even after two years, a faint scent of Beatrice's blood still remained in the small clearing. There had been so very much of it.

Phil scrambled off his back, and Nico shifted to human.

He took her hand and steadied her for a moment. "Now, that wasn't so bad, was it?"

Her eyes narrowed. "Quit speaking to me as if I'm a child."

"I will if you will."

"Your point is taken." She studied the small clearing, the dark woods beyond, where the moonlight barely penetrated. The wind sighed through the trees, branches scraped together and the scurrying of small animals sounded in the undergrowth. "Where, exactly, did her body lay?"

Nico pointed to the base of a large oak tree, the enormous roots covered in green moss, shaping small caves and hollows. The ghost-hunter walked forward and placed her hand on a large root. "Here."

"Yes."

"Call her."

Nico took a deep breath. He'd wanted this, hadn't he? "Beatrice. Are you still here? Will you come?"

Phil tilted her head at a rustle behind him. Nico glanced at the were-snake in surprise. His keen hearing didn't often allow anyone to sneak up behind him. Sarah shifted to human and slid forward.

They waited in a silence that stretched far too long, until Nico couldn't bear the disappointment that rose in him. "Do you see anything?"

The ghost-hunter shook her head.

"Why won't she come?"

Phil turned to him. "I told you, I can't command a spirit to appear. I only see them when they do. It might comfort you to know that she's gone to the other side. Whatever happened here, she came to terms with it, and is now at peace."

"Are you sure?" growled Nicodemus. "We can come back . . . try again."

Phil sighed. "I can't feel the slightest hint of even a memory of her spirit, Nico. I'm afraid it won't be of any use."

Nico shifted to wolf, threw back his head, and howled his frustration. For a brief moment he'd actually thought that he would find Beatrice's killer and clear his own name. He should have known it wouldn't be that easy. Nothing in his life had ever been easy.

When he lowered his head, his eyes met Philomena's. She rushed toward him and threw her arms about his neck, burying her face in his fur in sympathy. Nico felt himself calm. When she'd looked at him, he hadn't seen a trace of fear in her face, despite his howl, which had made even the were-snake cringe.

Phil believed in his innocence. He had that much consolation, at least.

Chapter Eight

Phil awoke that night to a cold that made her breath turn to white mist. The warrior with the blue sword stood at the foot of her bed, glanced at the fireplace and then over his shoulder.

"He's makin' his rounds again," Tup said, his thin little face watching her with solemn intensity. "Ye'd best hurry if ye mean to follow him."

This time Phil had a general idea of the warrior's route. She called out to Sarah but didn't bother to wait for her assistant. She sprang out of bed, grabbed a fairylight and ran for the stairs, tumbling down the circular tower with only a fleeting regret that she'd forgotten to put on her night robe. She waited in the gloomy main hall for another glimpse of the warrior, hoping that Sarah had heard her call and would follow. Her assistant had acted peculiarly when they'd retired for the evening, unable to suppress wide yawns of fatigue. Perhaps the work at the farm had tired her more than she was accustomed to. At least, Phil hoped that was the reason.

She caught the slight flicker of the glow of the blue sword from the corner of her eye. She ran for the library just in time to see the ghost disappear down the stairway again. She took a deep breath and followed. By the time she reached the kitchens she had to push her hand against the stitch in her side.

"Not the cellars," she murmured. But the blue sword

winked from within as if to mock her. Phil followed more slowly this time, aware of the sound of her breath in the stillness of the rooms. She had lost sight of the warrior's spirit but went down to the dungeon nonetheless, hoping she wouldn't witness that battle again.

Her ears rang in the deep silence of the chamber. She waited for another vision and when it didn't come she couldn't tell whether she felt relieved or not. There might have been a clue in that deadly battle that she'd missed the first time.

Phil stepped forward, avoiding the worst of the spider-webs, hoping they were all unoccupied. She thought a spider in her dress would be decidedly worse than a hayfairy.

Tup materialized on top of a black-stained table. "He went in there, ye know." He pointed at the door that led to the tunnels. "I've been keepin' an eye out for him since ye tried to follow him the last time."

The door stood open, a dank smell coming from within, the rusted lock still lying where she'd last seen it. Perhaps Nico had forgotten to tell his brother to have the lock replaced. Perhaps Royden was so ill he hadn't been able to take care of it yet.

Phil cautiously approached the black opening. "Have you followed him inside, Tup?"

"Not on yer life. Crikey, do ye think I'm barmy? Even ghosts can get lost, ye know."

She supposed he was right. "But you've followed the warrior here before?"

"Oh, aye. Ye asked me to find out what I could, but he won't talk, ye know. He runs about on his own business and then disappears down here. That's all I've been able to find out."

His voice sounded so distraught that Phil turned and held out her hand to him. Tup floated forward, his translucent fingers wrapping around hers. "This is my problem to solve,

Tup. So don't you worry. You've already done more than enough by keeping me company in this dreadful place."

His eyes grew luminous. "I'd do anything for ye, Phil, ye know that. Yer the only mum I've ever known."

Philomena's heart twisted and she longed to throw her arms around the lad. But he was old enough that he'd shy away from the embrace. And besides, she would be holding nothing but empty air. "Well, you were right not to follow the warrior in there. If you should get lost, whatever would I do without you?"

Tup smiled as he faded, his energy spent for the night.

Phil sighed and faced the door. Who knew how many miles of tunnels lay beneath Grimspell? Tup was right; she'd be barmy to try to follow the ghosts inside. Yet if the warrior made his rounds every night, that meant he'd have to come out of the tunnels as well. If she could follow him in, he could also lead her out.

A hiss echoed off the dungeon walls and Phil smiled. "I only considered it for a moment."

"Didn't you ssay that a tunnel collapsed on Ssir Nicodemuss?"

"Yes. If the tunnels are to be explored, it would require several men with beams to shore up the walls in case of collapse."

Sarah hissed again.

"You're quite right, it would still be an impossible task. I'll just have to find another way to solve this haunting."

Sarah followed Philomena back to their rooms, her sliding footsteps slower than usual. Phil closed her bedroom door behind them and faced her assistant. "Is something wrong, Sarah? You don't seem quite yourself."

She lowered her head, swaying a bit. "It'ss time for my shed."

"I thought so. Well, then, you must try to get some extra rest. And take more baths—that helps, doesn't it?"

Sarah nodded. "But I don't like to neglect you."

"Nonsense. We've been through this before. I can manage until you are . . . whole again. Go on now, off to bed." Phil knew the extent of Sarah's fatigue by the way she followed her order without argument. Philomena washed the dirt and cobwebs from her feet before crawling into her own bed.

Phil's sleep was undisturbed for the rest of the night, except for dreams of riding a wolf through a forest, tangled up with visions of jumping into a golden stack of grass. When Phil awoke the next morning she slowly realized that none of it had been a dream. How disconcerting.

Before she could ponder the thought further, the bedroom door cracked open and Sarah slipped into the room. "Would you be coming down to luncheon, my lady?"

"Botheration, I slept rather late, didn't I?"

"I musst admit," Sarah murmured, "I did too."

"Good. You look much more rested. And I don't want you helping in the kitchens today. I'm sure the rest of the servants will understand."

Sarah made no comment, just pulled a day dress out of the wardrobe and held it out to her mistress for approval. A dove gray frock, with prancing unicorns embroidered about the neckline and sleeves. Phil nodded and performed her morning toilet with haste, then made her way down to the dining room.

Royden rose when she entered the room. "I'm afraid we've already dined."

Edwina glanced at her empty plate and gave Philomena an unapologetic smile.

"I'm so sorry," Phil said as she took a seat. "I don't normally sleep this late." A footman brought in a plate and she began to uncover the dishes sitting on the table.

"It's perfectly all right," Edwina said. "One must make allowances for age. Why, my mother often dozes off in the middle of the day."

Phil chose some cold venison and sliced herbed potatoes and attacked them with vigor. "Has Sir Nicodemus already eaten, then?"

"He left early this morning," Royden answered. "He'll be working at the home farm until the harvest is in. Probably about a fortnight."

Phil tried to hide her disappointment. Of course, she couldn't expect him to take her with him every day. After all, she had a job to do. But she had so enjoyed the farm. Surely, that's why her stomach had plummeted. Not because she'd miss Nico. How could she miss a man she barely knew?

"He usually sleeps there as well." Royden grinned at Phil. "But he assured me he'll be home every night to join us for dinner."

Edwina rose. "The seamstress is waiting for me, Roy. Wait until you see the gown she has crafted with the cloth that Nico brought me. I'm sure it will quite take your breath away." She leaned up and pecked him on the cheek, then glanced at Phil. "I'd ask you to take a look, but I'm sure you're not interested in the current fashions." And with a glance at Phil's simple dress, she sailed out of the room, her hoops bouncing with her stride.

Royden collapsed back into his chair and stared after his wife with a frown of confusion on his face. But Phil understood the girl's hostility. If Nico were to marry, Edwina would be supplanted as mistress of Grimspell. Not that Nico would ever consider Phil as a possible wife. A temporary bedmate, yes, but she was entirely too old for him to marry. A titled man needed heirs and a younger woman was more likely to survive childbirth, which was why it was perfectly acceptable for a man to take a younger wife. But not the other way around.

Phil concentrated on her food until she heard Royden give a tired sigh. "Did you happen to see any more spirits last night?"

Phil glanced up, studying his face. Wrinkles of exhaustion seamed his smooth skin and the circles under his eyes had grown even darker. "Yes, I did. And I think you dreamed of them."

He nodded.

Phil took a drink of her watered wine. "Oh. I should mention that when Nico took me on a tour of the castle I saw one of your ancestors battling a dragon in the dungeon."

Royden raised a brow, whether from the mention of the ghosts or her slip of Nicodemus's nickname, she couldn't be sure. "The castle has a long history, but I've never read anything about dragons. How did you know it was one of our ancestors?"

"He shifted into a wolf."

"Ah." Royden leaned back in his chair.

"Perhaps if you told me some of the castle's history it would help me solve the puzzle of your angry ghosts."

"There are books in the library that you might want to read," he replied. "But I've been through them and didn't find any clue to our current problem. The castle has been in the family for generations, always with a direct descent. In some cases, there's been more than one son who inherited shape-shifting abilities. The only odd thing that I could discover is that within the last few generations, the owners didn't die here."

Phil tilted her head. "Your father isn't buried on the property?"

"Nor my grandfather."

"Botheration. I was hoping that we could appeal to their spirits for answers. All the ghosts I've encountered here are so old that I can't make any direct contact with them."

Royden sighed and uncurled his lanky frame from the chair. "My father might have been able to help us. He seemed to know a lot of secrets about the castle. I think he planned on telling his heir one day, but I'm sure he didn't expect to die so young." He gave her a sad smile. "Perhaps you'll find something I overlooked. You're welcome to make use of the library today."

Phil nodded, pushing away her plate. Yes, perhaps she could find some answers that way.

Royden gave her a small bow and shuffled toward the door, his footsteps that of a much older man. Phil half turned in her chair. "Can your duties wait, Royden? You might consider returning to bed."

His smile met his soft brown eyes this time. "I appreciate your concern. It's very kind of you."

Phil spent a very frustrating day searching through tomes with yellowed pages. She'd found nothing useful. Not even a mention of the tunnels beneath Grimspell. Sarah had kept her candles replenished but had left several times during the day to return to their rooms and soak in a bath.

Phil sat in an enormous leather chair surrounded by piles of books and even a few old scrolls. She rubbed her tired eyes, glancing over at her silent companion. The young man adjusted his spectacles and shifted on the sofa, holding his book a bit closer to a transparent candle. She'd tried to speak with him, but he was like all the other castle ghosts: nothing but a memory performing the same action over and over.

She sighed and squinted at the clock on the mantel of the ornate fireplace. Her heart leapt a bit as she realized it was nearly dinnertime and she would see Sir Nicodemus. If nothing else, she'd managed to learn today that he came from a long line of heroic men. Indeed, most of the records held accounts of the brave acts of his ancestors, either in defense of the castle or the crown.

The library door opened and Sarah slid into the room.

Her glossy black eyes had taken on a shade of milky white, and she moved slowly as she began to unbury Phil from the books surrounding her. "Sir Nicodemuss hass returned. They are waiting for you in the dining room."

Philomena smiled. "Well, I'm rather wrinkled, but I shan't make them wait, especially since I was late for luncheon." When she stood, Sarah pulled a fabric brush from her pocket and began to smooth the wrinkles from Phil's skirts. "How do you always know what I'm going to need, Sarah?"

Her assistant graced her with one of her rare smiles, the sharp points of her teeth glinting in the candlelight. She didn't reply, but Phil hadn't expected her to. When Sarah nodded that Phil looked respectable, she accompanied her mistress down the long hall to the dining room and then left to return to her soaking.

Phil stopped in the doorway and caught her breath. Nico sat at the table, laughing at something Edwina had said. He had recently bathed, and his white-brown hair was slicked back from his face, making his cheekbones even more prominent. His work at the farm had darkened his complexion to a golden brown and enhanced the muscles in his arms and shoulders. But Phil decided the shallow dimples by the sides of his mouth would be her complete undoing.

Why did he make her feel as if she'd been lonely her entire life until she'd met him? Why, she had a legion of friends and acquaintances and had never for one moment thought she lacked for companionship. Yet looking at him now made her feel as if the time she'd spent without his company had been completely wasted.

He must have felt her staring at him. Nico bounded out of his chair so quickly that the footman had to scurry to catch it before it fell over. The baronet crossed the room in a few strides and took her hand, brushing his lips over it. "Phil," he murmured.

He acted as if he'd missed her as much as she had him.

Phil couldn't pull her hand out of his grasp; it felt entirely too delicious. They stared at each other for the longest moment.

Edwina turned. "Why, Philomena, whatever on earth have you been doing? You look as wrinkled as a prune."

Phil turned her gaze on that sweet face. She really would have to figure out how Edwina did that. The girl could make the most cutting remarks with such a sweet manner and smile that one would feel boorish taking insult.

Phil pulled her hand from Nico's hold and took her place at the table. "I have been reading up on the castle's history, trying to discover some clue to your haunting."

"And have you?" Royden inquired, his hand trembling as he set down his fork.

Philomena sighed. "I'm afraid not. There's not a single mention of the tunnels."

Royden frowned, Edwina gasped, and Nico scowled. Royden managed to speak first. "Do you mean the tunnels beneath Grimspell? Why didn't you mention this earlier? What would they have to do with the haunting? No one's been in them for years."

"Last night I followed one of the castle spirits into the dungeon," she replied.

They all fell silent for a time while the servants brought in silver platters of stuffed pheasant and chafing dishes of soup and vegetables. Royden filled his plate sparingly, as usual, while Phil and Edwina spooned up generous helpings. Nico just stared at the silver candlesticks that graced the table, though their fancifully crafted shapes of frolicking elves were a strange thing to mesmerize him. Phil looked at him in concern, watching his aura darken as the shadow of his wolf fell over his handsome features.

"You know, Phil," Royden said, "now that you mention

it, I do think it's odd that there's nothing in the history of the castle about those tunnels. I wonder if there might be something in Father's trunk."

Phil's ears pricked. "What trunk?"

Royden leaned forward. "Father used to keep his private papers in an old leather trunk. Maybe he has something in there that mentions the tunnels." He frowned and sagged back against his chair, as if that little burst of excitement had drained him. "Although we went through it right after he died and I don't remember seeing any history books. It mostly held personal mementoes. Did you see anything, Nico?"

Phil didn't wait for Nico to answer. "But there may be something else in there that could shed some light on what's happening. I would so like to take a look for myself."

"If it would help get rid of my nightmares, you have my blessing. I'll have Dickens dig it out of the cellars. I think that's where we stored it."

Phil smiled with eagerness. She almost felt as if she were on a treasure hunt. She glanced at Nico and blinked. His aura had darkened to almost black. She couldn't imagine why he might be so angry.

Phil took a bite of her pheasant.

"Royden, you will not give Philomena Father's trunk," Nico announced.

Philomena swallowed. "Why ever not?"

His fists slammed atop the table and Edwina jumped. "Because I don't want you having anything to do with those tunnels, that's why."

"I think you're overstepping yourself, sir."

"The hell I am." His voice had lowered to a deadly growl. One of the servants squeaked and bolted from the room. Cheevers quivered in his boots but managed not to follow. Phil shivered and felt surprised by the odd reaction she had. The anger of his were-self didn't frighten her.

On the contrary, it excited her in a way she'd never quite experienced. Before she had a chance to explore this strange realization about herself, he spoke again. Well, growled, actually. "I am your employer, madam, and the master of this castle. I have every right to insist that you obey my orders."

Phil considered. "There may be nothing in the trunk regarding the tunnels, and something that could help me with your haunting. I understand that these are your father's personal things and that you may find a stranger going through them upsetting, but we must consider the benefit." There. He couldn't argue with such a calm, reasonable reply.

"On the contrary, I don't consider you a stranger. And I fear that if you find anything, you will act before considering your personal safety."

Philomena took another bite of pheasant. It was really quite good. No one spoke while she swallowed. Indeed, she appeared to be the only one eating. "I have no intention of going into the tunnels."

"You were just there last night."

"But I didn't follow the ghost inside." Phil didn't mention that she'd been tempted. Only Sarah knew that, and she was up in her room. "Surely that proves you can trust me."

Royden finally joined the conversation. "I must say, she's quite right, Nico. And I'm bloody well tired of not sleeping at night. She hasn't done anything to make us doubt her word."

Nicodemus considered, the golden flecks in his eyes glittering in the candlelight. Phil raised a brow. He had asked her to trust in his innocence; surely he could reciprocate in something so insignificant by comparison.

"I think Nico's right," Edwina piped up. How she managed to sing so beautifully when she possessed such a shrill speaking voice was beyond Phil's comprehension. Ah, yes, of course. Magic. "Those tunnels are dangerous and she shouldn't go anywhere near them." She shivered dramatically.

"What proper woman would want to go beneath the castle anyway? I'm sure it's damp and full of cobwebs."

"Please do not speak of me as if I'm not in the room."

Edwina's porcelain complexion flushed a beet red. "Since you're not listening to your common sense, I am appealing to Nico on your behalf."

"On the contrary. I have years of experience and common sense to draw upon, as you so often point out." Phil turned to Nico and fixed him with a steely gaze. "This is far too much fuss over such a minor request. Botheration, you would think the trunk was filled with gold. Do you want me to find out why your brother is being haunted, or not?"

Sir Nicodemus's aura had lightened to gray as he stared back and forth from her to Edwina. He chose that moment to make a major production out of choosing his dinner from the silver dishes, arranging his meat and asparagus on his plate with a precision that he normally didn't bother with. He took a bite of pheasant and glanced up at Cheevers. "It's too well done. Will you fetch me some meat that's worth consuming?"

Cheevers bobbed his head and left the room. Phil narrowed her eyes at Nico. The man appeared to be all too aware that it had now come down to a matter of will between herself and Edwina. His answer would shift a balance of power that Phil hadn't even known had existed until this moment.

How could she expect him to choose her over his brother's wife?

Nico leaned toward her, his charisma an almost tangible thing. "I give you my permission to look through my father's trunk . . . on one condition."

Philomena smiled. Edwina really must resist grinding her teeth. They'd be nothing but nubs by the time she reached Phil's age. "And what is your condition?"

"That you come to me with anything you may find that has to do with Grimspell's haunting. *Before* you investigate further. Are we agreed?" He held out his hand.

"Agreed," Phil replied, grasping his hand and giving it a hearty shake. When she loosened her grip, he tightened his. She could almost feel a sudden energy flow from his body to hers. Her eyes widened as she felt herself drown in his golden-flecked gaze. She had underestimated his attraction for her, thinking it must be some passing fancy from a young man who had spent too much time alone the past few years.

On the contrary, he wanted her badly. She could feel her body respond to it with an excitement that had her quivering in her chair. She could see it within the intense focus of his dark brown eyes. The man didn't just want to bed her. He wanted to possess her body with a desire that she'd never felt before. She'd been a fool to allow him to kiss her.

"You shouldn't let a stranger go through your father's private belongings."

Phil blinked. Nico growled. "I've made my decision, Edwina. It's not your place to question it."

The girl let out a startled breath. Philomena wanted to smooth her hurt feelings, but she couldn't tear her gaze away from Sir Nicodemus.

"The villagers are gossiping, you know."

Edwina's voice cut through their concentration like a knife. Nico glanced at his sister-in-law in surprise, allowing Phil to study the young woman as well. Her words had been sweet enough to clog the throat.

"What will my mother say when she comes to visit and sees the two of you?" Edwina blinked. "Royden, they are so obviously infatuated with one another. The villagers already whisper about the woman we hired who can talk to ghosts, but can you imagine the scandal if it got about that your brother actually bedded her?"

Phil rose. "If you will excuse me, it seems I have lost my appetite."

She gathered her skirts and sailed to the door. "Good night."

"Phil," Nico growled.

But she didn't stop to hear what he might have to say. She flew up the stairs, the tower making her a bit dizzy, but didn't stop running until she'd reached the privacy of her room. Phil panted a bit. She'd done more running in the past few days than she'd done in a year in London. Well, her visit would strengthen her constitution, if nothing else.

She checked in on Sarah. The were-snake had somehow managed to curl most of her massive body into the curved tub, and glanced up at her with milky white eyes. Phil didn't approach her or say a word. Sarah got testy during this time.

Phil closed the door softly and managed her toilet by herself. She yawned while crawling into bed, but the evening's conversation kept replaying itself in her head. What a private family they were, to be so concerned about their father's mementoes. But she must try to understand that here in the country they led a very sheltered life.

She rolled over and rearranged the feathers in her pillow. It had to be her imagination that made her hand still burn where Nico had held it. But she hadn't imagined his lust for her. That had been entirely too real, and she had to consider what she would do about it.

Phil tossed and turned, and when a castle ghost appeared she was still wide awake. She sat up with surprise, grabbing the fairylight and clutching it to her. The medieval peasant with the waving scythe appeared this time, and with a regretful glance at Sarah's door, Phil shrugged into her robe and followed him. Perhaps he would lead her to a different place than the warrior had. A place that she'd be able to explore to discover some answers. The sooner she left the temptations of Grimspell castle, the better.

Chapter Nine

Nico ran through the enchanted forest, trying to clear the frustration from his mind. The moon shone so brightly to his wolf eyes that he could see every twig and nymph. His paws barely touched the earth as he followed his old trails, his nose catching the scent of night-blooming azzinas, damp oak leaves, and the spoor of rabbit, deer, and orcrich. But not a whiff of a beast that could murder a human with teeth and claws the size of a were's.

Nico spun to a halt, his nose quivering, tail high. The scent of orcrich had made his mouth water. But the underlying smell of a slynk, a bloodthirsty scavenger that preyed on the villagers' flocks, interested him more. Exactly the challenge he needed tonight.

His nose dipped and he tracked his prey, the wolf part of him completely absorbed in the hunt, his human brain still fumbling with his thoughts. He had overreacted to Phil's request to go through Father's trunk. But he worried that the clever woman would find something that he'd overlooked. Something about the tunnels.

Nico leaped a fallen log, sniffed for the trail again. What was it about the tunnels that made him overreact? Had his childhood misadventure affected him so strongly? He'd barely given it a thought over the years until he'd told it to Phil. And yet . . .

His muscles tightened as he found the trail again, with a stronger scent this time. Nico slowed his pursuit to a stealthy walk. And yet he'd always felt uncomfortable in his home, and that feeling seemed to originate from those tunnels. Something just felt so *wrong*.

He swiveled his ears, catching the sound of chirping orcriches. Still, he should have trusted Phil, especially since she appeared to be one of the few who trusted in his innocence. But for the first time in his life he felt fear . . . and it wasn't for himself. Just the thought of her getting lost in those tunnels, never to find her way out again, made his wolf growl with fury.

Nico strangled the noise in his throat. Beyond a stand of trees stood an open meadow, and he could see the slynk stalking the orcriches. He lowered his belly almost to the ground, his paws cracking nary a twig as he crept forward.

He did trust Philomena, and his foolishness would have been forgotten if Edwina hadn't chosen to voice her own fears. He couldn't remember ever being so furious with his sister-in-law. Oh, she was right about the tunnels, but entirely wrong when it came to his pursuit of Phil. He didn't give a damn what his neighbors thought.

One of the birds sensed him and the entire flock raced for the trees. The slynk spun, sighted Nico, and ran in the opposite direction. Adrenaline surged through Nico, and the thrill of the chase overrode his human thoughts as he followed the scavenger.

Slynks might have been fast sprinters, but they didn't have the stamina of a wolf. Nico could run all night.

Eventually the slynk tired and Nico pounced, taking its neck in his jaws and cracking it with merciful swiftness, tearing open the warm flesh and gorging on the rich, salty flavor.

When he finished, he threw back his head and howled his triumph. Now there was one less scavenger to steal the villagers' livelihood. An answering howl sounded through the trees and Nico knew another of his pack had found a successful hunt tonight. He recognized the rich timbre of Hexword's song.

Nico made his way to a moonlit pond and shifted to human, quickly shedding his clothes and climbing atop the flat boulder that jutted over the water. He stood for a moment, the thrill of the hunt still raging in his blood. The cool air caressed his naked skin and he felt gloriously free. And powerful. He stretched his arms up to the heavens, his muscles stretching and rippling. Then he dove into the water. The chill of it made him gasp as he broke the surface. Several water sprites tried to coax him into play, their dragonfly wings buzzing about his face and ears. But Nico didn't want to play. He wanted something much more serious.

Her face shimmered in his mind. The feel of her silky hair between his fingers. The warmth of her trembling lips beneath his own.

The wolf still shadowed him, sang to him to take his mate, to hunt her as he'd hunted so successfully tonight.

Nico rose out of the pond and sluiced the water off his skin. The cold hadn't dampened his fever. He threw on his clothes and made his way back to the castle, not altering his course for a moment.

But when his feet took him to Phil's bedroom door he stared down at them in bewilderment. What would he say to her?

His wolf answered. He would make it clear to the ghost-hunter that he would pursue her regardless of what anyone else thought about it. That the only decision that mattered would be hers, and she would make it tonight.

His wolf howled inside of him, and Nico smiled. He rapped on her door. When she didn't answer, he tried the handle. She'd left it unlocked. Nico took that as an invitation and stepped inside. Despite the gloom, his eyes had no difficulty seeing that her bed lay empty.

The beast growled with disappointment, and this time

the sound echoed within the empty chamber. She was out chasing ghosts again. He shouldn't be so annoyed; after all, that's what he'd hired her for. But his wolf blood still sang its mating song, and he thought he might go moonstruck from it.

Nico spun and shifted to wolf, following her scent. Roses and vanilla. He headed for the tower stairs, but halfway down the hall, the door onto the landing opened and Phil stood within the halo of a fairylight. He shifted to human just outside his own bedroom door and waited for her to come to him.

She wore a smile as she neared him, but it faded with each step she took. Phil stopped a few paces away, keeping her distance. She tried to keep her tone light, but Nico heard the uncertainty in her voice. "It appears that we've both been hunting again tonight," she whispered.

"And were you successful?" Nico murmured, keeping his voice low as well. He didn't want to wake anyone.

She blinked, her eyes a smoky gray in the fairylight. "I followed a different ghost this time—not the warrior . . . the one with the scythe. But he led me to the same place. Is something wrong?"

His eyes traveled the length of her. Her robe gaped open and beneath it she wore a gown of some sheer material that laced together from neck to navel. The ties had come undone and the cloth had parted to reveal the valley between her breasts. Nico stared at the shadow of her nipples beneath that thin covering until they puckered beneath his gaze. He suppressed the wolf's howl of triumph. He didn't even need to touch her.

She gasped and Nico closed the distance between them and kissed her. Her mouth was open beneath his and he took full advantage of her weakness, slipping his tongue inside and exploring all her sweetness. For a split second she froze in surprise and then she melted beneath him, tilting her head to give him deeper access. Nico shifted forward and put his arms around her warm body, pulling her against his chest. A low rumble started in the back of his throat as he felt her breasts press against him. He pushed the robe off her shoulders, pulling down the sagging neckline of her gown.

She tore her lips from his, her breath shallow and ragged, her eyes as round as a startled doe's. His hands caressed her bare shoulders, slid along the silky skin of her collarbone to her neck.

"I'm still hunting," he murmured.

She sucked in a breath. "What do you mean?"

"How long do you think you can continue this game of yours? You ask me to kiss you one moment and then tell me to stay away the next. You must make a decision, Phil. I'm not an ordinary man—I can smell your desire and it's driving me mad."

"I can't . . ." Her voice trembled. "I can't deny that I'm attracted to you, Nico. What ordinary woman wouldn't be?"

"Then what is it? Surely you can't be falling for that tripe about our difference in age. You're not a woman who worries about the opinions of others."

She stepped back, trying to put some distance between them. Nicodemus scowled and stalked her. "Tell me, Philomena. Tell me that you don't care about what others may think. Tell me that you'll spend the night with me."

Phil licked her lips. "I only care how it will affect what *you* think."

He frowned in confusion, trying to make sense of her words. But then she tilted her head in thought and quickly changed tactics, as if afraid that he might just ask her to explain.

"I'm old enough to know," she said, "that with certain actions, there are consequences."

Nico lifted his hand and brushed the backs of his fingers against her soft cheek. She leaned into his touch. She could talk all night—it wouldn't change a thing. No matter what she said, he would have her beneath him before the sun rose. Her eyes widened with awareness. She'd been hunted and caught, with no way out. But she'd been stubborn; he'd give her that.

Nicodemus let his hand stray to her throat. "And you aren't willing to pay?"

She gave a nervous laugh. "On the contrary. I believe the . . . satisfaction would be well worth the price. But are you willing, Sir Nico? Have you thought of the consequences to you?"

He smiled. "Let me worry about myself, Phil." He could feel the pulse of her rapid heartbeat at the base of her throat. Nico leaned down and nuzzled her neck, breathing in the scent of her, his body rigid with desire. The anticipation would kill him.

He straightened and swept her up in his arms, surprised at her slight weight. Nico carried her into his bedroom and locked the door behind them. Phil's assistant had the uncanny ability to show up at the worst times and he wasn't about to risk an interruption.

Nicodemus carried her to the bed but couldn't force himself to let her go yet. She dropped the fairylight, and it bounced on the oriental carpet, the glowing dust inside the orb flaring with a burst of glittering sparkles. Her hands touched his cheeks, her fingers as soft as butterfly wings. She swept the hair away from his face, tilting his head so she could meet his eyes. Her own were glazed with passion and a hint of something else. Something that made his wolf retreat a bit.

She kissed him then, a gentle press of her mouth against his, a hesitant sweep of her tongue across his own. He could think of nothing but the tenderness of her lips, the soft touch of her hands in his hair. He had wanted nothing more than to rip off her clothes and bury himself inside her . . . and yet now he found himself caught up in the sensation of a kiss he didn't want to end.

But she released his head and Nico slowly lowered his arms, setting her feet carefully on the floor. She swayed while he sat on the edge of the bed. Then he recaptured her in his embrace, pulling her between his legs, his thighs straddling her hips. She placed a hand over her heart and took a step back. He let her, although he couldn't stop the wolf's growl that rose low in his throat. He watched her through the fall of his hair.

Nico had never particularly cared whether his bedmates accepted his beast. He'd taken his lovers to his bed in much the same way that he devoured his meals, his goal one of satiation and nothing more. But she continued to hold back, and for some reason he wanted more from her. He wanted her to know the brutal nature of his beast. And he needed her to accept it.

"I hunted tonight, Lady Radcliff. I caught my prey between my jaws, snapped its neck with my teeth and enjoyed the sweet taste of my kill. Does that frighten you?"

Her breath left her in a rush. "No, it doesn't."

Nico lowered his mouth to her bare shoulder. So sweet, so soft. She had beautiful shoulders, as white as cream. He ran his mouth over them, making her shiver. His hands slid up to the already loosened neckline of her gown. He had wanted to tear it off of her a moment ago, and yet now he found himself slowly, gently drawing it lower on her shoulders, until the tops of her breasts lay exposed to his hungry gaze.

His hands curved around and under her breasts and he gave them a gentle squeeze. Her breasts were heavy and full in his hands, so very perfect. He lowered his mouth and kissed the tops of them. His shaft had been hard for some time, but now his trousers felt particularly tight.

Nico left her breasts long enough to yank on the flimsy gown, exposing her hardened, dark nipples. Before she could finish her gasp of surprise, he had his hands under her breasts again, lifting them and kissing every inch of that soft, sweet flesh.

He'd never wanted a woman as much as he wanted her.

Nico leaned forward and kissed her lips, then her cheeks and nose, and when her eyes fluttered closed, he kissed the lids. Her robe sagged down her back and it took but a nudge for it to fall to her feet. Her gown had puddled around her hips and he hooked his fingers inside, drawing it down the length of her legs. He sat back and raked her with his gaze, the reality of her lovely, naked body much better than anything he could have imagined. Such luscious curves.

Her hands fell to her sides and she lifted her chin.

"You're beautiful," Nico blurted, and then flushed because he'd sounded like some bumbling lad.

But Phil didn't seem to mind. Indeed, she gave him such a radiant smile that he couldn't move for a moment. Her hands reached for the buttons of his linen shirt and she took her sweet time unhooking them, until he growled and tore at the rest of them, flinging his ruined shirt across the room.

"Nico," she admonished, making his name a caress.

He caught her hips and held her gently, although he wanted to crush her in his arms. Nico slid his hands to her back, noting every curve and muscle, stroking that soft skin with his large rough fingers. He caught her bottom in his hands and squeezed, loving the feel of her muscles.

Phil moaned and dropped her hands to his shoulders, the light touch of her fingers causing his skin to ripple in response. She slowly traced the planes of his chest, until Nico gritted his teeth against the sheer torture of her touch. She leaned forward and explored the ridges of his back while he buried his face in her hair, breathing in the warm scent of roses. Then her hands went back around to his chest and circled his nipples, the pads of her fingers making them harden to tight peaks. His shaft nearly burst his trousers.

Just when he thought he couldn't take any more, she crouched, pushed his arms to his sides and laved her tongue over his nipples. His hips thrust forward of their own volition. Then she sucked at his right nipple and his left, and he thought he might come undone.

Nico grasped her shoulders and pushed her back. "This isn't necessary," he panted. "I already want you more than I can stand."

She looked up at him with a frown. "Who says I'm doing this for you?"

He crushed her to him and ground his mouth atop hers. Nico filled his hands with her bottom again and thrust her against his groin, wanting to feel her against his shaft. "Clothes," he growled. He pushed her away and stood, tearing at the buttons of his breeches. Philomena stumbled backward and watched him with eyes wild enough to match his own. One of his buttons popped off and launched across the room, hitting a bare patch of floor and rolling along the smooth surface.

"Nico," she breathed again. His name on her lips had the uncanny ability to ensorcell him. His hands stilled and she laid her smaller ones atop them, pushing them away, her fingers taking over the task of his stubborn buttons. He sucked in a breath as each delicate movement she made increased the fire in his loins. His shaft sprang free and she gasped, staring at him for the longest time. Then he heard her swallow and she eased off his trousers.

It took only the lightest pressure of her hands on his shoulders for him to sit back down on the edge of the bed. Phil ran her fingers up his ankles to his knees, sifting through his fine hair, until she raised goose bumps on his skin. Nico spread his legs wider and she continued her exploration of the skin inside his thighs, until she reached the two rounds of flesh beneath his shaft and stroked until they rose up into his body.

Her hair trailed a silken path along his skin as she rained kisses down his chest and stomach until she reached . . .

Nico sat up and looked down at her head. She kissed the tip of his shaft, her hair tickling the inside of his thighs. Damnation, he had thought she might be experienced with men, but he never would have guessed to what extent. He felt a trickle of relief that he wouldn't feel guilty about seducing the woman, and then her tongue circled the tip of him and coherent thought fled. His entire being focused on the feel of the light, wet, warm touches of her mouth trailing up and down his shaft. The sheer ecstasy when she finally encased him entirely and lowered her head with the movement.

Nico tangled his hands in her hair, lifted her head up from his lap and stared at her enchanting face. He could stand no more. Phil's wide eyes were glazed with passion, a shimmering dark gray by the dim fairylight. He tried to read the expression in them and his heart squeezed a bit. Tenderness, wonder and . . . curiosity? He hadn't the willpower to stop and analyze those emotions. He brought her mouth against his, plunging his tongue inside, hard and frenzied, mimicking what he intended to do to her.

Nico fell back on the bed, bringing Phil with him, intending to roll over and mount her with all the lust she'd aroused in him. But she sighed into his mouth, pushing his hands above his head, lacing her fingers in his own. She planted her knees on the sides of his hips. The small woman's strength was negligible compared to his, but Nico felt as pinned to the mattress as if bands of steel held him down.

Phil sat up and he watched her breasts bounce, admiring

the fullness of them, the way her dark nipples stood out in contrast to the rest of her creamy skin. He licked his lips and lifted his head for a taste, but they slipped past his reach as Phil shifted down his body. When she moved her hot opening over the tip of his shaft, his feet slammed against the floor as he reflexively tried to ram inside of her. She lifted away from him and he shuddered.

"Nico," she whispered.

His beast retreated and he took a deep breath, watching her through half-lidded eyes. Phil gently lowered her body onto his, her hot wet sheath encasing him by such slow degrees that Nico felt sure his wolf would howl with frustration and demand he take her fully. Instead he found himself savoring each exquisite movement she made. She would take him a bit further inside herself and then retreat, sliding ever so deliberately up and down his shaft. The cool air would touch his skin and then her heat would cover him again.

Nico sighed and reached for her, the pads of his fingers tracing her breasts, the outline of her nipples. He had never explored the softness of a woman's skin so completely. But perhaps only Philomena felt like the petals of a flower, her skin more delicate than even a fairy's wings.

She had taken him almost fully inside of her when she suddenly froze and made a small sound, her eyes widening in alarm. Nico frowned. "Phil," he murmured, catching her cheek in his palm. She leaned into his hand for a moment and sucked in a breath, then lowered herself onto him fully.

The muscles in Nico's legs and arms locked with the feel of her tight wetness surrounding the entire length of his shaft. He traced a finger down her breast and across her rounded stomach until he reached the curls between her legs. He parted her folds with one hand while the other continued his attention to her breasts.

Phil shivered.

Nico found her center and stroked it, the tiny nub swelling beneath his touch. He forced his touch to nothing more than a bare sweep across the silky wet skin. Phil tensed, her eyes staring into his with bewilderment.

And then her head tilted back and she groaned, her body twitching over his with the force of her release.

Nico curled his arms around her back and pulled her flat on top of him, until he could feel her breasts against his chest and could place soft kisses on her brow. He slid his hands down to her hips and began to rock her across his body, matching the rhythm that she'd already set, luxuriating in the wet tight feel of her.

Phil made small whimpering sounds against his chest, and Nico smiled. He kept himself inside of her as long as he dared. But when she clamped his shaft with her own inner release he couldn't hold back any longer. He pulled her off of himself and rolled over barely in time, his body ramming against the bedding from the force of his own climax.

When he finally came back to earth, every muscle in his body felt limp, but he reached out one arm and gathered Phil close to him before he sighed and allowed himself to relax. His head was turned toward her, his face half buried in her hair and he breathed in her scent, amazed by what she'd made him feel.

Nico's arm lay over her ribs and he held it slightly aloft so that he wouldn't crush her. He heard her quiet sobs before he felt them. "Phil? Did I hurt you?"

"No." She drew in a ragged breath. "I just didn't know it could be that . . ."

"Neither did I," he replied, something stirring inside him as he gazed down at her soft face. His lust had dissolved into pure affection for this woman at his side. "Stay the night with me. At least until dawn breaks."

She shivered.

"Phil?"

"All right. I don't want to leave you either."

Nico smiled into her hair. Even in the summertime there was always a nip in the castle at night. "Are you cold?"

"A bit."

He covered her with the edge of the bedding before he rose with an extreme display of willpower, lit a candle, and went into the washroom. He wet a cloth and cleaned himself, frowning at the dark color that stained the rag. Nico picked up another cloth and went back into the bedroom, yanking the bedding off of Phil and holding the candle over the spot where they'd lain. A small dark stain colored it as well.

He blinked stupidly at it a moment longer. "Philomena?"

She sat up, the wealth of her hair falling over her beautiful breasts. "Yes?"

"I thought you said that I didn't hurt you."

She tilted her head. "I felt only a bit of pain for a moment but it went away."

He cursed under his breath. "You were a virgin."

"Of course."

The imp had the temerity to sound offended. Nico's mind whirled in confusion. "But the things you . . . How could you know . . . ?"

She shivered and he cursed again, setting down the candle and sweeping her up into his arms. He pulled down the bedding and slid her inside. "Still cold," she said, smiling up at him. Nico crawled in beside her and gathered her next to him, warming her with his body heat. She gave a sigh of complete contentment and closed her eyes.

"Phil," he rumbled.

"Yes?"

"Where did you learn the things you did to me?"

"What things?"

Nico felt surprised that his wolf hadn't risen in response to his frustration. And then he realized he hadn't felt the nature of his beast since she'd . . . "The things with your fingers and lips and tongue."

He felt her shrug. "Oh. That."

"Yes, that."

She spread her fingers through the hair on his chest, exploring the contours of his muscles. "It's my house in London, you see. It used to be a brothel."

Nico groaned. "And I suppose it's haunted?"

"Yes." Her fingers swirled the fine hair around his nipples. "In the past few years, a certain ghost named Fanny has appeared quite regularly."

He tried to ignore her wandering fingers. He thought back to their first meeting in her parlor. "She was there the night we met, wasn't she?"

He could feel Philomena's smile. "So, you aren't so insensitive to the spirit world, after all."

"On the contrary. I'm just sensitive to *you*." Nico tilted her face up to meet his eyes. "I thought I was taking an experienced woman to my bed."

She blinked. "I don't see how that matters."

"It does. To me." He had seduced a complete innocent. He had wanted nothing more than a casual affair, a satiation of his extraordinary lust for the ghost-hunter. An experienced woman would understand that. Now . . . now he couldn't be sure how he felt about her. Only that something had changed with the realization that she'd never given herself to another man before.

Or perhaps something had changed when she'd shown him how to make love without his beast. With more tenderness than he had ever known.

Phil snuggled her head onto his chest and Nico placed his hand over her fingers and closed his eyes. He would think about it tomorrow, when he didn't feel as if every muscle in his body had been stretched and pummeled. When he didn't feel quite so absolutely satisfied.

When he awoke, he immediately sensed something had changed. Phil. He stared at the empty place beside him. She'd promised to stay with him all night, and he could only think of one thing that would take her from his side. With a frown of annoyance he got out of bed and pulled on his trousers, determined to hunt her down and fetch her back. He wanted her again. Badly.

Nico shifted to wolf, his nose to the floor, following her scent. It led him into the cellars, down to the dungeons.

Nico heard a low whining growl and realized it came from his own throat. Philomena lay on the dungeon floor, her eyes closed, her face as pale as one of her ghosts. The tunnel door stood open, and an eerie wind made her white gown float around her body and her hair swirl like a ginger halo around her head.

Nico shifted to human and gathered her in his arms. She didn't stir, and his heart stopped while he studied her. The soft rise and fall of her chest made him close his eyes and press his cheek to hers in profound relief. The ghost-hunter hadn't needed to go into the tunnels for disaster to find her, but Nico growled and kicked the door shut with his foot anyway. He had told Royden to put a new lock on it, but apparently he would have to take care of that himself.

Nico spun and carried Phil out of the dark chamber, calling for a doctor as he pounded up the stairs.

Chapter Ten

Philomena awoke to the most ghastly headache. Sunlight streamed into the room like beams of torture. A strange man stood over her, his hazel eyes blinking at her from behind wire-rimmed spectacles.

"I'm Dr. Darknoll. How do you feel?"

"I'm pleased to meet—what happened?"

Sarah's glossy black eyes wavered into view. Phil could just see the slight rippling of Sarah's skin from the start of her shed, but at least the worst part had passed. "You had an accident, Lady Radcliff."

Ah. Memories of last night sprang into her mind, and Phil felt her face go hot. Nico. Smooth skin, hard muscle, tangled limbs. The place between her legs throbbed to remind her and she suddenly felt him in the room. She sat up, then winced and gingerly investigated the back of her head. "I do believe there's a lump."

"You took a bad fall," the doctor said, lifting the lids of her eyes and peering into them. His breath smelled of garlic and onions. "But it appears that you're going to be just fine."

"That's a relief," Royden said.

Phil squinted across the room. Royden sat on the fainting couch, a bored-looking Edwina at his side. Nico stood next to the fireplace, his arms crossed in front of his chest, the gold flecks in his dark brown eyes glittering dangerously. His wolf shadowed him.

Philomena's heart did a flip at the sight of him and she helplessly began to babble. "Yes, but it begs a question, doesn't it? How on earth did it get there? Because I certainly don't remember falling. I recall a brief moment of pain as I stood in the dungeons, staring at those tunnels. *Then* I must have fallen . . . but I was alone, and I don't remember encountering a spirit. And an apparition doesn't have enough strength in the material world to cause such an injury."

Dr. Darknoll stared at her in horrified consternation. "Err, well. A blow to the head can confuse your memories. You may return to your regular . . . duties tomorrow. I advise you to rest today." He gathered his tools and stuffed them into a well-worn carpetbag and headed for the door. "Now, I have a birthing to attend. Master Royden, you will let me know if the sleeping draught I gave you is effective?"

Royden nodded and Phil raised a brow at Sarah. "Ssir Nicodemuss insisted that hiss brother consult the doctor while he wass here," her assistant whispered.

Philomena nodded. Perhaps it would help, although she had her doubts. Some opiates could make people more open to spiritual energy. When the doctor walked out of the room, her eyes were drawn to Nico again. His aura had darkened to a black cloud, and he looked ready to implode. He moved to her side and growled into her ear, "You will not leave your room again without someone with you, do you understand?"

A rush of pure desire swept through her. And this time, she knew exactly what her body ached for. Before she found her voice, Nico turned and stormed out of the room.

"You scared the blooming daylights out of him, you know," Royden said. "Don't look so upset. A day of hard labor at the home farm will calm him down."

Edwina plucked at the lace on her sleeve. "Perhaps we

should look for another solution to your problem, Roy? It appears that things are getting entirely out of hand." She rose, a graceful rustle of silk and petticoats. Phil scowled, certain that the girl referred to Nico's increasing affection for her and not Phil's well-being. Edwina glanced at her and stifled a yawn. "I'm only concerned for Lady Radcliff, of course. Her clumsiness might cause her even more harm."

When Phil refused to rise to the bait and protest that she wasn't the slightest bit clumsy, Edwina yawned again. "Nico woke everyone last night with his howling. I'm sure you'll both excuse me. I'm sorely in need of my beauty rest." She pecked Royden on the cheek and swept out of the room.

Sarah hissed.

"Fluff up my pillows, will you, Sarah?" Phil said. "Aah, much better. Now, Master Royden, surely you don't agree with your wife? Not when I feel as if I'm on the verge of solving your mystery."

The doubt faded on his face and he turned hopeful eyes on her. "What do you mean?"

Phil breathed an inner sigh of relief. For a moment there, she had thought he might just dismiss her, and she could use the money that they'd offered. It had nothing to do with the thought of not seeing Nico again. Nothing whatsoever.

Philomena sat up to accept the cup of spicy tea that Sarah handed her and used it as an excuse to think. She couldn't exactly tell Royden that she'd spent most of the night in his brother's room. That a new ghost had appeared—this time a lady in a medieval gown with long trailing sleeves—who had led Phil on a lively chase through the castle that had ended in the dungeons. Perhaps the castle had more ghosts than she had ever dreamed.

"Lady Radcliff?"

"Forgive me, Royden. I think that knock on the head

has rattled my brain a bit." She gave him a self-deprecating smile. "So far, I have encountered different spirits in different rooms."

"Such as?"

Phil spilled a spot of tea. She just wouldn't mention the ghost-lady. "Well, there's the peasant and warrior in my room, a priest in the chapel, and a bespectacled lad in the library. My thought is that there may be many more ghosts in other rooms and that one of them may lead me to the source of the disturbance." She didn't hasten to add that she feared they might already have done so. With Nico's aversion to going in those tunnels, she hoped that wasn't the case. Perhaps an old forgotten graveyard or secret passageway between the thick stone walls could provide the answer to their problem.

"My plan is to sleep in a different room each night and discover just how many spirits this castle contains." She handed Sarah her cup and settled back against the cushions.

"But Nico . . ."

Phil waved a hand. "Sarah will be at my side, of course. Your brother has nothing to object to." Well, other than the fact that he wouldn't be able to seduce her into his room again.

The room wavered a bit at the thought. She'd had an affair. Lady Philomena Radcliff, the rather odd but attractive spinster who talked to ghosts but was invited into the homes of the cream of London's society, was no longer an innocent virgin. She blamed Fanny and the irresistible temptation that was Sir Nicodemus Wulfson.

And her blasted curiosity.

"Master Royden, when may I look through your father's trunk?"

He frowned, making the lines of fatigue around his eyes even deeper. "It's deuced odd, but the butler can't seem to find it. I thought we had stored it in the cellars. But I assure you that as soon as we find it, I will have it brought to you."

"Thank you." Phil's eyes fluttered closed as sleepiness overcame her.

She pulled the bed coverings up to her chin. Botheration, she couldn't remember feeling more exhausted. Perhaps it was the knock to her head, but she suspected a night of lovemaking to be the more likely culprit. How could Fanny manage it with so many different men? Perhaps it had been an entirely different experience for the doxy. All technique and no . . . feeling.

Phil smiled. She couldn't regret making love to Nico. She now had the most marvelous memories to cherish and would take them with her back to London and relive them, moment by moment. The ferocity of his beast . . . the tender heart of the man.

"You will tell me if she needs anything?" Royden said.

She'd forgotten he was still in the room, but her eyes weighed a ton and would not open.

"Yess, ssir."

The door opened and closed, and Phil rolled to her side, clutching one of the pillows to her breast. It would be best for her to finish this assignment and return to London as quickly as possible. Away from the temptation of gold-flecked eyes and smooth muscled skin. Of wild growls and gentle touches. Warm lips and soul-stealing pleasure.

A week later, Phil stood in the dungeons of Grimspell castle with a hissing Sarah at her side and a hovering Tup near her left shoulder. "Every single ghost has led us to these tunnels," she snapped.

"It appearss that the answer to the mystery liess within."

"Which is more than vexing," Phil replied. "Considering that Sir Nicodemus will never allow me inside."

"And he's jolly well right," Tup piped in. "Go in there and ye would be lost in a blink."

Phil stared at the door, which Nico had chained the day after she'd had her little accident. She couldn't get inside without the key anyway. She turned and made her way back to the cellars, her companions following.

Phil stopped in the cellar nearest the dungeon and stared in irritation at the piles of boxes and trunks stored in the room. She held up her fairylight and peered into the gloom. The room had to be as large as the dungeon, although the ceiling looked a bit lower. "How could they find anything in this pile?"

Tup walked over to a wooden crate, his footsteps making no impression in the dirt whatsoever. He placed his skinny arms on his narrow hips and scowled. "Crikey, Phil. If ye could just tell me what this missing trunk looks like, I might be able to help. I ken just float right into 'em."

Phil smiled. "What a capital idea. Now, why didn't I think of that? I shall speak to Royden on the morrow. Come to me tomorrow night and I shall describe the trunk for you in detail, Tup."

He snorted. "And where will ye be sleeping this time? I don't like that chapel place, I can tell ye."

Phil made her way through the kitchen. She suspected Tup hadn't taken to the priest, who had lectured the lad on the evils of stealing on the night that they'd slept in the chapel. The only meals the boy had eaten on the streets of London had probably been snatched from a costermonger's cart. Phil felt the Lord would make allowances in times of need.

"I think we will return to our original guest rooms," Phil replied.

Sarah gave a hiss of relief.

Phil understood exactly how she felt. Despite the bedding that they'd cushioned the floors with, it had been a most uncomfortable week, sleeping in the different drafty rooms of the castle.

Phil picked up her skirts and went up the tower stairs. The only benefit to their accommodations was that Sir Nicodemus hadn't had an opportunity to seduce her again. Although, Phil couldn't be sure if Nico would have even tried. He'd worked hard at the home farm all week, his head nodding from exhaustion at dinner, the only time they'd spent in each other's company. His wolf had constantly shadowed him and he'd barely spoken a word to her, which had suited Phil just fine.

But she wondered at the way she'd catch him staring at her during dinner. As if he pondered some great mystery and she lay at the heart of it.

Phil shrugged off the fancy and concentrated on her job. As she had expected, each room in the castle had carried the memory of a different ghost. And they had all led her to the tunnels.

Phil turned to her companions when she entered the bedroom hallway. "Just because I don't like the answer doesn't mean it's incorrect. There's something inside those tunnels that has upset the castle ghosts. Now I will just have to discover a way to find out what it might be."

Tup frowned. "I wish I could help more."

"You've been an extraordinary help to me already—" He vanished before Phil could complete her sentence.

Sarah led the way back to their guest rooms and Phil followed, her footsteps dragging. She felt sure her unnatural despondency was due to her inability to solve the castle's haunting and had nothing whatsoever to do with the baronet's sudden disinterest in her. Nothing whatsoever.

When Sarah opened the door to her bedroom Phil eyed the huge tester bed eagerly. Perhaps all she needed to feel quite herself again was a good night's sleep on a comfortable surface. She kicked off her slippers and crawled onto the bed, sighing at the sheer pleasure of feather ticking, and had just closed her eyes when a pounding on the door woke her.

Sarah entered Phil's room through her connecting door, blinking sleepily and hissing all the way across the room to answer the knock. Phil had opened her mouth to tell her that a portion of her old skin had fallen off her face and hung in a tattered strip when Sarah flung open the door.

Sir Nicodemus stood outside. He stared at Sarah, his eyes slowly widening, and then flicked his finger against his jaw. "You have a bit of, um . . ."

Sarah turned and fled back into her own room. Phil sat up and clutched the covers to her chest.

"She's amazing, isn't she?" Nico said, sauntering into the room. "I was hoping that I'd find you here."

Philomena stared at him in utter stupefaction.

"I've decided that you deserve a day off. Come on now, out of that bed." He tore the covers from her fingers.

What had happened to the brooding young man of all last week? He looked like a different person. Phil glanced at the windows. Being up all night and sleeping during the day had muddled her sense of time, but it still looked almost dark outside. "It can't be morning yet."

"Yes, it is, my dear ghost-hunter. It's just overcast." His gaze raked her from head to toe and Phil couldn't suppress a shiver of reaction. "Good, you're already dressed. I've decided to show you the enchanted forest today."

Phil glanced down at her rumpled clothing. She hadn't worn a nightgown all week, since she knew she'd be investigating at night and the maids had an annoying habit of wanting to clean the grates during the day while she slept. So she'd worn her most comfortable dresses, with flowing lines and little boning to shape them. "But shouldn't you be at the home farm? I thought Royden said it would take you a fortnight to harvest the grass."

He grinned at her, a wolfish expression that made her heart skip a beat. "Not this year."

Phil's jaw dropped. He'd done the same work in half the time? No wonder he had looked so exhausted at night. And why had he worked so hard? So that he could be with her? What an arrogant, silly thought.

He put his finger under her chin and shut her mouth. Phil tried not to react to his touch. But those large hands had touched her in the most intimate places. Those fingers had aroused her to the heights of pleasure.

"Come on, Phil, hurry up. I don't want Sarah following us."

She glanced at her assistant's closed door while Nico grasped her arm and bodily hauled her out of bed. "Why not?"

He rolled his eyes at her. "You can't be . . . All right, there are places I want to show you, and only you." He bent down and picked up her slipper, grabbing her ankle and shoving the slipper onto her foot.

"These are hardly appropriate for a walk in the woods," Phil protested while he crammed on the other shoe.

He glanced up at her through the curtain of his hair. His work on the farm had bleached the pale streaks to a pure white and shaded the brown in his hair to a lighter hue. His face had darkened to bronze, making the golden flecks in his brown eyes appear to glow by contrast. His teeth looked startlingly white when he smiled at her. "You won't be doing much walking."

Well. Phil couldn't make sense of that extraordinary statement until they stood outside the castle door and he shifted to wolf, butting against her side in a gesture that she understood only too well.

Phil scrambled onto his back, burying her fingers in his thick coat, remembering to pull up her knees. He leaped from the top of the stone steps onto the ground, making her stomach plunge into her throat and forcing a laugh of surprise from her. His nose lifted and scented the morning air, and Phil found herself doing the same. But all her puny human senses could detect was the sharp smell of impending rain, the sweet scent of lavender and elfclover, and the musty smell of the fallen leaves that Nico smashed beneath his paws.

And then the were-wolf lowered his head and leaped forward. Phil didn't have a moment to absorb anything but the feel of his fur clenched within her hands, the strong muscles moving beneath her body, the wind slapping at her skin. He made a few more amazing leaps, presumably over fallen logs . . . or tall trees, for all she knew. Phil couldn't be sure through the tears in her eyes caused by the force of their flight.

But every time Nico leapt, her stomach would flip and she couldn't hold back the laughter that flew from her lips.

Her wolf finally slowed and Phil sat up a bit and looked around the forest. Enchanting, indeed. The wind blew through the leaves, a sound between a sigh and the rush of waves across the shore. Crimson vines that looked as if they had feathers sprouting from their stems crisscrossed the branches of several trees, creating a gown that would rival any in London. Birds flew from vine to vine, their jeweled plumage glowing with violet and sapphire.

She felt Nico's muscles tense beneath her. Phil lowered her upper body onto his back. He walked silently now, as if stalking prey.

Nico passed between two enormous oaks at the entrance to a narrow ravine, and Phil sucked in a breath. The sides of the gap had natural terraces, and tiny cabins of sticks had been built atop every one. Rope ladders hung down from the earthen steps, connecting each of the buildings to one another and making a spiderweb pattern to the trees above their heads.

Stickmen sat on miniature porches, staring at the visitors as Nico strode by. Some picked up tiny spears and bows, casually notching the arrows and holding them at the ready. Phil didn't move, afraid she might make a gesture that appeared threatening. Nico passed through their settlement as if he didn't notice their suspicion.

Phil breathed a sigh of relief when they rounded a corner and melted back into the forest. But, oh, it had been worth it to see that miniature enchanted dwelling hidden in the forest. Their homes were better than any dollhouses she could imagine.

Nico increased his pace again until they came to a stand of willow trees and then stopped and sat.

Phil slid off his back onto her bottom. "You could have just told me to get off."

Nico shifted on his hands and knees in front of her. "And how would I do that? Should I have barked at you?"

Phil smiled and dusted off her hands. "You have a point. What were those birds?"

"We call them dragobirds—"

"Their wings looked like tiny jewels. How do they fly?"

"Magic." He closed the distance between them until his mouth lay but a breath from her own. "I knew you would like them."

"And . . . and the stickmen's village." Phil stared at his lips, remembering how soft and warm they had felt against her skin. "They didn't like us passing through their village, did they?"

"They don't like strangers, but they know me so they accepted you. I will have your kiss of thanks now."

Phil tried to pull away from him but her body wouldn't respond. "I think we need to talk."

"Hmm, yes, but first . . ."

His mouth covered hers and Phil realized that despite her resolve that they would never suit, she had no resistance to him whatsoever. She felt as if she'd been starved all week and she couldn't deny the sustenance of his kiss any more than she could have denied a feast after fasting for a week.

Nico swept her lips with his tongue and she tilted her head, opening her mouth on a sigh. She could feel his lips curl upward because of her surrender, knew that he was aware of his own power over her. And Phil didn't care. She slid her hands over his muscular shoulders and kissed him back with a tender fierceness that shocked her.

Nico chuckled, a rumble that shook her to the core. She'd never felt such wild emotion, such longing that deprived her of caring for little else but him.

Nico pulled his mouth away from hers and stared into her eyes. "Easy," he whispered, his breath harsh, his eyes glazed with feral passion. Then he blinked and smiled, the two dents at the edges of his mouth making her insides melt. "I can't believe I just said that. I can't believe that I haven't held you in my arms for an entire week. I never want to go through that again, Phil. I can't. Promise me that—"

Nico spun to face a tangled growth of bushes on their right. He growled while he shifted; his were-form appeared to grow even larger than usual. His coat bristled, a line of fur standing upright across his back. His lips pulled back and revealed deadly fangs while his growl lowered to a deadly, menacing sound.

Phil pressed her hand against her mouth, felt her eyes widen with true fear. She hadn't realized until this moment how truly frightening Nico's wolf could be. How lethally dangerous. He could easily rip apart a human with his strength. Those jaws could tear open a man's throat—or a woman's. No, she wouldn't think such foolish thoughts. He had not killed his fiancée.

Something moved within the bushes. Something black, with eyes that glittered just as dangerously as the baronet's.

Nico lowered his snout, his body stiff with suppressed fury as he stalked toward that black shape.

Phil felt her heart lurch into her throat. She scanned the small clearing, looking for a weapon. She spied a stout stick small enough for her to wield but large enough to cause some damage, and lunged for it.

That black shape flew out of the bushes at the same time that Nico launched himself toward it. The two beasts met in the air. Nico looked like nothing more than a mass of snarling teeth and muscled fury. Phil resisted the urge to cover her ears; the sound of his wolf rage surely had to echo through the forest for miles. When they hit the ground Nico landed on top of the other beast. A black wolf, slightly smaller than the baronet himself.

Phil closed her sweaty hand over the stick.

Nico pinned the black wolf, his jaws going for its throat. Another growl erupted from the bushes, and Nico's teeth snapped on empty air as he turned to face the new threat.

Phil stood, despite her wobbly legs, and brandished her weapon as another beast leapt at Nico. Dear heavens, not another were-wolf. This one looked as big as Nico, with similar brown and white streaked fur but with the blackest eyes Phil had ever seen. All of them had at least twice her body weight, even the smaller black one, and that weight looked to be nothing but pure muscle and fang.

The brown wolf halted before he reached Nico, lowered his head, and snarled. The baronet rumbled back at him, unmoving from his position atop the black wolf. Phil took two steps, swinging her stick behind her, ready to bash the brown wolf on his hindquarters.

And then the black wolf whined and bared its throat.

Nico shook his head as if to clear it, then met Phil's eyes and barked at her. She froze. He turned his attention back to the brown wolf and growled low, this time not in anger, but in warning. The brown wolf yipped, lowering its ears and tucking in its tail.

Nico lowered his head and licked the black wolf's face. And then the very air seemed to waver as all three shifted to human at once.

Phil stared at Nico, who now lay sprawled atop a young lady with hair as midnight black as her fur had been. Her brown eyes held a dark beauty, her face a feral quality that would fire any man's lust. When she swept the hair from her face, her movements displayed the same carnal grace that Nico possessed.

A flush of jealousy rocked Philomena. The newcomer was young, lithe, a better match for Nico than Phil could ever hope to be.

Chapter Eleven

"Jane," Nico growled, "what are you doing in the bushes, spying on me?"

The girl glanced over at Phil. Her eyes flickered with some emotion that Phil couldn't quite decipher, then looked back up at the baronet. "I wasn't spying."

"I told you not to come into the woods. You know that your were-wolf resembles the beast that killed—"

"We have to hunt, Sir Nicodemus," interrupted the man who had been the brown and gray wolf. As a human he lacked most of his brownish coat, his hair almost purely gray. But his black eyes sparkled with the same thoughtful intelligence.

Phil dropped the stick from nerveless fingers. "Beatrice's killer resembled a black wolf?"

Nico glanced at her. "A few villagers thought they saw a black wolf the night of the murder. It's probably nothing more than rumor, but until we know for sure, I worry about Jane's safety."

Philomena swallowed, trying desperately not to look jealous by his concern for the other woman. But, botheration, he still lay on top of the girl and Jane seemed to be quite content with the position. Still, Phil gave Nico a look, raising her brow at him. He flushed and scrambled to his feet.

"Allow me to introduce myself," the gray-haired man said, giving Phil a graceful bow. "I'm Sir Edgar Hexword of Hallows Hall." He gestured toward the girl. "And this is my daughter, Jane. We are Nico's pack."

Phil absorbed that last statement with what she considered amazing alacrity. "How do you do? I'm Lady Philomena Radcliff—"

"The ghost-hunter," Jane said. "I've been ever so excited to meet you. Nico said he would introduce us, but it's been over a week and he still hasn't come 'round."

"Ha," the baronet crowed. "So that's why you were spying."

"I wasn't . . . oh, very well. I've never seen a ghost-hunter before and I didn't know you'd be, well, doing what you were doing."

Nico's lip twitched. "If you hadn't been spying, you wouldn't have seen something inappropriate for little girls."

Jane's lower lip stuck out in an enticing pout and Phil revised her opinion. The girl wasn't just beautiful; she was stunning. "Nico, you're not that much older than I am. Quit treating me like a child."

He glanced at Philomena, the gold sparkling in his brown eyes, reminding her of the conversation they'd once had. Phil smiled and a shiver of something passed between them. Jane felt it, because her brow lowered and she launched herself at Nico. "You're worse than a big brother."

She would have bowled over any ordinary man. But the baronet just caught her up in his arms and swung her around, making them both laugh. Phil's chest twisted painfully at their easy camaraderie. How could she have allowed herself to get involved with such a young man? Jane would make him a much more suitable wife, and she could easily see that they were fond of each other. Jane might even already be in love with him. Phil's relationship with Nico would only complicate things.

"Set me down." Jane laughed, giving him a playful slap.

Nico obliged, and Phil couldn't help noticing that although his wolf shadowed him, his aura glowed brightly.

"Lady Radcliff, I have so many questions for you."

Phil opened her mouth.

Jane waved a graceful hand. "Oh, not just about ghosts and such, although I find them extremely fascinating. But I'd also like to know about the latest fashions in London."

Phil glanced down at her dress. "I'm not sure if I'm the right person to consult, Miss Jane. I prefer the style of the Pre-Raphaelites and don't keep current with the fashions of the aristocracy."

She didn't dampen Jane's enthusiasm. "Oh, I would so love to hear about the movement and see the rest of your wardrobe. I find it quite sensible to do without these dratted hoops, especially when I have to shift. The boning always causes lumps in my coat, you see."

Philomena did see and found herself completely charmed by the young woman. Surely Nico already had to be in love with her. Why had he pursued Phil? She colored, afraid that she knew the answer. He had needed the physical release. Fanny had taught her that much. Jane opened her mouth again.

"But first you must come to our home for dinner, right, Papa?"

"We would be honored," Sir Edgar replied, his eyes roaming over Phil with appreciation. He stepped toward her, his full lips curved into a smile. Phil swayed toward him a bit. He might be a decade or more older than she, but was handsome in a distinguished way. When he picked up her hand and gave it a gentle squeeze, Phil caught herself staring into his eyes a bit too long.

A low growl startled them both. Sir Edgar gave her a regretful smile and dropped her hand. Phil glanced at Nico and was dismayed to see that the shadow of his wolf had turned black. Jane frowned and stared at all three of them, her soft brown eyes flickering with thought. Then she appeared to come to some decision and she smiled. "That settles it then."

"Perhaps," Nico said, grabbing Phil's hand and pulling her away from Sir Edgar. "Lady Radcliff has yet to solve the mystery of our ghosts and she does her hunting in the evenings. We will see if she has the time."

Phil wanted to argue, but he squeezed her hand and she desisted. Jane scowled, but when Nico glared at her she dropped her eyes and shrugged. Sir Edgar looked at the two of them, his face creased with sad disappointment.

"Take your daughter home, Hexword," Nico snapped. "And don't let her wander these woods alone."

The man nodded, amazing Phil with the easy manner in which he accepted Nico's superiority. He grabbed his daughter's arm and led her away. She rolled her eyes and threw Nico one last glare before they disappeared into the forest.

The small clearing fell silent. Then the sky rumbled far to the north and the wind picked up again, rustling the tree branches with sighs and creaks.

Phil glanced beneath her lashes at Nico. "She's beautiful."

"Who?"

"Miss Jane, of course."

His aura darkened even more. "And I suppose you think that Sir Edgar is handsome?"

"Good looks seem to be a trait among you were-wolves." His hand tightened and Phil tried to twist out of his grasp. "What did Sir Edgar mean when he said that they are *your* pack?"

"I'm alpha. That hierarchy extends to our human forms."

So that's why Sir Edgar obeyed him so readily. Phil huffed in exasperation. "Do let go of my hand, Nico. You're squeezing too hard."

He stared down at his hand in surprise, then slowly released her fingers.

"Still," Phil continued, "it was rather high-handed of you to refuse my invitation."

"Why? Because you want to see Sir Edgar again?"

Oh, botheration about Sir Edgar. Why did Nico seem so interested in him when all Phil wanted to talk about was Jane? And his possible feelings for her? "Why, yes. He seems a pleasant enough sort of fellow. But really, it was Jane whom I felt bad for. She seemed so eager for a bit of society."

Nico put his finger under her chin and lifted her head, looking into her eyes as if seeking some hidden truth. "You wanted to spend some time with Jane?"

"Yes, of course. She's so beautiful and charming, don't you think?"

"I suppose. She's like a little sister to me."

"Is that all?" His finger burned her skin. "I mean, have you ever considered . . . have you ever wondered . . ."

"What?"

Phil couldn't stand the suspense. "Are you in love with her?" she blurted.

He blinked in genuine astonishment. "With Jane?"

"Yes, of course, with Jane. She's in love with you, you know."

Nico threw back his head and laughed, his aura fading to a dull gray. When he looked down at her again, his eyes fairly sparkled. "Don't be ridiculous. Jane and I have known each other since we were children."

"Then you don't think . . . I mean, is it possible that Jane might have been jealous of Beatrice? That maybe the villagers really did see a black wolf the night of her death?"

Nico seemed to consider it for half a breath, then shook his head. "It's not possible. She's my pack and I'm alpha. She wouldn't dare defy me."

Philomena couldn't be so sure. How could he truly

know what the were-wolf might be capable of? Although Phil had to admit that the girl didn't seem capable of such an act. But love could make people do things they otherwise might not.

"No," the baronet continued. "It's some other animal, or another wolf from a different territory. I just have to find a scent strong enough to follow." He swept the hair away from her face. It had fallen out of her bun some time ago, and she probably looked a fright. "Enough about Beatrice. I want to forget about it for just one day, Phil. I'd like to only think about you."

"Me?" Botheration, the word came out as a squeak. But when this man turned his attention on her she felt like a mouse trapped by a very large hungry cat. A bit of annoyance gave her some armor. "You've barely spoken two words to me all week and today you suddenly show up at my door and——"

"So you missed me?"

"I didn't say that."

His eyes softened. "You didn't have to. And we need to talk, but not here. Come, I want to take you somewhere special." He captured her hand in his and began to tow her toward the massive weeping willow trees. For a moment Phil considered refusing him. But he was right; they needed to talk. She had to tell him that they must end this affair before anyone got hurt. And she felt dreadfully curious about what he had to say.

He parted the yellowish green branches as if he swept aside draperies, and Phil stepped beneath that canopy. It felt as though she entered into another world. Tiny pricks of light sparkled from each branch, like a waterfall of green stars surrounding her. Without that light she would have been plunged into complete darkness even if the sun had been shining outside. The layers of branches were that dense. She took another step. Some type of moss covered the ground so thickly that it felt as if she walked on cushions. Bouncy cushions.

"Is this real or an illusion?"

Nico let the drape of branches fall together behind him. "It's real, although magic created it. The willow-nymphs infuse their trees with a phosphorescence that glows." He held out one of the branches and Phil peered at it. Tiny green globes grew along the length of it.

"Why, they're like miniature fairylights," she breathed.

Nico dropped the branch. "Only there isn't any fairy dust inside." He shoved at the moss beneath his feet. "And there isn't any feather stuffing in here either, even though it feels like it."

"It's bouncier than feathers."

He smiled at her, the greenish light casting his features into an unearthly glow. "I knew you'd like it, Phil. I haven't shared this place with anyone else before, yet somehow I knew I had to share it with you."

She could drown in his eyes. Philomena could gaze at him for years and always find something new within his face to explore and enjoy. She might have made a mistake in coming with him today.

Nico strode to the other side of the tree, his footsteps lighter than usual, and parted another curtain of branches. Phil thought she heard Tup call out to her and barely listened to Nico's next words.

"The willow-nymphs know I'm immune to their magic, so they don't meddle with me. But they can . . . Phil?"

She spun, looking for the source of Tup's voice. The note of fear in it made her heart thunder. What would her ghostly lad be doing beneath the willows? Why would he follow her today? When the branches on her right parted with their own volition and Tup cried out again, she didn't hesitate. Phil stepped through to emerge beneath another willow's canopy.

"Philomena, wait," said Nico, but the branches snapped closed behind her, cutting off his voice. She could still clearly hear Tup calling for her while the branches continued to part open a path from tree to tree. She wondered how many willows grew in this grove. Surely enough to create a confusing maze of passageways.

Phil could dimly hear Nico trying to follow her, the sounds of his muffled curses and the breaking of limbs. But she couldn't slow down to wait for him when Tup sounded like he needed her.

She plunged through another tree's canopy and could only stop and stare in sheer astonishment.

Tup stood next to the trunk of the willow and his form didn't waver or appear insubstantial. "Hullo, Phil."

"Tup? What's happening? You look so . . . alive."

He blinked his large round eyes at her, that saucy grin of his appearing on his dirty face. "I am alive. At least, in here I am."

Phil took a dazed step forward, and then another, until her bouncing steps closed the distance between them. "How?" she breathed, reaching out to touch his wild hair. The strands tickled the palms of her hand.

"Stay with me," Tup said. "And I can be your real boy forever."

She fell to her knees and held out her arms. How many times had she wished to hug him? To hold him close and let him feel how very much she loved him?

Tup stepped into the circle of her arms and Phil bit back a sob. He felt so skinny, his arms and ribs nothing but bones. But now she could put some meat on him and he would never go hungry again. And she would teach him to read and buy him toys to fire his imagination. She would help him grow into a strong man and he would make her so proud.

Phil smiled into his messy hair. How very warm and

alive he felt! She crushed him to her, pressing kisses on his dirty cheeks. She could stay like this forever.

"Phil," Nico gasped, crashing through the fall of branches.

"Look," she said, "it's Tup. He's come to life for me."

"Damnation," the baronet muttered. "Fiona, stop this right now. Phil is my guest and what you're doing is cruel."

For a moment the glamour stayed with Philomena. She had no idea what Nico was talking about.

"Listen, Phil," he said, and she felt the warmth of his hand on her shoulder. "The willow-nymphs don't like intruders and Fiona delights at treating them to her illusions. She's been known to trap people here until they starve to death, spinning a weave of their heart's desire."

"Oh, Nico, you're wrong. See, feel him. He's real."

"I can only see a vague outline of his form because illusions don't work on me. I'm so sorry. I never thought Fiona would try to enchant you while I was here." He waited a moment, then growled loudly enough to shake the branches surrounding them. "I'm warning you, Fiona."

A tiny squeak of alarm came from the leaves above them. Phil glanced up and saw a little green face with enormous emerald eyes and a pointed chin.

The warm bundle in her arms began to fade. "No," Phil cried. "Nico, don't take him away." But the lad disappeared and her arms lay empty. Like they had been all of her life. Tears sprang into her eyes and she leapt to her feet and spun. "Damn you. Bring him back."

"I can't, Phil. He was never really here."

She slapped him. He took the blow across his face without moving an inch. "I should have warned you sooner," he said.

Phil wished he'd gotten angry, or stopped her from hitting him, because his stoic acceptance only made her want to weep. "He felt so alive."

"I know."

Phil forced herself to accept reality. "He was nothing but an illusion?"

"A wish from your heart, nothing more."

Nico's lovely eyes looked so sad for her, as if he understood her pain. Phil fell into his arms; only her strength of will prevented her from sobbing into his linen shirt. She could only feel profound relief that Nico was real. That the warmth she felt from his body truly existed in her world.

"Come along, now," he murmured, leading her away from Fiona's tree. Perhaps Nico had frightened the nymphs because the rest of the branches parted before them without any assistance from him. By the time they emerged from the thirteenth tree, Phil had her heart in hand again. She pulled away from Nico and he cocked a brow at her, but didn't protest.

Phil stepped out of the canopy into a glade that made her stop and stare. "How much of this is illusion?"

"Does it matter?" he replied.

Perhaps to Nico, who might only see it as a vague outline, but to Phil . . . "Not a whit."

A pool of clear water sat in the middle of the glade, fed by several springs that appeared to flow from the top of an enormous crystal boulder that jutted out over the surface of the pond. White falls of water hid the cavern beneath the boulder and Phil imagined that the crystal surface would fairly sparkle in the sunshine.

The overcast day only appeared to make it glow.

Not that she could see much of the sky. Gorchids grew to enormous proportions all around the edges of the pool, their stems so heavily laden with blooms that she could barely see the green of their leaves. Pale lavender flowers with ruffled edges vied with star-shaped sepals enclosing frilly white petals. Clusters of deeply pink flowers with burgundy insides grew next to vibrantly blue-spotted petals with tiger-striped tops. Phil took a few steps out onto the mossy bank and breathed deeply. The combined perfumes made her feel almost drunk with delight.

A gust of wind curled through the glade and the flowers danced, the sound of their petals rubbing together like a delicate symphony. Phil had never heard the like. Some loose petals floated into the pond, creating a soft carpet of color on the rippling surface.

She reached down and trailed her fingers in the crystal water. It felt surprisingly warm. Phil crouched and scooped up the liquid and bathed her face, removing the last vestiges of sorrow from her encounter with an illusory Tup. She sat back on the spongy moss and closed her eyes, allowing the peace of the glade to soothe her.

"What an enchanting place," she murmured.

"I knew you'd like it," Nico said. "Come on, let's go for a swim. It was hot beneath the willows."

Phil glanced over her shoulder and gaped. "What on earth do you think you're doing?"

Nico's chest was bare, all that golden brown skin gleaming even in the cloudy daylight. His boots and shirt already lay on the carpet of moss and he'd started to undo the buttons of his trousers. "I always swim in just my skin. Don't you?"

"Certainly not."

"Ah, then you're in for a treat, ghost-hunter." His trousers puddled around his ankles and he kicked them away. His drawers followed a scant second later. He was so incredibly beautiful. It was one thing to see glimpses of him by candlelight and quite another to see the entire length of him bared in the outdoors.

She felt incredibly wicked.

Nico didn't appear to be the least bit self-conscious. "Come on, Phil. The water is always warm here." He strode past her and she couldn't take her eyes off him, despite the flush that rose to her cheeks. Every muscle in his body rippled beneath that smooth skin, outlining his thighs and calves and . . .

Well, she hadn't known how large the muscles were in a man's buttocks.

He waded waist-deep into the water and turned to her. "How can you be so shy after what's already happened between us?"

"I . . . I thought you wanted to talk."

Nico flashed that wolfish grin. "I do. After we go swimming."

Phil sighed. He seemed so young and impulsive. So enormously appealing.

"I assure you that we're quite alone, so there's no reason to be afraid."

"I am not afraid." Oh, botheration, she certainly was. But not for the reasons he might be thinking.

Sir Nicodemus took two menacing steps toward her, the water swirling around his waist. "You're coming in, with your clothes on or off. I imagine soggy skirts will make for one uncomfortable trip back to the castle, though."

Phil narrowed her eyes. "You wouldn't dare."

He splashed water at her. "Try me. Come on, you know you're dying to find out what it feels like to swim without so much as a stitch on."

How had he come to know her so well? Because truly, the curiosity to find out what it felt like nearly overwhelmed her. She felt sure the confines of a bath couldn't quite compare, and the swim gear that women were required to wear was bulky and uncomfortable, with as much material as their regular clothing.

Phil glanced around. If there were nymphs in the trees, they stayed hidden beneath their canopies. Nico was right; this place was entirely secluded. She doubted anyone could get through that growth of willows unless the nymphs let them.

She stepped out of her slippers, slipped off her stockings, and buried her toes in the moss. It felt cool and moist. Her medieval style gown laced down the front, with a silk sheath beneath that peeked out from her sleeves and at her throat. It took her but a moment to undo the laces and step out of it, but she hesitated at removing the sheath. She only wore a thin chemise beneath it and in this light it would reveal entirely too much of her. She settled for removing her pantalets, then glanced up at Nico beneath her lashes.

His dark brown eyes had glazed with emotion and his features had an intensity to them that made her catch her breath.

"This feels entirely too brazen," Phil said.

Nico gave her a lopsided grin and spun to face the opposite direction. "Does this help?"

He had a beautiful back, a straight spine and curves of muscles by his shoulders. The clear water revealed entirely too much of him to her view. She could clearly see the smooth rounds of his bottom.

Phil stared in disbelief at her sheath and chemise now bundled in her hands. She'd taken them off without even consciously thinking about it. The wind curled between her thighs, tickling the tiny hairs on her legs and arms. She had never, ever been naked outdoors before. It felt quite liberating. And made her feel terribly brave.

She tossed her clothing on the ground. She no longer had the willowy figure of her youth. She was rounded and full, and in the light of day Nico would see her every fault. Perhaps then he would understand that a younger woman had much more to offer. Phil lifted her chin. "You may turn around now."

Thunder accompanied her words, as if the rising storm echoed her fears.

Nico spun and a slow smile of appreciation curled his lips. "My god, you're stunning, aren't you? Come here."

The man was daft. Phil waded into the pond, the cool water swirling around her skin and caressing her in the most intimate places. Nico didn't wait for her to come to him. He strode forward and grasped her around the waist, hauling her into deeper water.

The sky rumbled again.

"Hold your breath," he commanded, and then pulled them both under the surface. She kept her eyes open, the water so clear she could see every strand of hair that floated around his face. The glow of his brown eyes. He caught her own wayward locks in a fist and brought her lips toward his. Oh, my. The contrast of the cool water and his hot mouth, the weightlessness of their bodies as they clung to each other, the sheer exuberance of kissing this man, made her heart soar and her entire body come alive.

Phil regretted having to come up for air. She swept the water back from her forehead and smiled at Nico. He slicked back his wild locks and for a change they stayed in place. His wet eyelashes stuck together, making his eyes look larger, the tiny glints of gold in them more pronounced. Drops of water trickled down his handsome face and Phil leaned toward him, licking the droplets from his lips.

He growled lazily and swam closer to shore, his eyes never leaving hers. Phil followed as if some invisible string attached her to him. He stood on the gravelly bottom of the pool, just his head and shoulders above the water, and greedily reached for her. "Wrap your legs around me," he commanded.

Phil put her hands on his shoulders and lifted her legs, the water making her movements languid and the weightlessness making it easy to lift herself up to him. Her ankles met behind his back.

"Tighter," he murmured, his lips feathering the lobe of her ear.

Phil shivered and squeezed. The action brought her

most intimate place against his and she became acutely aware of his desire. He gave a low moan and lifted her bottom until her breasts were above the water, dipping his head to lick the beads that clung to her nipples.

The cool liquid swirled around her, making the contrast of the heat of his body whenever he touched her a shock by comparison. Phil pressed her breasts against his mouth, demanding more, and he obliged, taking her peaks into his mouth and suckling until she threw her head back with a moan. A raindrop pelted her forehead, a shock of cold that added to the torrent of sensations that shook her body.

He slid her up and down his shaft and she felt her slick inner heat making the contact slippery. Phil instantly wanted him inside of her. She caught his face between her hands and he lowered her until she could reach his mouth. She boldly swept her tongue inside, showing him what she desperately craved.

He pulled back and looked into her eyes. "I'm sorry, Phil, but I've waited a week for this. And it felt like a lifetime. I can't wait any longer."

Nico lowered her onto his shaft with a swiftness that took her breath away. Then his firm hands squeezed her bottom, and he lifted her. The rain came down in earnest then, pelting their heads and faces, and Nico copied the rhythm of the storm. Phil held on for dear life, the sky pounding her from above and Nico pounding her from below. The force of her body shattering with pleasure took her by surprise and she screamed his name, the wind drowning her cry and carrying it away.

Nico thrust deeply inside her and stayed there, his body rocking as wave after wave of release made him crush her to him. Phil felt a deeper response tighten all her muscles with a low throb of gratification.

He whispered her name in her ear and kissed her then, a mingling of rainwater and heat and the taste of Nico.

"It's raining," she shouted over the sudden boom of thunder.

"You don't say." His lip quirked and he gave her one last kiss on the forehead before he waded to shore. Phil's legs were still wrapped around his, and when they emerged from the water she felt the pull of gravity and dropped them. She wobbled for a moment, then spied her clothing, and sprinted forward.

Sopping wet.

Then Nico took the clothes from her, picked up his own sodden pile, and headed for a willow tree. Phil followed, blinking against the rain in her eyes, goose bumps rising on her flesh. He held open the branches and she crawled inside, flushing as she realized he had quite a view of her bare bottom.

The sheltering branches of the tree muted the storm outside and the moss felt dry beneath her feet. Despite the close air, Phil shivered. Nico ducked back outside and returned with two gorchid petals. He shook off the rain and placed the largest on the ground, and Phil settled herself on top of it. It felt like padded velvet. Then Nico wrapped the smaller petal around her shoulders.

"Better?"

Phil smiled and nodded.

"I'm taking our clothes to another tree to spread them out to dry. And then I'm going to bring us some food. I worked up quite an appetite." He laughed when Phil blushed, kissing her rosy cheek before venturing out into the rain again. Apparently the elements didn't bother him as much as they did Phil. He was probably used to it.

Phil tucked up her legs and huddled inside the gorchid petal, wondering what on earth he might bring them to eat. She hadn't the stomach for raw meat, couldn't be sure that she'd be able to get used to it. Loving Nico would not always be easy.

Botheration. She couldn't be in love with him. She must not allow herself to think that way because her heart wouldn't be able to stand the pain when she returned to London.

Phil's eyes widened as a sudden realization hit her and she clutched the petal closer. He hadn't pulled out of her when he'd found his release. She had a dreadful image of standing in a church with her belly bulging in her wedding gown and Nico reluctantly reciting his vows, the black shadow of his wolf looming over him.

But she hadn't given it a thought while they had been making love. It appeared that neither of them had had the good sense to at least try to be careful. They couldn't risk it again.

Nico ducked into the shelter, his body gleaming slickly with rain. Phil closed her eyes against the sight.

"Aren't you hungry?" he said. She heard him crouch next to her and she opened her eyes to see what he offered. Nico held out a shiny green leaf laden with berries and some pale pink fruit. "Granafruit. Try it."

Phil's stomach rumbled, and she picked up the fruit and bit into it. The tartly sweet flavor exploded in her mouth. "It's delicious."

He settled beside her, picking up one for himself. "It only grows in this forest. I often wonder who cultivated it." Then he shrugged, and they both ate in companionable silence, the storm outside shaking the branches, making the tiny green lights dance around them.

Phil licked her fingers, her stomach full. "How long do you suppose it will take our clothes to dry?"

He gave her a hooded look. "Until the rain lets up we should stay put. Are you anxious to get away from me, Phil?"

The intimate way he said her name made her heart flutter. "Yes. I mean, no. It's just difficult to speak with you when you're not wearing anything."

"Is it, now?" His voice lowered suggestively. She shivered and he frowned. "You're still cold." He moved next to her, wrapping his arm around her shoulders, pulling her into his warmth. "Better?"

Certainly not, but she wouldn't admit to why. He tucked her head under his chin and smoothed a damp strand of her hair between his fingers. "I missed you."

He meant the last week, when he'd barely said a word to her. Phil sighed. "You came to your senses and realized you'd made a grave mistake. What I don't understand is why you changed your mind and brought me here today."

She felt his muscles clench.

"Is that what you think?"

"Of course." Phil closed her eyes, memorizing the feel of his smooth skin next to her, knowing that she'd never experience this pleasure again. "We're playing with fire, Nico. The longer we continue this affair, the more complicated it will get."

"You're probably right."

Phil's heart dropped and she chided herself for a fool. And then he spoke again.

"That's why I think you should marry me."

She froze. "We can't. Oh, Nico, can't you see into our future a bit? You need a younger woman, someone like Jane, who can bear you lots of children and—"

"Enough." He pulled away from her and clasped his large hand under her jaw, making her look at him. "I've done nothing else the entire week but think about our future. I've turned it around in my head every way I could, but the only thing I come back to is that I can't imagine a future without you."

"You're confusing lust with love."

"The hell I am. I just don't want one without the other. I admit that at first I thought that what I felt for you was nothing but a physical attraction. And then we made love and it confused the hell out of me. It took me nearly a week to realize what had happened. Damnation, Phil, don't you see how perfect we are for each other? I was engaged to a young, silly, flighty woman. You're wise and calm and—"

"Stop." She didn't want to hear about his former lover. "I can't marry you, Nico. It's as simple as that."

"Is it?" His mouth covered hers. She tried to pull away but he gathered her into his strong arms until she felt herself melt against him.

He pulled her down and snuggled her body against his, covering them both with the petal. The warmth made Phil's eyes heavy, and she fell asleep to the sound of pattering rain and Nico whispering endearments in her ear.

Chapter Twelve

Phil climbed out of bed the next morning with stiff muscles and a slightly stuffy nose. She didn't know how long she'd slept beneath the willow, but as soon as she awoke, Phil had insisted that Nico take her back to the castle. He didn't argue, and she didn't care for the smug smile on his face. Their clothes were still wet and cold, and the rain hadn't stopped. Sarah had hissed at the sorry sight of the two of them when they'd returned to Grimspell. Philomena had taken her supper in her room and had had no difficulty falling right back to sleep.

Now she blinked in the morning light and peered into her mirror, grimacing at her red nose. Fortunately, she'd never been prone to sickness, so she hoped the head cold wouldn't get any worse.

Sarah slid into the room and helped Phil dress, informing her employer that the master and his mistress were having luncheon in the pavilion.

"There's a pavilion?"

"Yess. You musst get out of the housse more, Lady Radcliff."

Phil bit back her reply. Whenever she'd left the house it had been with the baronet, and she'd vowed to avoid being alone with him again at all costs. She had no willpower against his seductions. One of them had to be sensible.

Phil hurried outside and stepped into bright sunshine. Last night's storm had cleared the air for a beautiful day.

She followed Sarah's directions, taking the white-pebbled path around to the back of the castle. The forest in this area had been tamed and a manicured lawn stretched before her, filled with bushes cunningly shaped into different animals. She wondered how many of them had been modeled after the household staff.

A lovely pavilion sat nestled between two towering oaks, a rounded creation of white trellis and latticework. Manicured rosebushes surrounded it and rows of flowers had been neatly planted around them. The lawn stood in stark contrast to Nico's secluded glade of riotous gorchids, and she thought that Edwina had likely had a hand in such obsessive tidiness.

It was still a pretty picture, and Phil slowed her walk, enjoying the warmth of the sun on her face and the swish of her skirts along the path. But she felt his eyes on her and when she neared the pavilion, Nico caught her up in his gaze. Those dark brown eyes told her how much he appreciated the way she looked in her pale blue flowing dress. The glitter of gold told her she would look even better out of it.

Philomena narrowed her eyes in warning, letting him know that she wouldn't tolerate any of his advances. But she privately allowed herself to admire the broadness of his shoulders and the cut of his coat. The way the sunlight made his hair look like a mix of cream and coffee. How his smile made those two little dents appear near the corners of his mouth.

Nico and his brother stood as she walked up the stairs into the pavilion. Edwina ripped her eyes from Nico's face and scowled at Phil. Her happiness from Nico's apparent disinterest in Phil last week faded in an instant. Edwina's nose lifted and she appeared to scent the chemistry that crackled between Nico and Phil.

Nico stepped forward and took her hand, guiding her to

the empty seat next to his. She hoped that Royden and Edwina didn't notice how natural it seemed for him to touch her now.

"Good afternoon, Lady Radcliff," Royden said, his voice raspy and tired. "Did you enjoy our forest?"

Phil felt her cheeks get hot. Royden's tired brown eyes held no hint of a double meaning. She studied him in concern, for he looked as though he'd aged ten years in the past week. The doctor's potion didn't appear to be helping him. If anything, he looked even worse.

"Your enchanted woods are fascinating. Nico took me to see the dragobirds and the stickmen's village—"

"Ugh," Edwina said, giving a delicate shudder. "Those nasty little things. They are forever sticking to one's skirts. And did you encounter any of the tree nymphs? They are even worse, always pelting one with acorns."

Royden smiled and patted his wife's hand. "Edwina doesn't like the forest. It's too untamed for her."

Nico shifted in his chair and Phil knew *he* interpreted a double meaning in his brother's words. She dismissed the conversation, nodding at Cheevers as his hand hovered over the chocolate pot. The footman poured her a cup and Phil accepted it along with a plate of pasties.

"Oh, dear," Edwina moaned, eyeing the cup of chocolate.

Phil prayed for patience.

"Lady Radcliff, are you sure you want chocolate? My mother says that once you reach a certain age, it's best to avoid particular foods. They are a threat to one's figure." She smoothed her hands over the front of her corseted gown, which drew everyone's attention to her flat belly and very tiny waist. "I don't have to worry quite yet, of course. But Mother always has unsweetened tea."

"That's very wise of her, I'm sure," Phil replied. She would not let the girl ruin her cup of chocolate. She would not let guilt . . . Phil took a sip. Ah, divine.

"Edwina, quit being so contrary," Nico said. "I'm amazed that Lady Radcliff has shown such tolerance for your silliness."

Edwina shrugged her shoulders, as if to say that she'd only been trying to help, and concentrated on her plate.

Royden sagged back in his chair. "How goes the search for our ghosts, Philomena?"

"Only too well," she replied. "I've never experienced so many spirits in one location before. It's quite odd."

"Grimspell has a long history," Nico said, his eyes hooded as he stared at her.

Phil carefully set down her cup. "Yes, but to have so many spirits linger is unusual." She debated whether to tell them that all the ghosts had led her to the tunnels beneath the castle, and decided that Nico's childhood experience would just make him overreact to the discovery. No, it would be best to see what more she could find out about the tunnels before she mentioned them again. "Royden, have you managed to find your father's trunk yet?"

His eyes fluttered open and he frowned. "No, it's deuced odd. I thought we had stored it at the front of the cellar room. But Dickens hasn't been able to find it and has been forced to go farther back into the rooms than he should."

Nico subtly shifted his chair closer to Phil's. "So, it appears that we have another mystery to solve. I'm afraid that you may be forced to bear our company even longer, Philomena."

He looked entirely too pleased at the prospect. Sir Nicodemus obviously had not taken her refusal of his proposal to heart. He looked determined to change her mind. But Phil had no intention of giving him the opportunity. She would go mad if she spent any more time in his company than necessary. Even now his sexual charisma had her heart pounding and her hands sweating.

Phil tried to ignore her traitorous body's reaction to the

baronet. She addressed her words to his brother. "What does your father's trunk look like? Does it have any distinctive marks?"

"You can't mean to search for it yourself?" said Edwina. "Why, the cellars are positively crawling with spiders and vermin."

"I have some otherworldly help."

"Tup?" Nico asked, his thigh rubbing against her skirts.

"Who?" Royden said, his eyes fluttering again. He seemed to be struggling to keep them open.

"You remember, Roy. At the séance? It's her spirit guide." Nico picked up the folds of Phil's sleeves. "That's a lovely dress. I don't understand why the Pre-Raphaelites' leanings haven't swept London like a storm."

Lovely dress, indeed. Phil knew very well that he had no interest in fashion whatsoever. He merely needed an excuse to fiddle with her person. And he'd emphasized the word *storm*, and she had no doubt he intended to remind her of yesterday's weather, and what they had been doing in the rain. As if she needed any reminders.

Yes, she would go mad if she had to deny herself another encounter with the handsome baronet. But already she worried that they might have produced a child and it would be several weeks before she knew for sure. Any further . . . adventures would only increase the risk.

Now, whatever had they been discussing? Oh, yes. "The trunk, Sir Nicodemus. Can either you or Royden describe it for me?"

"It's about so big," Nico answered with a smile, spreading his arms wide, unconsciously showing off the breadth of his shoulders. "It has my father's name engraved on the front of it, Sir Syrus Wulfson."

"And it's banded with two leather straps," added Royden. "Do you really think a ghost will have a better chance of finding it?"

"Tup is very clever," said Phil, feeling a smile at just the mention of his name. She wished the willow-nymph could have truly made him flesh and blood again. "He can't read, of course, but he will be able to recognize the pattern of the letters. And he doesn't have to shift any boxes. He can flow right through them. I think he will have a better chance—"

"Whatever is wrong with Dickens?" Edwina interrupted. "Why, his face is as red as a beet."

Philomena watched as the portly gentleman skidded to a halt at the steps of the pavilion, gasping for breath. In his black and white suit, his human form resembled his werepenguin far too closely. Phil smothered a grin.

"Please forgive me, Sir Nicodemus." Dickens took a kerchief from his pocket and mopped his face. "But I felt you should be warned. The magistrate is here to see you."

"Father," Edwina muttered. "I wonder what he wants."

Phil tilted her head at the girl's expression. She didn't appear one whit pleased to see her father.

Dickens glanced at Edwina. "Your mother has also accompanied him, mistress."

Edwina rolled her eyes.

Nico had gone quite still. "Why would it be necessary to precede their visit with a warning?"

"Quite, sir." Dickens sucked in a few more deep breaths and shook his clothes as if smoothing his feathers. "Lord Magift is here on official business, sir. I don't wish to upset the ladies, sir. Shall we talk privately?"

Nico glanced at Phil and Edwina. "Spit it out, man. I'm sure the ladies can endure it."

Dickens' voice dropped to an ominous whisper. "There's been another murder, sir. Yesterday, sir, in the forest. Because of . . . well, I'm not privy to all the details, but I thought you should have some warning. Sir."

Phil resisted the urge to dash her chocolate in the butler's face. Why did he feel it necessary to warn Nico? Unless this murder was similar to Beatrice's?

Sir Nicodemus's wolf shadowed him. His dark brown eyes had hardened and the gold glints shimmered dangerously. "Thank you, Dickens. Please ask the Lord and Lady Magift to join us."

"What can this mean?" Royden asked, as the butler retreated.

"It means that I shall have to entertain my mother," Edwina said glumly. Then she glanced back and forth between Nico and Phil, finally settling her blue eyes on Phil with a calculated gleam.

Phil tried not to worry about that look. She wondered about the poor person who had died last night. Speculations about Nico's guilt over Beatrice's death would surely be sparked anew by this dreadful event. The baronet looked as if he relived a nightmare. Phil took his hand under the table and gave it a squeeze of reassurance. Nico didn't respond. He barely blinked as he watched the approach of Lord and Lady Magift.

They were a handsome couple, both gray-haired and blue-eyed, although Lord Magift had precious little hair left on his balding head. Lady Magift dressed in the height of fashion despite her country living, in a gown with hoops so wide that her husband had to walk several feet from her side. When they were introduced to Phil, the magistrate gave her a bow of one equal to another due to their matching titles, but his wife stuck her tiny nose slightly in the air as she eyed Philomena's dress.

"Will you join us for tea?" Edwina asked, with a tone of forced politeness.

"Thank you, darling," her mother replied, navigating her skirts through the opening of the pavilion. Both Royden and Nico scooted their chairs over to make room for the lady's voluminous hoops.

Lord Magift stood at the bottom of the wooden steps. "I'm sorry to say that I've come on official business."

"So we've heard," Nico said, meeting the man's eyes with deliberate intensity.

"Ah, bad news travels fast as always," Lord Magift replied. "It's a travesty, I tell you. The girl was quite young, as pretty as . . ." He shuffled his feet, but continued to hold Sir Nicodemus's gaze. "I hate to have to ask you this, Wulfson, but can you account for your whereabouts yesterday afternoon?"

Royden half rose to his feet but quickly collapsed back into his chair. "How dare you, sir. You may be my wife's father, but that doesn't give you leave—"

Lord Magift raised his hand to stem Roy's tirade. "I meant no disrespect, son. But the marks on Arabella's body are identical to the ones on Miss Beatrice's. I'm only asking the question that the villagers will be demanding an answer to."

"Arabella?" Royden said. "The rector's daughter? Gads, she was such a lovely, sweet girl." He fell back in his chair, his pale face sagging into premature wrinkles.

The magistrate's eyes never left Nico's. "Well, Sir Nicodemus?"

Nico glanced at Phil and his mouth hardened into a grim line. An ominous silence froze them all in place for a moment. Even the birds ceased to chatter.

"Of course he can account for his whereabouts," Philomena interjected. Why didn't Nico say anything? "He was in the forest yesterday, that's true. But he was with me the entire time."

"The entire parish doesn't need to know it," Edwina hissed.

"Was he, now?" said Lord Magift, his blue eyes shifting to Phil, his bushy gray brows raised in surprise.

Lady Magift let out a small noise, narrowing her eyes as

she stared from Phil to Nico. Then her mouth dropped open. "Surely you were escorted?"

Phil shrugged. "I'm past the age of requiring a chaperone, madam."

"I've tried to warn them, Mother," Edwina said. "Can you imagine the scandal this would create?"

"Enough," Nico growled, his fist slamming on the table, sloshing cups of chocolate and tea. "My association with the ghost-hunter is no one's business but my own. Including you, Lord Magift."

Phil leaned toward him, trying to catch Nico's gaze, but he wouldn't look at her. "I can prove that you didn't have anything to do with this girl's death."

"And would you be willing to testify to his whereabouts in an open court?" the magistrate demanded.

"Why, yes, of course," Phil replied. How could the man even doubt that she'd fail to help Sir Nicodemus prove his innocence?

Nico finally looked at her, the hard line of his mouth softening for a moment. "I don't think you realize what you're saying," he murmured. "They will ask you questions—many of them. They will want to know exact details about what we did together yesterday, to prove that you're telling the truth. They'll want specifics, Phil, and you'll have to tell them if you testify on my behalf."

Philomena frowned. A public hearing would expose her affair to the entire country. Even in this backwater parish, the London papers would sniff out a scandal involving the gentry. A horrible image of a *Punch* magazine cartoon of her and the baronet flashed through her mind. "I hardly think my reputation matters when it could save you from the gallows."

Nico's brown eyes softened as he studied Phil. "Perhaps you will reconsider my marriage proposal."

Edwina and her mother gasped.

The magistrate cleared his throat. "I'm sorry, Sir Nicodemus. I just had to be sure I had proof of your innocence. I'll do everything in my power to prevent Lady Radcliff from having to testify. With that in mind, I would like you to come view the body. Perhaps your keener senses will detect something I might have missed."

Nico's eyes hardened, and his wolf shadowed him again as he rose to his feet.

Royden stood, as well. "I'll go with you."

"You can barely stand," Nico pointed out.

Roy gritted his teeth and managed to cease wobbling. "I'm going."

The baronet shrugged. "As you wish." He took Phil's hand and pressed a kiss on the back of it, bowed his head at Edwina and Lady Magift, and led the men down the gravel walk.

"Well, I declare, this is a dreadful business," Lady Magift announced.

Phil wasn't sure whether she referred to the murder or Nico's suit. Edwina kept glancing from her mother to Phil with a look of anticipation on her face, her hands clasped tightly together in her lap as if she had to prevent them from clapping in glee. Philomena squashed down the cowardly temptation to make her excuses and flee.

"Did Nico really ask you to marry him?" Edwina inquired, purposely directing the conversation away from the horror of the murder.

Phil couldn't decide whether to be relieved or not. She picked up her cup and sipped, waiting for Lady Magift to take the bait. The wind sighed through the trees and the birds began to sing again.

"I'm sure she has no intention of accepting such an outlandish offer," Lady Magift said, patting Edwina's shoulder in reassurance. "Do you, Lady Radcliff?"

Phil raised a brow. Of course she had no intention of

accepting, even to salvage her reputation, but she wouldn't give the other woman the satisfaction of saying so.

"Will you have your man pour me some tea, Edwina dear?" the baroness continued. "No sugar, of course." She eyed Phil's cup of chocolate with disapproval. "At our age, we must consider our health, mustn't we, Lady Radcliff? We can no longer rely on the vigor of youth."

"We are of an age, Lady Magift," Phil said. "Surely you don't consider yourself so frail?"

Cheevers let out a strangled quack. Phil had forgotten the footman was still standing at his post and shot him an amused look.

The baroness narrowed her blue eyes. "Not at all. But there is a certain . . . dignity that an older woman must maintain as an example to the younger."

Bravo.

"Perhaps London society is just shockingly fast compared to our little corner of the world," Edwina prodded.

Lady Magift kept her eyes fixed on Philomena. "I'm sure your friends in London would frown upon such a marriage."

Phil tilted her head in thought and seriously considered what her friends might think. "Perhaps. Although, well, I imagine most of the younger women would be annoyed that a so-called spinster had taken such an eligible bachelor off the market. And now that I've seen your reaction, Lady Magift, I have to wonder if my older friends' spite might just be from jealousy."

Phil watched in fascination as the other woman's lips narrowed into a tight, white line.

"Are you insinuating that I might be jealous of you and Sir Nicodemus?"

Phil shrugged. "He's an incredibly handsome man."

"And an animal!"

"Mother," Edwina gasped, completely appalled. Her

expression had altered from triumphant glee at having someone side with her opinion of Nico's suit to a worry of concern at her mother's outburst.

Phil carefully set down her cup. She didn't mind that the lady had tried to insult her; she'd had enough experience from the aristocratic circle to defend herself. But the insult to Sir Nico made an unusual rage flare up inside of her. "He is more of a gentleman than many of the finest lords in London. I confess that that type of ignorant attitude by the common folk didn't surprise me, but I would suspect better of the gentry. We are, after all, quite accustomed to magic."

Lady Magift opened her mouth to defend herself and then snapped it shut, looking entirely confused by the turn in conversation. She tried to recover her composure by taking a sip of tea.

Edwina looked quite put out and when Phil changed the subject, the young lady gave a rather watery smile of relief and stuffed a biscuit into her mouth.

"Edwina has a beautiful gift," Phil said. "Her singing voice is simply divine. May I inquire as to yours, Lady Magift?"

The woman glanced at Edwina and eagerly latched on to the new topic, as if speaking of magic would smooth the insult she'd made to her daughter's brother-in-law. "I can make plants grow. It's quite a useful type of magic for the country. Bargest House has the most productive acreage in the parish."

"Nico mentioned your house before," Phil said to Edwina. "It struck me that it sounded familiar." She paused, thinking. "Of course, now I remember! Isn't it named after some ghostly dog? But I think the Bargest is usually associated with Yorkshire, which is why I didn't get the connection right away. I read a book about it once—"

The china rattled and Lady Magift's teacup rolled across

the table, splattering tea everywhere. She rose swiftly to her feet. "Oh dear, it seems that I have spoiled the linen."

Phil glanced at the table. Nico had already done a splendid job of that earlier. But Edwina blushed and asked Cheevers to bring another setting.

Phil rose, determined to take advantage of the opportunity. "As much as I'm enjoying myself, I'm afraid I must get back to work."

"Ah, yes. What an interesting magical gift you have, Lady Radcliff. Talking to the dead."

Phil had grown used to the sneer that accompanied the lady's words and didn't let it bother her. "Yes, it is." She circled the table toward the pavilion door. Botheration, she'd tolerated enough of this woman's company to prove her mettle.

"It's a shame though, isn't it?"

Phil stopped in her tracks. She shouldn't turn around. She really shouldn't. "What is?"

Lady Magift didn't appear to mind speaking to the back of Phil's head. "Why, the way you use it, of course. If I had such a talent I assure you that I could execute it in a far superior manner."

Phil's skirts swished as she spun. "We do the best we can with our gifts and circumstances, madam. Now, if I possessed your gift, I would use it to feed the masses of starving children that populate the streets of London, but since I'm not privy to your limitations, I would never be so arrogant as to say so. Unless I am forced to rudeness, as your comments have goaded me to do."

Edwina's mouth had dropped open and Lady Magift looked as if she'd been whacked over the head. Well, perhaps she'd needed it. Why did those who offered the harshest criticism rarely have the fortitude to withstand it themselves? Phil sighed. She seldom lost her temper, even with the most ignorant people, and always regretted doing so. "If you will excuse me."

As she walked out of the pavilion she saw Cheevers give her a low bow of respect.

Phil spent the rest of the day in the cellars, determined to find that trunk. Her heart had continued to feel heavy for Nico, imagining the horror he must be reliving with this new tragedy. If she could solve the mystery of the castle ghosts, she could at least bring peace to one aspect of his life.

Tup emerged through a large crate. The cellars were so dark that Tup had little trouble materializing to her down here. "Can I see the picture again?"

Phil nodded and showed him the paper where she'd written Sir Syrus's name.

"I'll be blowed, but I think I found it."

Philomena's heart leapt and she forgot to chastise Tup for his language. "Where?"

He turned and pointed down a narrow passage between the boxes. "All the way to the back of the room. It's almost as if someone was tryin' to hide it. Can ye figure that?"

Phil shook her head. She'd been searching through the crates and furniture and trunks stored toward the front of the room, since it seemed logical that the more recent items would be placed there. The recesses of the room held storage that looked as if it dated back to the dark ages. Why would the trunk be stored all the way back there?

Sarah slithered into the room, a dinner tray in her supple arms.

"Is it that late, then?" Phil asked, sweeping the straggling hair from off her forehead. She didn't wait for her assistant to answer. "Did Sir Nico come home for dinner?"

"No, my lady. But you musst eat."

Phil waved her hand. "Later. Tup thinks he's found the

trunk, Sarah, and he's been a strong lad to search for it this long. I can't risk him fading before he shows it to me." She reached down and picked up her lantern. "Lead on, Tup."

The boy grinned and floated down the dark passage, Phil right on his ghostly heels. Sarah hissed a sigh but followed directly behind. His immaterial form went right through the cobwebs, but Philomena felt their sticky nets cover her face more than once.

She feared that Tup's strength would give out before he could show her Sir Syrus's trunk, and she couldn't bear to wait another day.

"Phil," Tup whispered, bringing her up short. "Is this it?"

The lad pointed. His ghostly fingers had faded to near transparency. Phil crouched and held her lantern in front of the chest, wiping off the dust from a metal plaque on the front of it. "Sir Syrus Wulfson," she read aloud. "Oh, Tup, you *have* found it."

"Jolly good," he whispered. "I'm so bloody fagged."

"Well done, my clever lad." Phil felt a touch on her cheek as light as a breeze, and then he faded. She couldn't remember a time when he'd managed to stay with her so long, and she felt so grateful for his friendship. Her smile turned to a frown as she studied the old trunk. The lock had been broken. Perhaps Royden or Nico had lost the key. "Sarah, will you hold the lamp, please? Yes, just above the trunk."

Phil grasped the two bands of leather at the top and pulled open the chest. Botheration. The entire contents had been left in a scattered mess, with loose papers stuck between old books and tattered journals and antique ornaments and heaven knew what else.

Sarah hissed.

"Quite," Phil agreed. "About that dinner, Sarah. Would you mind fetching it while I begin? This will take longer than I thought." She took the lamp from her assistant and began to sort through the mess while Sarah slinked away to do her bidding.

Phil used the top of an empty crate to pile the books in one spot, the journals in another, and the loose papers in a smaller pile. On another crate she piled the personal belongings of Sir Syrus: some of them worth a small fortune; a few that he appeared to have kept for sentimental reasons; and some that she couldn't fathom at all. An ordinary rock, some feathers, a pair of worn dice.

She wished she could call his spirit, so he could explain some of the contents to her. Which of his ancestors had used the curved sword? Where had he purchased the glass obelisk with the strange carvings? What lady had gifted him with her silver perfume box? Phil opened it and inhaled the scent of gardenias, so strong even though the bit of sponge inside had decayed after all these years.

"My lady?"

Phil jumped, then let out a little laugh. "I swear I feel a bit guilty. As if I'm rummaging through someone's private life." Sarah's black eyes glittered in the lamplight as she handed Phil a meat pasty. "Botheration, I suppose I am. But it's necessary. I'm positive Sir Syrus would approve."

"May I help?"

"Oh, yes, or I shall be here all night." Phil took a bite of her pasty and chewed thoughtfully. "You may look through his books while I start on the journals. Put aside anything that has to do with the history of the castle."

It took Phil several hours to scan the contents of the journals. Most of them had to do with Sir Syrus's youth and his travels. Sarah had gotten only halfway through the books, for she read slowly, mouthing the words.

Phil looked through the remaining books. They were mostly about foreign lands and languages. She tried not to allow her hopes to sink as she read through the loose papers, which appeared to be letters regarding the estate, written while Sir Syrus had been away on his travels.

She found no information about the tunnels or the history of the castle. "We shall just have to go through everything again," Phil said. Her eyelids drooped. "Tomorrow. Let's pack it away for now, Sarah."

Her assistant gave a nod of relief and started stowing the books back in the trunk. Phil set the collectibles inside, taking care to see that not even one of the feathers got damaged. She wouldn't allow herself to feel discouraged. They would go through everything again tomorrow and—

Phil picked up the stack of journals and one of them tumbled from the pile, its pages falling open. The angle of the lamplight picked up a bit of gold color that winked at her. She set down the rest of the journals and fingered the bit of gold in the crease of the last page of the book. It looked like a bit of ribbon. Phil picked up the frayed edge and tugged, and it grew longer, until she held the wrinkled length of a girl's hair ribbon in her hand.

"Sarah, look at this." Phil handed her assistant the ribbon and studied the crease of the book.

"I wonder why he ssaved this? It'ss like the rock and feathers—ssomething he valued for the memory."

"Yes, of course," Phil replied impatiently. "But somehow he'd hidden it inside the journal." She bent the back cover of the book as far open as she could. "Bring the light closer."

Sarah put it right next to the book and Phil blinked at the comparative brightness. "Look, this last page is twice as thick as the others, and I just thought it was extra support for the booklet." Phil picked at an edge near the fold of the spine. "But see here, this is where I pulled the ribbon from. The last page has a hidden pocket!"

Phil quickly picked up another journal, and indeed, the last page appeared almost three times as thick as the others. A subtle difference but only if one looked for it. She carefully pulled open the pocket and slid out a drawing of a woman in the most outlandishly bare costume. "Well," she mused, "I don't imagine this is a picture of his wife."

"Or perhapss it iss."

Phil smiled and picked up another journal, which held a letter that was clearly from his wife, and her face grew hot as she read it. "You may be right, Sarah. It appears that Sir Syrus had a . . . healthy relationship with his lady."

Phil carefully replaced the letter in the pocket and went through three more journals, most of them containing such intimate documents that she quickly returned them to their hidden places. The last page of the next journal she opened felt extra thick. She sucked in a breath and withdrew an envelope. When she turned it over her hand shook, but she clearly made out the royal seal on the outside.

"It's from Prince Albert."

Phil stared at Sarah, whose glossy eyes had widened as far open as she felt her own had.

"It might be nothing more than an old invitation to a ball," Philomena breathed.

"But it bearss hiss personal sseal."

Phil held it to the light again and picked at the wax. "The impression is half melted. It appears that it was opened and then resealed." If not for that seal, she would have read it on the spot. But one didn't ignore the sanctity of the crown's private seal. She quickly stuffed the envelope in the seam of her dress. "I may not have found anything to help solve the mystery of the castle ghosts, but it may comfort Nico to know that his father held some importance to the crown."

She patted the letter beneath the folds of her skirt and then frowned. "I just pray that it does indeed contain something comforting."

Chapter Thirteen

After Nico and the magistrate had inspected the girl's body, Nico spent the rest of the day searching the forest, looking for the slightest clue to the beast that had torn apart Arabella in the same manner it had Beatrice.

But the storm in which he'd found such pleasure with Phil had removed any traces of the beast's scent or track— if there had been any to follow in the first place.

Nico bounded up the low rise of a hill, his paws crunching fallen leaves, his ears flat to his head. The trees thinned around an enormous boulder and he leaped up the craggy surface of it, lifting his head to the fading moon and howling out his frustration to the night.

This was his territory and another beast had dared to harm those within his domain. He could not let it happen again. He would not. Nico felt his beast steal into his human soul and he welcomed it, just as he had when Beatrice had died. He plunged back into the forest, his world narrowing to the scents in his nose and the shadows of bush and branch and the hunger in his belly.

The black beast that threatened his wood had left no trace, but the rabbit and orcrich and deer . . . Ah, his mouth watered at the scent of deer, his nose down and his body quivering with the thrill of following fresh spoor through tree and glade. He crouched beneath weeping branches, his feral eyes fixed on the stag that stood at the edge of the pond. The soft surface beneath his wolf's paws would hide the sound of his stealthy approach; the wind that blew through the sweetly aromatic growth would cover his scent. The stag lowered his head to drink, thinking himself safe in the quiet dark of the night.

The wolf crept forward, muscles bunched in anticipation of his attack. He would leap for the throat, tearing open the soft warm flesh. He could already taste the sweet saltiness of blood, the delicate feast of the still-beating heart.

The stag sensed him and spun, lowering his horns at the threat. The wolf grinned, knowing his prey had no chance against the strength of his jaws, the speed of his attack. The night held its breath for a moment as the wolf gathered himself for a mighty leap. There was nowhere for his prey to run, with the pond behind him and the enormous growth of flowers twined as thickly as any net on nearly all sides.

The flowers. A petal floated down and rippled the surface of the water and a name whispered inside the wolf's head. Philomena.

Nico leapt. The stag braced his front hooves, then snorted with surprise as the wolf vaulted over him to splash in the cold water behind.

Nico shifted to human and came up for air, gasping at the coldness of the water. The stag had come to drink from the glade where he'd made love to the woman of his heart. His soul. He pictured her face, remembered the gentleness of her touch. Her soft sighs of pleasure as she wrapped her legs around him and welcomed his body into her own.

Nico smiled when the confused stag took one last look at him and disappeared beneath the branches of the weeping willows. The wolf growled inside him at the sudden abandonment of his prey, reminding him how simple it was to lose himself in the beast, as he had when Beatrice had died.

But now he had Philomena. Just her memory could

overcome the lure of the wolf, could turn him back into a man.

Nico walked out of the pond and straight home, his clothes dripping a trail through the forest floor until they half dried upon his back. He needed the ghost-hunter like he needed the very air to breathe. He had to touch her to banish the rest of the beast from his soul.

He had to hold her in his arms to reassure himself that the wolf would never rule him again.

His boots squeaked all the way up the tower stairs and his wet clothing chafed, so he headed for his room to change.

He blinked at the light when he opened the door to his room, adjusting his sight to the glow of the candle on his bedside table. Nico froze for a moment, staring at the woman asleep on his bed, as if he'd conjured her up from his very thoughts. She was fully dressed in one of her flowing gowns, her hair spilling out of her bun, her arms hugging something to her chest.

Nico went to her as if in a dream, lowered his head, and placed a soft kiss on her lips. She sighed and he kissed her again, inhaling her scent, feeling the last vestiges of his wolf slip away.

Her eyes opened with a start and she smiled. He couldn't resist kissing her again, but this time more deeply, as she opened her mouth beneath his, welcoming him as always. She raised her arms to his head. "You're wet."

Nico stood up and grinned. "I went for a swim."

Phil glanced around the room and frowned. Then those beautiful eyes widened and she sat up, clutching a piece of paper to her chest.

"What a nice surprise to find you in my bed," Nico said, removing his boots.

"I . . . I needed to talk to you. And I wasn't sure when you might get home, so I thought it would be best . . . are you all right?"

Nico stripped off his damp coat, his eyes riveted on her lovely face. "The marks on Arabella's body were made by the same beast that killed Beatrice."

"Are you sure? Of course you are—oh, Nico, I'm so sorry."

He removed his soggy cravat and flung it on the floor. "I spent all day searching for some trail, hoping that this time I would find something." Nico dropped his waistcoat on top of the growing pile. "But there was nothing. And the only thing that saved me from despair was the thought of you." He unbuttoned his shirt.

Her cheeks colored. "Sir Nicodemus, I had no intention of making this appear like an invitation. It's just that I got sleepy and the chairs in your room are horribly uncomfortable—please stop doing that, sir."

Nico peeled off his wet linen shirt. "Doing what?"

Her eyes roamed the contours of his chest. "Disrobing. I have something terribly important to show you and . . ."

He slowly unbuttoned his trousers, enjoying the way his actions made her forget her words. Made her forget everything but him. "I need you." Nico peeled his trousers down his legs and stepped out of them. "When you enter a man's room, my lady, you should be prepared for the consequences."

Her eyes lowered to below his waist and she swallowed. "No. No, you see, I have decided that we can't risk being together again. Neither of us has any restraint, and the consequences . . ."

Nico strode over to the bed and stroked her cheek. "You are right on one respect. I have no restraint when it comes to you." He bent down and kissed her again.

"Nico," she mumbled into his mouth, and then her arms were around his shoulders, her palms as hot as flames as she caressed his chill skin. He unbuttoned the bodice of her dress and pulled the sleeves down her shoulders. She moaned when he cupped her beautiful breasts and rolled her nipples between his fingers.

Her tongue stole into his mouth and he grinned, one hand still playing with her breasts, the other dragging up her skirts. His hand found the top of her stocking and traveled up her thigh to her pantalets, finding the slit in the drawers with ease. When he touched her soft heat she bucked against him and reached for his shaft, her fingers grazing the tip of it. Nico sucked in a breath.

He tore his mouth from hers while he spread the opening in her drawers, his tongue finding her nub as easily as his fingers had. He suckled her. She clutched the hand that covered her breast and held on as if for dear life. He thrust a finger inside of her and didn't stop tasting her until he felt a fresh burst of wetness from within her sweet folds.

Then he was on top of her, whispering in her ear, telling her how badly he needed her. The head of his shaft rubbed her wet opening until she whimpered. Nico slid inside, the thin cloth of her drawers an added friction to the slick, tight feel of her. Her legs slid up and he felt the sharp heels of her boots against his bottom and it nearly made him come undone.

But he gritted his teeth and plunged inside her again and again, until she arched her back with release. Nico dove deep and finally allowed himself his own release, bucking against her as wave after wave of spasms racked his body, while he whispered her name into her ear over and over until he finally came back to earth.

He curled his arms under her and rolled onto his side, cradling Phil against his chest. "I didn't even manage to get you out of your clothes," he murmured.

"Oh, Nico." Her breath caught on a hitch. "I should have known better than to wait here for you. When we're alone together it's like a spark on kindling. There's no resisting the sudden flame."

Nico smiled. He liked the sound of that. "I suggest that you just stop resisting."

She looked up at him and he kissed her nose.

"Honestly, Nico," she said, her gray eyes shining with intensity. "We have to stop doing this. Every time we make love, we increase the risk."

Nico stilled. He only dared to hope that she meant falling in love with him. "The risk of what?"

She ran a finger over the side of his neck. "At least the first time we were together, you took some sort of precaution against conception. But since then . . . well, it appears that we lack any willpower whatsoever."

Ah. Nico tried to look innocent. If she had confessed her love to him—therefore admitting it to herself—he might have done some confessing of his own. But he didn't think it would be the right time to tell her that he'd been fully aware of what he'd been doing when he had spilled his seed deep inside her.

He wanted her beside him forever. He knew he loved her and that she loved him as well, despite her fears. And those fears made her doubt his love, made her somehow think that it wouldn't last.

"Would it be so bad?" he asked. "I saw the way you looked when you thought Tup was a real boy that you could love and raise. I know you value your independence, Philomena, but haven't you regretted that you'll never have a child of your own?"

"That's not fair," she said, pulling out of his arms. "Blast those willow-nymphs and their vivid illusions. I won't raise a bastard, Nico, nor will I force you to marry me."

He raised himself up on one arm, staring down at her in exasperation. "But you know damn well that I *want* to marry you."

"You think that now. Because you're young . . . and I'm just afraid . . ."

Nico sighed. "I know," he murmured, kissing the top of her head. He decided that his decision to make her pregnant had indeed been the right one.

Philomena wiggled away from him and sat up, pulling up her bodice and tugging at the bunched-up skirts about her waist. "So then. You agree that we can no longer continue this—botheration! The envelope. What happened to the letter?"

Nico smiled lazily, admiring her still-exposed lovely legs. "What letter?"

Phil scrambled off the bed and shook out her skirts. "I had it in my hands when you kissed me and then I forgot everything but you." She shot him an accusing look.

Nico hadn't the slightest inclination to apologize.

"It's why I waited for you tonight," she continued, taking the candle by the bedside over to a candelabrum and lighting every single wick. He narrowed his eyes when she brought it back to the bedside, holding it over the rumpled linens and examining them. Nicodemus stretched, satisfied when her gaze was unconsciously drawn back to his body.

Phil licked her lips. "Nico, please stop. This is terribly important."

He sighed and pulled out the crinkled paper that had been poking him in the back. "Is this it?"

"Thank heavens." She set down the candelabrum and climbed back on the bed. "I found your father's trunk. And better yet, I found something hidden inside of it."

Nico glanced at the black-bordered envelope. It was addressed to his father. He turned it over. It bore the prince consort's seal. "You say it was hidden?"

Phil picked up a pillow and covered his groin. "I'm sorry, but I can't concentrate . . ." She picked up another pillow and covered half his chest. When she reached for another one he grasped her wrist.

"Where did you find this." It wasn't a question.

"Tup found your father's trunk buried in the back of the cellars. I found that envelope in a hidden pocket in one of your father's journals. I was looking for an account of the castle's tunnels, but instead I found this."

Nico dropped her arm. "You seem to have an unhealthy obsession with those tunnels."

She suddenly became absorbed in buttoning up her bodice. "I didn't want to mention it until I was sure." Phil kept her head lowered, her voice muffled. "Every ghost I followed ended up in the entrance to the underground tunnels, Nico. Every one."

"And that means?"

She peeked up at him. "It means that whatever is causing the castle spirits to haunt your brother must lie inside those tunnels."

Nico growled low in his throat at the thought.

She nodded at the envelope. "Aren't you going to open it?"

Nico stood and put it on the bedside table and strode into the washroom to splash water on his face and steel himself for what the letter might say.

Back in the bedroom, he pulled on a clean pair of trousers while Phil used the washroom. Nico took a deep breath, picked up the envelope, and sat in one of his "uncomfortable" chairs. He carefully cracked the wax seal and began to read.

He felt Phil come back into the room. She didn't stand behind him and try to read his letter. Instead she settled on the rug with a rustle of skirts and leaned against his thigh. His hand went to Phil's hair and she laid her head on his leg while he rubbed a strand that had fallen from her bun, acutely aware of the soft, silky feel of it. He couldn't seem to keep his hands off the woman.

When Nico finished reading he rose and tossed the letter into the banked coals of the fireplace and watched it blacken and curl into flame.

"I was hoping that it would bring you some comfort," she whispered.

"It did."

"Then why did you burn it?"

Nico turned. He could lose himself in the wide gray depths of her eyes. Her hair was still mussed from their lovemaking, her lips still swollen from his kisses. Her beauty always astounded him. He strode to her and held out his hand, helped her rise to her feet. "You'll be happy to know that you didn't fail."

"I . . . what do you mean?"

He couldn't let go of her hand. "You found the secret of Grimspell's tunnels. Although the truth of them may be more than you bargained for."

His words didn't prevent her eyes from shining with anticipation. "What do you mean?"

"Phil, this can go no farther than this room. I'm trusting you with a secret that I wouldn't tell my own brother."

She nodded gravely. "I give you my solemn vow that I won't tell another soul."

"Have you ever heard of the legend of Merlin's Relics?"

"Not that I recall. My reading is somewhat limited to my profession—ghostly lore and such. What would some old legend have to do with the castle?"

Nico towed her back to the chair and sat, pulling her onto his lap. She was too eager to hear what he had to say to resist, and he smiled at the feel of her bottom between his legs. "When I was a boy, my father told me about the legend. He said it would be important to me someday, but I had no idea what he meant. I'd actually forgotten all about it until I read that letter."

Nico's smile faded as the full implication of the letter struck him. No wonder he'd always felt uncomfortable in his own home. "Merlin created thirteen magical relics in different jewels, each one containing a powerful spell. So powerful that even the queen has no defense against them. Most of the relics have been lost over the centuries, and not knowing where they are terrifies the royalty. Because shape-shifters are immune to magic, we are the only peer who can withstand the relics' spells. But we can sense them and often track them down. I thought that father had told me the story because the village children had been taunting my beast-nature that day and he was just trying to make me feel better. But now I know he had another purpose. I can feel it even now."

Phil reached up and began to stroke his cheek soothingly. "Feel what?"

"The relic. That maze of tunnels was dug to bury it. For generations my family has guarded it from discovery, to prevent it from being used against the crown. The secret was passed down from one heir to another. Except I had to learn it from Prince Albert himself. He wrote my father to thank him for the family's loyal service. To assure him that he hadn't forgotten what Father guarded and that he trusted him with the realm's safety."

"But why would the prince leave something so dangerous here?" Phil asked.

"My family has guarded it for generations in complete secrecy. Why risk exposing its existence by having it moved?"

"I suppose you are right." Phil swept the hair away from his eyes and he fixed them on her.

"And now you know the secret as well. But as my future wife, you needed to know in order to tell our son in case anything happens to me. I don't want to repeat my father's mistakes."

Phil colored and dropped her hand. "We cannot be sure that I carry your child."

Nico leaned back against the upholstery and closed his eyes. Daft woman. If there were any justice in this world, his seed would be growing in her womb right now. His thoughts went back to the prince's letter. "Damnation, I've felt it for years and had no idea what it was. Even beneath tons of earth and stone, the power of Merlin's Relic is so strong that I can almost smell it. Mind you, it's not that the stone is evil itself, but the power it can unleash reeks like some unpleasant odor."

The ghost-hunter stood and brushed down her skirts. "No wonder you've always hated those tunnels. I wonder if the relic has anything to do with the castle spirits?"

Nico shrugged and opened his eyes. "There's only one way to find out."

Phil froze in the act of shoving hair back into her bun. "What do you mean?"

Nico rose and began to put on the rest of his clothing. "Father must have a map to those tunnels somewhere, and if he kept this letter in the trunk, it's only logical that he'd keep the map within it, as well."

Phil nearly shook with excitement. "Why can't we just go exploring without it?"

"Those tunnels are a maze purposely designed to confuse and trap the unwary. Without the map, we could spend years searching for the relic, and we don't have the time. Royden was very fond of Arabella, and I'm afraid that seeing her body like that made him even more ill. The sooner we stop those spirits from disturbing him, the better."

"Do you think the relic has something to do with Royden's illness?"

Nico shrugged. "We shall see." Now that he knew the source of his discomfort, the thought of going into the tunnels didn't bother him. On the contrary, he now had an overwhelming desire to see the stone vault that contained the relic, to which the prince had alluded in his letter. The prince had reminded Father to check for any cracks or faults in the stone that might unleash a trace of power onto an unsuspecting world.

Suddenly Nico's life had a larger purpose, and he embraced it with relish. He had been born an animal for a reason. Perhaps now he could consider it a gift and not a curse.

They left his bedroom and moved silently through the dark castle. Phil followed him down into the cellars, a quiet presence at his back. But he could feel her intense excitement. Did she even realize that her love of the hunt raged fiercer than his? Nico stopped at the cellar doors. "Which one?"

She stepped forward and plunged into a pile of crates and boxes and old furniture. Nico followed and nearly bowled her over when she stopped up short.

"Tup?" Her head tilted to the side and Nico willed himself to see what she did. To no avail. "Oh," she continued. "All right, I found a letter from the prince to Sir Nicodemus's father." She paused. "Quite. We think there's a map of the tunnels in the trunk as well." She listened again. "Yes, you can help us look, but don't tire yourself."

Her voice held such gentle concern that Nico caught her arm and spun her in a hug. "You'd make a wonderful mother."

She didn't say anything, just stepped away and gave him the most curious look. When he grinned back at her, she spun on her heel and led him forward again, finally coming to a stop near the back of the cellar, scuffs in the dirt floor showing him clearly where his father's trunk lay.

Nico fingered the broken lock, thinking that Phil had been a bit overzealous in her attempts to get inside, and threw open the lid. He breathed in the scent of his father, still lingering among his things after all these years.

The first time Nico had gone through his father's trunk

had been shortly after he died, and Nico had only given the contents a cursory look. Now he scanned every page of his father's journals and books and studied each trinket, looking for any sign of a map. Phil helped him search, Tup apparently looking over her shoulder and making a nuisance of himself.

Philomena's messy bun suddenly tumbled completely down. "Tup, you put those pins back right this instant," she demanded, slapping closed the book she'd just finished perusing. "I don't care a fig if you like it better this way, young man."

Phil's hair began to rise on its own and twist into a cone above her head. Nico grinned at the sight, then realized how easily he'd come to accept the ghost-hunter's spiritual companions. Although he had a bit of an advantage in visualizing Tup, since he'd seen the willow-nymph's illusion.

Phil's cone of hair untwisted and tumbled down around her face. The blanket of her hair muffled her words. "You are the most willful scamp. Whatever shall I do with you?"

The teasing softness of her voice made Nico feel a warm spot somewhere inside his chest. He set down the puzzle box he'd been studying. He'd managed to get the thing open but nothing had been inside. "We've gone through everything twice, and I don't see anything resembling a map. Tup, do you think you can see inside the walls and floor of the trunk? I'd hate to have to pull it apart looking for some secret compartment."

A deafening silence greeted his words. Phil swept the hair back from her face and stared at him in stunned amazement.

"What?"

"You just spoke to Tup."

Nico snorted with impatience. "So? Will he do it?"

Phil reached out and stroked the air. "No one's ever . . . well, Tup says that he already has. While we were going through the other things. He says there's no map hidden in there, and he's been a bit bored." A smile lit her face. "It's why he's been rather troublesome."

Nico directed his eyes toward the spot of air that she'd stroked. "Thank you for helping us."

Phil blinked. "Oh, I'm sorry. He's faded. I'm surprised he managed to stay with us this long." She stifled a yawn with her hand. "You've made quite a friend of him, you know. No one has spoken directly to him except me since he passed."

Nico studied her face. "You need to go get some sleep, Philomena."

"But we haven't found the map."

He closed the distance between them, gathering her loose hair in his hands and massaging his fingers through the silky mass. "Don't be so stubborn, Phil. That's because it's not here. I don't know what happened to it. Perhaps my father decided to hide it somewhere else. But I promise you that we'll search the castle until we find it."

She leaned into his hand. "But your brother . . . Nico, we can follow the castle ghosts. They've all been leading me to the tunnels."

Nico considered it for a moment, and then shook his head. "No. It's safer if we have the map, especially if we want to get back out again. I don't have as much faith in your ghosts as you do, Phil."

"But aren't you worried that the map is missing?"

"The relic is still here and safe. I can feel it. We'll solve this mystery, Phil, but I also have other pressing concerns."

Her face crumpled and she nodded. "Yes, of course. Nico, this may not mean anything, but are you aware of the legend of the Bargest?"

"As in Bargest House?"

"Exactly. There's a legend about a black spirit dog by that name. And since those two girls were mauled by a beast—"

"Are you saying that a ghost might have killed them?"

"I don't see how. Spirits could frighten someone to death perhaps, but they don't have enough corporeal strength to physically harm someone in that way. I just thought . . ." She swayed on her feet.

"You did right to tell me. It won't hurt to have a talk with the Magifts about this legend." He clasped her shoulders to steady her. "You're so tired you can barely stand. Go get some rest and then you have my permission to search wherever you wish. Just bring Sarah with you while you're going about it."

A muffled clang from the kitchen filtered into the room. Cook was up and making the morning meal.

The ghost-hunter frowned at him. "And what about you? You're not going to rest, are you? And you've had less sleep than I."

Did she know him that well already, or did she just have good instincts? Nico leaned down and caught her lips in a kiss. "I have an errand to run first."

When she opened her mouth to argue again, he gladly covered her words with another kiss. Without any conscious thought of his own, the kiss deepened and he lost himself in the sweetness of her lips, until he held her tightly to his chest, her feet completely off the ground. His heart thundered in his ears. "I'm likely to do that until you agree to go to bed. And if we continue, I can't guarantee that you'll be going alone."

"Nico." She sighed his name. He loved when she did that. "Set me down and I promise to go to my room."

He stroked his mouth across her cheek before he released her and, with regret, watched her leave the cellar. He wished she wouldn't see him as some youth who didn't know the difference between lust and love.

Nico left the cellar a bit later, after going through the trunk one last time. Despite his assurances to Phil, he was worried that they hadn't found the map. He couldn't be sure that his father had not decided to destroy the map or hide it somewhere else. But he could still feel the relic and would have to be content with the knowledge that it was safe for now. Besides, he knew Philomena would eventually find the map. She had an uncanny knack for the hunt.

He'd never had anyone with whom to share his burdens before, and he felt a profound sense of relief that he could trust Phil to help him.

By the time he reached the road leading to the village, the cool morning air had revived him. First he would find out the local gossip, and then he'd head for Bargest House. After searching for answers for two years, Nico was desperate enough to pursue even an unlikely lead.

He headed for the only pub in town and wasn't too surprised when he found it packed to the rafters, since the villagers had taken the day off for Arabella's funeral service. Silence descended on the room as Nico waded through the smoke and alcohol fumes toward a dark back corner. He called for a pint, keeping his mouth shut and his ears open. Eventually the brew relaxed the men and they began to talk amongst themselves again. The magistrate had his own methods for getting information, but Nico knew that anything that went on in the shire would eventually be talked about in the pub.

But the men didn't mention the murder until Mr. Jenkins walked into the room accompanied by two other men, who insisted on buying the rector several drinks to ease the pain of losing his daughter. Nico felt sorry for the man. He looked as if he could indeed use an afternoon of drinking himself into a stupor.

"My poor Arabella," Mr. Jenkins moaned. "She was such a sweet girl, wasn't she, men?" All heads nodded in agreement while the rector took another swig of his ale. He slammed his tankard on the scarred, wooden table. "This is the second time those animals killed one of our own. How long are we going to stand for this, I ask you?"

A few men sitting near Nico cast him a frightened glance.

"Now, guv'nor. We don't know as to what's gone and done them in," slurred a man standing at the oak bar.

"It was one of those animals," the rector replied. "But you're all too scared to do anything about it."

"Ole man Harlow says he saw a black wolf in the woods last night, right enough," a crofter said.

"Aha!"

"I saw one too," admitted a local carpenter, his clothing a bit more polished than the others. "But that doesn't mean a wolf attacked your girl."

Nico hunched over his drink. The same rumors had been circulating when Beatrice died, and he had agreed with the carpenter. But now it made him wonder that a black wolf had been seen again on the night Arabella had been murdered. Jane was the only black wolf that he knew of in the area. No. He quickly dismissed his suspicion. He would know her scent anywhere and he hadn't smelled it on either girl. It had to be another wolf from another shire.

"Well," huffed another crofter who sat near Nico. "We know it's not our master, 'cause he's not a black wolf."

Nico appreciated the man's attempts on his behalf, but he knew it would do little good.

"In the dark, any wolf looks black," Mr. Jenkins said.

"No," the carpenter countered. "I tell you the beast was as black as night, and moved through the forest with barely a sound."

The rector grunted. "We should do the Lord's work and run them all out of the shire."

Nico growled, low in his throat. Conversation stopped and the rector squinted over at his dark corner. Nico rose.

He'd found out what he needed to know. And he had to warn Jane and her father.

Nico could hear the floorboards beneath his feet squeak in the silence of the pub. Mr. Jenkins saw him approach and his eyes bugged out of their sockets.

"Until we find evidence against the real killer," Nico said, "I suggest you keep your prejudices to yourself." He glanced around the room. "If any of you so much as harm one hair on any of my pack, I will see to it that you hang. As surely as I will see that the beast who harmed these women hangs."

He waited a moment for one of them to challenge him outright. But they still had respect for his title, if not for his nature, and they cast down their eyes. Nico tossed some coins on the table and strode out of the pub, his heart heavy and his thoughts dark. He had once called most of these men his friends.

But they were afraid, and he knew what fear could do to some men. When he reached the road leading to Hallows Hall, he shifted to wolf and ran like the very wind. He didn't wait for the butler to answer the door; he just shifted to human and pushed it open, his boots pounding across the marble-floored entry.

"Hexword," he growled. "Jane," he bellowed.

She peeked over the banister of the stairs above him. "Goodness, Nico. Whatever is the matter?"

Nico flew up the stairs and gathered the girl into his arms. He hadn't realized that he'd been worried she'd come to some harm until he found her whole.

Jane laced her fingers in his hair and hugged him back. "This is quite some greeting. I think I rather like it."

Nico grasped her tiny waist and set her back down. "Where's your father?"

"He went into Norwitch. He won't be back until this evening. What's happened?"

"There was another murder yesterday." Nico tightened his hold as she swayed. "Don't faint on me, Jane."

"I . . . who?"

"Arabella Jenkins."

Jane's sweet face turned as white as a sheet and Nico guided her over to a satin-cushioned bench, keeping his arm firmly around her as he settled her beside him. He waved away the maid and butler who'd appeared. "I'll take care of her." They followed his orders as befit the servants of his pack.

"Listen to me, Jane." Nico lowered his voice. "The marks on Arabella's body match those on Beatrice's. There's talk again of a black wolf on the night of the murder. Did you stay out of the forest like I told you to?"

Jane's soft brown eyes widened. "Of course I did. When have I ever disobeyed . . . oh. You can't think that I . . . ?"

Nico shook his head. "Of course not. But there's talk in the village, and I didn't like what they said. Until things calm down, I want you and your father to keep to your house, do you understand?"

She nodded, her black curls swaying. "Of course. I'll tell father as soon as he returns. Poor Arabella."

Her eyes brimmed with tears and Nicodemus gathered her into his arms. "It will be all right, Jane. I'll find out who did this, I swear. It has to be another wolf from an outlying area and I'll keep searching until I find him. In the meantime, I want to make sure that you're safe."

"You do love me, don't you, Nico?"

He blinked as she pulled back and stared into his face. "Of course I do, Jane. You're like a—"

She covered his mouth with her own. Nico couldn't have been more shocked if she'd slapped him. For a moment he couldn't move, couldn't breathe. Her tiny tongue darted into his mouth, a probing kiss that couldn't be considered even remotely sisterly. He shoved her away from him. "Don't ever do that again."

Tears spilled down her rosy cheeks. "It's that ghost-hunter, isn't it? Are you . . . are you in love with her?"

"Damn it, Jane. Even if I weren't, I could never consider you as anything other than my sister. I thought you knew that." Nico inwardly groaned. Phil had been right and he hadn't seen it.

Jane pulled a pocket scarf out of her skirt seam and wiped away her tears. "I hoped your feelings would deepen and change. I thought that after Beatrice died, you might turn to me."

He raised a confused brow. "But we don't have to mate with one of our own kind."

Jane rolled her eyes at him. "Oh, Nico." She sat back, straightened the flounces of her skirt, and then gave him a sad smile. "Well, you can't blame a lady for trying, now, can you? How was my kiss?"

"I—what?"

"My kiss. You're only the second man I've ever kissed in that way, and I just want to know if I'm proficient at it."

Nico forced his head to stop spinning. Women. "Who was the first?"

Jane fluttered her fingers in the air. "Never you mind. Just answer the question."

"You will make some man very happy one day."

She nodded. "I know. Now, have you asked the lady to marry you yet?"

Nico growled. "She said no."

Jane patted his hand. "Don't worry, I'm sure you can change her mind. As a matter of fact, why don't you bring her for dinner? If I'm to be confined to the house, you can at least provide some sort of distraction. And perhaps I will put in a good word for you."

"Does that mean . . . we're all right, then?"

"Of course we are. We shall pretend this moment never happened."

He breathed a sigh of relief and stood. "I'll bring her, then. Tomorrow evening, at seven."

"Excellent. Father and I have both been looking forward to getting to know her. And now I'm more anxious than ever to do so."

The butler opened the door for Nico, and he made his way to Bargest House. When he arrived to find Lord and Lady Magift out for the day, he returned to the forest. He would call on them tomorrow, but in the meantime, perhaps he'd overlooked something. He shifted to wolf and returned to the site where Arabella had been murdered.

Chapter Fourteen

Phil slept most of the day. She awoke to find a tray of fruit, crackers, and cheese next to her bed, along with some cold tea. And a note. She ignored the food and snatched up the letter.

It was short and to the point, just as she would expect in a letter from Nico. He would be gone all day searching the forest and wished her success at her own hunting. He had accepted an invitation from the Hexwords for dinner this evening and hoped she would join him. He had signed it: *Love, Nico.*

Her heart did a crazy flip at the endearment, and she felt tempted for a moment to allow herself to succumb to the fantasy that his love would stay true. That they would live happily ever after, regardless of their difference in age and lifestyles.

Phil carefully refolded the letter and tucked it under her pillow, then reached for the tea. Mint, sweet and tart on her tongue, and still delicious cold. She glanced around the room, at the medieval tester bed, the enormous fireplace, the gothic arches carved into the wardrobe. When had this castle come to feel like home?

Nonsense. She was just trying to convince herself that she belonged here. That she could make Nico a satisfactory wife. Phil reached for a piece of fruit.

Sarah glided into the room and pulled a dress from the wardrobe. "You showed Ssir Nico the letter?"

Phil licked plum juice from her sticky fingers. She trusted Sarah implicitly, but she'd made a promise to Nico not to mention Merlin's Relic. "Yes. There was supposed to be a map of the tunnels in that trunk, Sarah. Nico and I went back and looked, but it's not there. Mmm, the blue muslin, I think."

Sarah held out the dress with its embroidered neckline and hem and Phil stepped into it. The sleeves and bodice fit snugly, and the skirt flared only slightly. It should be perfect for a day of hunting.

"Sir Nicodemus thinks his father might have changed his mind and hidden it somewhere else," Phil continued as she pushed her feet into her ankle boots. "I do hope he's right, and that he didn't destroy it."

Phil sat in the vanity chair while Sarah brushed out her hair and said, "Perhapss it wass sstolen."

Phil winced as Sarah twisted her hair into a bun. "That would be even worse."

Sarah blinked her glossy black eyes at her. "Why?"

"Because then Sir Nicodemus may not let me search the tunnels and I shall never find out why the ghosts are haunting Royden."

Sarah put one last pin into Phil's hair and stepped back. "Then we will look for the missing map today?"

"Yes."

By the time Phil returned to her room that evening she felt ready to admit defeat. They had searched all day and had only managed to explore a tiny portion of the castle. And she couldn't even be sure that the map still existed.

Sarah and Beth prepared her bath, the castle maid adding heated water to the tub until wisps of steam floated on the surface. Phil sank in up to her neck, sighing with pleasure and inhaling the sultry scent of the elfspice that Sarah had added to the water. Her frustration eased and by the time she'd finished her toilette and stood gazing at herself in the cheval glass, she felt ready to endure an evening at the Hexwords'.

Phil wondered how much of her anxiousness today had really been caused by dread of this evening. Oh, not that she didn't like Sir Hexword and Miss Jane—on the contrary, they both seemed like charming people. It was just that the age difference between Nico and herself felt more pronounced around them. Phil's sentiments coincided with Sir Hexword's and Jane . . .

Jane was in love with Nico.

Philomena scowled at her reflection. Despite the care she'd taken with her appearance tonight, she couldn't hope to compete with the girl's youthful beauty. The ivory satin dress with its heavy boning made her appear a little svelte, at least. And the tiny satin roses that Sarah had twined into her elaborate coiffure made her reddish brown hair look richly dark by comparison. She pulled on the matching ivory gloves, which went up to her elbows.

"Masster Royden wishes to ssee you in the withdrawing room before you leave," Sarah hissed.

Phil sighed. She hadn't had an opportunity to tell Royden about the discovery of the trunk. She had hoped that she could provide him with some answer to the mystery by this evening, and although she regretted that she couldn't, he still deserved to know that she'd made some progress.

Phil followed Sarah down the stairs, careful of her flowing skirts. If Sarah hadn't hissed a warning, Phil would have plowed right into Edwina in the entrance hall.

"Lady Radcliff," the blonde-haired girl said, "may I have a word with you?"

Phil raised a brow at the formal address, but nodded and waved Sarah on to the withdrawing room. Edwina rocked her crinoline for a moment, her dress swaying like some delicate bell. Then she colored, her rosy cheeks emphasizing the beauty of her complexion. "It's about my mother."

Philomena could only stare at her in bewilderment.

Edwina scrunched up her face. "My mother has always criticized my magical gift. She's always telling me that if she'd been blessed with such a voice she would sing even better than I do . . . and even if I manage a perfect performance, she can find something to complain about."

"Then she's not listening," Phil said. "Your voice is simply the most beautiful thing I've ever heard, and if you don't believe me you should come to London and perform. The appreciation of your audience would convince you."

Edwina's tentative smile twisted into open-mouthed horror. "Oh! I could never go to London. It's simply not safe."

Phil refrained from pointing out that a girl had just been murdered in Grimspell's forest.

"Besides," Edwina continued, "my mother's opinion is all that really matters. It just never occurred to me—or to her—that her magical talent wasn't beyond reproach either. It was quite a liberating experience for me." Her mouth twisted. "And for Mother. Well done, Lady Radcliff."

Phil nodded, and unsure how to respond, gathered her skirts and continued back down the hall. It had been rude of her to point out Lady Magift's own shortcomings and in good conscience she couldn't accept Edwina's praise for it. But it did give her an understanding of the girl's character, and she gave Edwina a smile as they entered the drawing room.

Phil took one look at Royden, however, and her smile quickly faded.

"Forgive me for not rising," he whispered. Despite the warm evening, a fire burned in the grate and blankets had been piled over his recumbent body. Pillows had been propped up behind him on the sofa to keep his head upright.

"What has happened?" said Phil, seating herself on a mahogany chair carved with climbing clematis. She leaned forward to hear him, for he barely spoke above a whisper.

"I seem to have caught a fever and can't get rid of it." He shivered and raised a shaking hand to his head. "I have a devil of a headache."

"Have you been getting any rest?"

"I'm afraid not. The ghosts have been quite insistent lately. I hope you've made some progress."

Edwina offered Royden a glass of port, but he waved it away. The girl stared at her husband in concern.

Philomena tried to instill confidence in her voice. "I have made some progress."

"Tell me."

"I found your father's trunk."

Edwina gasped and dropped the tumbler of wine, then moaned about the spot it would leave on the rug. Sarah slid from a shadowed corner and quickly began to mop up the mess with a handkerchief.

Royden ignored the interruption. "Dickens finally located it for you?"

"No. I used a little spiritual help to find it. It was stored in the back of a cellar."

"That's odd," Royden whispered. "Why would Dickens put it back there?"

Phil shrugged. "I'm not sure."

Edwina swooped to Royden's side, insinuating her skirts between him and Philomena. She sat on the edge of the couch and frowned at Phil. "I must insist that you cease this conversation. It's making my husband feel worse."

Philomena nodded at Royden. "She's right. You must allow Nico and me to investigate this mystery. In fact, I think it would be best if you left Grimspell for a while. The ghosts might not follow——"

"How dare you?" Edwina hissed.

Phil tilted her head at the girl's overreaction. "I beg your pardon?"

"You're trying to roust us from our own home, and I will not stand for it."

"I meant nothing of the sort," Phil soothed. "It's just that I'm not sure how long it might take to discover the source of the spirit's disturbance . . . and just look at your husband, Edwina. I'm not sure how much longer he can go without some sleep."

"Precisely." The young woman reached over and patted her husband's cheek. "Can't you see that he's too ill to be moved? Why, taking him from his home may only make him worse."

"Or it will make him better. We won't know until we try."

Edwina narrowed her eyes at Phil. "You've been planning this all along, haven't you? First you take advantage of Nico's infatuation with you, and now that you have him snared in your web, you can't wait to take my place as mistress of Grimspell."

Philomena stood, shock and dismay spurring her movements. "That's the furthest thing from my mind, Edwina. I have every intention of returning to London as soon as I have finished with this case. My only thought is for Royden's health."

Royden reached out a shaky hand and grasped his wife's arm. "Don't be so silly, dear. Perhaps the ghost-hunter is right. I would give a ransom for one night's good sleep. Do you really think they might not follow me, Phil?"

Philomena gripped the back of her chair and sighed. She didn't think she'd ever met a more insecure, confusing girl than Edwina. "Spirits are capable of haunting a person, but more often than not, they're attached to the place where they died."

"But where will we go?" Edwina murmured. "You

cannot suggest that I go home, Royden. You know what it's like for me there." Tears began to pool in her soft blue eyes. "No, this is out of the question. Don't listen to her, Roy. This is a dreadful idea."

"On the contrary," interrupted a deep, masculine voice from the doorway, "I think it's a jolly good idea. And I don't think we have any choice."

Phil's fingers clutched the chair back even harder. Sir Nicodemus wore a pale gray velvet coat that made his sun-bronzed skin look even darker, his brown eyes even more fathomless. His gaze swept her from head to toe, his full mouth curling with appreciation.

And then he stood at her side, lifting her hand to his lips. She felt the heat of his mouth even through her gloves. "Good evening," he murmured.

Phil just stared at him like some buffoon. He looked devastatingly handsome, a man in his prime bursting with vigorous health. A man entirely in command of the situation . . . and her heart. She shook off the thought and pulled her hand out of his grasp.

"You wouldn't make us leave, would you?" Edwina pleaded.

Nico turned and studied his brother. "You look like hell, Roy."

Royden's lip quirked. "Feel like it too."

"Do you think you can manage a trip to the village? The doctor has a spare room he reserves for patients and he offered the use of it when he was here."

Royden glanced at his wife, whose little hands had curled into fists. "Come on, Edwina. It will be like a holiday."

"Living among the peasants, while she pretends to be mistress of my home?"

Nico seemed to swell in size, nearly bursting the seams of his coat. "She *will* be the mistress of *my* home, if I have my way. You would be wise to remember that."

Edwina shot one last glare at Phil, then dropped her head. "Well, then. It seems that I have no choice."

"I'll make all the arrangements tomorrow," Nico said, raising his brows at his brother. Royden nodded his agreement. "In the meantime, our hostess will be wondering where we are, Phil."

"Of course." Philomena gathered her skirts and nodded at Sarah, who had hidden back in the shadows. Her assistant slid to her side. Nico frowned, but Phil would not be caught out again without a chaperone.

Sir Nicodemus took Philomena's arm, laced it through his own, and led her out of the castle. The sun had just begun to set, so the horses would still have plenty of light to see the road. A light breeze stirred the loose curls around Phil's face and carried the scent of oak and wildflower from the forest.

When she caught sight of the carriage that awaited them, she realized that the flowers she had smelled had not come from the forest. An old barouche waited in the drive. It had been lovingly cared for over the years, with a high sheen to its polish. Streamers of roses twisted with lavender and honeysuckle had been draped around the tops and corners of the carriage. Bouquets of magnolia and faun's lace topped the four corners of the cab and even Samuel and Charles, who stood impatiently in their traces, had ribbons and roses twisted in their manes and tails.

"How lovely," Phil murmured.

Nico smiled with arrogant pride. "I may not be able to cast an illusion over my equipage, but you'll drive like a princess anyway." He handed her into the open door, along with a bemused Sarah. He scowled when Sarah sat next to Phil, but took the seat opposite them with fatalistic grace.

The carriage was well sprung, and despite the bumpy road they had barely a jostle. Phil tried to enjoy the ride but her thoughts kept drifting back to Royden. His failing health worried her. "I think you should talk to Dickens about your father's trunk," she said. "And why it was stored in the back of the cellar."

Nico glanced at Sarah.

Phil hastened to reassure him. "Sarah knows that a map was supposed to be in the trunk and that it's missing."

He nodded, aware of what she had omitted from her story to Sarah. "I've already spoken with Dickens. He said he'd stored it in the front of the cellar and has no idea why anyone would have moved it."

"Then perhaps one of the other servants knows something about it. That broken lock worries me . . . anyone could have gotten inside the trunk."

Nico frowned. "I thought you had broken it."

"No. I had assumed you and your brother did, shortly after your father died."

"I had a key, Phil." He crossed his arms over his chest. "I don't like the sound of this." His gaze drifted to Sarah and he hooded those dark eyes. "Never mind. I just want to quit worrying about everything and enjoy the evening. Can you manage that, my curious ghost-hunter?"

His wolf shadowed him and Phil knew he spoke more of the murder than the missing map. With her concern over her own task, she hadn't thought about his other problem. She reached over and patted his hand with her gloved palm. He caught her fingers and wouldn't let go, staring into her eyes with enough heat to make her squirm.

Sarah hissed and Sir Nicodemus dropped Phil's hand, lounging back in his seat with a sardonic grin on his face. "I rather like you, Sarah, despite your excellent abilities as a chaperone."

Sarah only blinked her glossy black eyes at him, her lips narrowed into a thin line, but Phil knew her assistant well enough to know that he'd pleased her.

Naturally. His charm could overcome the most frigid of

women, including making a spinster believe in happily-ever-after. Phil turned and stared out the window the rest of the trip, trying to ignore a man whose very presence dominated the inside of the carriage.

She had little success and breathed a heavy sigh of relief when the conveyance swayed to a stop. Phil burst out of the carriage in an unladylike display of haste, breathing in the fresh air with relief as she studied the Hexwords' home. It sat on a hill with what must be a stunning view of the valley behind it, and the building almost glittered in the sunshine from some natural marbling in the stone. Rose petals littered the ground around the manor, like a scented blanket of snow.

She should have guessed that Jane would live in a home that matched her beauty. Nico took Phil's arm and led her up the stairs, Sarah following behind.

"I've always preferred this house to Grimspell," Nico began.

"I certainly do not," Phil interrupted. "Grimspell is full of history and character, something no modern construction can hope to emulate."

The butler opened the door, bowed deeply to Nico, and led them inside.

The hall had marble floors, frescoed walls, and gilt ceilings. The curved staircase glittered with a golden banister, and plush oriental carpets created puddles of softness down the length of the hall. Delicate sculptures and vases shone from nooks in the walls.

"Besides, Grimspell is a castle," Phil said defiantly.

Nico smiled down at her and she couldn't resist the urge to look up at him. The softness in his eyes, the two tiny dimples from his smile, held her completely immobile. She fantasized for a moment that they lived in a world without prejudice, where circumstance did not dictate a suitable marriage partner. That they were truly a couple visiting friends for the evening, before going home to their shared bed, discovering new ways to pleasure each other—

"Nico," Jane said, her voice shattering Phil's daydream. The shape-shifter came down the staircase in a glory of ruffles and satin and lace. Despite Jane's earlier protestations against a crinoline, she wore one almost as wide as Edwina's, making her appear to float across the floor as she approached them. She threw her head back for just a moment, exposing the creamy whiteness of her throat in contrast to the black shimmer of her hair.

Nico reached out and took her gloved hands in greeting, and Phil stepped away from his side.

"You look very nice," Sir Nicodemus said.

"Thank you."

"You remember Lady Radcliff? And this is her assistant, Sarah."

The girl's soft brown eyes dismissed Sarah and lit as she turned to Phil. "I'm so glad you're here. Come, let's go sit down, shall we?"

Phil ignored Nico's outstretched arm and followed the girl unescorted, frowning in confusion. Nico's greeting to Jane had lacked the easy camaraderie of when they'd met in the forest. Perhaps it was the formality that Jane felt the occasion deserved, but Phil wondered if something had happened between them.

Which was entirely none of her business.

Sir Hexword stood as they entered the drawing room, his muscular figure enhanced by the cut of his elegant coat. His thick gray hair waved softly over his forehead and his intelligent black eyes glittered in the candlelight.

Sir Hexword briefly tipped back his head, exposing his throat in the same manner that his daughter had, and Jane realized that the girl hadn't done it to show off the elegance of her neck. They had both been acknowledging Nico's superiority in the pack. She found it all quite fascinating.

Jane motioned Phil to a chair, but Nico grasped her arm and dragged Phil down next to him on a plush settee. She couldn't have broken his hold without making a fuss. She shot him an annoyed glance, but he just grinned back at her unrepentantly. As usual, Sarah took a seat in a shadowed corner of the room.

"Welcome to our home," Sir Hexword said, resuming his seat.

Phil glanced around the elegantly appointed room. A wealth of gilt and furniture and bric-a-brac dizzied her senses. "Thank you. It's kind of you to invite me."

A lavishly uniformed footman entered the room with a tray of port and brandy, and as soon as everyone held a drink, Jane leaned toward Phil from the chair she'd taken opposite the settee. "Now, let us dispense with the formalities, Lady Radcliff. Tell me about the ghosts at Grimspell."

Phil smiled. She really liked this girl. She couldn't understand why Nico had never fallen for Jane's obvious charms. "They're mostly from the medieval period, of all the curious things."

Jane's eyes widened. "Why is that curious?"

"Well, I would just think that there would at least be a few more recent ghosts and I can't account for it."

"What do you think, Father?"

Sir Hexword eyed the amber liquid in his glass. "I don't know much about ghosts, mind you. But based on the brutality of the Middle Ages and the population in the castle during that time period, I don't think it's surprising that it would be haunted by many of their spirits."

Phil smiled, pleased to discover that he was as intelligent as his eyes had suggested. "Excellent reasoning."

"History is a hobby of Father's," Jane said.

"Truly?" Philomena smiled at him. "I'm fascinated with history myself. I can't tell you how thrilling I found it when I first stepped into Grimspell castle."

Sir Hexword nodded eagerly. "I think Grimspell is what first inspired my fascination with history. Since then I have visited all the castles in the area, and even farther afield."

Jane's gaze flew from Phil to her father and a crafty look passed over her face. "Father is writing a book, Lady Radcliff."

"Truly? How fascinating. About castles, I presume?"

"The local ones, mostly, with a bit of Norwitch history thrown in." Sir Hexword stood and held out his arm. "Shall we continue our discussion over dinner? With your permission, of course, Sir Nicodemus. It's a rare treat to find another amateur historian."

Phil glanced at Nico, who looked a bit disgruntled. But he couldn't decline without being rude, so he nodded and followed them into the dining room with Jane on his arm.

Despite it being Sir Hexword's house, Nico sat at the head of the table, with Jane on his right and Sir Hexword on his left, with Phil next to him and Sarah on her other side. Phil spent the dinner discussing the architecture of Grimspell and describing the clothing that she'd seen on the castle ghosts. Despite Sir Hexword's interest and intelligence, she found herself missing Nico's exuberance and charm, the casual touch of his hand fiddling with her skirts or her hair.

She glanced up at Jane and Nico quite often, especially when their laughter threatened to bring down the chandeliers from the gilt ceiling. Their heads were often bent together as if they shared private confidences.

By the end of the dinner, Phil found that her servings of apple crumb, Nesselrode pudding, and sugared strawberries tasted flat.

"Would you like to see my collection?" Sir Hexword asked, unaware of her downcast spirits.

Phil had lost track of their conversation and had no idea as to what collection he referred. But she nodded anyway, suddenly eager to be away from the table.

Sir Hexword wiped his mouth on a napkin and rose. "If you two will excuse us, I'd like to show Lady Radcliff my collection."

Sir Hexword held out his hand and Phil took it.

She rose and glanced at Nico. Jane's shoulder almost brushed his while she leaned over and snatched the strawberries from his china plate. They looked so comfortable with each other. So suitably matched in age and temperament and . . . character.

"You make a charming couple," Phil said. Jane froze in the act of popping a strawberry between her red lips. "I wouldn't be surprised if your childhood friendship blossoms into something more." There, she'd said it. She'd pushed Nico toward Jane as his right and proper partner. She couldn't quite believe her audacity, but it was the right thing to do. Wasn't it?

Sir Hexword led her from the room, but not before she heard Nico's parting words. "Jolly good try, Phil." Her heart soared despite herself.

Sir Hexword led her down the hall to his study with Sarah hard on their heels. They entered an enormous book-lined room with French doors that opened onto a garden. His collection of history books astounded Phil. But a breeze drifted through the open doors and drew her toward them first. "What a charming garden."

She felt Sir Hexword come up behind her. "I went to Italy several years ago and tried to re-create the gardens I saw there. I brought the statuary and fountains home with me."

"You've traveled a great deal, as well. You're a fascinating man, Sir Hexword."

"Perhaps. But not as fascinating as Sir Nicodemus, I fear. It won't work, you know."

Phil turned in surprise. "What do you mean?"

He smiled sadly. "Pushing Nico away. He always gets what

he wants, and trying to change his mind will only make him more stubborn."

Phil felt her face heat. She drew away from Sir Hexword, back into the room, running her fingers across the spines of a neat row of books. "Do you have anything on spiritual matters in your collection?"

"Such as?"

"Local legends. Or better yet, legends pertaining to Yorkshire."

He gave her an odd look. "I've never had much interest in that area of study, but I do have a few volumes . . . yes, this shelf over here." He pulled out and handed her a few books.

"Thank you," Phil said as she accepted them. She longed to dive into them right there, but didn't want to appear rude. However, her eagerness must have shown on her face.

"Please peruse them at your leisure," Sir Hexword offered. "I think I shall step outside for a cigar."

As Sir Hexword moved to the garden, Phil curled up in the leather chair in the corner, Sarah settling on a padded stool near her side. Phil quickly lost herself in her reading.

An indeterminable length of time passed before she became aware of her surroundings again. She shut her book. She'd hoped to find something about the legend of the Bargest. But there was nothing about the spirit in Hexword's books.

Philomena stood and stretched. "What happened to Sir Hexword?"

"He hassn't returned from the garden," Sarah replied. "Perhapss he rejoined the otherss."

Phil hesitated. If Jane had any sense whatsoever, she would have taken Phil's hint and pursued Nico with a vengeance. Phil was in no hurry to see if Jane had acted on her suggestion.

So instead of seeking out her hosts, she stepped through the French doors and into the night, the air warm and fragrant, the stars shining down with brilliance. The skies over London never looked like this. The sculpted paths led her onward, past stone benches carved with the faces of beasts, hidden alcoves of miniature templelike structures, and myriad flowers that she vowed to come back and see in the daylight. Darkness turned their brilliant colors to shades of gray.

Sarah touched Phil's arm, held her finger over her thin lips, and canted her head as if listening for something.

A low growl erupted from the bushes to her left. Philomena froze. Had Nico come out to the garden to fetch her? Could she hope that he sought her out for a few moments alone together?

"Nico?" she whispered. The growl rose in intensity. No, not Nico. He would never growl at her like that. "Sir Hexword?" She couldn't imagine that her gentle host would play with her in this manner, but he was the only one she knew to be in the garden.

Sarah shifted to her were-form, her mouth open and her tongue flicking, smelling the night.

The bushes shivered and Phil slowly faced them, then backed up until her skirts met a stone bench. "This isn't funny," she said.

Sarah hissed and slithered between Phil and the bushes, her triangular head swaying back and forth.

The bushes parted and Phil's heart stopped for a moment. The beast gleamed as black as night, a stark contrast to the white glint of its fangs and the glow of its red eyes. It slowly emerged from the bushes, head low and purposeful. A wolf. A black wolf.

Sarah hissed and the wolf leaped, catching the were-snake's head in its jaws, shaking her assistant from side to side. In that moment, Phil knew. Knew she'd wind up as dead as the other two girls, making Nico even more of a suspect in their murders.

Sarah tried to wrap her coils around the wolf but it was too fast, leaping straight up in the air when necessary. Eventually Sarah stilled, and the wolf spit Sarah's head out of its jaws.

Phil shook with horror. It had all happened so quickly.

The wolf made a feint at her, and Phil collapsed backward onto the stone bench. The beast's mouth stretched into a canine laugh, tongue lolling. Phil felt a trickle of anger through her terror. She knew the deadly speed of the were-wolves; it could pounce on her before she drew another breath.

The wolf toyed with her, like a cat to a mouse.

Phil slowly leaned down, her fingers clawing at a handful of dirt. Her aim must be true. It wouldn't stop an attack, but it might slow one. The wolf's muscles bunched and it leaped. Phil threw her handful of dirt right into those ghastly red eyes and opened her mouth to scream, but before she could utter a sound—

Another wolf hit the side of the black one in midair. A wolf with a brown coat liberally streaked with gray. Sir Hexword. The two beasts rolled down the path, snarling and snapping.

Phil rushed to Sarah's side. She'd already shifted back to human. Philomena sank to the ground, pressing her hand against Sarah's neck. She felt the beat of her pulse and released a breath on a sob.

Then fury ripped through Philomena. She glanced around for a weapon and silently cursed Sir Hexword for the tidiness of his garden. She scrambled to her feet, tore a branch off a sculpted tree, glanced at the flimsy weapon, and threw it down. Phil desperately searched the darkness.

She picked up a small stone gargoyle and hefted its weight in her hand while she advanced on the combatants.

The snarls and growls made her wish she could cover her ears.

The wolves looked like a solid mass of seething fur and wouldn't separate long enough for Phil to use her weapon. Sir Hexword was trying not to hurt the other wolf. But his caution would get him killed.

Phil raised the statue and took aim. Those red eyes focused on her for a moment. Phil launched the stone as hard as she could. The gargoyle spun in the air, landing squarely on the black wolf's nose.

Phil's flush of triumph lasted only a moment. The wolf shook off the blow and launched at Phil again. Sir Hexword made a giant leap and landed on top of it before it could reach Phil.

A howl that seemed to make the night air shiver made Phil look behind her. Nico's wolf ran in their direction, the fur along the ridge of his back upright and bristling.

The black wolf yelped, turned, and disappeared into the shadows.

Nico seemed to be mad with rage, turning on Sir Hexword with a vengeance.

"No," Phil shouted. "He tried to save me."

Within a heartbeat Nico had Sir Hexword pinned to the ground, his fangs at the smaller wolf's throat. He bit down and Sir Hexword howled.

Phil ran to them. "Nico!" she cried. "Stop!" Sir Hexword lay still, as if accepting his fate. Phil curled her fingers into the fur on Nico's back and pulled. Tears burned her eyes. "Please, Nico. Make the beast go away."

Nico's wolf shuddered for a moment. He unclenched his fangs and retreated, shifting to human. He held out his hand and Phil took it, watching as Nico slowly calmed.

"Shift," he commanded Sir Hexword. The older man

shimmered to his handsome self, clutching his throat. "How badly are you hurt?"

Sir Hexword grimaced. "Shallow puncture wounds."

"My apologies." Nico squeezed Phil's hand.

"Sarah's hurt," she said. But when they turned, Sarah stood behind them, swaying unsteadily on her feet.

"I'm all right," Sarah assured them. "My head jusst spinss." She lowered her glossy black eyes. "I'm ssorry, Lady Radcliff. I didn't protect you."

"Yes, you did," Phil replied. "You bought me time."

Nico squeezed Phil's hand again. "What happened?"

"I was walking in the garden, Sarah heard a noise, and the next thing I knew, we were being attacked."

"I didn't believe the villagers with their tales of a black wolf," Nico growled. "But we cannot continue to deny the truth. I caught only a glimpse of her, but it looked exactly like Jane's wolf."

The older man shook his head in denial. "But it didn't smell like Jane. It looked like her, yes, but . . ."

"Wasn't she with you?" Phil asked.

"We had an argument," Nico replied. "She ran out of the house. And then I went to look for you." He turned back to Sir Hexword. "Go find her. Bring her home. Perhaps there's some other explanation, but she'll have to go before the magistrate for questioning."

Hexword nodded and shifted, put his nose to the ground, and started toward the bushes where the black wolf had disappeared.

"Hexword," Nico said. The brown and gray wolf turned his head. "If you don't bring her back, I'll go after her myself."

Chapter Fifteen

Nico woke the next morning to the sound of Edwina's shrill voice outside his door. He sat up and shoved the hair from his face, blinking in the morning light.

"Be careful with that lamp, Cheevers," Edwina said. "That belonged to my great-grandmother."

Nico growled softly as he padded to his door, opening it to a scene of complete chaos. Half of the furniture from Royden's bedroom crowded the hall. "Edwina. What are you doing?"

She spun, a tiny frown marring her smooth complexion. "I'm moving us out of the castle."

Nico crossed his arms over his chest. He had little patience for his sister-in-law's theatrics this morning, not after the night he'd had. After they'd left Hallows Hall, they'd stopped in the village to have the doctor look at Sarah. Then Nico had made arrangements for Royden to stay at the doctor's house.

When they'd arrived back at the castle and he told Edwina that they would be able to move Royden out on the morrow, she'd cried and complained until Nico had lost his patience and stormed from the library.

By that time, Phil and Sarah had already retired. Despite the doctor's assurances that her assistant would be fine, Phil had insisted that Sarah sleep with her just in case the were-snake suffered any aftereffects from her injuries.

Which meant that Nico had to sleep alone, when he

had wanted nothing more than to hold Phil in his arms all night, reassuring himself of her safety. Instead he'd tossed and turned while he dreamt of her being mauled in the same way that Beatrice had. The thought of how close he'd come to losing Phil made his were-wolf shadow him all night with the urge to hunt down Jane himself.

Even now, he suppressed a howl of fury.

"Well?" Edwina demanded, her booted foot tapping impatiently. "If I recall, you said you wanted us to leave first thing in the morning."

Nico focused his gaze on her. "Quite. But is it really necessary to bring your entire bedchamber with you?"

"I only thought of your brother's comfort. It's bad enough being ousted from one's own home, but to ask him to sleep in a strange bed—surrounded by someone else's belongings—is the outside of enough."

Nico sighed. "Edwina, this is only for a short time."

Her big blue eyes shimmered with tears. "Do you mean it?"

"Of course I do. As soon as Phil finds a solution to our ghost problem, you and Royden will come home." Her face twisted with some new emotion at the mention of the ghost-hunter and Nico quickly swung his gaze to Cheevers. "Move everything back later. For now, put their trunks in the cart and meet me back up here in half an hour."

The footman bobbed his head and Nico stepped back and closed his bedroom door, resisting the urge to slam it. By the time he'd finished washing and getting dressed, he'd regained some of his patience. He had a feeling he would need it today.

Cheevers helped him get Royden down the stairs and into the cart. One look at his brother's face convinced Nico that despite Edwina's feelings of insecurity, he was doing the right thing. Royden couldn't even stay upright in his seat.

"Make him a pallet in the cart," Nico told Cheevers.

"It's not necessary." Royden sagged and gave Nico an abashed smile. "I mean, jolly good idea."

Nico settled his brother in the back of the cart and took his seat next to a red-eyed Edwina. Thankfully, she didn't say a word the entire trip to the village, but her sniffles were loud and pointed.

The overcast sky shrouded his forest in gray shadows and when they entered the village, it appeared somber as well, as if muffled in a blanket of gloom. Samuel and Charles pulled the cart up to the doctor's home and Nico leaped down from his seat and offered his hand to Edwina. She eyed it long enough for her to be satisfied that she'd insulted him, then allowed Nico to help her down.

He'd just rung the doctor's magical bell, the sounds of Mogow drums vibrating throughout the house, when Edwina screamed.

"You've killed him."

Nico ran to the back of the cart as Edwina scrambled up into it. She threw herself dramatically across Royden's chest.

"I told you we never should have moved him," she cried. "But you wouldn't listen—"

Nicodemus ignored her. Royden looked too still and deathly pale. Nico leaped into the cart, his heart hammering with dread, and pressed his fingers against his brother's neck. Relief washed through him. "Roy? Wake up, old chap."

Royden's eyes fluttered open and then rounded with amazement. "I fell asleep. Nico, I fell asleep! The cart was rocking and—bloody hell, I haven't slept in so long I forgot what it felt like."

Nico smiled. "It appears that our ghost-hunter was right. The castle spirits can't reach you outside the keep."

Edwina looked disgruntled and relieved all at the same time. "Well, I don't see how he's going to get any rest with those dreadful drums pounding every time someone comes to the door."

The doctor saved Nico from responding by peering over the edge of the cart, narrowing his eyes behind his spectacles. "I assure you, dear lady, that your husband will not be disturbed. I'm afraid that I'm a heavy sleeper and that the drums are necessary to wake me up at odd hours, but I will deactivate the bell while you are here."

Edwina looked only slightly mollified.

"I visited Mogow some time ago," the doctor continued, unaffected by her discomposure, "and I must admit that I found the culture quite fascinating. Are you familiar with the island, dear lady?"

Edwina blinked.

"Ah, excellent. I'll look forward to our evenings together, then, when I can share my travel adventures with you. The magic of their witch doctors is quite fascinating— headhunting and all that."

Edwina threw Nico a mutinous frown and he quickly jumped from the cart. "I'll need to help Royden inside."

"Oh, of course, my apologies. My patients often tell me that I can talk them to sleep. Perhaps that will be helpful to your brother." He chuckled and led them into his house, past his office and up a flight of stairs to a cozy room with smiling masks covering the walls. Roy fell asleep again the moment Nico lowered him onto the bed.

"Well, it appears that your brother won't be needing my services," the doctor mused, tucking Edwina's arm through his own and patting her hand.

"I wish I had thought of this earlier," Nico replied, watching the wrinkles smooth from his brother's forehead as his heavy breathing filled the room. "He might sleep for days. I hope it won't be too much of an inconvenience."

"Nonsense. I will just have the pleasure of this lady's company even longer," said Dr. Darknoll, patting Edwina's hand again and leading her from the room. "I've been lonely since my daughter married, my dear. She was fascinated by my collection of Mogow shrunken heads, as I'm sure you will be."

Before Edwina could form a reply, a message sprite whirred into the room, whispered into the doctor's ear, and then flashed back down the stairs in a flurry of irides-cent wings.

The doctor turned and frowned at Nico. "I'm afraid you'll have to see my collection at another time, Sir Nicode-mus. The magistrate is looking for you. No, don't look so upset, dear lady. I shall take *you* to see those heads right now."

Nico muttered a hasty good-bye, avoiding Edwina's gaze. Spending time with the lonely doctor seemed a small price to pay for her husband's restored health.

Nico pounded down the stairs, told Samuel and Charles to take the cart home, and ran for the woods, shifting to wolf as soon as he reached the trees. Bargest House lay on the other side of the river, beyond his own home farm. He crossed open fields and copses of oak and ash and leaped several streams before he arrived at the magistrate's home.

Nico shifted to human and strode up the graveled walk. Despite the leering gargoyles carved into every column and corner, he had once liked the sprawling manor better than Grimspell. Perhaps it was the statues of hunting dogs at every turn that had made him feel at home. But now that he knew why he felt uncomfortable in his castle, he decided that Bargest House really possessed a somewhat sinister façade.

Or perhaps Phil had made him see Grimspell in an en-tirely different light.

The butler opened the massive front door the moment Nico's boots hit the steps, and led him into Lord Magift's study. The paneled rosewood walls gleamed in the sun-shine that poured through the floor-to-ceiling windows, and unfortunately, sparked an answering shine from Lord Magift's balding pate. He sat behind a kidney-shaped desk, his fingers tapping a rhythm on the arms of his leather chair.

A royal had spelled the room to intimidate those whom the magistrate interrogated. To Nico, the illusion appeared like nothing more than a translucent curtain of color, but more than one ruffian had spilled all his sins at the sight of devils cavorting behind Lord Magift's chair, hell's flames ripping up the walls, stern schoolmasters waving switches, and even a rather stern-faced illusion of Queen Victoria.

Nico strode into the room and came to an abrupt halt at the sight of Hexword and Jane ensconced in the high wing-backed chairs facing the magistrate's desk. Jane's midnight hair straggled down the sides of her face, and her eyes looked red and puffy. Hexword appeared to have aged ten years overnight.

"Nico," Jane gasped, her bottom lip trembling.

He resisted the urge to comfort her, as he had done since they were children and she'd gotten her first scrape on her knee. She looked so tiny and vulnerable in that big chair. Only the thought of Phil being almost mauled stopped him.

Nico swung his gaze over to Hexword. "You brought her back."

The older man's lips twisted. "She was home when I returned. Jane insisted that we tell the entire story to the magistrate."

"Hoping for some leniency?"

Lord Magift cleared his throat as if to say something, and Nico shot him a look. This was his pack. His responsibility.

Jane's tears tracked a new path down her cheeks. "I . . . I didn't try to harm Phil. I didn't kill Beatrice or Arabella."

Sir Hexword leaned forward. "We were just telling Lord Magift that my daughter has no motive for these attacks, Nico. And . . . and it was dark. You can't be sure it was Jane's wolf."

Hexword was just as blind as Nico had been. The answer had been staring Nicodemus in the face all these years, and he'd refused to see it. "I'll give you your motive. Did you tell them where you were last night, Jane?"

She dropped her head. "In the forest."

"And why did you run off into the forest, Jane?"

Hexword's face creased into a frown, and the light faded from his eyes as he stared at his daughter. Nico's gut churned. The two people closest to him were being destroyed right before his eyes. But he had to stop the killings, and the only way to do that was for the truth to come out.

"I . . . I tried again," Jane whispered. "After the ghost-hunter made it clear that Nico and I would be more suited—that she wouldn't accept his hand in marriage—I hoped that Nico would finally turn to me." Her eyes narrowed as she looked up at the magistrate. "But he rejected me. Again. And I couldn't bear it anymore. So I fled into the woods until—"

"Until you saw Phil standing alone, and your beast took over." Nico couldn't stop pressuring her. It was as if he needed to hear her admit her crimes before he could totally believe in them.

"No." Jane rocked back and forth in her chair. "I ran until I could run no more. Then I fell asleep, and by the time I returned home, you all had left."

"Did you see anyone in the forest to corroborate your whereabouts?" Lord Magift interjected. At the girl's dejected shake of the head, the magistrate leaned back in his chair and steepled his fingers. "Love is a strong motive for murder." His sharp eyes glanced at Nico. "And you say she was in love with you when Beatrice was attacked?"

"Yes, I believe she might have been."

"But what about Arabella?" Sir Hexword said. "She had no romantic interest in Nico."

Nicodemus frowned. Hexword was right. He'd barely

spoken two words to the rector's daughter. Jenkins had her so frightened of shape-shifters that the girl ran the other way whenever she saw him.

"It could have been a clever ploy," Magift said. "To throw us off the scent, so to speak."

And Nico had seen Jane last night. Phil could have died. The thought of losing his ghost-hunter nearly threw him into a rage. Nico's head spun. He had to push aside his feelings for Jane to get to the truth. "You're a clever hunter, aren't you, Jane? How did you disguise your scent? How did you erase your tracks so thoroughly over the years?"

"But I didn't . . ." Her soft brown eyes met Nico's. "You don't believe me, do you?" she whispered. "You truly think that I could have done such horrible things." Jane wrapped her arms around her shoulders and her body appeared to wither into the chair. "Then it doesn't matter. No one shall believe me, if you don't."

"Don't worry," Hexword said, leaning forward and catching up his daughter into his arms. "It will be all right, Jane."

"Well," Lord Magift said, "a trial will solve the matter."

Jane's sobs filled the room and twisted at Nico's gut. "She will have a fair trial, Magift. I know how most of the gentry feel about shape-shifters."

The magistrate nodded. "I'll make sure of it. And you'll be there to testify." He lowered his voice. "I'll be taking her to Norwitch prison for the time being. I don't have anything here that could hold her, if she became determined enough to escape."

Nico nodded. Most cells weren't strong enough to hold a determined were, and magical wards didn't work on them.

"She won't try to escape," Hexword snapped. "And I'm going to Norwitch with her."

"Why?" Nico growled. "Why did you let your beast control you, Jane?"

She looked up at him in surprise, but Nico refused to meet her gaze and allow her to see his fear of his own beast.

Nico shifted to wolf and howled, his voice rocking the walls of the manor. He ran from the room, Magift's butler just managing to open the door in time for Nicodemus to fly out of it. Nico's heartbeat thrummed in his ears and his paws moved almost in synchrony to the sound. When he reached the confines of his forest he leaped over rock and bush, swam the familiar streams and ponds, but still couldn't outrun his fear.

Not this time.

Jane had proven that his fears weren't groundless. That the feral nature of the wolf could overcome a shifter's basic humanity. The need to mate—to kill—might consume him one day. Might strip him of his preconceived notions of his own decency. He could never run fast enough or far enough to destroy the beast inside him. He could never tame the wolf. Jane had betrayed him in more ways than she knew.

Nico's paws scrabbled in the leaves as he came to an abrupt stop just outside the crumbling walls of Grimspell castle. Perhaps he couldn't control his beast, but he reminded himself that the ghost-hunter had tamed his wolf. He'd come to her time and again with his beast raging, and with a word, a caress, she'd managed to calm his soul. No one had ever done that before.

He didn't need to fear his beast as long as he had Phil. She completed him like no other person ever had and made him a better man. An entirely human man.

Nico wearily trudged up the drive. It had been a hell of a night and an even more hellish day, and he needed Phil in his arms more than he needed to breathe. But she could be anywhere in the castle, searching for that map, and he wouldn't hunt her down as he had so many times before. He wouldn't allow any part of his beast to pursue her.

He shifted to human and went straight to his room. To bathe, to pace, to wait.

He had almost given up and was about to seek her after all when he heard a light tapping on the door.

"Nico?"

The knob turned. He backed up several steps. The door slowly swung open and she stood there in nothing but a thin gown and a hesitant smile. A rush of pure triumph surged through him, and it was all he could do not to catch her up in his arms.

"Oh, good, you're still awake." Phil slipped into the room and closed the door behind her. And locked it. "Are you all right? You didn't come down to dinner and the servants have been gossiping all day about Jane Hexword being arrested and confessing to every crime that's ever befallen the villagers . . . Nico, why are you looking at me that way?"

"You came."

She cocked her head. "Of course I did. You must be dreadfully upset about Jane."

He shook his head, letting his hair fall over his eyes. "No. You want me, Phil."

"Do I?" she asked with an impish grin.

"You locked the door behind you."

"Did I?" She walked toward him, her eyes taking in his shirtless chest, his half-buttoned trousers. "You look deliciously rumpled." Her hands covered his biceps, trailed a hot path down to his stomach. She undid the buttons of his trousers, pulled them off. He closed his eyes when he felt her wet mouth on his calf, her tongue trailing a line up his thigh. He knew—he hoped—where her kisses were headed and tensed in anticipation. Phil ran her tongue over his hip bone, up to his stomach, and back down to the other one. As if she explored the taste of each inch of his skin. Her gentleness humbled him, made him forget the shadow of his wolf, the betrayal of his best friend, the missing map, and even the presence of the relic.

Her tongue stroked the length of his shaft and Nico forgot everything but Phil.

She made love to him with her mouth until he didn't think he could endure it any longer without exploding. Then she stood and backed away. Nico caught his breath, lost it again when she reached up and removed her gown. She looked into his eyes and froze for a moment.

"You're the grandest thing I've ever seen," he said.

She smiled and crawled up on the bed, her hand extended out to him. Nico strode to the bed and in one fluid movement covered her body with his own. The urge to take her then, to claim his mate, to possess her with a ferocity that matched the instincts of his wolf nearly overwhelmed him.

"Nico," she breathed, her hands on his shoulders, tangling in his hair.

He banished his wolf, held himself immobile atop her. He wanted nothing more than to show her the same tender love that she had shown him.

"Tell me, Phil." He lifted his hips until his shaft stroked the inside of her thighs.

Her eyes clouded with confusion for a moment and then she smiled and almost made him come undone. "I want you."

"Ah, dear girl, not quite enough." He placed the tip of his shaft against her opening, gritting his teeth when he felt how very much she really wanted him. Hot, wet. He sucked in a long breath.

Phil curled her legs around his back, grasped his bottom and tried to push him into her. Nico felt his lips curl but couldn't be sure whether he grinned or grimaced.

"All right," she gasped. "I need you."

Nico lowered his head and her mouth opened hungrily

beneath his kiss. This time he knew he smiled. He allowed her to pull him inside her, but only a bit. Only enough to hint at the pleasure he could give. He drew back and in, until he set a gentle rhythm that had her straining toward him, trying to pull his entire length inside of her.

Ah. Nico felt the strength of his gentleness, the heady delight of her sweet opening clenched around the tip of him.

"Nico, please."

"I love you, Phil."

"Nico . . ."

He lowered his voice to a whisper. "Trust me, Phil. Trust me with your heart."

She swept her fingertips along his jaw. "Yes, Nico. I love you . . ."

He slid inside even deeper. Phil murmured her love for him over and over and he matched the rhythm of her words, rewarding each endearment with another thrust, until she shook and arched her back and cried out the words again with her climax.

He finally allowed himself his own release, and he'd never before felt anything like it. The pleasure swept him up on a gentle tide and rocked him for so long that he didn't think he'd ever come up for air. It felt overwhelming and enduring and . . . tender. Just like Phil.

The pleasure spread throughout his heart and soul. He never would have guessed that true love could be so bloody fabulous.

He rolled over and cradled Phil against his side. He'd meant to force her to realize her own feelings. He'd never expected to come to even more realizations himself. "You don't tame my beast, Phil. I tame it for you."

She turned to her side and looked up at him. "Of course you do, Nico. You're one of the strongest men I've ever known."

Nico smiled. "It was about time you admitted that you love me."

She went very still. He could almost hear her thoughts tumbling around in that pretty head. "I just have so many doubts."

He pulled her closer, until her arm lay across his chest, her leg atop his thigh, and her head beneath his chin. "I have none, my dear ghost-hunter. Yours will have to be enough for both of us." Nico's eyes drifted closed. He'd gotten precious little sleep the last few days and felt as if he could sleep for a fortnight. "Besides, you'll have plenty of time to get used to the idea of loving me."

"What do you mean? Nico, don't you dare fall asleep."

He yawned. "Well, first you have to solve our problem with the ghosts. Then we'll need to wait to see if you're carrying my heir."

She shifted and he felt her breath on his lips, her breasts on his upper chest. He cracked his eyes open in appreciation.

"Your heir," she whispered.

Nico smiled. Her hair haloed her face in a mass of tangled curls, color flushed her cheeks, and sleepiness hooded her eyes. So many shades of beauty in one small woman. It might take him a lifetime to discover them all.

"You knew perfectly well what you were doing all along, didn't you?" Phil scolded.

"You know," Nico mused, "when you speak to me as if you were my nursemaid, all sorts of naughty visions come to mind."

Phil made a strangled sound, but when she spoke again she'd completely changed the tone of her voice. "What if I'm not with child?"

"It won't be from lack of trying." He cradled her cheeks with his big hands.

"I mean, how do you propose to keep me here, then?"

"I'll think of something. Don't be afraid, Phil. I have no intention of letting you go." He pulled her face down and kissed her until he felt all her muscles go lax, and then he tucked her close to his side again. "I'm so damn tired. Stay the night with me, Phil. I want to wake up in the morning with you beside me."

She wiggled and shifted and then let out a long sigh of contentment. "I already told Sarah not to wait up for my return."

Chapter Sixteen

Philomena dreamt of the warrior with the blue sword. He battled the dragon again, but this time when he shifted to wolf and sank his blue teeth into the red scales, the larger beast managed to shake him off.

"Get up," Phil shouted, clutching the bed linens to her chest.

The warrior shifted to human and looked up at her from where he'd fallen on the dungeon's flagstones, his face so similar to Nico's that her heart squeezed in her chest. The light in his blue sword flickered out. His leg lay beneath him, twisted at an odd angle. The dragon belched a flame of crimson-yellow fire at the warrior, and just before it enveloped him, he held out his hand to Phil. "I cannot prevail this time. Come—"

She closed her eyes against the sight of flesh charring from bone, but another spirit took his place and Phil realized that she could still see, despite her closed lids. She had no earthly defense against dreams. The medieval peasant waved his scythe, the sharp blade moving closer to her throat with each pass, until she could feel the whisper of the cold metal against her skin.

"We bring him warning and he runs away," the peasant shouted.

The bespectacled boy from the library appeared on her right. "Why didn't the messenger warn our lord?"

The priest appeared on her opposite side. "You are all we have left."

"Hurry, hurry! Before it's too late," cried the spirit of a woman brandishing a cleaver.

And then more spirits appeared and joined the woman's cry until Phil covered her hands over her ears to drown out the deluge of voices. But they shouted inside her dreams, and there was nothing she could do to stop—

Phil woke and sat up, her hands still over her ears, her breath misting before her face from the icy chill that accompanied the spirits ringed around the bed. "You're still here."

She dropped her hands and dragged the bed linens up to her neck to cover her nakedness. Grimspell's ghosts watched her for a moment, then, as one, they again began to shout at her to hurry, hurry. Phil glanced down at Nico, whose bare chest rose and fell in deep slumber.

"Phil," rang a familiar voice above the tumult. She turned her head. Tup sat atop the fireplace mantel, his eyes rounded with fear, his hair sticking out even more wildly than usual. "There's somethin' very wrong tonight."

She suppressed the urge to tell him that was obvious and instead reached for her gown, slipping it over her head while juggling with the bedcovers. "They were in my dreams."

Suddenly Nico's eyes opened, and he reached for her. "What's wrong?" The ring of spirits around the bed crowded even closer.

"With Royden gone, they sought ye out," Tup said.

"But I'm more sensitive. I can still see them, hear them. I can't wake up from the nightmare like Royden could."

Nico sat up and caught her shoulders. "The ghosts are in *your* dreams now?"

Phil turned and tried to make out his features in the darkness. "Worse. They are clustered around the bed, urging me to hurry. They want me to follow them."

Tup floated down from the mantel to the foot of the bed, facing the hostile spirits, using himself as a barrier between them and Phil. "I'll try to hold off the blighters, but somethin' has driven 'em crackers. Somethin' bad."

Nico lit a candle and held it up as if the light could help him see the spirits. "Get out of here," he commanded.

Phil sighed. Arrogant man. "Nico, I hardly think that's going to work. Tup says there's something very wrong with them tonight. That something bad—"

The warrior spirit reached for Tup. Her brave lad threw his fists, but they bounced off the man's chest and he barely seemed to notice. He picked up Tup with one arm and threw him over his shoulder like a sack of flour, gave Phil one last meaningful glance, and headed for the bedroom door.

"Botheration," Phil shouted, scrambling out from under the covers. "Leave Tup alone!"

The warrior and his wiggling burden faded through the door. Phil tried to follow, but Nico grabbed her arm. "Where do you think you're going?"

"Your wicked ancestor has my Tup. I'm going to get him back."

Nico set down the candle on the bedside table and shook his head. "Oh no, you're not. I know where they're trying to lure you. They might lead you into the tunnels, but I don't trust them to get you back out again."

Phil struggled vainly against his grip. When he still refused to release her, she took a breath and stilled. "Don't you understand? I have no choice. They need my help, Nico. I can't turn my back on them, or on Tup."

Nico's jaw clenched with pure stubbornness. "I won't allow you to be put into danger."

"This is what I *do*, Nico. If you truly love me, you'll have to accept that."

He sprang out of bed and struggled into his trousers.

"I'll take that as a challenge, lady. And *you* will accept this as proof of my sincere feelings for you."

Phil headed for the door. She opened her mouth to reply but spirit fingers grasped at her, tugging on her gown and yanking on her hair. With that uncanny speed of his, Nico reached the door before she did, opening it before the demanding spirits slammed her into it.

The ghosts tugged her down the hall and Nico followed, then suddenly turned back around and went back the way they'd come. Within a heartbeat he'd returned to her side, steadying her against the pull of the ghosts. "Sarah. The key."

Phil should have thought of fetching her assistant herself. And that they'd need the key for the new lock on the tunnel door. But the ghosts' panic had begun to infect her as well, making her heart slam inside her chest, her throat close with empathic fear.

Whatever frightened them must be dreadful indeed.

Her bare feet slapped the cold stone stairs and then she stumbled on her gown. If Nicodemus hadn't been there to support her, she'd have fallen headfirst down the spiral stairwell.

"Stop pulling her," he growled, his dark eyes wide as he tried to visualize the beings that swirled around her. "She'll be of no use to you if you break her neck."

The hands quit touching her. Phil breathed a sigh of relief. The bespectacled lad twisted his hands together, the priest fingered his cross, and the peasants clutched their homemade weapons. But they didn't pull at her again, though their cries for her to hurry increased in volume.

When they reached the dungeons, Nico opened the door and then disappeared again. Phil hesitated at the threshold, her eyes widening at the sight of the black wraiths swirling about the room. Their spirits were so old that nothing was left but a shadow of their beings, and she could only make out the outlines of dragons, monsters, and demons.

Nico appeared again at her side, a bucket of whitewash in one hand and a lantern in the other. He narrowed his eyes at the expression on her face. "Now what?"

"I . . . I'm not sure. Dark wraiths. Something has disturbed the deeper spirits of the underworld . . . or has made them extraordinarily excited." She felt a shiver crawl up her spine.

But her slightly more solid companions ignored the wraiths, hurrying into the dungeon, beckoning her forward. Phil took a deep breath of the fetid air and coughed, but valiantly followed. The wraiths felt like a cloud of lightning, their forms moving through and around her, making the hair stand up on her arms and the back of her neck. Nico kept his arm around her and watched her face with concern, not the least bit affected by the charged energy roiling about them.

"They *are* excited about something," she murmured. "And expectant. Oh, Nico, I don't think this is good." Phil reached the tunnel door and stared at the chains that appeared to have been ripped apart and flung on the cold floor. "No, I don't think this is good at all."

Nico cursed and retrieved the broken lock, the metal bar twisted from its casing. "Someone with inhuman strength did this. Someone with the strength of a were."

"Ssince your castle iss crawling with weres, ssir," Sarah hissed, "there are sseveral possibilities." She bent down and helped Phil step into a pair of leather slippers.

"You caught up with us quickly," Nico said.

Her assistant nodded with sinuous grace and before anyone could protest, she slid in front of Phil, shifting to her were-form as she did so, her tongue flicking eagerly to test the air. Her dark skin quickly vanished in the blackness of the tunnel.

"She's got more courage than sense," Nico muttered with a trace of a smile.

The castle ghosts urged Philomena onward and she could hear Tup calling out to her from beyond the darkness. Why didn't her lad disappear? Could the blue warrior keep Tup substantial against his will? She prayed that his spirit wouldn't be irreparably damaged.

Nico stayed by her side, the light of his lantern and his strong arm helping her to avoid tripping over the scattered rocks on the loose dirt floor of the tunnel. She silently thanked Sarah for her forethought in bringing her shoes.

Soon the walls of the tunnel narrowed, and Nico stepped in front of her, his warm back a barrier against the constant demand of the ghosts. They came to a branching of several other tunnels. "Which one?" he asked, his voice deep and low.

Phil felt a tug on her left sleeve. "The left." Nico stopped, dipped a finger into the bucket, and painted a white arrow pointing in the direction they'd come. No, he didn't trust her ghosts one whit to lead them back out.

It felt as if she walked for hours, stopping every few minutes for another deceptive branch in the tunnels. Phil wondered where the other tunnels led, if anywhere at all. Did they just circle around like some mad labyrinth? A moment of panic stole her breath at the thought. To be so trapped and lost . . . she could imagine Nico as a young lad, blindly wandering these black tunnels, and her heart constricted with agony for the memory of that lost boy.

Phil bumped into Nico's back as he stopped again. He reached into the bucket and painted his arrow, took a step and then stopped again. Phil looked around his arm. "What is it?"

Sarah slid toward them, her large black eyes glowing in the lamplight. She shifted to human. "There'ss a fall of rock blocking the tunnel ahead," she whispered. "But it lookss like someone hass cleared a way through it. Recently."

Phil felt Nico stiffen. He followed Sarah to a large tumble of rocks, holding up his lantern and studying the narrow entrance that had been cleared through the blockage. "This must have taken months to dig out," he murmured.

Sarah nodded. "I'll go through firsst."

"No. Stay here with your mistress and I'll—damn the woman."

Sarah had already shifted to snake and eased into the passage.

Nico set down the bucket and handed Phil the lantern. "Stay here." And then he crawled in after Sarah.

Phil shook her head and set down the lantern, following right on his heels. She couldn't see a thing, but she didn't think she could manage to crawl in the tight space and hold the lantern at the same time. She felt when Nico emerged on the other side and the passage cleared in front of her. Despite her slow caution she tumbled out the other side, unable to suppress a yelp of surprise as she fell.

Nico caught her before she hit the ground. "Neither of you listen very well, do you?"

Phil didn't bother to respond. They seemed to be in a larger tunnel, judging by the echo of his voice, and the passage ahead appeared to glow, the ethereal bodies of the castle ghosts winking in and out of the light.

Nico set her on her feet. "I'm not sure what that light is yet, so I'd advise you not to touch it."

Phil suppressed a smile at his change from giving orders to advice, and nodded in agreement. He took her hand and led her into the bluish glow and they both peered closely at the walls. It appeared to be some sort of moss; a growth of narrow stalks that oozed a blue sap of light.

Nico shrugged at her glance, his face an unearthly blue. Apparently he'd never seen the growth before either, and Phil didn't have the time to ponder the mystery as the castle ghosts suddenly united in a scream of fury. She covered her ears, which didn't do a bit of good at blocking it. Her body vibrated from the sound. Nico frowned with worry, his mouth opening to speak, but at Tup's sudden cry, Phil's feet seemed to move of their own accord, running down the glowing blue passageway.

Nico caught up to her in a blink, but he didn't try to stop her; he just kept pace at her side, his arm held out to steady her in case she fell. But the floor smoothed out to hard rock and Phil didn't stumble a bit, her feet flying surely and swiftly down the tunnel, as if she'd come this way hundreds of times before.

The walls widened, again and again, and she slowed as she approached a jagged opening. Her heart pounded in her ears as she crossed the threshold into a large cavern. Nico caught her around the waist and brought her to a stop. Phil's knees trembled and her mouth opened as she stared in wonder.

The walls of the cavern looked like layers of steps, climbing upward until they disappeared into blackness. Rectangular stones, carved with images of warriors and crests and sometimes just a name, patterned the top of each step. In a few places the stones had fallen out, revealing tattered cloth and bone. Phil couldn't even guess at how many burial chambers ringed the room.

But the largest stone coffin sat in the center of the floor, an enormous slab covering it. Phil blinked at the light shining from beneath a narrow crack in the lid, a crack that had been wedged open with a steel bar. A steel bar held in the smooth, white hands of Nico's sister-in-law, Edwina.

Phil blinked stupidly at the girl, who was so intent on her task that she hadn't noticed them yet. Edwina's face burned red from her exertions as she pushed and tugged on the bar, trying to shift the stone lid of the coffin open even farther. She wore a white dress layered with ribbons and bows, her hair swept up with similar satin pieces. Despite the streaks of brown dirt across her skirt and bodice, and the straggles of hair loose in her coiffure, she looked daintily feminine . . . and quite incongruous for the task at hand.

"Edwina?" Phil gasped.

The girl glanced up, black shadow wraiths swirling around her arms and shoulders, plucking at her sleeves and hair, urging her onward as surely as the castle ghosts had urged Philomena into this cavern. "It's mine," Edwina said, her mouth twisting into an ugly smile. "You're too late."

"Keep her talking," Nico whispered as he shifted to wolf.

"What's yours?" Phil asked, although she had a good idea. But did Edwina truly know what she sought? Did Nico even know what power the relic contained?

"That's the real reason you came to Grimspell, isn't it?" Edwina demanded. "To find the relic before I did. Well, you're too late. I win."

From the corner of her eye, Phil watched Nico slip into the shadows. "You found the map."

"Of course I did," Edwina crowed. "When I married Royden, I only thought to get away from my mother and father. I had no idea he held the means of lifting my curse until I found that map in his father's trunk. Roy's love will truly set me free."

Phil had no idea what she was talking about, but Edwina had quit pushing on the rod while they spoke, and from the other side of the room she saw Sarah in her were-form advancing on the girl as well. She needed to give Nico and Sarah time to reach her.

"What curse, Edwina?"

"I thought you had already figured that out," she replied, glancing down at the crack in the coffin lid. The gray light that leaked from the stone turned her delicate features into a visage of death. "You're the ghost-hunter. You study the spiritual legends . . . you mentioned it to Mother."

Philomena frowned in concentration. Edwina wedged

her fingers into the crack of the stone and started to push her hand inside. What was taking Nico so long?

Phil had to keep Edwina talking, for heaven knew what would happen if the girl managed to touch the relic, and she'd already shoved her arm halfway inside the coffin.

Edwina suddenly squealed and yanked her arm out. The wraiths surrounding the girl roared in protest, and Phil stumbled backward from the sound. In that moment she noticed Nico's were-form poised on a step behind Edwina and the dark shape of Sarah's snake creeping around the corner of the stone casket. A wraith that appeared more substantial than the rest, a large black dog with glowing red eyes, raked its claws through Edwina's blonde hair, making several white ribbons tremble.

Edwina clutched at her head, her blue eyes widening with horror. "There's a skeleton in there . . . ugh, ugh . . . it's still got hair on it." She shuddered, but plunged her arm back inside the coffin. "But he's here, he's here again. I must be brave. I can't let him take me."

"Your mother spilled her tea when I mentioned the legend of the Bargest," Phil said, staring at the wraith that shadowed the girl. "Your home is named after a monstrous black spirit-dog. But it's nothing but a ghost unless . . . Good heavens, is it possible? Can the curse allow it to enter your body and give it corporeal form? Oh, Edwina. Don't tell me you're haunted by a Bargest."

Nico whipped his head around to stare at Phil, realizing the implications. He must have made some sound because Edwina glanced over her shoulder.

"Don't move," she commanded. "You don't want to hurt me. Terrible things happen when people try to hurt me."

Nico shifted back to human, frozen in his crouch. "You killed them, didn't you? Beatrice and Arabella. No wonder I could never find a scent or a track."

Edwina glared at him, then turned her attention back to

her task, her arm now up to her shoulder within the crack. She ignored Nico and directed her words toward Phil. "It wasn't me. I'm not haunted, ghost-hunter. I'm possessed. I thought for sure that you, at least, would figure it all out. But no, you were too absorbed with the castle ghosts, too intent on finding the relic before I did. I tried to warn you away."

Phil took several cautious steps toward Edwina. "You're the one who hit me over the head that night."

Sarah had reached the girl's feet. She gently crept under Edwina's skirts, barely ruffling the material, forming a circle of scales beneath the hoops.

"I didn't mean to hit you so hard," Edwina said. "But I couldn't risk you finding it first. I knew it would only be a matter of time before you talked Nico into exploring the tunnels, especially after you managed to convince him to move us out of our own home. And it took me a dreadfully long time to move the stones that blocked the tunnel."

"But why didn't you tell me, Edwina? I might have been able to help you," Nico interjected.

She looked up at him in disbelief. "No one can lift the curse. Don't you think I've tried? Father even tried to beat it out of me. He chained me—so when the dog came it wouldn't kill him—and then he'd beat me within an inch of my life. I prayed it would work, but it didn't do any good. It only made me hate Father."

"He knew?" Nico muttered, his handsome face twisted with betrayal.

"Of course he knew," Edwina snapped. "And he's wrong; I didn't do anything to bring on the curse. Just because it hasn't come to anyone in our family for generations . . ."

Nico growled, stilling the wraiths and castle ghosts. "He should have told me. Instead he made it appear that I was responsible for their deaths. And now Jane. Damnation . . . Jane! You'd let her pay for the crimes you committed."

Edwina's head whipped around. "It wasn't me, I tell you. I didn't kill them; the beast did."

"But you should have been locked up so the Bargest couldn't do any more harm."

The girl's eyes glittered with satisfaction. "See, that's why I didn't tell you. I'd go mad if I were locked up. At least Father understood that. And now you understand why I need the relic. It contains the most powerful magic in the world, and with it, I can surely break the curse. I don't want that beast to ever touch me again. I hate it when it makes me kill." Tears began to track down her cheeks. "It's so ugly . . . so messy."

Despite herself, Phil felt sorry for the girl. She couldn't be sure what she would do in the same situation. To be locked up for the rest of one's life would be horrible. But to be forced to kill would be even worse. She could feel Edwina's terror and horror, and tears sprang to her eyes.

"But you don't even know what kind of magic the relic does," Phil said. "You might make it worse."

Tup patted her on the cheek. Phil blinked. The blue warrior had released her lad, and he hovered at her shoulder. The castle ghosts now appeared to be more interested in holding back the black wraiths that threatened to overwhelm Edwina, doing their best to hold off the largest one. The Bargest.

Edwina's shoulder flexed as she began to search inside the casket again. But Sarah must have tightened her coils beneath the hoops, for Edwina's eyes widened in surprise as she suddenly toppled over. Her arm nearly tore from its socket as it was yanked out of the stone coffin. Within a blink, Nico shifted to wolf and leaped, straddling the prone girl.

"No," Edwina shouted. "Get off, you're hurting me. He's near, I tell you. Don't make him come."

Like a spring suddenly released, Philomena sprinted for the stone box. She had just laid her hand on the cold dusty surface when the Bargest let loose a howl of triumph and broke through the castle ghosts' defenses. The black dog's shadow melted into Edwina's prone body. Her eyes widened, her back arched, and she let out a groan of sheer agony.

Her transformation looked nothing like a were shifting. It was unnatural, slow and painful. When Edwina's bones cracked, Phil thought she might be sick. The girl's eyes grew into wide pits of red fire, her tiny nose and full mouth twisted into a long muzzle. Her porcelain skin grew wiry tufts of black hair while her limbs lengthened and sprouted wicked claws. The material of her dress ripped as her body grew, ribbons and bows flying from it like thrown confetti. Fangs grew from Edwina's mouth until she opened her black lips and howled.

She looked exactly like Jane's wolf, except for the glow of her red eyes.

Nico threw back his head, in surprise or horror, Phil couldn't be sure. But Phil knew the beast wasn't made of magic and that Nico wouldn't be immune to those claws and fangs. When Hexword had fought the Bargest in Jane's garden, the beast hadn't been furious, hadn't been surrounded by black wraiths to fuel the power of its earthly manifestation. Nico had no idea what he was up against.

The castle ghosts fought the wraiths even harder, the swirl of their spiritual battle like a tornado above the stone coffin.

Phil opened her mouth to scream a warning when the Bargest twisted, throwing off Sarah and tossing Nico into the air. Sarah uncoiled and raised her sleek body high, her tongue flicking and her triangular head weaving. Phil ran toward Nico, who'd landed hard on a stone step and lay still.

"No, Phil," Tup whispered. "There's only one way ye can help."

Philomena ignored the boy. Nico might be hurt . . .

But that shaggy wolf's head rose and in one fluid motion he leaped onto all fours. In a blink Nico pounced on the Bargest and they rolled across the floor, the snarls and snap of teeth echoing loudly in the stone cavern. Although the dog's claws and fangs almost glittered with hard clarity, its form wavered, and at times it seemed as if its paws floated just above the stone floor. Sarah slithered after them, watching for an opening in which she could help Nico.

"The Bargest will kill them this time," Phil whispered.

"There's more danger than ye know," Tup replied.

She turned and looked into her lad's face. What could be more dangerous than a furious dog spirit? "What do you mean?"

A roar of pain shook the walls. The Bargest rolled free of Nico, its red eyes flashing with triumph. Phil covered her mouth in fear. One of Nico's paws bled, the red drops spattering the rocky floor. His ribs heaved with exertion as he stared into the Bargest's eyes.

Fury quickly replaced Phil's fear. She looked wildly around for a weapon and spied the steel bar that Edwina had used to shimmy open the stone slab atop the coffin. She raised the hem of her gown and sprinted, then closed her hands around the cold steel and yanked it out of the crack.

Sarah had flung her body around the black beast. Phil turned around just in time to see the dog clench its jaws around the snake's head and shake her viciously. Phil leaped forward and swung her weapon, managing a glancing blow to the dog's withers. The Bargest yipped and dropped Sarah, backing away from Phil in surprise. Sarah shifted to human and lay still, but Philomena noticed with relief that she still breathed.

Phil's arms had started to shake, but she kept her weapon up, standing protectively over her prone assistant. Tup hovered near her side, his spiritual form flicking in and out of existence.

And then the black dog turned his attention away from them and looked into Nico's eyes again, and the fear that threatened to overwhelm Philomena multiplied a hundred-fold. Something passed between the two animals, some shared understanding that she couldn't fathom. The Bargest threw back its head and howled. Nico didn't take advantage of the bare throat exposed to him. Instead, he lifted his own shaggy head and joined in the Bargest's song.

It was wild and feral and glorious. It promised rich hunting and power beyond imagining.

The castle ghosts halted their attack, turning their pale eyes toward the two beasts. The wraiths grinned and spun like tops. Phil shuddered. "The Bargest wants Nico to join him. He's calling out to the wildness in him."

Tup pulled at his hair, making it stand out even more than usual. "No, no, it's worse. Crikey, don't ye see? The Bargest wants to trade Edwina for Nico. If Sir Nicodemus accepts the curse willingly—" He disappeared for a moment.

"Nico," Phil screamed. The animal's song cut off in mid howl. Those golden-flecked eyes turned to her and the black dog spun and glared. "Don't listen to the beast. Don't let the wolf rule you. I . . . I need you."

Nico's eyes cleared and his love for her shone in them. But Phil could feel the tug on Nicodemus's soul, the lure with which the Bargest enchanted him. Her stomach twisted, knowing that what she'd always dreaded had so quickly come to pass. Nico's love for her wasn't strong enough. It would never be strong enough to overcome the beast in his soul.

Nico's gaze alternated between hers and the glowing red eyes of the dog.

"What am I going to do?" she whispered to herself.

Tup answered, "Have faith in him . . . and use the relic."

"What?" His words shocked her enough to make her turn away from Nico's spiritual battle with the Bargest.

Tup floated toward the stone casket, hovered over the crack in the lid. "Can't ye feel its power, Phil?"

She could, and it terrified her. And yet Phil found herself walking toward the coffin, peering into the gray light filtering out of the stone crack. A low, angry growl sounded from behind her, and she glanced back at the Bargest. The dog gathered its legs to launch itself at her, but Nico sprang first, slamming into the beast and tumbling them into the far shadows of the cavern.

Phil couldn't allow the Bargest to destroy Nico, physically or spiritually. And the only thing powerful enough to stop it was the relic. She put her fingers inside the opening.

As she touched the coffin, the dark wraiths let loose a howl of fury and swarmed her. Sharp needles of pain tore at her eyes and face. Icy cold ripped through her body as the wraiths plunged inside her. Philomena screamed from the onslaught. It was the castle ghosts who responded to her cry. They pulled back the swarm, one black shadow at a time, until she felt she might manage to breathe again.

Gratitude warred with confusion. Weren't the castle ghosts supposed to be protecting the relic? Keeping it out of the hands of anyone who would use it for their own evil purposes?

Tup dove beneath the stone lid, his tangle of hair popping out of it a moment later. "The girl didn't dig deep enough."

Phil dreaded what he might mean. She stole a glance over her shoulder. Sarah still lay where she'd fallen, but her glossy black eyes opened and she nodded once at her mistress, as if she gave her approval. Phil couldn't make out Nico or the Bargest in the dark shadows, could only see the flash of the dog's red eyes. But she could hear the whine of an injured animal and it tore at her heart.

Phil turned back around and plunged her arm inside the

coffin. Dust coated her fingers, eddied up her arm, and made her nose burn. Her fingers brushed cold bone, wispy fine hair.

"Lower," Tup directed from inside the box.

She felt knobby things, which disconnected at her touch, falling apart like clods of dry earth. She recoiled, then frowned at her squeamishness. When Tup commanded her to dig, she dug. Past the bone and through . . . she didn't know what, didn't want to know. She felt every hair on her neck prickle.

And then realized the sensation came from icy breath at her nape.

She slowly turned her head to find red eyes staring into her own. Foul breath washed over her face. The Bargest's black muzzle opened, a growl vibrating through its throat until she could swear she felt her skin quiver. Phil felt her heart stop. The dog licked her face, as if savoring the taste of its next meal, saliva dripping from its fangs. Oh, dear heaven, was it Edwina inside that spirit—or Nico?

And then the Bargest grunted and spun. Sarah had shifted back to her were-form and managed to wrap her body around the dog's back legs. It snapped at her assistant, grazing the smooth scales, then pulled its legs free and pinned Sarah down in turn.

Phil closed her hand around a hard knob in the coffin.

The sudden silence in the chamber made her ears ring. The castle ghosts released the black wraiths and they all turned to stare at Phil. The Bargest shook its head and looked at her in bewilderment.

Phil pulled her hand out of the casket and stared at the shiny object she held. She blew off the dust and debris to reveal a band of gold with a sparkling blue stone set into the bezel.

She hesitated for a moment, then slid the ring onto her finger. It fit perfectly.

The blue warrior went down on one knee and the other castle ghosts quickly followed suit. The black wraiths bowed their heads. The Bargest released Sarah and sank to all fours, rolling over to expose its neck and belly to her.

"What's happening?" Phil whispered. Tup faded, his energy spent. She couldn't remember when he'd managed to stay material for so long.

After an interminable silence, the blue warrior floated to her feet, his knee slightly sunken into the stone floor. "What do you wish of us, Master?"

Phil blinked in surprise. "Why haven't you spoken to me before?"

He looked up at her, his face so similar to Nico's that she glanced at the Bargest. Was she too late? Did the Bargest encompass Nico's soul even now?

"Look around you, lady," the warrior said. "The ring gives you a direct connection to me now. To all of us."

Phil looked past his form to the steps. Shapes began to emerge from behind the carved stone markers. Her eyes went up to the next step that circled the cavern. Even more ghosts began to wake, ghosts that experience told her had been at peace for thousands of years. They began to float down from the darkness of the ceiling, drift up from the stone floor beneath her feet, until the enormous chamber swirled with the spirits of the dead.

Phil's knees went weak. This wasn't right. Those who had gone to their rest deserved the peace to stay there. After years of helping the poor souls who couldn't cross over finally reach the spiritual world, she knew what a travesty it was to yank them back to a semi-life that would only bewilder and torture them.

"We gave up our own rest," the warrior continued, "to guard that which would disturb the peace of the Otherworld. You hold in your hand the power to command all the ghosts that have gone before . . . you have within your means an unconquerable army, lady. What is your command?"

Phil locked her knees to prevent them from giving way beneath her. What a terrible, terrible power. She wanted nothing to do with it. Yet she had unleashed it and the ghosts swirled about the room, waiting for her command.

Sarah had shifted back to human and when Philomena's gaze met hers, her assistant only blinked at her and shrugged. Of course, she couldn't hear or see the ghosts. Only the Bargest was strong enough to be visible to other humans. And then Phil's gaze shifted to the Bargest. Of course.

Would she be freeing Edwina's soul . . . or Nico's?

"My first command," Phil said, trying to stop her voice from trembling, "is for you to be at peace." She pointed at the Bargest, and the blue stone winked to life on her finger. The dog howled in fury and began to writhe. Phil watched with bated breath while the spirit left its host, allowing Edwina to transform back to herself. The blonde girl crouched where the dog had once been, naked and bloody, looking around in terror. Her eyes rolled back into her head and she slumped over in a heap. Sarah sighed and got to her feet, cradling Edwina's head in her arms, patting her cheeks.

Phil's heart threatened to explode with hope. Had her love been enough to help Nico resist the lure of the Bargest's curse? Or . . . no, she couldn't allow herself to think it. Surely he couldn't be dead. Her eyes searched the chamber, but she couldn't see past the myriad spirits crowding the room.

Phil opened her mouth to tell the spirits to go back to their rest, and then snapped it shut again. She'd spent most of her life helping restless spirits to return to the Otherworld. In the process, she'd carried final messages of love to the bereaved, revealed secrets that a spirit needed confessed, and had even helped several ghosts find and convict their murderers. And now she had almost eradicated the world of all spirits! The enormity of the power of the relic overwhelmed her. She chose her words with care. "I command all the spirits that were at rest, to be at rest again," she shouted.

The warrior sighed. "We chose wisely in you, my lady."

Phil blinked. The castle ghosts *had* kept the black wraiths at bay so she could retrieve the relic. Perhaps she should feel flattered that they considered her less of a threat than Edwina, but she preferred that the relic hadn't been unearthed at all.

Slowly, the spirits that had risen when she'd put on the ring disappeared. The dark wraiths had already faded with the Bargest, but the castle ghosts remained, silent and watchful.

She saw Nico stagger from the shadows, blood streaming from his paw and neck. He shifted to human, and despite his battered appearance, he was the most magnificent thing she'd ever seen. First she had thought him cursed, then dead. But he strode toward her, proving that his love for her had been strong enough to overcome the wolf's call.

Phil caught her breath on a sob and took a step toward him. Within a blink his strong arms wrapped around her, and it took all of her will not to burst into hysterical tears. Instead she blinked her burning eyes and just held on to him in sheer relief.

"Are you all right?" he murmured.

"Are you?" Phil stepped out of his arms, taking his wrist and frowning at his bloody hand. Several puncture wounds from the Bargest's fangs oozed blood. She had streaks on the front of her gown from the blood that trickled down his chest from his neck. She looked around wildly.

Sarah had recovered Edwina's torn dress and tossed it over the girl's naked body, but her many petticoats still littered the floor. Phil began to tear one into strips. "I've been a fool," she muttered. "I should have had faith in you."

Phil took her makeshift bandages to his side and stanched the flow of blood from the gashes in his neck. "Can you ever forgive me?" she whispered.

"Ah, Phil. There's nothing to forgive." Phil's eyes burned and she took the rest of the bandages and wrapped his injured hand. She should have realized that he was a cut above the ordinary man. That his love wouldn't be swayed by her gift of talking to ghosts. That the difference in their ages had nothing to do with their hearts. When she finished, his fingers closed over hers.

She looked up at him and kissed his handsome mouth. "Let's have no more doubts between us."

"Does that mean you'll marry me?" he asked.

Phil laughed, but only because she couldn't cry. If she started, she might never manage to stop. "Yes, Sir Nicodemus Wulfson, I will gladly marry you."

"That's better." He straightened up and then winced from his injuries. "Now, what are we going to do about *that*?"

Phil glanced down at her hand, where the blue gem twinkled prettily. "I haven't the faintest idea. I suppose we could put it back."

Nico glanced over at Edwina, who still lay slumped in Sarah's arms. "It may be too late for that. What else does it do?"

Phil suppressed a shiver. "It raises the spirits of the dead. All the spirits, Nico, even those at peace."

He didn't appear to be as intimidated by the power of the ring. His mouth twisted in an ironic smile. "Well, I suppose there's no one else who could appreciate it as much as you, ghost-hunter."

"Perhaps." Phil stepped away from Nico and faced the blue warrior, who still knelt near her feet. She didn't want the ring, but since she had it . . . "Is there some way I can help you and the other castle ghosts be at rest, as well?"

Nico started, as if he'd forgotten that the spirits still remained. But he turned and followed the direction of Phil's gaze as if he could see his ancestor too.

"That's not so easy, my lady," the warrior replied. "We have sworn a vow to guard the relic, and although we have kept it from evil hands, we would still be loath to relinquish our duty."

Phil cocked her head in thought. It seemed that his trust of Phil only extended so far. Did the castle ghosts fear that she'd change her mind? That the lure of enough power to rule the world would be too much of a temptation for her to resist for long?

Perhaps they were right. If she had the chance to use the ring for a good cause, she would. And who was to say that the good she accomplished with it would change a course of events for the better? How could she know all the weavings of fate to predict how such power would affect others? She couldn't change the world in such a large way. She was happy with the little bit she could manage on her own.

Phil's head spun. The relic was too dangerous even in the hands of someone who had only the best intentions. And she knew herself well enough to know that she didn't *always* have the best intentions.

"I would not have you forsworn," she said. Phil eased the ring off her finger. "But I would have you at peace." She handed the relic to the warrior. She knew then that she'd made the right decision, because the ring didn't drop through his ghostly hand. Indeed, it changed to partial shadow and the warrior closed his fingers around it.

Nico sucked in a breath and Sarah let out a startled hiss.

"I think you could guard it best in the Otherworld," Philomena said.

The warrior stared at her in stunned surprise, then smiled. She'd never seen him smile before and it made him resemble Nico even more. "Indeed, we can, my lady."

Chapter Seventeen

Several weeks later, Nico stood in the Hall of Mages, hoping the prince would approve of Phil's decision to give the ring to the castle spirits.

The mousy clerk who had taken his petition for an audience waved Nico over to his desk, and the other people who waited in the Hall with him gave him looks of envy or speculation. Apparently the prince's letter to his father had given him a prompt audience with Prince Albert, the Master of the Hall of Mages.

A shudder shook the building, the fourth in less than an hour, and Nico shook his head at the magic that must be brewing within the walls. He felt extraordinarily grateful to be immune.

The clerk led him through a maze of halls and opened a door onto a cluttered study.

Prince Albert sat in a chair next to a blazing fire and Nico tried to hide his surprise. The man couldn't be more than a few years older than Phil, and yet he looked twice her age. The rumors of his illness were apparently true. "This is my son, Prince Albert," he said, nodding at the young man seated opposite him. "I'm training him to take my place as Master here."

Nico bowed to both.

The prince consort waved Nico to a chair and glanced at his son. "Bertie, this is Sir Nicodemus Wulfson. His family has protected one of Merlin's Relics for generations."

The younger prince's face widened with surprise. "Another hidden relic? Really, Father, you keep your secrets well."

"As should you," Prince Albert advised. "What brings you here, Sir Nicodemus? No problems with the relic, I hope?"

Nico winced. "Therein lies the story, Your Highness." Without further preamble, Nico launched into his tale, including his romance with the ghost-hunter, which the young prince took in with great enthusiasm. Nico's throat felt dry by the time he'd finished, and the prince consort's face had gone an unnatural shade of white.

"So, the relic is now in the Otherworld," he murmured. "I suppose it's safer there than anywhere on this earth . . . although I'd like to talk to your ghost-hunter about the possibility of retrieving it. What have you done about your sister-in-law and her father?"

A tumbler of water floated off a tea tray and hovered near Nico's face. He grasped it and took a sip, trying to appear as if floating glasses were nothing out of the ordinary. But he couldn't wait to get out of London and back to the country, where magic didn't inundate the very air. "I have removed Lord Magift from his position as magistrate and have put both of them in confinement. I thought it would be best if I left their trial and punishment to you."

"Well done. I'll have them transferred to the Magicians' Prison here in the Hall. They will stand trial among their peers."

Nico swirled the liquid in his glass. "My brother is most distraught over his wife's betrayal, Your Highness. He still harbors feelings for her, and for his sake, I would ask that you show some clemency."

The young Prince Albert slapped his knee. "I daresay that we should. How can we hold her accountable for the deaths when she was under a curse?"

The prince consort eyed his son with approval, although his voice sounded stern. "We cannot forget that she hid the curse and was willing to allow an innocent person to be convicted for her crimes, not to mention that she tried to steal a relic."

Nico's heart sank for Royden, but he knew the prince was right. Roy had some hard decisions before him, and Nico vowed to give his brother all of his support. "I'm sorry I failed in my duty to the crown, Your Highness."

Prince Albert waved his hand. "On the contrary. The relic is still safe . . . albeit in an entirely different location."

"And you solved a crime," the young prince interrupted. "And saved countless souls. I think you and your ghost-hunter's efforts deserve a commendation, Sir Nicodemus."

Prince Albert glanced at his son again with that odd combination of approval and censure. "I do believe, Bertie, that you will make a most fair Master."

The young man turned beet red under the praise. The gilded mantel clock struck the hour, and Nico surged to his feet. "If you will forgive me, Your Highnesses, your summons to meet with you came on a most auspicious day."

"How so?"

Nico bowed. "It's my wedding day, Master. And I fear to keep my bride waiting at the altar, in the event that she might change her mind."

The young prince beamed and rose, clapping Nico on the back. "Come along, man. I'll make sure you get to the chapel on time."

"Albert Edward . . ." his father warned.

The young man quickly ushered Nico out the door. "I say, Father, my magical experiments have been quite the success." And before his father could say another word, the young man had Nico out the door. They took a different route through the maze of hallways than the one by which Nico had entered, and when the prince directed him up a curving staircase with treads that moved of their own accord, Nico wondered what he might be getting himself into.

Prince Albert opened a door near the top of the stairs and Nico followed him out onto a balcony high above the city. The morning sky looked unusually clear, and Nico could see the sparkling water of the Thames beyond the mix of magical and mundane buildings. Fanciful illusions of colorful spires and flowers competed with those of steel and stone.

"Easy now, Venus," said Prince Albert. The answering snort made Nico turn toward the sound.

A white horse pawed the stone balcony, her abnormally long mane and tail swirling about her as if they stood in a storm wind and not a gentle breeze. Yet Nico marveled not from the beauty of the beast, but from the beautiful wings that flowed off her back.

Nico stepped closer, surprised that the horse didn't shy away from him. Except for were-horses, most beasts had a healthy instinctive fear of wolves. Instead, the beauty nickered at him, snuffling at his hair. The nearly transparent wings glowed in the sunshine, an iridescent mix of blue and silver. Golden brown veins formed an intricate framework throughout the front and back rounded wings.

Nico shook his head in wonder. Truly, the magic of the aristocracy astounded him.

The prince patted the ornate saddle strapped to the horse's back. "I say, what are you waiting for? Aren't you late for your wedding? Mount up!"

Nico tried to keep the horror from his expression. "I'm immune to magic, Your Highness."

"The wings are real. She won't fade on you, Sir Nicodemus."

Nico looked over the side of the balcony and swallowed. It was a long way down. But he couldn't keep Phil waiting. He'd only been half jesting when he'd told the princes that he was afraid his ghost-hunter would change her mind. And by the view below, the streets already looked crowded with traffic.

"My thanks, Your Highness," Nico said without a trace of irony. He grasped the swirling mane and vaulted into the saddle. Venus shook her head and danced prettily for a moment before she lifted straight up into the air, the sound of her buzzing wings drowning out Prince Albert's farewell.

Nico used the reins to guide her as he would any ordinary horse, but the movement that followed made his gestures more cautious. He flew over Buckingham Palace, the jewel-studded walls and the magical wards surrounding it making him narrow his eyes against the glare. The tower of the Hall of Mages quickly faded behind him, and he began to enjoy the freedom of flight.

If Phil hadn't been waiting, he would have tarried, amazed at the view of London from above. Instead he leaned forward to direct the horse lower and frantically searched for the small chapel near Phil's townhouse where they were to be married. Navigating the streets of London from a bird's view was quite different from doing so on the ground, but within a relatively short time, Nico spied the street and leaned his upper body over Venus's neck to tell her to land.

With barely a clatter of hooves, the horse stood in the fountained courtyard in front of the church. Nico ran his hands down Venus's silky mane in thanks and jumped out of the saddle. The mare made a bit of a show for the onlookers drawn by the sound of her buzzing wings, rearing her dainty hooves and making her mane and tail look like a white cloud surrounding her.

He might have delayed to watch her fly away, but he had the most beautiful woman in the world awaiting him. Nico ran for the church doors, pushed them open, and blinked in the comparative dimness inside the chapel. He brushed off the front of his coat and swept his hair back from his face as his eyes traveled down the aisle to the altar.

Nico could vaguely make out the forms of the clergyman and the parish clerk. Philomena's friends, arrayed in their medieval garb. Her assistant, Sarah, with that perpetual sway of hers. His brother, Roy, and Hexword, the new magistrate of Trollersby. Jane was conspicuously absent, whether because she was still in love with him or hadn't forgiven him for believing her to be a murderer, Nico couldn't be sure.

But the only one he saw with any clarity was Philomena.

The sun streamed through the stained-glass windows, outlining her in a soft light of gold and silver. She wore a silk gown of pale ivory that reflected the colors within the glass. Her hair tumbled over her shoulders, just the way he preferred it, tiny combs of pearl and diamond making the color look like polished mahogany.

Her eyes shimmered a soft gray as they met his, calm and gentle as always.

Nico felt a swell of emotion that nearly buckled his knees. He squared his shoulders and strode down the aisle, seeing nothing but his bride. He was still amazed that she'd consented to be his, despite his determination to make it so.

When he reached her side, he took her hand and a shock of excitement ran through him. Nico barely heard the service, his entire being itching with the urge for them to hurry. To make her finally his. Only when they signed the parish register in the vestry did he feel capable of drawing a deep breath, and other than his vows, he barely spoke a word to her until they were ensconced inside their carriage.

Even then, he had to kiss her first.

"You were late," Phil said, her mouth swollen from his attentions.

Nico eyed her hopefully. "Were you worried that I'd changed my mind?"

"Certainly not. I was worried that Prince Albert had you clapped in irons."

Ah, well. Nico felt an immense satisfaction that she no longer doubted his love. And that she belonged to him now. Forever. "The Master agreed that we'd made the best decision under the circumstances. And he will have Edwina transferred here to London for trial. I asked him for leniency for Roy's sake, and as long as Edwina keeps quiet about the relic, I think she may have a reduced sentence."

Nico leaned forward and nuzzled her ear. "Now, enough of that," he whispered. "This is our wedding day. You smell delicious." He trailed his tongue along the sweet curve of her lobe. "And taste even better. We really don't have to wait until after the wedding breakfast, do we?"

Phil shivered and laughed all at the same time. Delightful combination. "Nico, you must promise to behave. Everyone will gossip."

The carriage lurched to a stop in front of Phil's townhouse and Nico sighed and sat back. "You sure you wouldn't rather give them something to envy?"

Phil gathered her ivory skirts into her hands and gave him a smile that made his head spin. "Oh, my dear. They already do—that's half the problem."

Nico tried not to swagger as he escorted Phil up the walk. She made him feel like the most desirable man in London, despite his lowly social status.

The front drawing room overflowed with people, wine and food. Nicodemus watched Phil's face and then quickly scanned the room, trying to see what she did. But his wife was right, he was as sensitive to ghosts as a block of wood, and despite his fervent desire to see the spirits that haunted the former brothel, he couldn't see a shadow.

He escorted his bride into the throng of well-wishers, most of them Phil's friends or patrons. A quartette played on the terrace and Nico led Phil past the open French doors, sweeping her into a dance, if only for an excuse to hold her in his arms.

"It hasn't been so terrible," Phil said.

"What?"

She nodded toward the crowded drawing room. "My friends and acquaintances. Their reaction to our marriage."

Nico frowned. "You shouldn't be so worried about what other people think."

"I'm not. I'm just glad that I misjudged their character."

"Then I'm glad for your sake." A rush of warmth flowed through Nico. "I am so lucky to have found you," he murmured.

Philomena reached up and traced her fingers down his cheek and jaw. "And I, you."

Nico twirled her and settled her back into his arms. "How long before they'll leave?"

Phil looked over her shoulder into the drawing room. "Quite some time, I'm afraid. Consider the anticipation as thrilling as the act, love. It's the only way *I* shall make it through the day."

Nico threw back his head and laughed, his spirit so light and carefree that he felt he might fly as easily as Venus had. And indeed, throughout the long afternoon, he took Phil's advice, knowing that they would eventually be alone together, and that the wait only added spice to his desire.

And it worked . . . until Phil started to drive him mad.

At first she only seemed distracted, her gaze flicking past him to rest on an empty corner of the room. But her words began to fade in the middle of a sentence, and although it seemed that she purposely tried to ignore something over in the corner, her head would suddenly swivel in that direction and her cheeks would redden. Her friends didn't appear concerned by her behavior. He supposed they were used to it. And it didn't bother him that she saw ghosts; on the contrary, it only endeared her to him even more.

It was his wolf that made him watch her with predatory interest. His animal nature could smell her arousal and respond. By the time the party wound to a close, he couldn't take his eyes off of his new wife.

He watched her from across the room while she said farewell to the last remaining guests, steadying his glass of brandy as he casually leaned against the wall. He suppressed the low growl that rose in the back of his throat when she caught him watching and looked over at him. The slightly glazed look in her gray eyes set his every nerve afire.

Hexword stood next to him and said something, but Nico didn't understand a word of it. He handed the man his glass and strode across the room as Phil shut the front door behind her. Her body fairly vibrated at his touch when his arms closed around her. "What is it?" he asked, only a bit surprised at the huskiness in his voice.

"Fanny," she whispered, nearly choking on the name.

Nico felt his brows rise. Ah, the ghost who had shown Phil so many intriguing bedroom techniques. Who had taught her that lovemaking was something to enjoy . . . unlike most other society ladies, who had been taught to fear it. He owed a great deal to Fanny.

Nico's eyes scanned the drawing room. Hexword held Royden by the arm, caught Nico's eye, and began to drag his brother to the front door. Sarah supervised several hired maids in the cleaning up.

"I'll take him back to the hotel," Hexword said. "He's had a bit too much to drink."

Nico eyed his brother. The man was completely foxed. He frowned and hoped that the Master would indeed be lenient with Edwina. "Thank you, Hexword."

The older man nodded and said his farewell to Phil, and Nico closed the door behind them with a tired sigh. His wife immediately went back into the drawing room toward that blasted corner, where nothing stood but a potted palm, and cocked her head in studied concentration. Nico followed her as if Phil had a leash around his throat.

"Sarah." He hadn't meant to growl her name. "You can clean up later."

The were-snake glanced at her mistress, then calmly shooed the maids from the drawing room. "I will ssee to it that you aren't dissturbed." She sounded so smooth and un-ruffled, but Nico caught the gleam in those dark eyes, the half smile curving the thin lips as Sarah closed the with-drawing room doors behind her.

He never thought he'd become so fond of a snake.

Phil gasped and Nico closed his hands over her shoul-ders. "What do you see, Phil?"

Her cheeks colored and she trembled. "Fanny is more aware than the other ghosts here. This can't be a coinci-dence."

Nico's body tightened even more. Now that they were alone, he allowed his wolf to shadow him, allowed the beast some freedom. He wasn't afraid that his wolf would overwhelm him. Their love had proven to be stronger than the darkest forces on earth.

"I have waited all day, ghost-hunter. If you don't tell me what Fanny is doing, I'll go mad."

She turned and looked up at him, her mouth parted, her eyes glassy with desire. "It, um, involves a table."

Nico eyed the sturdy oak table holding the remains of their wedding breakfast and grinned. He took his wife into his arms and kissed her while he expertly unbuttoned the back of her silk gown, pulling it down her shoulders. He loosened the stays of her corset, just enough to yank the front of the garment down to bare her breasts. He didn't have the patience to remove all of her clothes. Yet.

While he lavished attention on her nipples with tongue and mouth, he begged her to tell him more. But she only moaned in reply, clutching at his head, burying her fingers in his hair. Nico straightened and scooped her up in his arms and carried her over to the table. He swept a corner clear and lowered his wife onto it, staring into her eyes. "What else?"

The ribbons in her hair trembled. "It . . . it involves sauces."

"Sauces?"

Phil's cheeks bloomed with renewed color. "The tasting of them. On various parts of the, um, body."

The experience in her eyes and the shyness of her voice fascinated Nico. Damnation, sauces. He glanced along the length of the table, but their breakfast had been light fare . . . .

He ran a finger through the frosting of their wedding cake. "I don't believe I've had a piece yet, Phil. Surely the groom should eat of his own wedding cake?"

"It's . . . a requirement."

Nico raised a brow.

"I'm sure it says that somewhere," Phil panted. "In some etiquette book or other."

Nico dotted her lips with his finger. "I'm certain it does," he murmured as he kissed her. The sweetness of the frosting made a delicious contrast to the salty flavor of her mouth and Nico's tongue swept inside until no trace of the sugar remained.

Fascinating.

But he wasn't one for too many sweets. He straightened and studied the table while he pushed Phil's skirts up around her waist. She wore satin drawers trimmed in lace and they distracted him for a moment. He'd waited all day to touch her. He spread the slit in the fabric and muttered a rather insincere apology when they ripped. He pressed his palm over her hot core. Phil threw back her head and groaned.

Nico suppressed a howl of dominance. She belonged to him. *This* belonged to him.

He reached for a decanter of brandy and poured a small amount into a glass, but didn't drink. Instead he dipped in a finger as Phil lifted her head. Those lovely gray eyes followed his every move as he circled her nipples with the alcohol. "I'm thirsty," he murmured.

Phil shivered.

"Are you?" Nico placed his wet finger in her mouth and she suckled. He felt his shaft jump in response at the same time her opening throbbed in his hand. Nico lowered his head and drank from her breasts, his finger still inside her mouth, her tongue a soft, wet instrument of torture. Brandy scorched his taste buds and competed with the sweetness of her skin.

Damn, but he loved Phil's ghosts.

He made his wife squirm. He made her beg. Then he straightened and reached for more frosting, easing her thighs a bit farther open. He spread it over her nub and along her lips and tasted that sweetness again while she cried out and nearly tore the hair from his head. Nico idly wondered if that was the reason why so many men went bald after several years of marriage. He fervently hoped so.

Nico brought his wife to the edge; he could feel the tightening of her muscles as she gained her peak, just on the verge of tumbling off into ecstasy. He untangled her hands from his hair. "Thirsty again."

"Nico!"

He reached for the brandy, dipped his fingers in again and went to his knees. It seemed as if her very skin heated the liquid, turned it into ambrosia. Nico satisfied his thirst, bringing Phil to a renewed crest, and he knew he couldn't deny her this time.

He knew he couldn't ask his body to wait any longer.

Nico stood and unbuttoned his trousers, his eyes never leaving his wife's. Then he pulled her toward him until her bottom hung over the edge of the table. The darling woman bent her knees, put her hands above her head and gripped the edge of the wood.

He growled when he entered her, fast, hard, her opening so wet that he slid deep inside with his very first thrust. Phil arched her back and cried out with her release, sudden and powerful. Nico didn't wait for her to recover. Couldn't wait. He plunged inside her again and again, rocking the heavy table, knocking over glasses and scattering fruit and sending dishes crashing to the floor.

And when Phil cried out for more, wrapping her legs around his back and digging in her heels, Nico let his beast have free reign. He felt himself swell inside of her, heard her startled gasp of surprise, and then lost himself in the pure pleasure of wild desire.

His release made him come undone. Nico's back arched, his head fell backward and he didn't have the breath to voice the sounds that erupted in the back of his throat. Fierce spasms swept through his body, so much pleasure it felt almost painful. And it went on and on, until he felt he had drained every bit of his essence into his wife. Philomena. Who echoed his tremors with her own release.

Nico looked down at her, his hair sweeping over his brow and cheeks. She looked up at him with eyes widened in amazement. The wolf inside of him snarled with arrogant satisfaction. Phil reached up a shaking hand and stroked Nico's jaw, and the wolf retreated to the farthest corner of his being.

Nico gently gathered her up into his arms, keeping himself inside her, loving the way they fit together.

Phil glanced at the floor, uttered a shaky laugh. "We've made quite a mess."

"I'll clean it up before the servants see it."

"No, Nico. Not yet. It's my turn, now."

It was his turn for his eyes to widen in amazement.

"Sugar and brandy," Phil murmured. "What will it taste like on your skin?"

He caught the back of her head and kissed her. Slowly, tenderly. "I love your ghosts, Phil."

She untied his cravat. "And I love your beast, Nico." She shoved his coat off his shoulders and her fingers flew over the buttons of his shirt.

Life with his ghost-hunter would surely be fascinating.

Chapter Eighteen

Nine months to the day later, Phil lay in the tester bed in her old room at Grimspell castle, her newborn baby held securely in her arms. Although Nico had insisted they keep her London townhouse—for nefarious reasons of his own—she loved being at Grimspell more. Nico had even agreed to move out of his room and into her old one since she loved it so much.

Phil unwrapped her baby and counted the fingers and toes again, smiling with satisfaction when they proved to be all there. Her child had a shock of white hair and a face too scrunched to tell whether he would resemble his mother or his father.

Philomena hoped that he would one day shift into a miniature little wolf, but she supposed she wouldn't mind if the lad turned out to be a ghost-hunter like herself. Her gift had eventually brought her the greatest happiness she could imagine.

Nico huffed in his sleep, still half sitting in the chair he'd pulled up next to the bed, his head draped over the side of the mattress where he'd collapsed after the baby had been born. She chided herself for worrying that she wouldn't be able to keep up with his youthful exuberance and ran her hands through his white-streaked brown hair, smiling as his exhausted breathing filled the room. Nico had spent more energy in worrying about the birth than she had spent in the actual doing of it.

Her baby made the most fascinating little moue with his tiny pink lips, and Phil smiled at him with delight. She had worried that giving birth at her age might be difficult, but other than the usual pain, it had all worked out rather splendidly.

Philomena sighed. She had worried about a great many silly things. She had thought she'd spend her mornings searching for new wrinkles, fearful that Nico would notice them. She had thought he was merely infatuated with her and that his love would fade. She had thought that she wouldn't have the strength to gentle his beast.

"How could I have doubted?" she whispered.

"Doubted what?" Tup replied, suddenly materializing at the foot of the bed.

Phil sat up, careful not to jostle the baby. Tup hadn't appeared for the last month, and before that his visits had become increasingly sporadic. "Where have you been? I've missed you."

Her ghost-boy gave her a rueful smile. "Ye have been busy, what with the baby comin' and all."

Phil cocked her head. Did she detect a note of jealousy in his voice? "I'm never too busy for you, Tup. When I think of how clever and brave you were when we faced the Bargest, well, I'm sure I don't know what we would have done without you."

The lad's spirit manifested even stronger, his face lighting up with joy. "Aw, weren't nuthin' much."

"Do you want to see the baby?"

Tup looked dubiously at the bundle in her arms and then shrugged. "Suppose I oughta." He floated to her side. "Looks kinda like a monkey."

Phil tried not to be offended. "He'll fill out, Tup. You'll see. Pretty soon the two of you will be sliding down haystacks together."

Tup ducked his head. "I don't think so."

Phil studied the boy. Something was seriously wrong, and yet at the same time strangely right. "Why not?"

"Because it's time for me to go."

She blinked stupidly at him. For years she'd tried to help him go to his rest, but he'd just smiled at her and stubbornly refused. And now here he was, telling her . . . "Why?"

He pulled at his spiky hair. " 'Cause ye don't need me no more."

"Me? Need you?" She'd always thought that the boy haunted her because he'd needed a mother. He'd been abandoned to die on the streets of London, which meant he never had much of a mother to begin with.

Tup's large hazel eyes suddenly looked older. "Haven't ye figured it out, Phil? I stayed tied to the earth because of yer need, not mine. And now that ye have yer own son, ye won't be needing me anymore."

Guilt washed through her. All this time, she had thought he needed her. And now Phil suddenly realized how very much she'd needed him. Tears gathered in her eyes and rolled down the sides of her face. The joy she felt at the birth of her child was now tempered with an overwhelming sadness at the loss of her Tup. But to have him finally go to his rest, botheration, wasn't that what she'd always wanted? "I shall miss you."

Tup sniffed. "I'll miss ye too. Yer the only mum I've ever known, and ye were a right good 'un."

Phil's breath hitched and she pulled her son to her chest.

"But don't be so sad. Ye'll be seeing me again one day."

It took all of her willpower not to burst into tears and beg him to stay. As she would one day do with the child in her arms, she had to let him go if she loved him.

"I love you, Tup. I always will."

"I know," he said, rather smugly. "Don't worry, now. Ye'll get along just fine, what with yer wolf-man and all."

Phil nodded, her lips clamped together for fear she'd start sobbing. He drifted closer, until she could feel the chill of his spirit. Tup kissed her cheek, an odd combination of warmth and cold. "I love ye too," he whispered.

And then he disappeared.

Her son started to cry, as if he didn't want Tup to leave either, and Phil kissed his downy head and then put him to her breast.

Nico woke and smiled at his son eagerly taking his nourishment, then frowned at the tears in Phil's eyes. "What's wrong?"

"Tup is gone. Forever."

Her husband didn't disappoint her. He had yet to disappoint. His handsome face softened in understanding and he crawled onto the bed and gathered Phil into his arms, careful not to disturb their nursing son. "Then you did well. It's what you've always wanted for him, isn't it?"

Phil nodded.

"You'll be busy with our son, after all." His voice lowered with a trace of anticipation. "And I have no doubt that you'll have plenty of other ghosts to vex me with."

Phil smiled through her tears. "I thought you said you loved my ghosts?"

He kissed her cheek. "You know I do. Did my teasing help?"

She nodded, turning her face to his for a kiss that warmed her to her toes. And then Nico tucked her head beneath his chin, fiddling with a lock of her hair as a quiet peace descended over them. Only the sounds of her son's satisfied grunts and the creaks of their castle disturbed the silence.

Phil's sadness over the loss of Tup lessened as the warmth of her child and Nico's arms around her stole into her soul.

Nico huffed in exasperation at a knock at the door. "Come in, if you have to."

Sarah slid into the room, her eyes eagerly landing on the baby. "When he'ss finished, do you want me to take him, misstress?"

Phil didn't want to let him go. But Sarah's face looked so hopeful that she couldn't bear to disappoint her. "Perhaps in another hour or so."

Those glossy black eyes lit with happiness and Sarah nodded in that sinuous way of hers. "Ssir Nicodemuss, I have some letterss for you." She glided over to their side, handing Nico the envelopes but never taking her eyes off the newborn. "He'ss a beauty, issn't he?"

Phil caught herself nodding with arrogant pride. Nico unwrapped his arms from around Phil and sat back in the chair by the bed. Sarah glanced at Nico and then quickly left the room.

"We'll have to have a dozen children to keep your assistant happy," he complained with a smile.

Phil smoothed her palm over the baby's fine hair. "She needs children of her own."

"Well, she *has* been spending a lot of time with Cheevers lately."

"Don't be . . . are you serious?"

Nico laughed. "Quite. A duck and a snake, who would have thought it?"

"Certainly not I." Phil's head swiveled toward him of its own accord. He went from merely handsome to entirely devastating when he laughed, and she couldn't resist looking at his face. His brown eyes met hers, the specks of gold in them almost appearing as if they danced with his humor. Her heart squeezed a bit and she tried to regain her composure. "Who are the letters from?"

He glanced down at the envelopes and frowned. "One is from Roy and I must say it's about time. Surely Edwina's trial has been settled by now and he can come home. The other one is from . . . Jane. Well, what do you know?"

Phil heard the hurt in his voice. Jane hadn't forgiven him for accusing her of murder, and until she did, Nico couldn't forgive himself. They'd returned to Grimspell after their marriage to find that Jane had left the shire for a grand tour of the continent. Nico had always thought of Jane as a sister, and Phil knew that he missed her and their old relationship.

"Which will you open first?"

"My brother's, of course." Paper crackled and tore.

Phil waited impatiently while he read the letter. "What does it say?"

"Hmm. Edwina received a lighter sentence than she probably deserved, thanks to young Prince Albert. Royden has decided to petition for a divorce . . . let's see. He says he can forgive her, but not forget. And he's . . . bloody hell. He's not coming home. Hopes I'll understand . . . he's going to the island of Mogow."

Phil rolled her eyes. "Dr. Darknoll."

"Apparently he regaled my brother with his stories when he stayed with him. Witch doctors—Roy's liable to lose his head."

His wolf shadowed him and Phil reached over and stroked his jaw until it faded. "He just needs time to heal, Nico. It doesn't matter where he goes."

"I suppose you're right." He swept the hair from his eyes. "I just hope he doesn't get into any trouble that I have to get him out of."

"You mean we. We make a rather good team when it comes to trouble, you and I. What does Jane write?"

Nico opened the next letter and read, a bemused look forming on his handsome face. "Little Jane has gotten married."

Phil breathed an inner sigh of relief. Sibling feelings or not, she felt glad that Jane had found someone to replace Nico in her affections. "To whom?"

"To another were-wolf. She always wanted to marry another wolf and I guess she found one. Jane wants to know if she can bring him home to see if I'll accept him in the pack."

"And will you?"

Nico shrugged. "Of course. If Jane chose him, he's good enough for me." Then he paused, a devilish glint in his eyes. "Although I'll make him work for it."

Phil smiled at the wolfish look on his face. Her wild husband who could only be gentled by her touch. How desperately she loved him.

He watched her and the baby through the screen of his hair, as if he didn't want her to see the vulnerability there. But he couldn't hide from Phil. She saw his soul in that gaze and felt humbled by it.

He reached out a muscled arm and carefully peeled the edge of the blanket away from the baby's face. He stroked his son's cheek, his finger looking brown and huge in comparison. "I hope the baby gets bigger fast, so I'm not afraid to break him."

Her child stopped suckling and promptly fell asleep. Phil lifted him and leaned forward. "The baby won't break, I promise. It's time you held him."

Panic warred with yearning until Nico finally held out his big arms. He took his son with a gentle reverence that made Phil's heart clench and she couldn't stop the tears that gathered in her eyes again.

"We can't keep calling him 'the baby,'" Nico said, his voice lowered to a soft whisper. "Have you decided what we should name him?"

"How would you feel about Nicodemus Syrus Wulfson?"

He looked up at her in surprise. "That's quite a mouthful. And wouldn't it get confusing?"

"I know, so I thought . . ." Philomena's breath caught. "We could call him Tup, for short. I think my spirit-boy would have liked that."

"Tup," Nico repeated, gazing down at his son with adoration in his eyes. "Yes, I think that will do. That will do just fine."

Win a majestic 5-carat London blue topaz necklace worth $130!

Kathryne Kennedy is giving away a necklace fit for a princess in celebration of the release of

Enchanting the Beast.

All you have to do is visit her Web site at

www.KathryneKennedy.com

and sign up for her reader newsletter.
A winner will be randomly chosen from those who have joined (current newsletter subscribers are automatically entered).

Only one entry per person. Contest ends July 31, 2009.

Void where prohibited by law. You must be 18 years or older to enter. No prize substitution permitted. This contest is subject to all federal, state and local laws and regulations.

☐ **YES!**

Sign me up for the Love Spell Book Club and send my
FREE BOOKS! If I choose to stay in the club, I will pay
only $8.50* each month, a savings of $6.48!

NAME: _____

ADDRESS: _____

TELEPHONE: _____

EMAIL: _____

☐ I want to pay by credit card.

☐ **VISA**   ☐ **MasterCard.**   ☐ **DISCOVER**

ACCOUNT #: _____

EXPIRATION DATE: _____

SIGNATURE: _____

Mail this page along with $2.00 shipping and handling to:
Love Spell Book Club
PO Box 6640
Wayne, PA 19087
Or fax (must include credit card information) to:
610-995-9274
You can also sign up online at **www.dorchesterpub.com**.
*Plus $2.00 for shipping. Offer open to residents of the U.S. and Canada only.
Canadian residents please call 1-800-481-9191 for pricing information.
If under 18, a parent or guardian must sign. Terms, prices and conditions subject to
change. Subscription subject to acceptance. Dorchester Publishing reserves the right
to reject any order or cancel any subscription.